Azophi's Wand

Alderbrian Press

Alderbrian Press

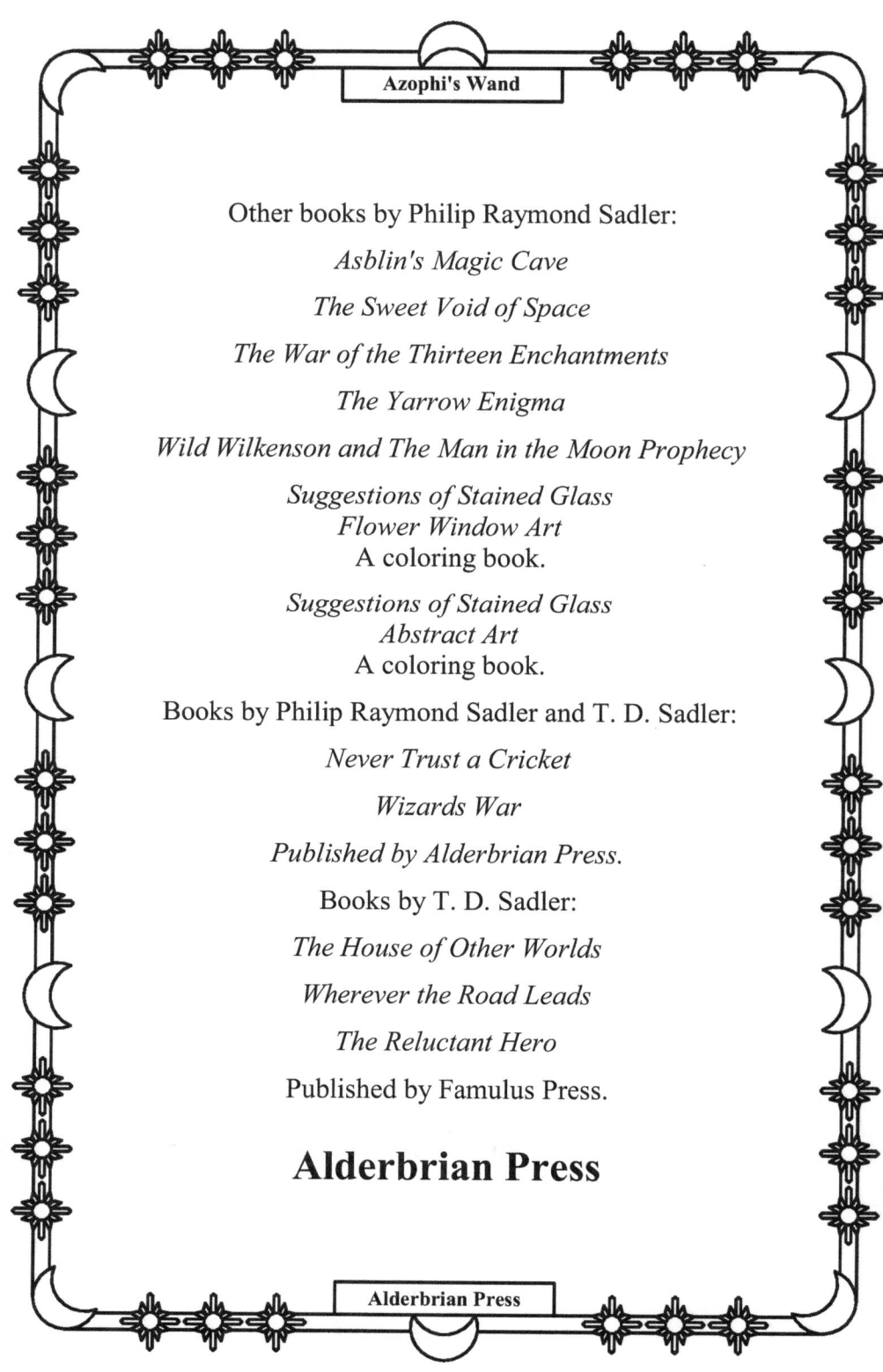

Azophi's Wand

Other books by Philip Raymond Sadler:

Asblin's Magic Cave

The Sweet Void of Space

The War of the Thirteen Enchantments

The Yarrow Enigma

Wild Wilkenson and The Man in the Moon Prophecy

Suggestions of Stained Glass
Flower Window Art
A coloring book.

Suggestions of Stained Glass
Abstract Art
A coloring book.

Books by Philip Raymond Sadler and T. D. Sadler:

Never Trust a Cricket

Wizards War

Published by Alderbrian Press.

Books by T. D. Sadler:

The House of Other Worlds

Wherever the Road Leads

The Reluctant Hero

Published by Famulus Press.

Alderbrian Press

Alderbrian Press

Azophi's Wand

by

Philip Raymond Sadler

Alderbrian Press

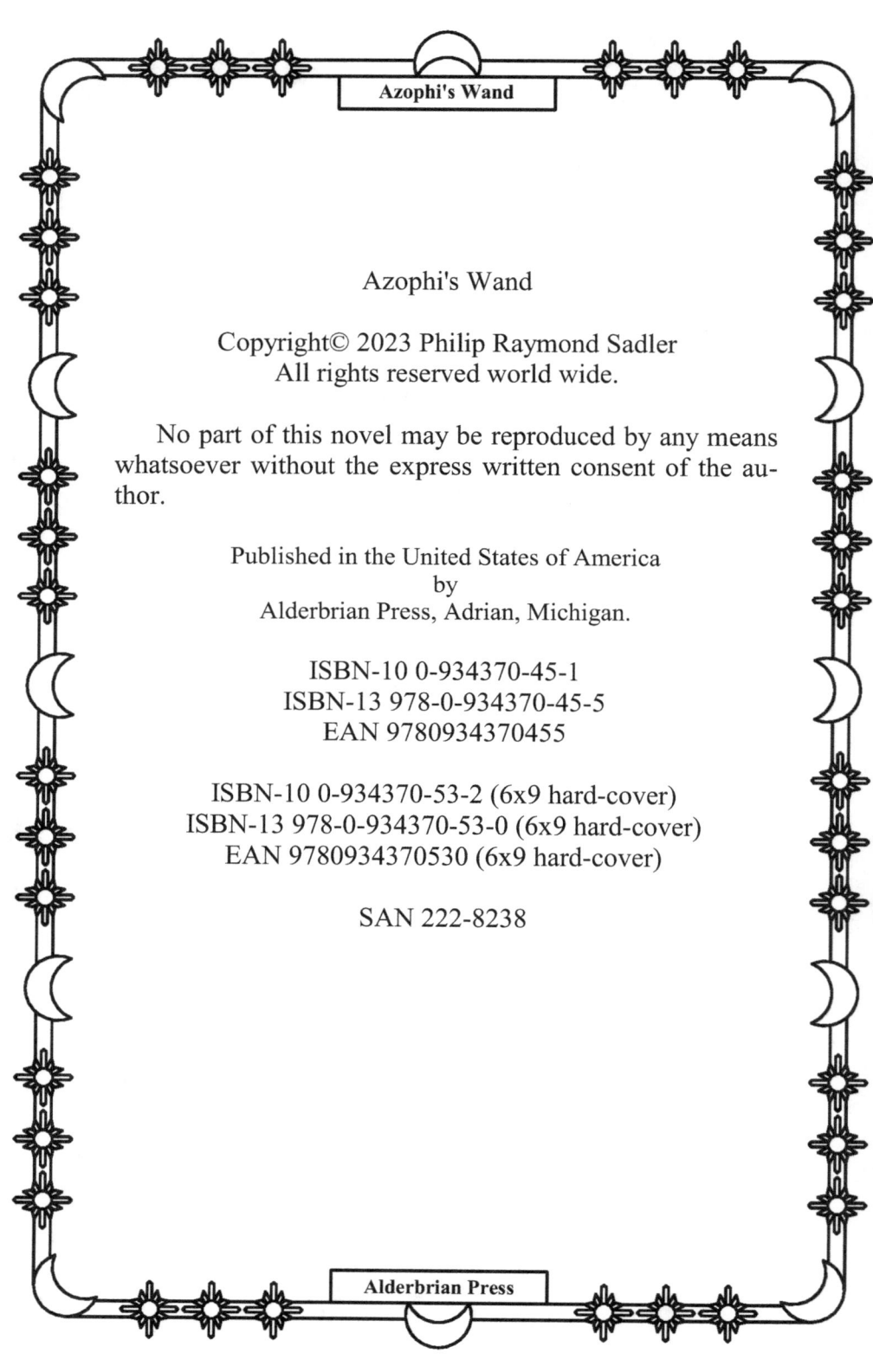

Azophi's Wand

Azophi's Wand

Published in the United States of America
by
Alderbrian Press, Adrian, Michigan.

ISBN-10 0-934370-45-1
ISBN-13 978-0-934370-45-5
EAN 9780934370455

ISBN-10 0-934370-53-2 (6x9 hard-cover)
ISBN-13 978-0-934370-53-0 (6x9 hard-cover)
EAN 9780934370530 (6x9 hard-cover)

SAN 222-8238

Alderbrian Press

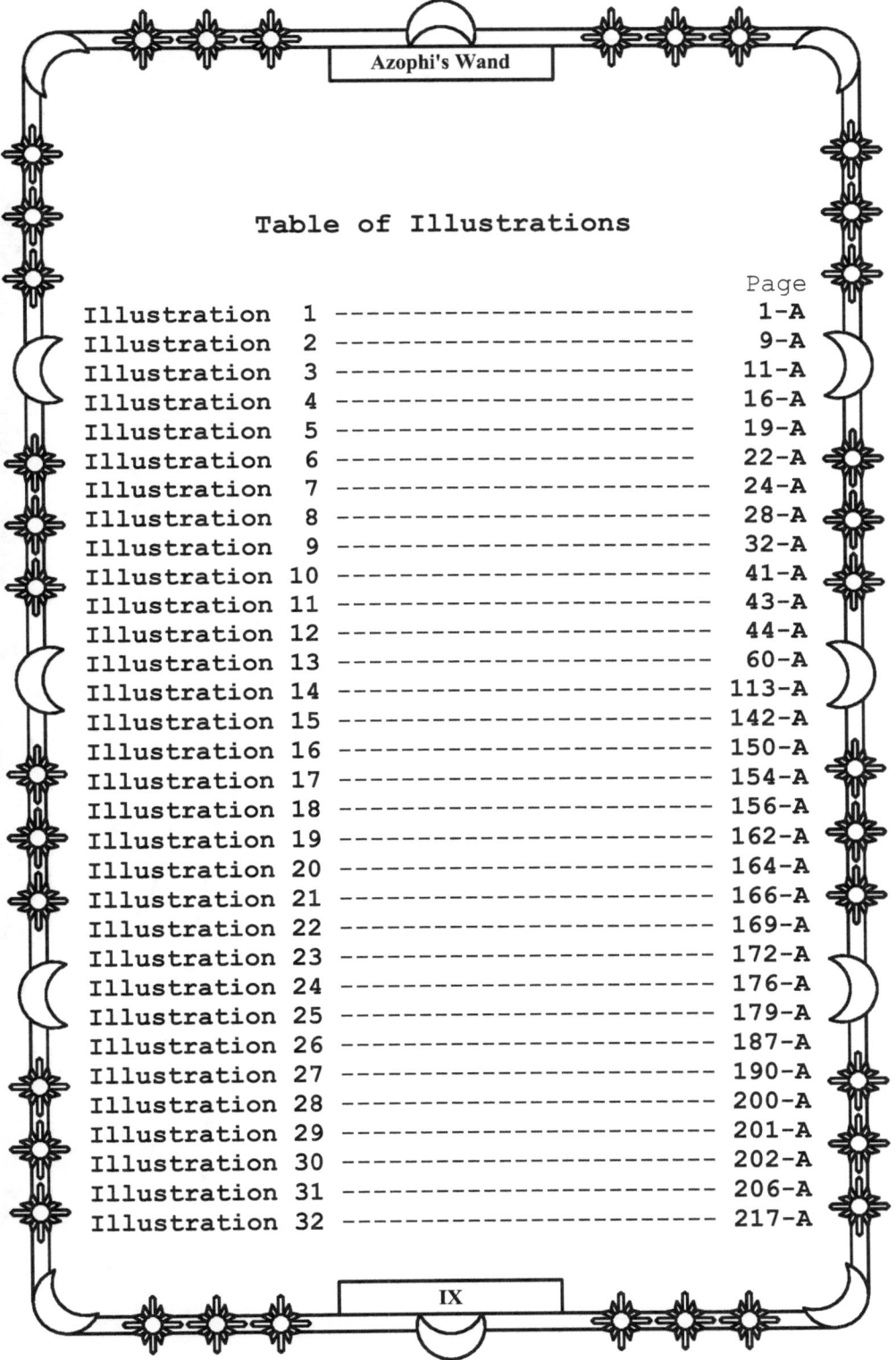

Azophi's Wand

Table of Illustrations

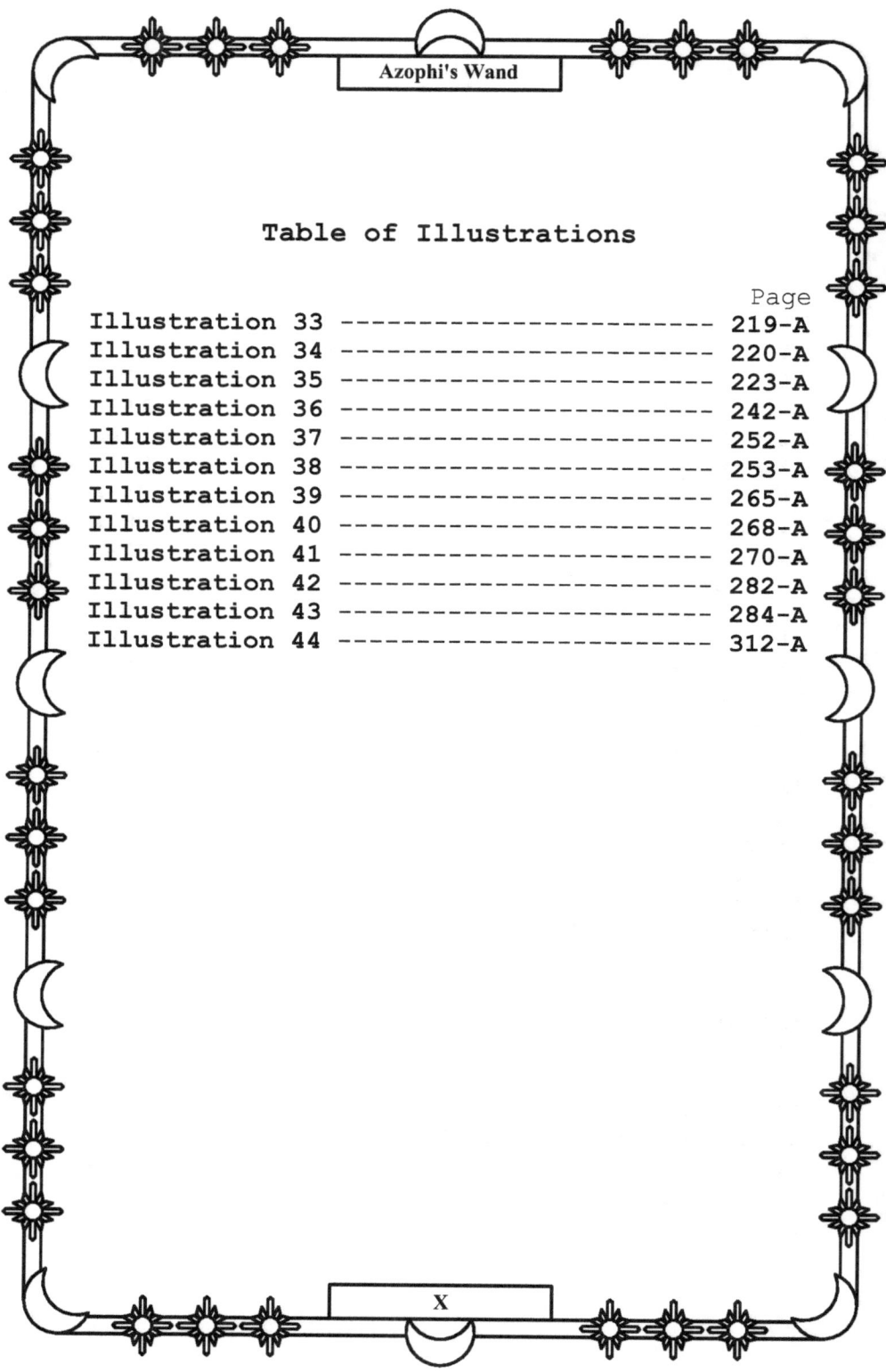

Azophi's Wand

Table of Illustrations

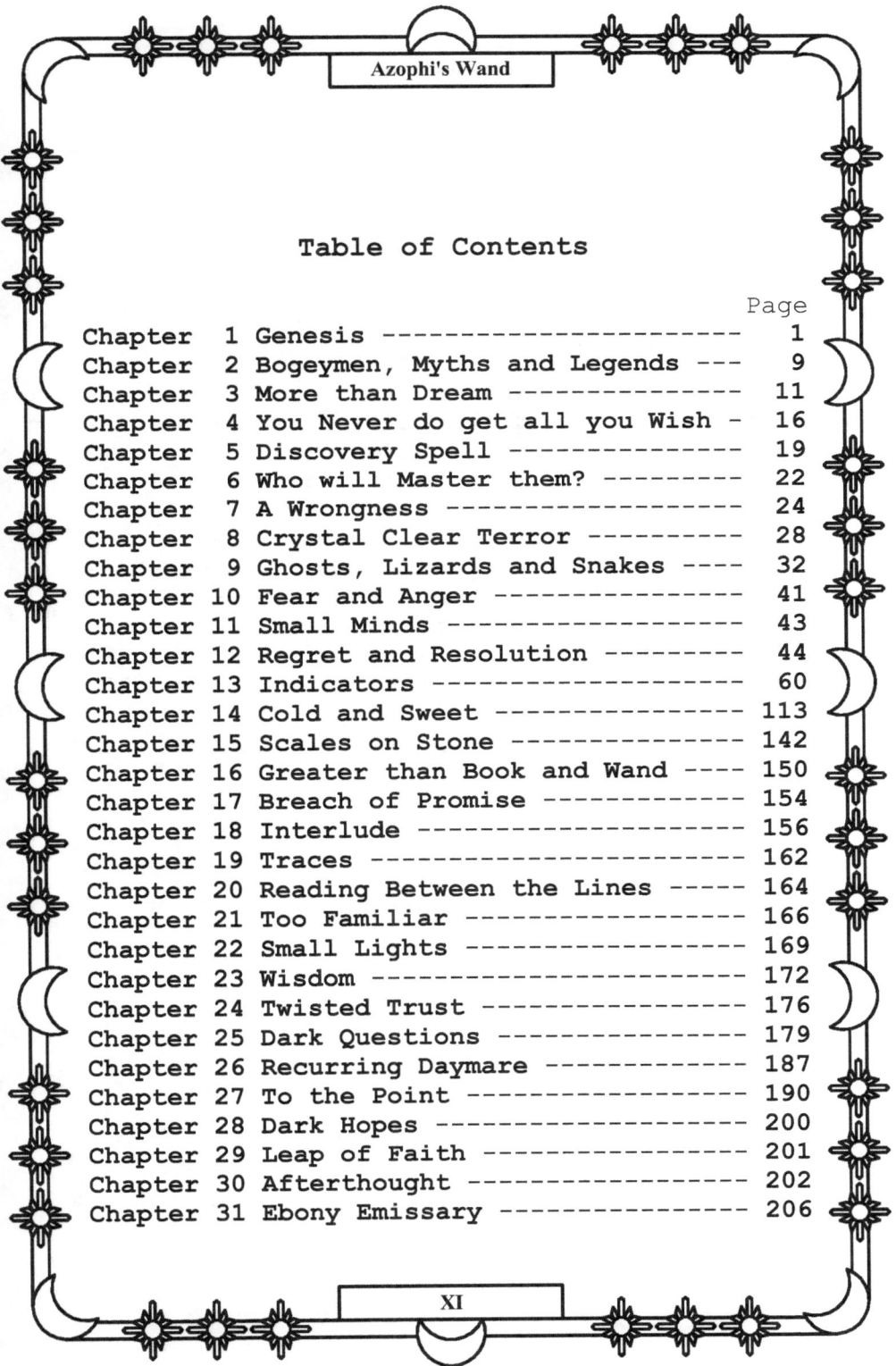

Azophi's Wand

Table of Contents

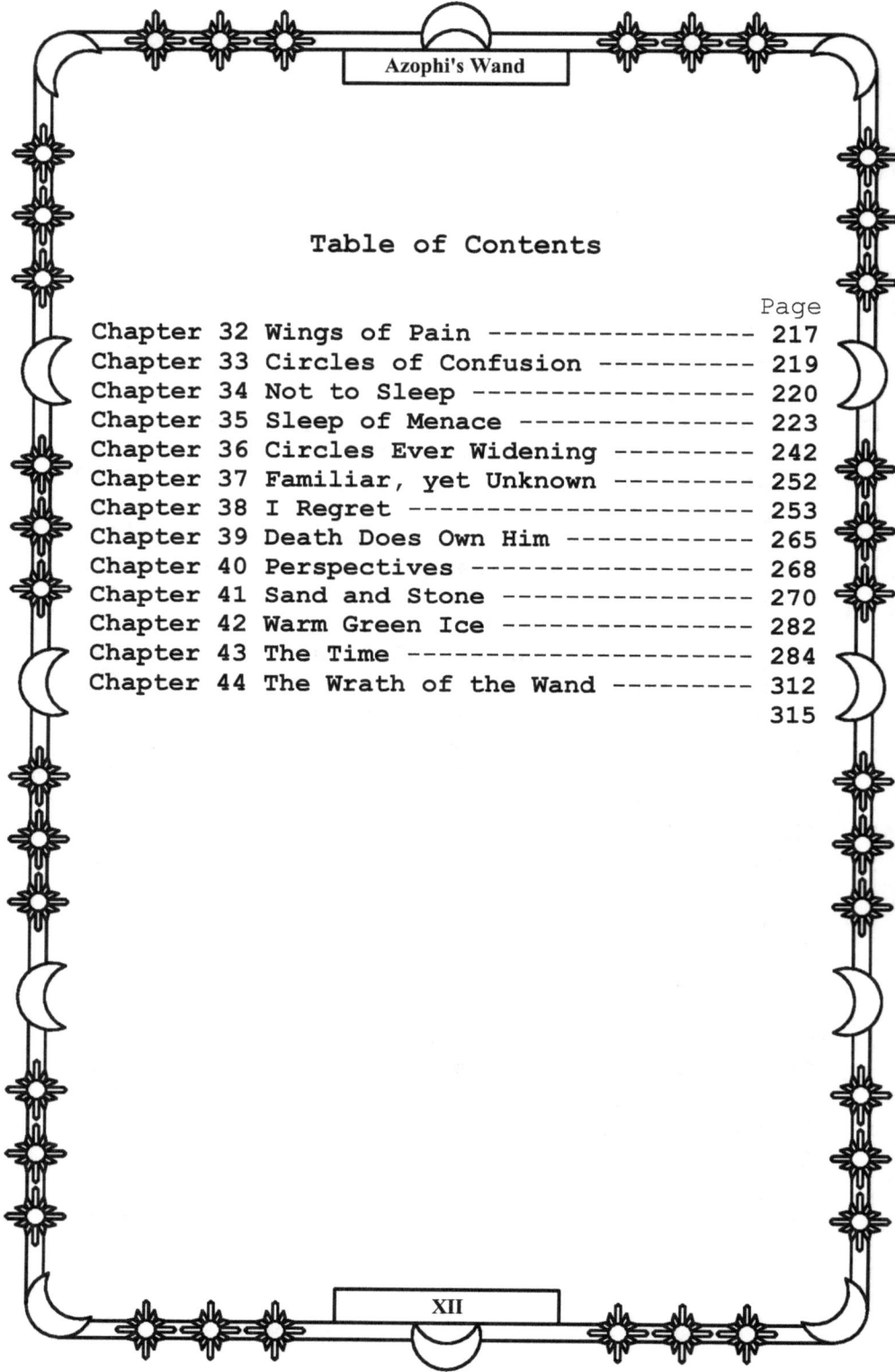

Azophi's Wand

Table of Contents

Illustration 01

Ortourian Beast Wrought Iron Window Grillwork

Copyright © 2019 Philip Raymond Sadler

1-A

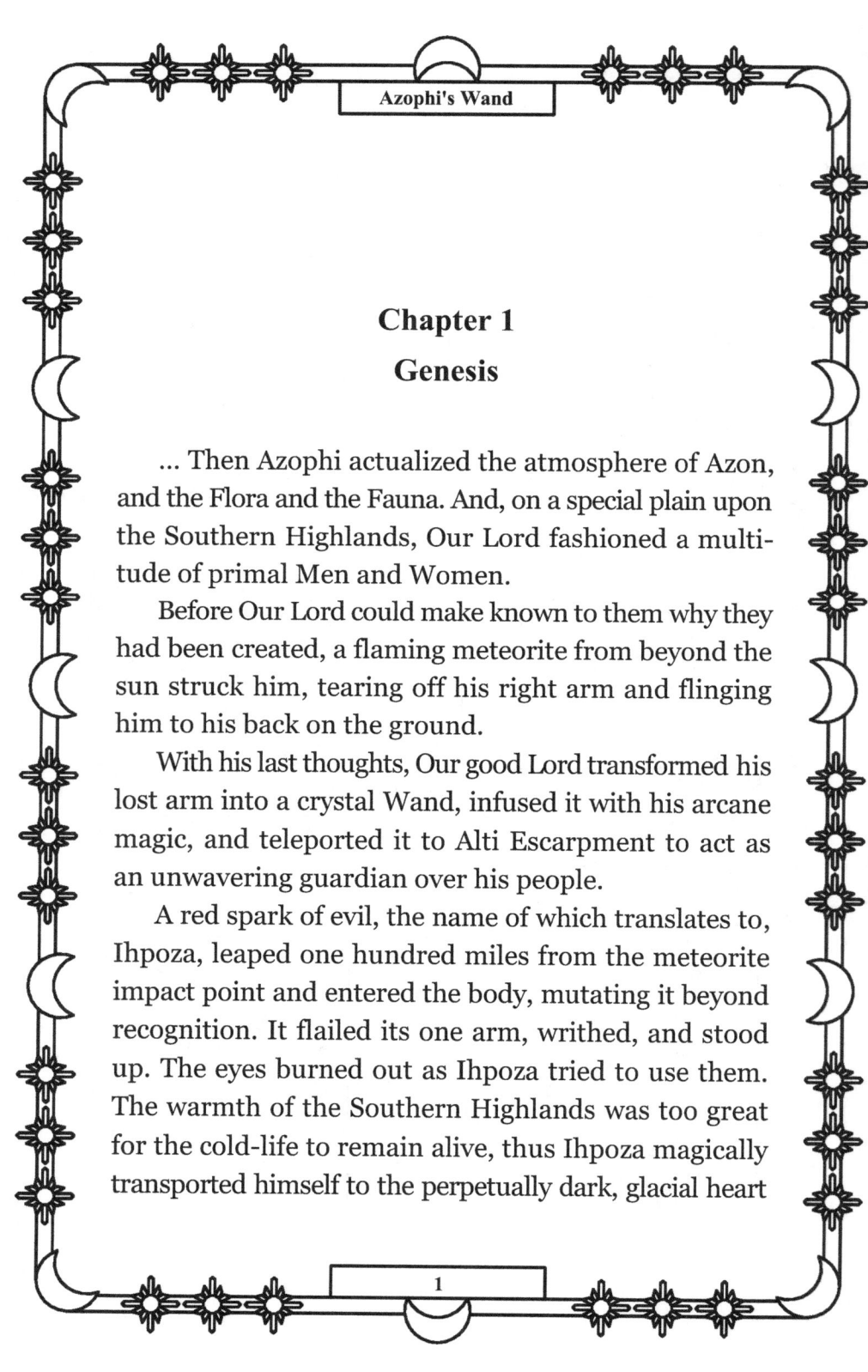

Chapter 1
Genesis

... Then Azophi actualized the atmosphere of Azon, and the Flora and the Fauna. And, on a special plain upon the Southern Highlands, Our Lord fashioned a multitude of primal Men and Women.

Before Our Lord could make known to them why they had been created, a flaming meteorite from beyond the sun struck him, tearing off his right arm and flinging him to his back on the ground.

With his last thoughts, Our good Lord transformed his lost arm into a crystal Wand, infused it with his arcane magic, and teleported it to Alti Escarpment to act as an unwavering guardian over his people.

A red spark of evil, the name of which translates to, Ihpoza, leaped one hundred miles from the meteorite impact point and entered the body, mutating it beyond recognition. It flailed its one arm, writhed, and stood up. The eyes burned out as Ihpoza tried to use them. The warmth of the Southern Highlands was too great for the cold-life to remain alive, thus Ihpoza magically transported himself to the perpetually dark, glacial heart

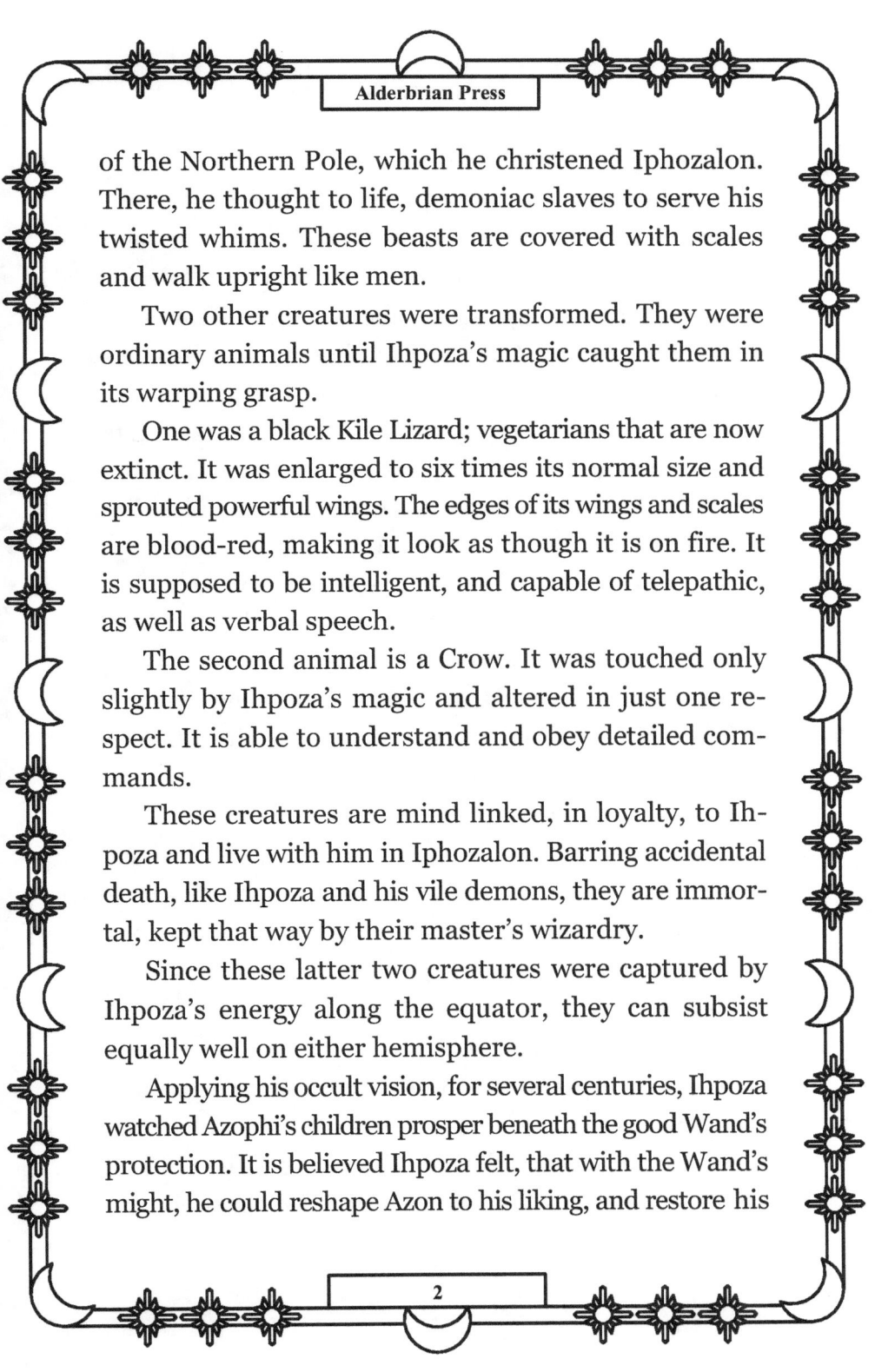

of the Northern Pole, which he christened Iphozalon. There, he thought to life, demoniac slaves to serve his twisted whims. These beasts are covered with scales and walk upright like men.

Two other creatures were transformed. They were ordinary animals until Ihpoza's magic caught them in its warping grasp.

One was a black Kile Lizard; vegetarians that are now extinct. It was enlarged to six times its normal size and sprouted powerful wings. The edges of its wings and scales are blood-red, making it look as though it is on fire. It is supposed to be intelligent, and capable of telepathic, as well as verbal speech.

The second animal is a Crow. It was touched only slightly by Ihpoza's magic and altered in just one respect. It is able to understand and obey detailed commands.

These creatures are mind linked, in loyalty, to Ihpoza and live with him in Iphozalon. Barring accidental death, like Ihpoza and his vile demons, they are immortal, kept that way by their master's wizardry.

Since these latter two creatures were captured by Ihpoza's energy along the equator, they can subsist equally well on either hemisphere.

Applying his occult vision, for several centuries, Ihpoza watched Azophi's children prosper beneath the good Wand's protection. It is believed Ihpoza felt, that with the Wand's might, he could reshape Azon to his liking, and restore his stolen body to its human form.

Marshaling his wizardry, Ihpoza fashioned an insulation sphere around himself and four of his demons and traveled to the Southern Highlands. He acted while the Wand was asleep. Imprisoning the Wand in a clear block of magic, he returned to Iphozalon intent upon discovering how to control the Wand's power.

There is slight proof the Wand created a Magic Life when it was captured. The purpose is not clear. The name translates to: Baylou. It has never been seen and its description has never been recorded.

Some say the Wand allowed itself to be abducted for a plan that is known only to the Wand. A scheme which has, of yet, not been executed by the Wand.

Others say the Wand and evil Ihpoza are evenly matched and neither can do anything to over power the other, or to change the way the world now exists.

Further it is recorded ...

Lie closed the dusty book and leaned back in his easy chair. "History! Hah!" he said, throwing the tome across the room. The book landed so that it was standing, face open, against the wall. "Legend!" Lie added, propping his feet on a stool.

There was a soft tapping.

When Lie opened the front portal, he saw dense fog. He stepped onto the cement porch and his foot struck something. He leaned down and picked up a gray, hand carved wooden box that looked a hundred years old. He

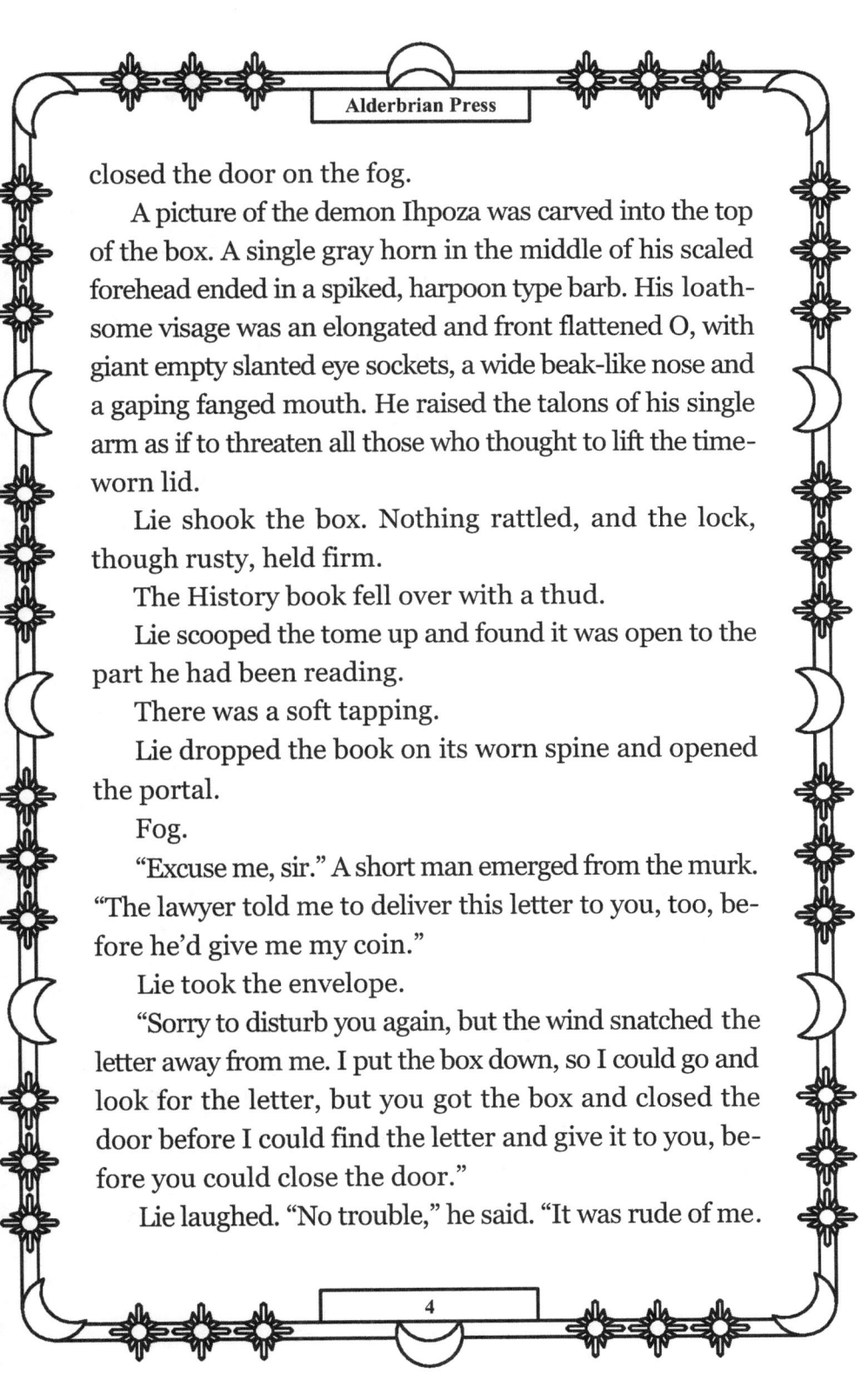

closed the door on the fog.

A picture of the demon Ihpoza was carved into the top of the box. A single gray horn in the middle of his scaled forehead ended in a spiked, harpoon type barb. His loathsome visage was an elongated and front flattened O, with giant empty slanted eye sockets, a wide beak-like nose and a gaping fanged mouth. He raised the talons of his single arm as if to threaten all those who thought to lift the time-worn lid.

Lie shook the box. Nothing rattled, and the lock, though rusty, held firm.

The History book fell over with a thud.

Lie scooped the tome up and found it was open to the part he had been reading.

There was a soft tapping.

Lie dropped the book on its worn spine and opened the portal.

Fog.

"Excuse me, sir." A short man emerged from the murk. "The lawyer told me to deliver this letter to you, too, before he'd give me my coin."

Lie took the envelope.

"Sorry to disturb you again, but the wind snatched the letter away from me. I put the box down, so I could go and look for the letter, but you got the box and closed the door before I could find the letter and give it to you, before you could close the door."

Lie laughed. "No trouble," he said. "It was rude of me.

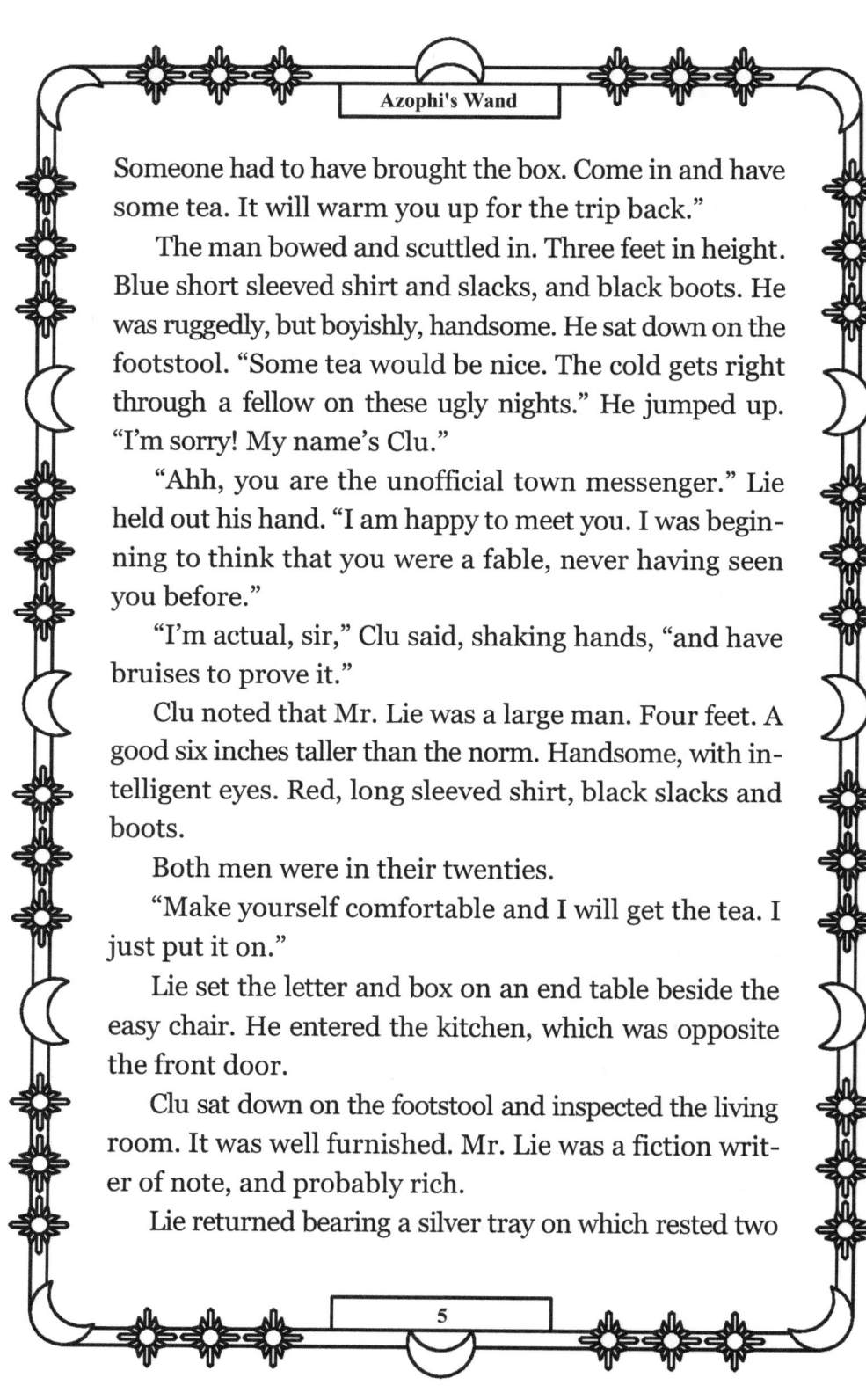

Someone had to have brought the box. Come in and have some tea. It will warm you up for the trip back."

The man bowed and scuttled in. Three feet in height. Blue short sleeved shirt and slacks, and black boots. He was ruggedly, but boyishly, handsome. He sat down on the footstool. "Some tea would be nice. The cold gets right through a fellow on these ugly nights." He jumped up. "I'm sorry! My name's Clu."

"Ahh, you are the unofficial town messenger." Lie held out his hand. "I am happy to meet you. I was beginning to think that you were a fable, never having seen you before."

"I'm actual, sir," Clu said, shaking hands, "and have bruises to prove it."

Clu noted that Mr. Lie was a large man. Four feet. A good six inches taller than the norm. Handsome, with intelligent eyes. Red, long sleeved shirt, black slacks and boots.

Both men were in their twenties.

"Make yourself comfortable and I will get the tea. I just put it on."

Lie set the letter and box on an end table beside the easy chair. He entered the kitchen, which was opposite the front door.

Clu sat down on the footstool and inspected the living room. It was well furnished. Mr. Lie was a fiction writer of note, and probably rich.

Lie returned bearing a silver tray on which rested two

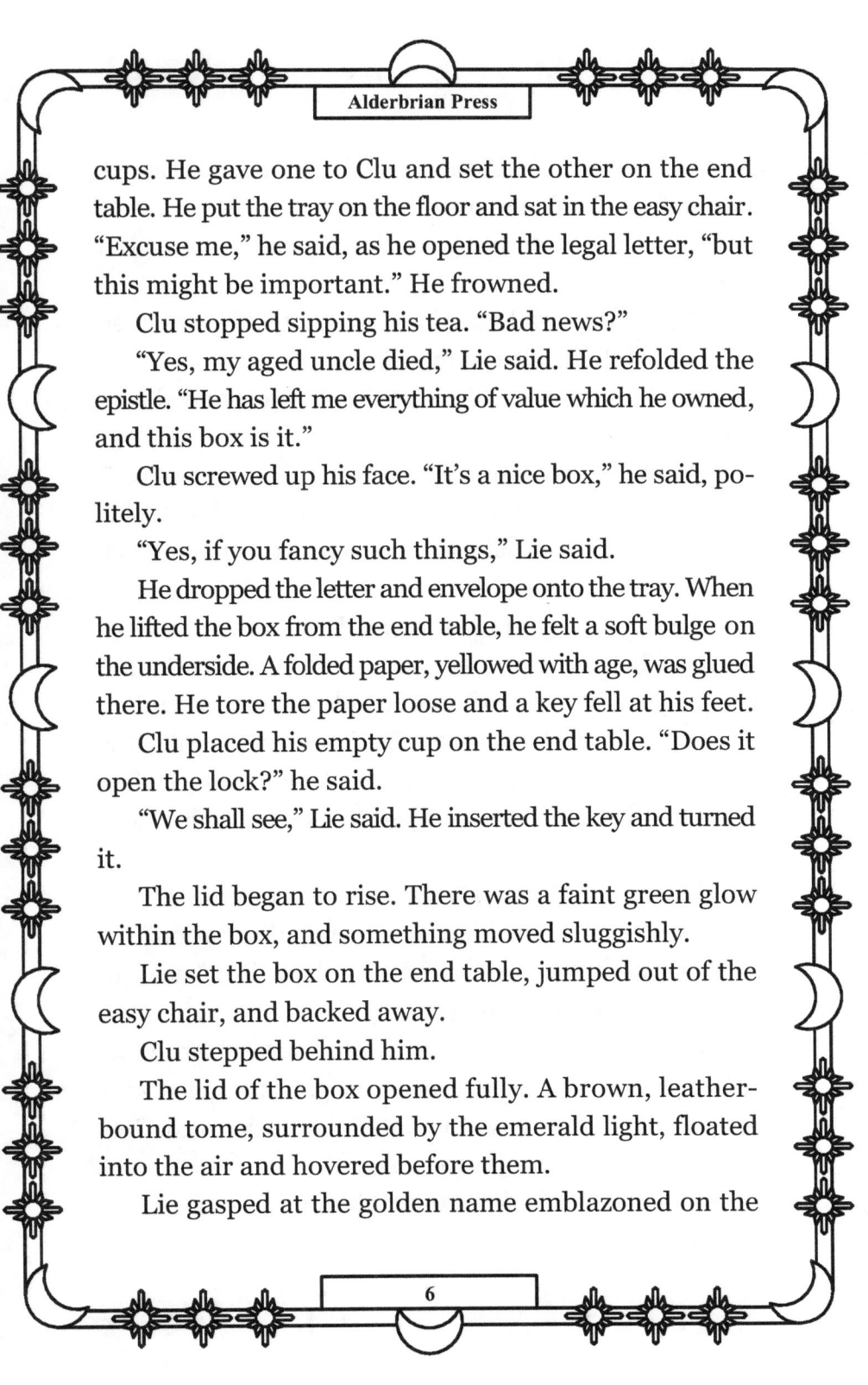

cups. He gave one to Clu and set the other on the end table. He put the tray on the floor and sat in the easy chair. "Excuse me," he said, as he opened the legal letter, "but this might be important." He frowned.

Clu stopped sipping his tea. "Bad news?"

"Yes, my aged uncle died," Lie said. He refolded the epistle. "He has left me everything of value which he owned, and this box is it."

Clu screwed up his face. "It's a nice box," he said, politely.

"Yes, if you fancy such things," Lie said.

He dropped the letter and envelope onto the tray. When he lifted the box from the end table, he felt a soft bulge on the underside. A folded paper, yellowed with age, was glued there. He tore the paper loose and a key fell at his feet.

Clu placed his empty cup on the end table. "Does it open the lock?" he said.

"We shall see," Lie said. He inserted the key and turned it.

The lid began to rise. There was a faint green glow within the box, and something moved sluggishly.

Lie set the box on the end table, jumped out of the easy chair, and backed away.

Clu stepped behind him.

The lid of the box opened fully. A brown, leather-bound tome, surrounded by the emerald light, floated into the air and hovered before them.

Lie gasped at the golden name emblazoned on the

book: Baylou Azophi. A single eye, lid closed, was carved, in relief, on the front cover.

Lie raised a trembling hand to touch the tome, but stopped short.

The Book's eyelid raised and a bright, glowing, green eye beheld them, almost angrily.

"No!" Lie shouted. "You are a myth! A childhood fairy tale! Not real!"

"Somebody's playing tricks on us, Mr. Lie. It must be!"

Baylou settled onto its back cover on the table, beside the chest, and closed its eye. It opened its cover and spoke in the air:

"This is what you must know. Read all that is written, and believe. In these pages, repose the truth, and the long awaited salvation of Azophi's sacred Wand!"

Lie was moved toward the Book against his will. This made him so angry, he slammed Baylou shut, locked it inside the chest, and dropped the key into his slacks pocket.

Clu stared at the box. "Was there something in the tea, Mr. Lie? Was it some kind of poison hallucination?"

Lie sat down heavily in the easy chair. "No," he said, trembling. "No hallucination."

Baylou misted into existence only inches before Lie, hovering at face level. Its green eye light was tinged with purple anger. "There is little time," the Book urged. "We must commence our journey, soon."

Clu slowly backed up toward the front door.

Baylou spun in the air to face him. "Hold!" the Tome said, coldly. "You must remain, for you are vital to Azophi's unfolding plan!" The door clicked as it was invisibly locked. Baylou's choler shine grew brighter. "Come and peruse what both of you must know!" the Book commanded.

Lie remained seated. "I will do nothing against my volition," he said. "Nothing!"

Baylou's angry glow vanished.

The door unlocked.

"I prefer not to compel you to do as you must," Baylou said, "but I shall, if it becomes necessary."

The Tome settled onto the end table and opened its front cover.

Lie and Clu drew nigh.

Baylou slowly flipped the gilt-edged, age-yellowed, black-lettered, rustling pages of its secret History for the men.

Illustration 02

Ortourian Beast Wrought Iron Window Grillwork

9-A

Chapter 2

Bogeymen, Myths and Legends

Baylou, perhaps asleep, lay closed on the end table.

Lie stood in stunned silence. He still found it hard to believe Azophi, Baylou and Ihpoza were more than childhood bogeymen and myths.

Clu stared at the Book, his expression, one of fearful excitement. "We must do what Baylou wishes," he said. "We must free the Wand."

"Why?"

"We have no choice."

"But, there is no real need. Ihpoza cannot intrude upon the Southern Hemisphere. He would be killed because his magic would fail after a few hours in the sun."

Baylou opened its eye.

"Why must we free the Wand?" Lie asked it. "Our crops are plentiful, our animals and people are healthy. There is no need to risk our lives in an unnecessary venture. And you enjoy limited powers. I read it in your pages. It would be foolish to go."

Baylou levitated from the table. "The action is necessary," it said. Its eye light swept over them like a wave of urgency. "With each day, Ihpoza's wizardry grows stronger. He will soon discern the secret of obtaining the Wand's powers and Azon shall be a wintry planet of evil!" The green light began to slowly rotate.

"Why do you come to us?" Lie asked. "Why must we be the ones to take on this task?"

Baylou remained silent but its light began to pulsate as well as spin.

"Why?" Lie demanded, shutting his eyes to the hypnotic illumination. "Why, damn you, why?" He angrily punched the Book in its eye.

Baylou staggered back in midair and the pulsating, spinning light receded into its pupil. "That is why I have selected you," Baylou Said. "You are both resistant to domination by Mind Magic." It lowered to the end table and closed its eye. "You must reconcile yourselves to the ineluctable. Tomorrow, we shall forgather supplies."

Lie started to speak.

Clu pulled on Lie's sleeve. "Baylou would not lie," he said. "Do we go?"

Lie stared at him. Clu seemed eager to do as Baylou ordered. So sure the Book was telling the truth. Did he truly comprehend the danger to his life?

"Well," Clu insisted. "Do we go?"

Lie smiled grimly. He had just fathomed the horror of Baylou's words, "Azon shall be a wintry planet of evil!" This had made up his mind. "Yes," he said, softly. "We will go."

Illustration 03

Ortourian Beast Wrought Iron Window Grillwork

Copyright © 2019 Philip Raymond Sadler

11-A

Chapter 3
More than Dream

In the dark center of Iphozalon lay an unmarred sheet of ice, shimmering with a blue light. This glacier spread for ten miles in every direction. In its middle stood a gigantic spired palace formed of the same frozen water. The deep blue glow of the palace could be seen for two hundred miles, but there was no one there to behold this luminous wonder besides its evil and soulless denizens.

The palace was almost as old as Azon, yet its odd, eerie towers showed none of the usual signs of the passage of time.

Within the palace, in his cavernous resting room, upon his ornately sculpted, glowing, blue ice bed, lay Iphozalon's master. He slept badly. He was suffering, for the tenth time, in as many hours, the same harrowing nightmare.

Ihpoza sat meditating on his shining, enchased, ice throne. The Wand of Azophi, in its gleaming, cylindrical clear-magic prison, stood nearby on the icy floor.

A ghostly Baylou appeared in the frigid air. The tome's wrathful eye began coloring Ihpoza with a hate filled green light.

Ihpoza attempted to rise to his feet, to flee, but could not, for he was being held in place by Baylou's radiant magic. A loud splintering of glass impelled Ihpoza's attention toward the magic prison. Terror raced through his brain.

Free of its bindings, the Wand arose from its ancient resting place and hovered over Ihpoza, illuminating him with a scintillating snow-white light, and burning him to ash with inescapable Magic.

Ihpoza screamed and awakened to discover himself safe and alone. The last eerie echoes of his cries sounded around him as he stood up and stalked through the doorway. Using telepathy, he angrily summoned his favorite slave.

The demon met Ihpoza in the hallway. It perused the Master's face and fell to its scaly knees to avoid peaking the Master's wrath. "The ill Dream has come again, my gracious Lord?" Favorite Slave said, subserviently.

Ihpoza paused and glared at it with his Magic Sight. "It is no longer a dream!" he bellowed, kicking Slave aside. "It is now a prophecy! Attend me! We must cast a spell to discover the enemy's plan!"

Favorite Slave scrambled to its taloned feet despite the pain that throbbed in its chest and followed a few slow paces behind its grotesque Master.

Only three objects adorned the colossal throne room: the Master's impressive ice throne and footstool, jut-

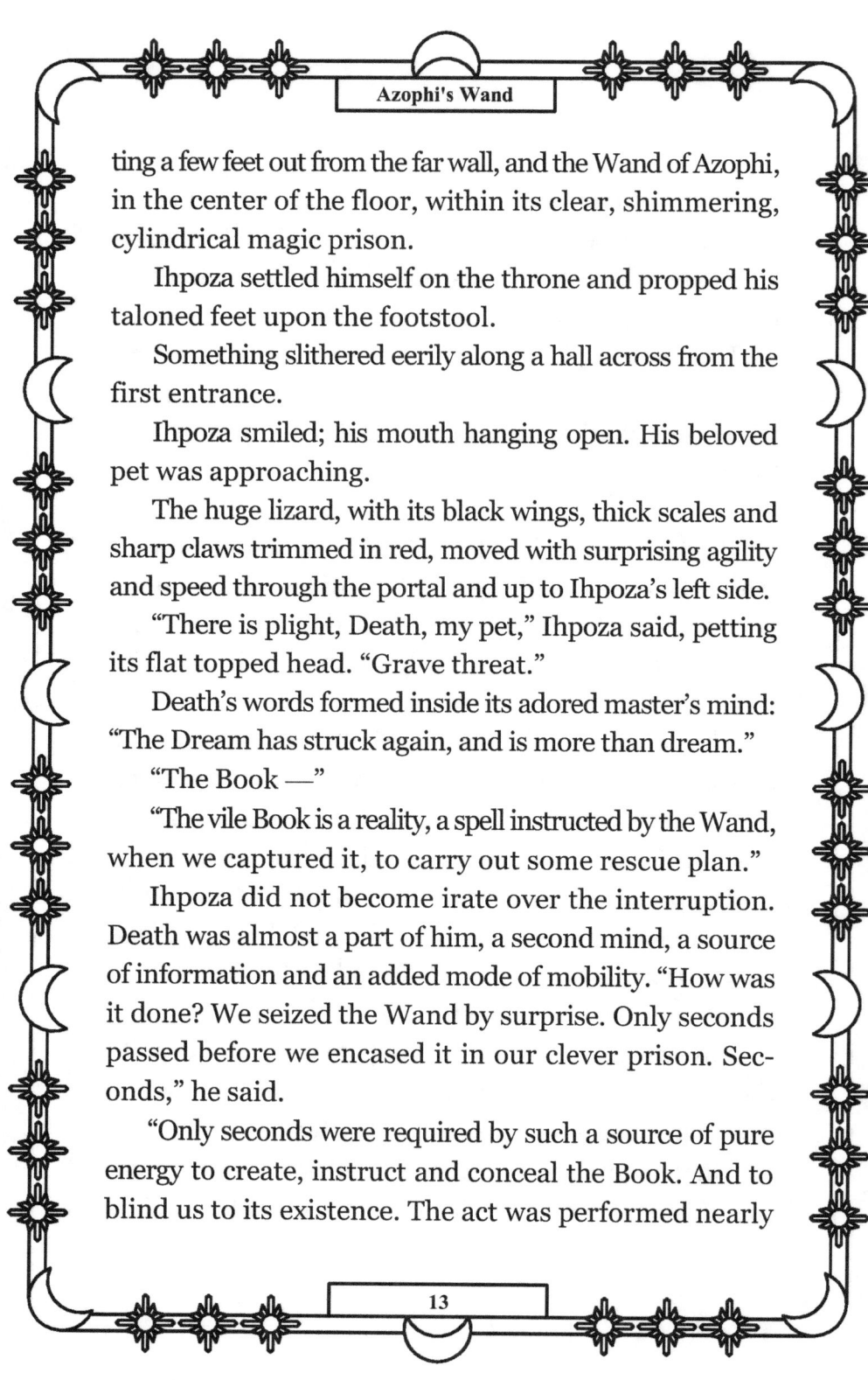

ting a few feet out from the far wall, and the Wand of Azophi, in the center of the floor, within its clear, shimmering, cylindrical magic prison.

Ihpoza settled himself on the throne and propped his taloned feet upon the footstool.

Something slithered eerily along a hall across from the first entrance.

Ihpoza smiled; his mouth hanging open. His beloved pet was approaching.

The huge lizard, with its black wings, thick scales and sharp claws trimmed in red, moved with surprising agility and speed through the portal and up to Ihpoza's left side.

"There is plight, Death, my pet," Ihpoza said, petting its flat topped head. "Grave threat."

Death's words formed inside its adored master's mind: "The Dream has struck again, and is more than dream."

"The Book —"

"The vile Book is a reality, a spell instructed by the Wand, when we captured it, to carry out some rescue plan."

Ihpoza did not become irate over the interruption. Death was almost a part of him, a second mind, a source of information and an added mode of mobility. "How was it done? We seized the Wand by surprise. Only seconds passed before we encased it in our clever prison. Seconds," he said.

"Only seconds were required by such a source of pure energy to create, instruct and conceal the Book. And to blind us to its existence. The act was performed nearly before the plan was thought. An instinct reaction, perhaps. And we were well deceived!"

"We have underestimated its intelligence."

"Yes, but we have imprisoned it securely. And beyond our hopes."

"Is it truly confined," Ihpoza mused, staring at the Wand, "or is it playing us for fools, to destroy us with the aid of the Book?"

"It is as helpless in its arcane restraint as you would be. I do not fully understand why so powerful a force is stopped by so weak a prison. Yet — It has something to do with the lack of air within the block. Perhaps the Wand needs the energy in the air, or in space, or in the light of the stars not filtered by the prison, before it can break free. I — do not understand. Not yet!"

Ihpoza squeezed the lizard's neck. "How soon can I control the haughty Wand? How can I control the Wand?" he asked.

Death flicked its forked tongue in and out. "I do not know. The old secret is illusive. It is simple. My instincts tell me this. Yet — The secret is unobtrusive and —" It shuddered, furious at its inability to solve the problem for its master.

Watching the conversation and hearing only Ihpoza's side, yet knowing the lizard spoke, Favorite Slave became jealous. It fell to its scaly knees and interrupted them: "You have forgotten the spell, my Master."

Ihpoza glared at the demon, then smiled cruelly. "It is

correct," he said. "You shall act your part now. Go to the end of our ice lawn and bring us a double handful of our snow. Quickly!"

Favorite Slave fled from the room, fearfully.

"Yes," Death telepathed. "The Wand is unable to work magic against us, but the repugnant Book may. We must uncover its plans and foil them."

Ihpoza continued to stroke the lizard's head, almost lovingly.

Illustration 04

Ortourian Beast Wrought Iron Window Grillwork

16-A

Chapter 4

You never do get all you Wish

Lie was awakened by the faint knocking. Disoriented, he wondered why he had slept on his couch. He recalled the eerie events of the previous night. He had given his guest the use of his bedroom as was customary.

"Who could be calling this early?" he mumbled as he stood up and went to the door. "Is Clu married and has his wife discovered where he is?" A prickly sensation shot down his spine.

Baylou was gone!

Lie unlocked the door and pulled it ajar.

The aged man in the green work suit was bearing a double arm load of packages. "I got the wares you ordered, sir," he said, cheerfully. "Where shall I put 'em?"

"I ordered!" Lie sputtered.

"Yes sir," the old man chimed. "Found your note under my shop door and made up your order, first thing. Note said you were leaving today, early, so I rushed. Where shall I put 'em?"

There was a slight movement of air from behind the door.

Lie read the total on the bill pasted on the first parcel. "Just set them on the porch," he said hastily, "and wait." He went to the end table by the couch, opened its drawer, plucked out the required number of coins, and paid the man. He kicked the bundles into the house, went inside and slammed the big door angrily. "You wrote that note, Baylou!"

"I enabled him to see a note."

"What?"

"I sensed you would need to sleep beyond eight o'clock, and take you until noon to gather supplies. So I did it more swiftly. We have limited time. I am trying to impress this upon you."

Lie nodded. "I — I will awaken Clu," he said. He knocked on the door and entered the bedroom. Baylou floated just behind him, at shoulder height.

Clu opened one eye. "Did the spooky Book go away, Mr. Lie?"

"No," Lie said sullenly.

Clu opened the other eye. "You never do get all you wish," he said, wistfully.

Baylou floated from behind Lie and said: "Come, I have prepared your breakfast."

They reluctantly followed the Book into the kitchen.

Clu had not even stirred the sugar in his tea when Baylou's eye glowed more brightly.

"It is changed," the Book said. "My existence is no longer hidden by my inactivity. Ihpoza will move to destroy us.

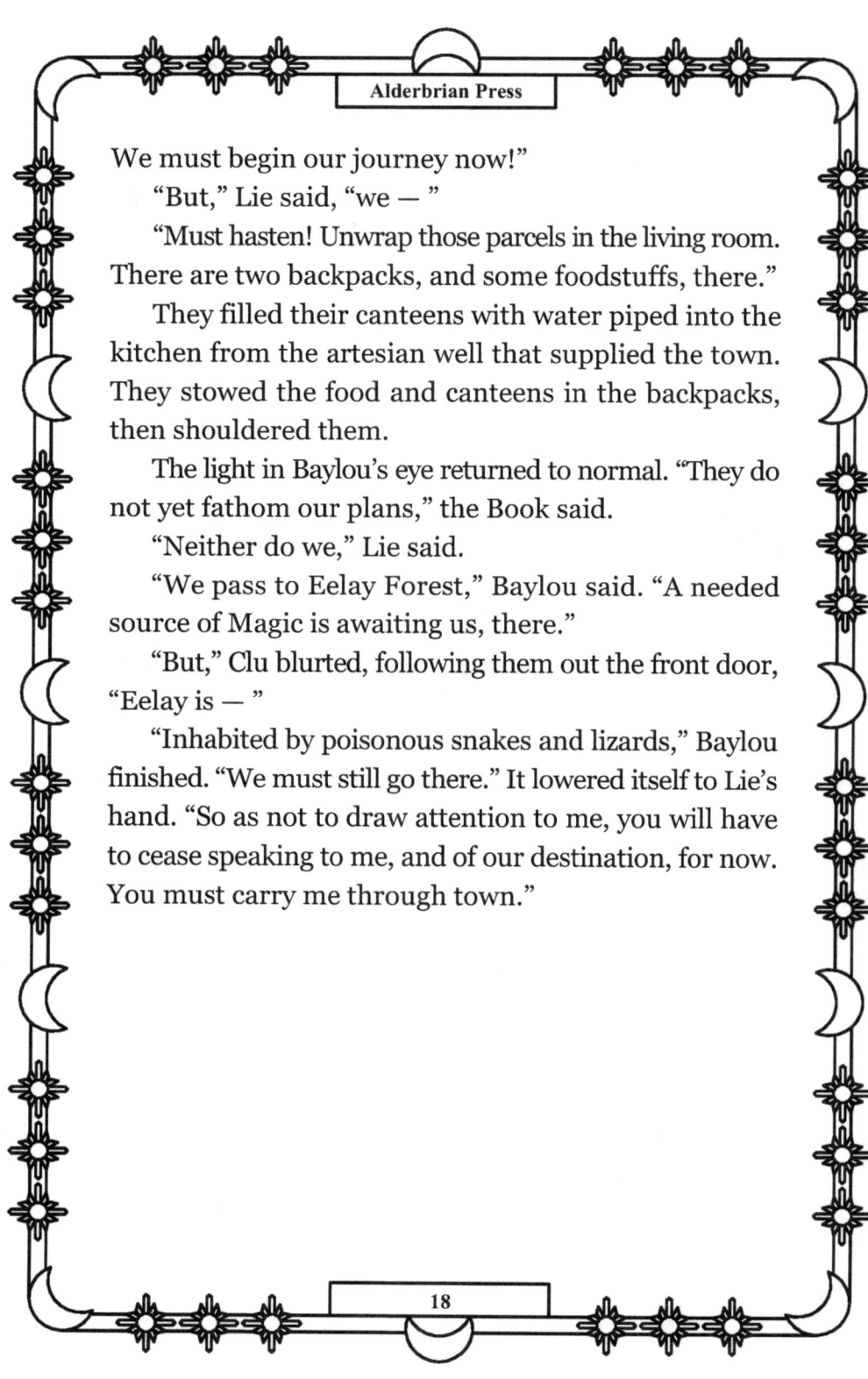

We must begin our journey now!"

"But," Lie said, "we — "

"Must hasten! Unwrap those parcels in the living room. There are two backpacks, and some foodstuffs, there."

They filled their canteens with water piped into the kitchen from the artesian well that supplied the town. They stowed the food and canteens in the backpacks, then shouldered them.

The light in Baylou's eye returned to normal. "They do not yet fathom our plans," the Book said.

"Neither do we," Lie said.

"We pass to Eelay Forest," Baylou said. "A needed source of Magic is awaiting us, there."

"But," Clu blurted, following them out the front door, "Eelay is — "

"Inhabited by poisonous snakes and lizards," Baylou finished. "We must still go there." It lowered itself to Lie's hand. "So as not to draw attention to me, you will have to cease speaking to me, and of our destination, for now. You must carry me through town."

Illustration 05

Ortourian Beast Wrought Iron Window Grillwork

Copyright © 2019 Philip Raymond Sadler

19-A

Chapter 5

Discovery Spell

Favorite Slave returned to the throne room and bowed low.

Ihpoza slapped the icy snow from the demon's hands, then kicked the beast onto its back. "That is to teach you never to speak when not spoken to. Leave us! We will consummate our Discovery Spell without the presence of one who lacks discipline!"

The demon scrambled to its feet, wrapped its arms around its flat scaly midsection, hunched over and fled from the throne room.

Death laughed in its master's mind. "How shall we spy upon our enemy?" it asked. "Shall we turn the ice below us into our eyes, dispatch the Crow, or shall I fly forth?"

Ihpoza stroked the lizard's flat head. "For now," he said, "we will use our ice. Later, if the Book is too immediate a threat, you shall go forth and destroy it."

"Why not send me now? The menace ended quickest, is the menace which inflicts the least pain."

"I do not wish to imperil the life of my only friend when other, less costly methods can be used."

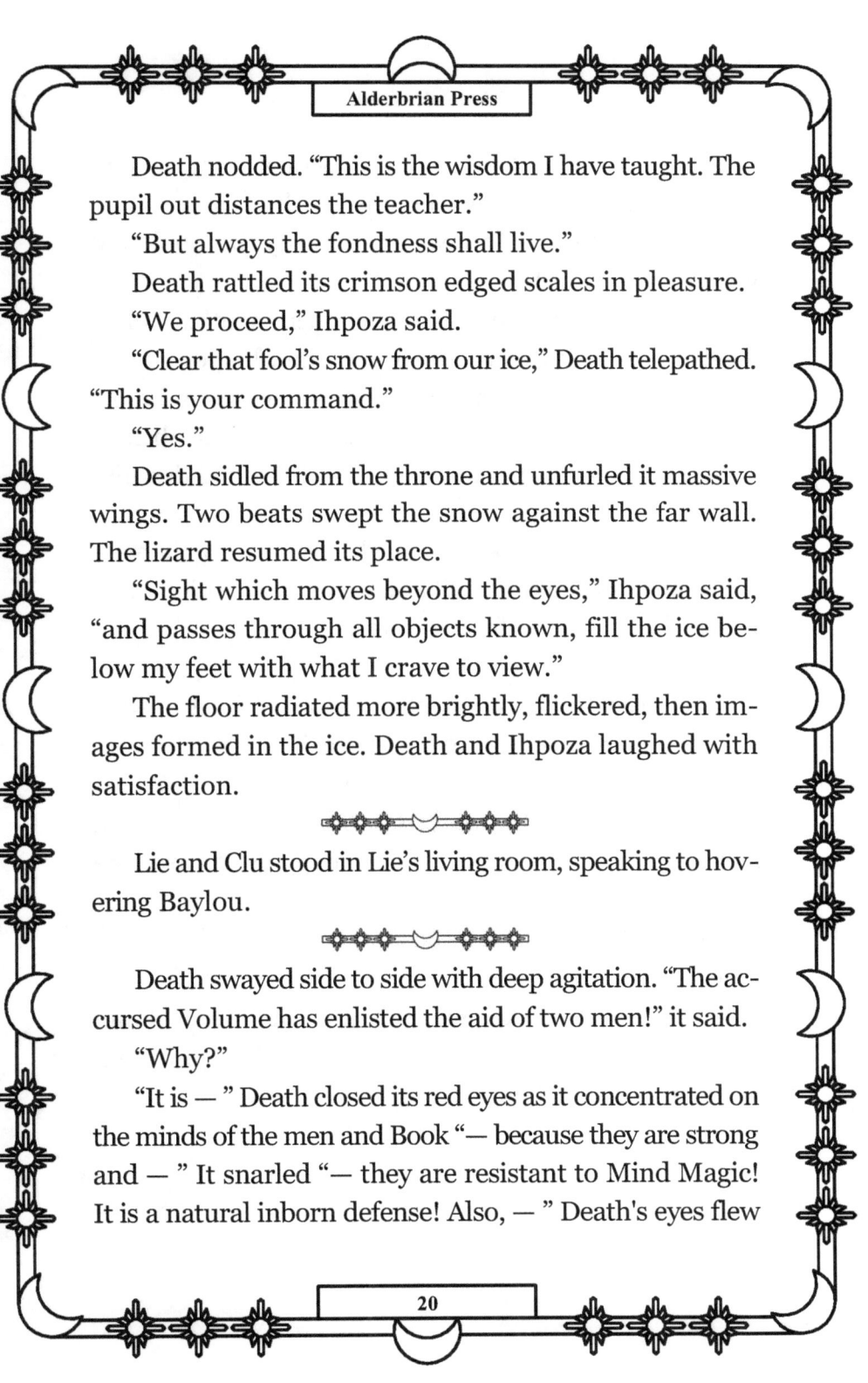

Death nodded. "This is the wisdom I have taught. The pupil out distances the teacher."

"But always the fondness shall live."

Death rattled its crimson edged scales in pleasure.

"We proceed," Ihpoza said.

"Clear that fool's snow from our ice," Death telepathed. "This is your command."

"Yes."

Death sidled from the throne and unfurled it massive wings. Two beats swept the snow against the far wall. The lizard resumed its place.

"Sight which moves beyond the eyes," Ihpoza said, "and passes through all objects known, fill the ice below my feet with what I crave to view."

The floor radiated more brightly, flickered, then images formed in the ice. Death and Ihpoza laughed with satisfaction.

Lie and Clu stood in Lie's living room, speaking to hovering Baylou.

Death swayed side to side with deep agitation. "The accursed Volume has enlisted the aid of two men!" it said.

"Why?"

"It is — " Death closed its red eyes as it concentrated on the minds of the men and Book "— because they are strong and — " It snarled "— they are resistant to Mind Magic! It is a natural inborn defense! Also, — " Death's eyes flew open with shock. "They amplify Baylou's magic as I do yours! That means they can amplify the Wand's magic! They must die before we can destroy the Book and control the Wand!"

Ihpoza smirked with his always open mouth. "Unless we can use them to our advantage," he whispered.

Death's trembling anger faded. It began to scheme. "We must know their intermediate moves, to control them."

"Yes," Ihpoza agreed. "We know their final destination."

"Iphozalon," they spoke, mentally, together, "our home."

They returned their evil attentions to the bright, distorted figures in the frozen water.

◈◈◈◡◈◈◈

"We pass to Eelay Forest," Baylou said. "A needed source of Magic is awaiting us there."

◈◈◈◡◈◈◈

Ihpoza returned the ice to its normal state and laughed, shrilly. "The Book did not sense our spying, my pet," he said.

"It is well," Death telepathed. "Now, we have the advantage."

"We do, indeed. And we shall utilize it. They will find more at Eelay than they expect, for we shall gift them their first, and last, great, tragic adventure."

Illustration 06

Ortourian Beast Wrought Iron Window Grillwork

Copyright © 2019 Philip Raymond Sadler

22-A

Chapter 6

Who Will Master Them?

Eelay resembled a green and black oil painting depicting towering, thorn covered trees surrounded by eerie gray mist.

They made camp a hundred yards from the edge. Not even the Book dared enter the snake and lizard infested forest at night.

Baylou stood on the grass, concentrating on the forest and mist as if it were listening to something the men could not hear.

Lie built up the fire the Book had ignited with a spark of magic.

Clu brought more sticks and dropped them on a reserve pile.

"That is enough."

"How is Baylou going to safeguard us, Mr. Lie? I really don't think it can."

"We will find out as soon as the Book pays attention to us again."

Baylou hovered near. "The Magic Cache is still there. It is active and is awaiting us," it said.

"How will you safeguard us from the snakes?"

Baylou turned toward Lie. "I shall control the snakes," it said. "They will show us the way."

"And the lizards?" Clu asked. He opened his backpack, took out a thin blanket and unrolled it on the grass. "Who will master them?"

"Lie shall."

Both men left off preparing for sleep.

Lie started to speak.

The angry cat howl of a lizard jangled their nerves. Its call blasted six times.

Another saurian, further away, responded.

"He can't control something that sounds like that!" Clu said, angrily.

"Those beasts move faster and weigh more than me," Lie said. "They see in the dark and never sleep. How can I direct them?"

Baylou faced the forest, taking the same listening position that it had earlier.

"Tell me!" Lie demanded.

Baylou did not respond.

"If our lives are not assured," Lie vowed, "we do not go in, Clu. We are of no value to the Book if we are dead!"

Illustration 07

Ortourian Beast Wrought Iron Window Grillwork

Copyright © 2019 Philip Raymond Sadler

24-A

Chapter 7

A Wrongness

Baylou's voice woke Lie and Clu at noon: "There is a trap set here."

Clu rolled up his blanket.

"Where is the trap?" Lie asked. "What is it?"

Baylou was still staring at the somber forest. It did not turn as it answered. "I am uncertain. There is a wrongness about Eelay."

"The trap's in the forest, then," Clu said. "And we can't go in, not knowing what and where in there it is."

Baylou faced him.

"You are wrong," the Book said.

"The trap is not in Eelay," Lie whispered. "It is Eelay."

"Yes," Baylou said. "Ihpoza's power of illusion is more adept than I have been warned."

"You mean, Eelay isn't real?" Clu said. He shouldered his backpack and started toward the forest.

Baylou blocked him. "It is not real," the Book said, "but the danger it conceals is, no doubt, a sudden death."

"But," Lie protested, getting to his feet, "you were speaking to the Magic that Azophi hid; speaking to it in there.

How?"

Clu nervously cracked his knuckles. "Can Ihpoza fool you with his illusions?" he asked.

"Yes."

"There is no real hope for us, then," Lie said, angrily, as he folded up his blanket.

"I was deceived temporarily," Baylou assured them, firmly. "I have detected the danger and can act against it."

Lie shouldered his backpack. "Then do so," he said, "or Clu and I are no longer your assistants."

"You react as a child," Baylou said. "You possess great resistance, but I possess superior power."

"I do not think so, or you would not have fallen prey to this illusion and could execute the Wand's rescue by yourself," Lie said.

Baylou's anger glow warmed their skin. "Why do you value your life so highly, knowing, that, if you refuse to help free the Wand, you shall have no life?"

"Why do you persist with this quest, when you cannot guarantee that we shall live to perform our purpose," Lie countered. "If Ihpoza has spun one illusion, he will spin others. One time, you will fail to detect illusion from reality, and we will die uselessly. What will become of Azon then?"

Baylou's anger receded into its pupil. "It is done," the Tome said.

"What is done?" Lie said, taken aback. "What trick is this?"

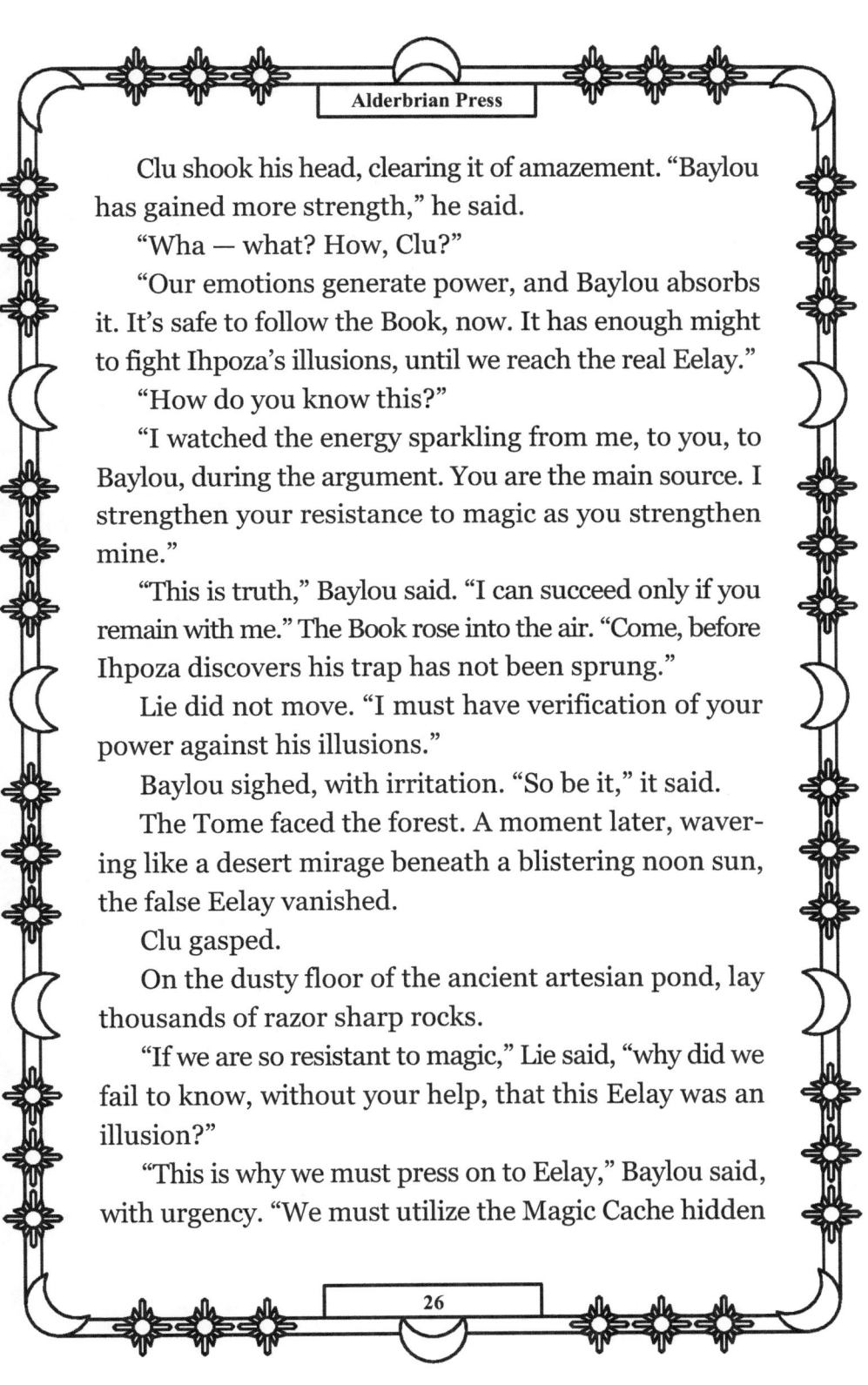

Clu shook his head, clearing it of amazement. "Baylou has gained more strength," he said.

"Wha — what? How, Clu?"

"Our emotions generate power, and Baylou absorbs it. It's safe to follow the Book, now. It has enough might to fight Ihpoza's illusions, until we reach the real Eelay."

"How do you know this?"

"I watched the energy sparkling from me, to you, to Baylou, during the argument. You are the main source. I strengthen your resistance to magic as you strengthen mine."

"This is truth," Baylou said. "I can succeed only if you remain with me." The Book rose into the air. "Come, before Ihpoza discovers his trap has not been sprung."

Lie did not move. "I must have verification of your power against his illusions."

Baylou sighed, with irritation. "So be it," it said.

The Tome faced the forest. A moment later, wavering like a desert mirage beneath a blistering noon sun, the false Eelay vanished.

Clu gasped.

On the dusty floor of the ancient artesian pond, lay thousands of razor sharp rocks.

"If we are so resistant to magic," Lie said, "why did we fail to know, without your help, that this Eelay was an illusion?"

"This is why we must press on to Eelay," Baylou said, with urgency. "We must utilize the Magic Cache hidden there to prevent Ihpoza from spinning more illusions, and to foil his further overriding of your intrinsic resistance. He does so, more than he should be able to. This could spell tragedy."

"You mean," Clu said, "Ihpoza may already control the Wand?"

"He may be toying with us, before he destroys this half of Azon," Baylou said.

The Tome led them away from the prehistoric pond.

Illustration 08

Ortourian Beast Wrought Iron Window Grillwork

Copyright © 2019 Philip Raymond Sadler

28-A

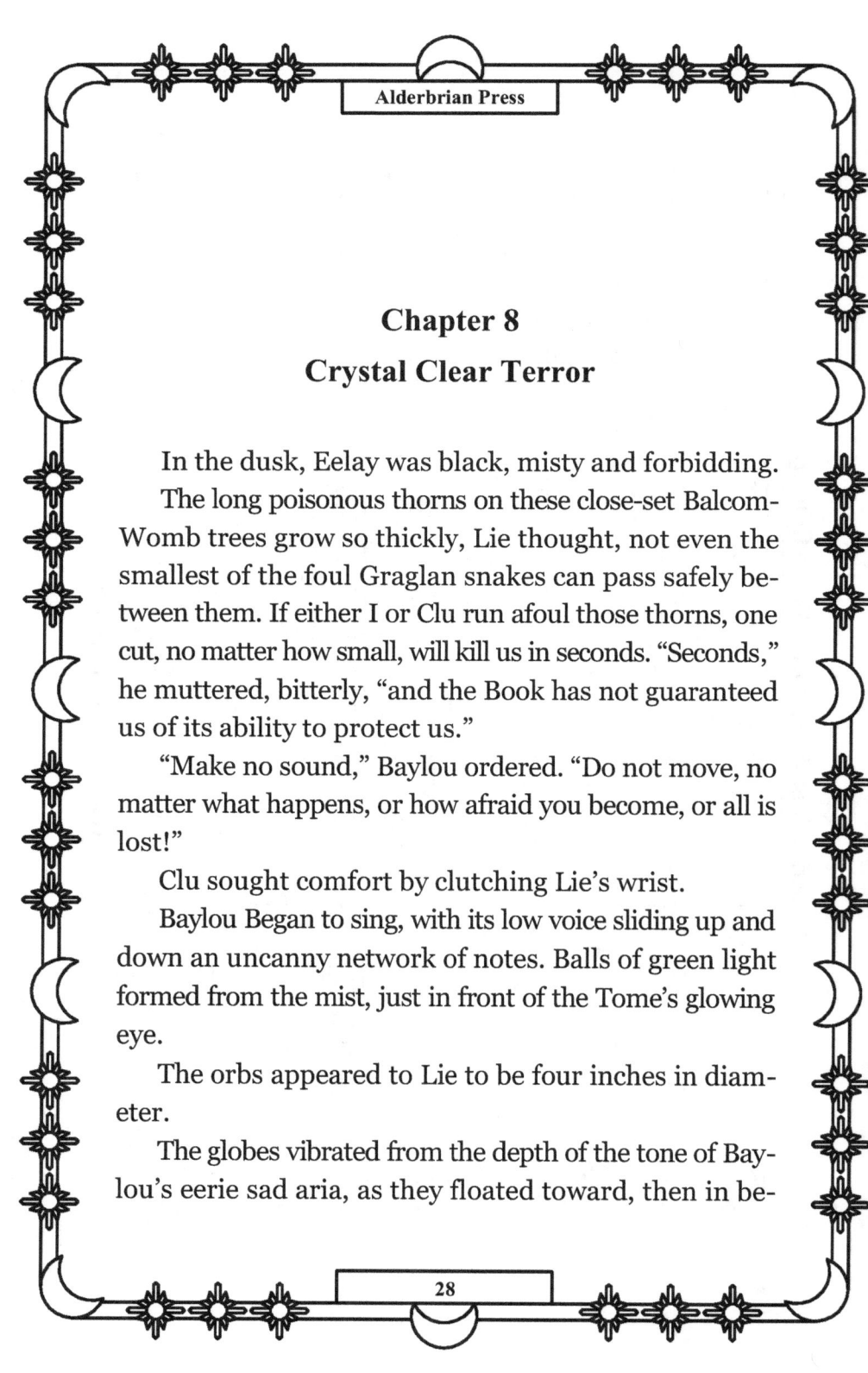

Chapter 8
Crystal Clear Terror

In the dusk, Eelay was black, misty and forbidding.

The long poisonous thorns on these close-set Balcom-Womb trees grow so thickly, Lie thought, not even the smallest of the foul Graglan snakes can pass safely between them. If either I or Clu run afoul those thorns, one cut, no matter how small, will kill us in seconds. "Seconds," he muttered, bitterly, "and the Book has not guaranteed us of its ability to protect us."

"Make no sound," Baylou ordered. "Do not move, no matter what happens, or how afraid you become, or all is lost!"

Clu sought comfort by clutching Lie's wrist.

Baylou Began to sing, with its low voice sliding up and down an uncanny network of notes. Balls of green light formed from the mist, just in front of the Tome's glowing eye.

The orbs appeared to Lie to be four inches in diameter.

The globes vibrated from the depth of the tone of Baylou's eerie sad aria, as they floated toward, then in between the BalcomWomb trees. The unearthly luminosity of the balls revealed the edge of the prickly forest.

Baylou's song became a long note of thunder, and the ground shook.

Lie's and Clu's eyes refused to focus.

The emerald orbs spread through dark Eelay, moving closer to its ebony heart.

The gray scaled serpents felt their treasure was threatened. They attacked the forty balls again and again but their sharp venom filled claws and fangs passed uselessly through the will-o'-the-wisps.

The light globes stopped their advance and Baylou's song changed until it sounded like dozens of children crying and wailing, each at a different octave.

The snakes became immobile.

Lie's vision refocused. What had been a blurred horror, now became a crystal clear terror.

Preceded by the orbs, the snakes began creeping from the forest like a wave of glowing red eyes. They moved stiffly, against their wills.

They are approaching us, Lie thought. If Baylou controls them, they should be moving away, out into the fields! His mind whirled. If Baylou commands them! He stared at the Tome from the corners of his eyes. It was still singing that unnerving crying aria. His fear increased. Baylou was motionless, as if it were being controlled. Possessed by Ihpoza? Lie attempted to budge, to call out to Baylou, but his body refused to obey.

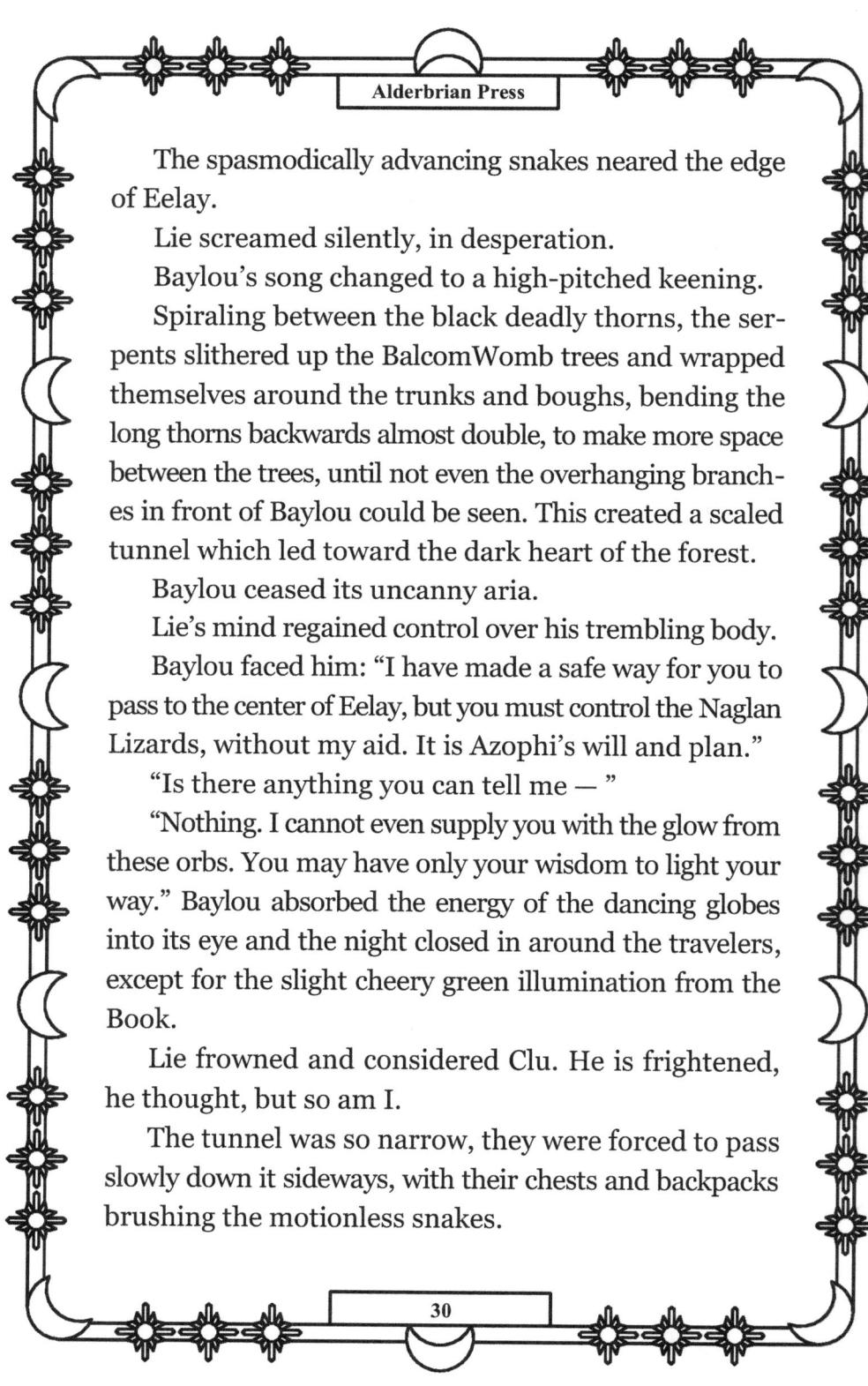

The spasmodically advancing snakes neared the edge of Eelay.

Lie screamed silently, in desperation.

Baylou's song changed to a high-pitched keening.

Spiraling between the black deadly thorns, the serpents slithered up the BalcomWomb trees and wrapped themselves around the trunks and boughs, bending the long thorns backwards almost double, to make more space between the trees, until not even the overhanging branches in front of Baylou could be seen. This created a scaled tunnel which led toward the dark heart of the forest.

Baylou ceased its uncanny aria.

Lie's mind regained control over his trembling body.

Baylou faced him: "I have made a safe way for you to pass to the center of Eelay, but you must control the Naglan Lizards, without my aid. It is Azophi's will and plan."

"Is there anything you can tell me — "

"Nothing. I cannot even supply you with the glow from these orbs. You may have only your wisdom to light your way." Baylou absorbed the energy of the dancing globes into its eye and the night closed in around the travelers, except for the slight cheery green illumination from the Book.

Lie frowned and considered Clu. He is frightened, he thought, but so am I.

The tunnel was so narrow, they were forced to pass slowly down it sideways, with their chests and backpacks brushing the motionless snakes.

Not even shimmering Baylou spoke.

The slimy smell of the motionless serpents was nauseating, and it was well-nigh as thick as the gray mist swirling outside the loathsome corridor.

Lie controlled his breathing, inhaling as little air as necessary.

In a short while, Baylou turned to Lie. "We come to tunnel's end," the Book said. It pressed itself up against the top of the serpent corridor to allow them to pass.

"You stay here?" Lie exclaimed, with dismay.

"Yes," Baylou said, sternly. "I can leave the tunnel only after you have succeeded in your task."

"But," Lie protested, "is it necessary that Clu be jeopardized? Must he come further with me?"

"It is Azophi's will," Baylou said, as it sadly closed its eye.

Angry at Azophi, Lie led Clu through the last inches of the protection of the viper passage, and into the waiting forest.

Illustration 09

Ortourian Beast Wrought Iron Window Grillwork

32-A

Chapter 9

Ghosts, Lizards and Snakes

Lie stood motionless until his eyes became accustomed to the darkness. He glanced back, but the tunnel had disappeared. He saw only BalcomWombs.

"We're going to die, aren't we, Mr. Lie?"

Lie forced a chuckle. "Have we not journeyed this far, alive?" he said, reassuringly.

"Yes, but with Baylou's help, not our own."

Something hard brushed the nape of Lie's neck. He spun around, eagerly. "Baylou — " A cold knot formed in his stomach. The ghostly lizard sailed eerily away from him on silk-like wings and vanished into the trees. When he turned back from watching the pallid beast, Clu was missing! Lie's heart throbbed. There was no movement, no sound, anywhere. He cupped his hands to his mouth. "Clu!" he shouted, terrified. "Where are you!"

"I'm here, Mr. Lie! Can't you see me? I'm right here!"

Lie felt a tug on his sleeve. A lizard materialized beside him, and soared into the lofty BalcomWombs, out of view, leaving Clu, in sight, unharmed.

"What's the matter, Mr. Lie? Is there something wrong

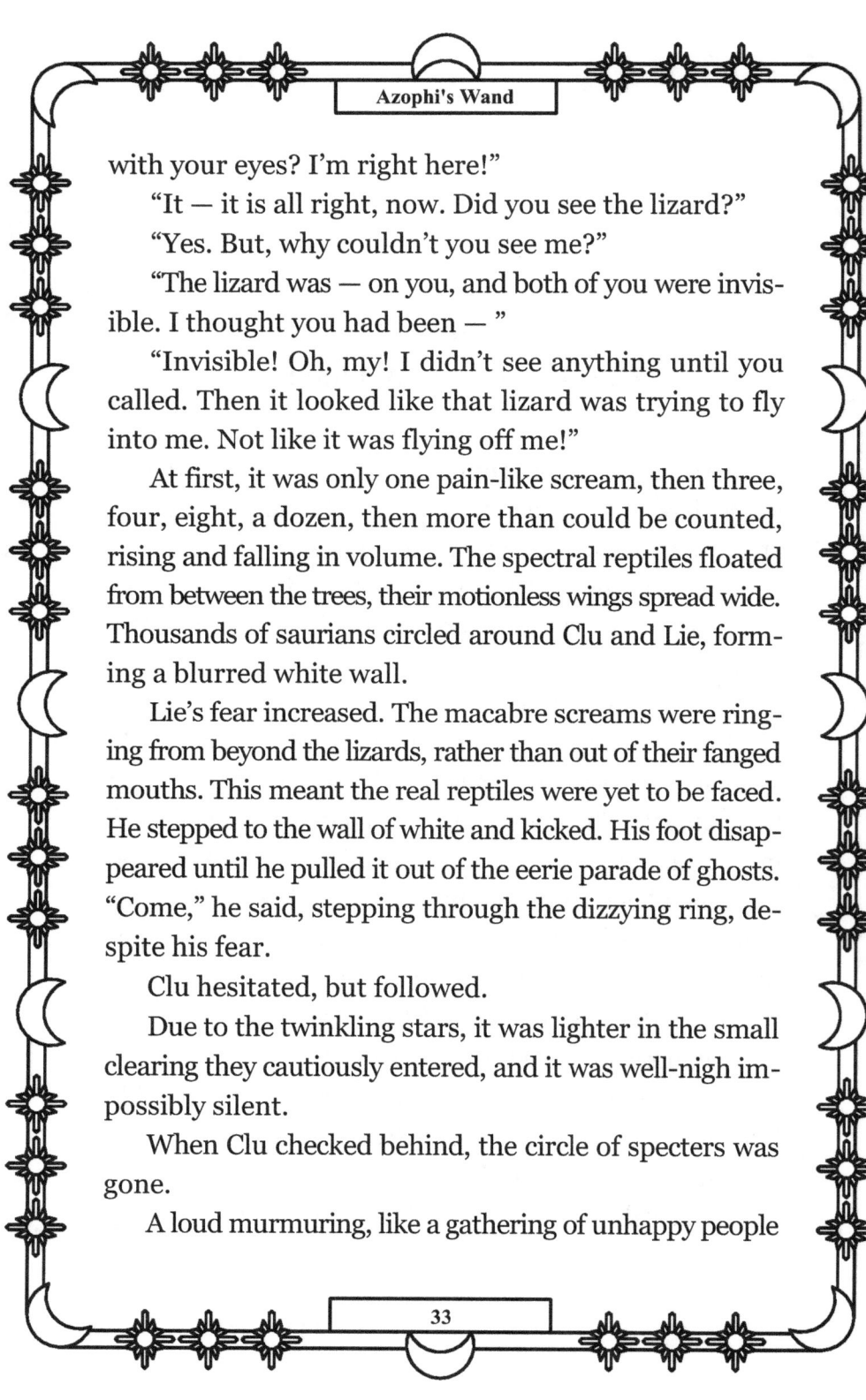

with your eyes? I'm right here!"

"It — it is all right, now. Did you see the lizard?"

"Yes. But, why couldn't you see me?"

"The lizard was — on you, and both of you were invisible. I thought you had been — "

"Invisible! Oh, my! I didn't see anything until you called. Then it looked like that lizard was trying to fly into me. Not like it was flying off me!"

At first, it was only one pain-like scream, then three, four, eight, a dozen, then more than could be counted, rising and falling in volume. The spectral reptiles floated from between the trees, their motionless wings spread wide. Thousands of saurians circled around Clu and Lie, forming a blurred white wall.

Lie's fear increased. The macabre screams were ringing from beyond the lizards, rather than out of their fanged mouths. This meant the real reptiles were yet to be faced. He stepped to the wall of white and kicked. His foot disappeared until he pulled it out of the eerie parade of ghosts. "Come," he said, stepping through the dizzying ring, despite his fear.

Clu hesitated, but followed.

Due to the twinkling stars, it was lighter in the small clearing they cautiously entered, and it was well-nigh impossibly silent.

When Clu checked behind, the circle of specters was gone.

A loud murmuring, like a gathering of unhappy people

at an internment, rose about them, and Baylou wavered into existence.

"Baylou!" Clu shouted, happily running toward the Book.

Lie grasped at Clu, but his fingers only brushed Clu's backpack.

Fiery light seared from Baylou's eye, encasing Clu in a square, hollow, block of clear magic. Clu screamed, flailed his arms, then became quiet, dropping to his knees and slumping against the inside wall of the block.

The Tome spun to face Lie.

Lie was already in motion toward Clu.

The volume issued its flame.

Lie threw himself to the moss, rolling side to side, then scrambled to his feet.

Baylou's emerald fire glared forth, dead on target.

Lie's mind whispered truth, and he stood his ground. The magic around both men sputtered like flares in wind, then vanished.

Baylou extended its bright eye into a foot long spear. Wailing like a madman, it swooped toward Lie.

Lie stepped aside and brought his fist down on the eye spear, breaking it in half.

Baylou was sent spinning, end for end. When it regained its air footing, it reformed its eye to its normal state, then swung at Lie, attempting to catch him across a temple with a corner of its cover.

Lie slugged the Book above its glaring eye. As the mad

Tome staggered backwards in the air, Lie rained blow after enraged blow into it, forcing it toward the edge of the clearing.

Baylou spun unsteadily around and crashed flat against one of the tall BalcomWombs.

Lie jammed a foot against the Book's back cover, impaling the Tome on the numerous poison thorns of the tree. The detonation of the eye knocked Lie stumbling backwards for a few feet. The greater explosion of the Book ripped the BalcomWomb to splinters and hurled Lie to his back on the moss. He sucked in air, rolled half over, and unsteadily helped himself to his feet.

The uncanny murmurings had continued throughout the confrontation. Now they increased in volume.

Lie ignored the mutterings, and the dizziness he suffered, and stumbled over to Clu. He knelt beside Clu and patted Clu's pale cheeks. "Please, do not be dead, Clu," he said. "Do not be dead."

The occult murmurings became angry and threatening. A slimy wind began circling Lie and Clu as had the ghost lizards.

Clu moved his arms feebly, but remained unconscious.

Wide, Blue-green rings of light coalesced around Lie and Clu and began pulsating, and spinning with the wind. Like forty wrathful nightmares, the Naglan Lizards hovered out of the darkness to circle the clearing, and the hated man who dared challenge their territory. Their wingless, incredibly green bodies reflected the pulsating light rings.

The center of the whooshing whirl wind was calm. Lie's mind drew an inspiration from this and spoke to him. He gathered insensate Clu into his arms.

The lizards decreased the circumference of their circle with terrifying slowness, muttering irately.

Lie's thoughts were clouded by profound fear and desperation but his subconscious spoke to him again, forcing him to calmly call back Baylou's earlier hard words: "... You must control the Naglan Lizards ... You must control the Naglan Lizards ..." Lie repeated the words aloud: "You must control the Naglan Lizards."

The lizards passed through the wind whorl and light loops. Their loud murmurings were repulsively nearly human. Like —

"Like the Book!" Lie shouted; wild hope rising in his soul. "Like the almost human voice of Baylou, whom I killed!"

Clu regained consciousness.

Lie nodded at Clu. "The light of my wisdom!" Lie said. "The light of my wisdom, to show me the way!"

Clu had taken in their situation and was sure their inescapable death had driven Lie insane. He threw his arms around Lie's neck and sobbed.

The Lizards howled like incensed cats and launched themselves at the men. The saurian's fangs dripped saliva, and their claws oozed venom.

Lie smiled, although the smallest doubt still played in his mind. "Stop!" he commanded.

Before the power word had even passed beyond Lie's trembling lips, the slimy wind and light rings disappeared. It was more the thought, than the action, which controlled the might. The Naglans were paralyzed in midair, their unnerving mutterings stilled in their emerald throats.

Clu looked incredulously at Lie, then the lizards. "Why?" he asked. He was unable to speak above a whisper, for fear his words might free the monsters from their spell. "How?"

Lie released Clu to a standing position.

"The Naglans not only guard the magic," Lie said, "they are the magic. This is what I needed to realize in order to control them."

Eelay filled with affection and, like a puzzling but welcome dream, Baylou floated from the snake tunnel.

Clu gasped, edging closer to Lie. "You're — you're dead!" he said. His thoughts raced as he recalled the suffocating occult flames that had flickered around him. He blurted: "You're the real Baylou! The other was — "

"A simulacrum of me from the minds of the Naglans," Baylou said. The Volume levitated around one of the motionless lizards. "You have followed your wisdom admirably, but have not yet completed your mission."

"What more must I do today, besides risk our lives?" Lie demanded.

Baylou raised to Lie's eye level. "You must release the magic within the Naglans, into me," the Book said.

Lie leaned to his right to avoid Baylou's power beam,

then struck the Book with both fists.

Baylou fell to the moss on its back cover.

Lie ground his heel into the Tome's green eye.

Baylou screamed and shot into the air at an angle.

Lie stumbled back, steadied himself, then ran to his right, hauling Clu after him, toward the trees.

Baylou's magic ray burned a scar into the earth behind them.

The Book drew upon its energy to attack again.

Lie clenched a fist against his heart and chanted: "Naglan Magic, will of Wand, Azophi's knowledge guide my hand!"

A thread of green magic sprouted from the nearest lizard and conjoined itself to the first knuckle of Lie's fist.

The false Baylou had failed in its second attempt to destroy Lie and Clu and fell heavily to the moss, splattering like hot wax.

Lie held his fist over his head. "Naglan Magic, you will fulfill the plans of Azophi's Wand!"

The energy thread parted from Lie's hand, burst into red flame, burned like a fuse, and struck the lizard's nose. The Naglan ignited, formed itself into a sphere, and trundled through the air, sounding like a boulder rolling over a wooden floor. The orb struck and ignited a second lizard, which formed itself into a ball. The two globes of non-consuming flame combined, and trundled around the ring of great lizards until each had been set afire and appended to the growing crimson orb.

Lie lowered his arm and the roaring globe of fire set-

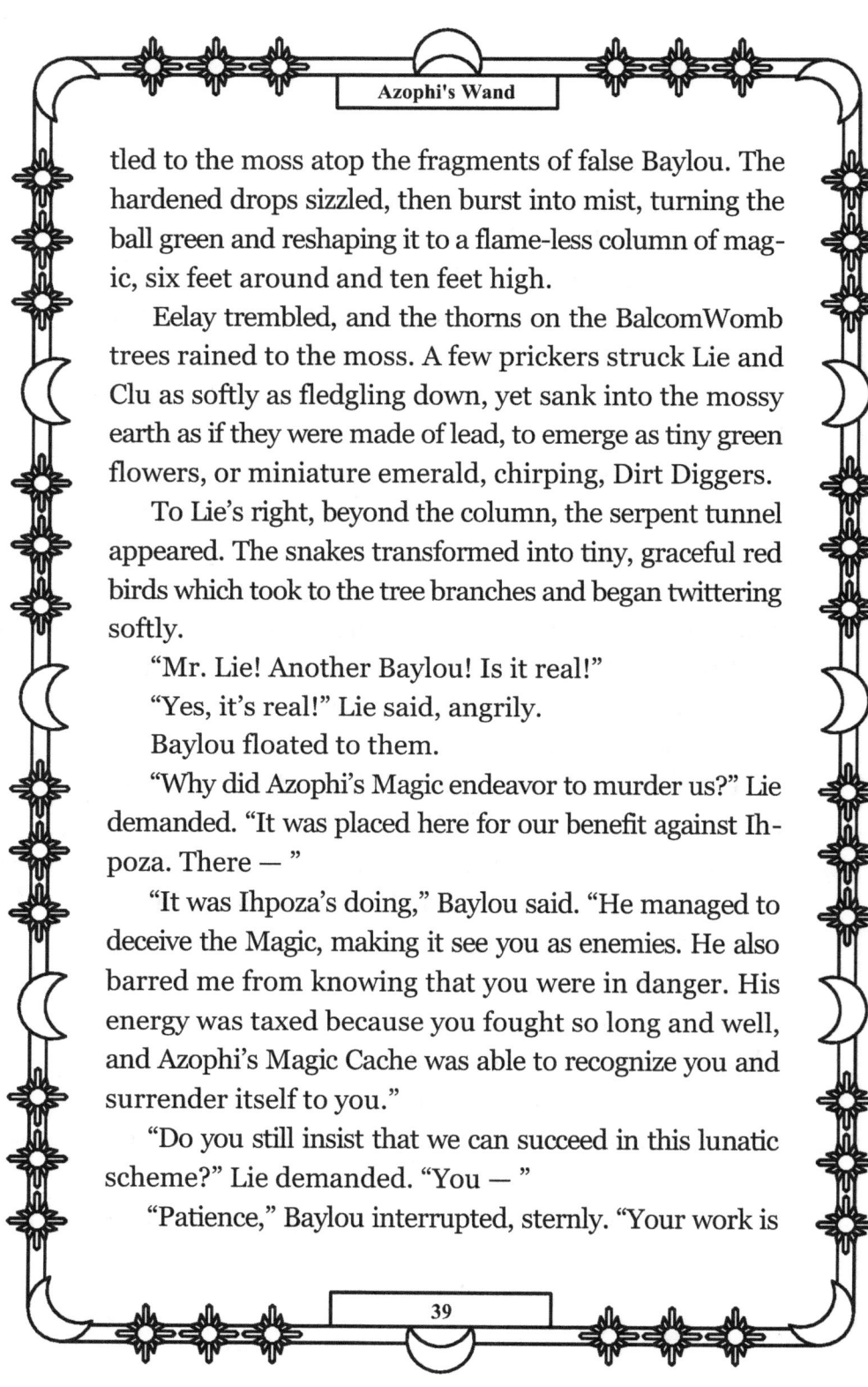

tled to the moss atop the fragments of false Baylou. The hardened drops sizzled, then burst into mist, turning the ball green and reshaping it to a flame-less column of magic, six feet around and ten feet high.

Eelay trembled, and the thorns on the BalcomWomb trees rained to the moss. A few prickers struck Lie and Clu as softly as fledgling down, yet sank into the mossy earth as if they were made of lead, to emerge as tiny green flowers, or miniature emerald, chirping, Dirt Diggers.

To Lie's right, beyond the column, the serpent tunnel appeared. The snakes transformed into tiny, graceful red birds which took to the tree branches and began twittering softly.

"Mr. Lie! Another Baylou! Is it real!"

"Yes, it's real!" Lie said, angrily.

Baylou floated to them.

"Why did Azophi's Magic endeavor to murder us?" Lie demanded. "It was placed here for our benefit against Ihpoza. There — "

"It was Ihpoza's doing," Baylou said. "He managed to deceive the Magic, making it see you as enemies. He also barred me from knowing that you were in danger. His energy was taxed because you fought so long and well, and Azophi's Magic Cache was able to recognize you and surrender itself to you."

"Do you still insist that we can succeed in this lunatic scheme?" Lie demanded. "You — "

"Patience," Baylou interrupted, sternly. "Your work is

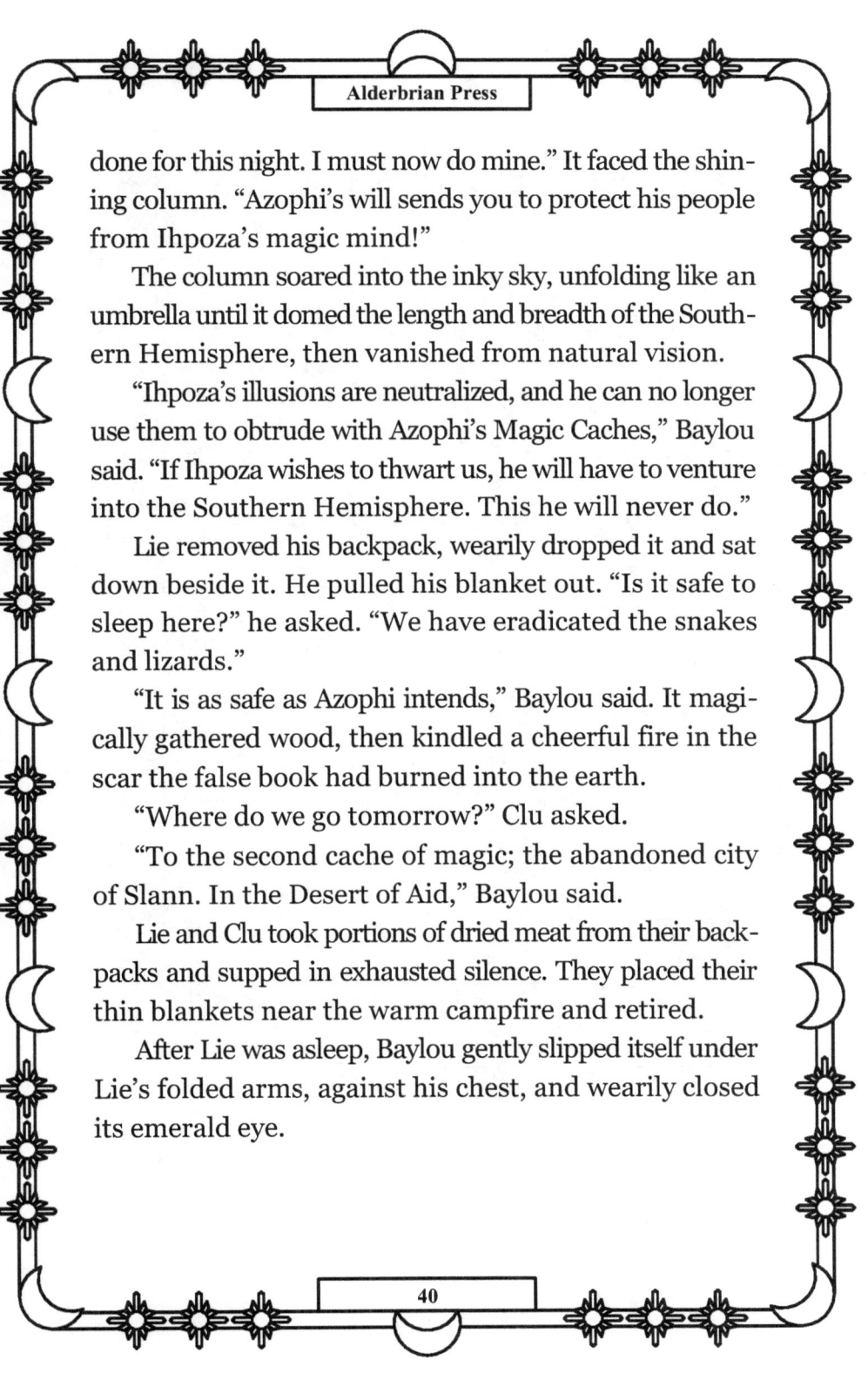

done for this night. I must now do mine." It faced the shining column. "Azophi's will sends you to protect his people from Ihpoza's magic mind!"

The column soared into the inky sky, unfolding like an umbrella until it domed the length and breadth of the Southern Hemisphere, then vanished from natural vision.

"Ihpoza's illusions are neutralized, and he can no longer use them to obtrude with Azophi's Magic Caches," Baylou said. "If Ihpoza wishes to thwart us, he will have to venture into the Southern Hemisphere. This he will never do."

Lie removed his backpack, wearily dropped it and sat down beside it. He pulled his blanket out. "Is it safe to sleep here?" he asked. "We have eradicated the snakes and lizards."

"It is as safe as Azophi intends," Baylou said. It magically gathered wood, then kindled a cheerful fire in the scar the false book had burned into the earth.

"Where do we go tomorrow?" Clu asked.

"To the second cache of magic; the abandoned city of Slann. In the Desert of Aid," Baylou said.

Lie and Clu took portions of dried meat from their backpacks and supped in exhausted silence. They placed their thin blankets near the warm campfire and retired.

After Lie was asleep, Baylou gently slipped itself under Lie's folded arms, against his chest, and wearily closed its emerald eye.

Illustration 10

Ortourian Beast Wrought Iron Window Grillwork

41-A

Chapter 10
Fear and Anger

The cheery chirping of the emerald Dirt Diggers ceased.

Clu was sprawled flat of his back, sleeping peacefully between Lie and the crackling campfire.

Lie lay on his right side, facing Clu. Lie was terrified. His eyes were mere slits. He was forcing his breathing to retain the slow and shallow rhythm of sleep so as not to betray his wakefulness. He clutched Baylou to his chest for comfort.

Three green scaled demons crept into the space between Lie and Clu. Ihpoza's assassins were encased in transparent suits of magic that insulated the evil saurians against the warmth of the Southern Hemisphere, and nullified the tell-tale sounds of their movements.

A pair of the monsters knelt in front of Lie. One aimed a dagger at Lie's throat, the other targeted its knife at Baylou's closed eye. The third saurian knelt beside Clu. The dagger it clenched in its claws glinted in the light of the campfire as the beast raised the weapon above its scaled head, preparing to strike, in unison, with its ghastly cohorts.

Lie rolled away from the monsters, and up to his feet, raising Baylou as a shield.

Baylou dispatched three bright red beams of rage at the startled gorgons.

The cold suits silently exploded, and the heat of the Southern Hemisphere slammed into the demons. They screamed in horror, and blasted into a fine, gray ash, which swirled in the air, and settled onto the green moss, covering their shiny, discarded daggers from view.

Lie sat down on his blanket to recover his nerves.

Clu was on the verge of tears. He sat up and hugged Lie's shoulders. "Are you all right, Mr. Lie?" he asked.

Lie stood the Book up on the moss. "Yes," he said. "Get packed, Clu, we are returning home."

Baylou shot into the air, its eye blazing purple rage. "No!" it commanded. "We must journey on to Slann!" The eye enlarged and its glow brightened. The light began to spin and pulse hypnotically.

Lie's mind clouded. He became frightened of losing his volition to the Tome. He punched Baylou just above the Volume's eye.

Astonished, the Book landed on its back cover on the moss.

When Lie's thoughts cleared, Baylou was gone.

Illustration 11

Ortourian Beast Wrought Iron Window Grillwork

43-A

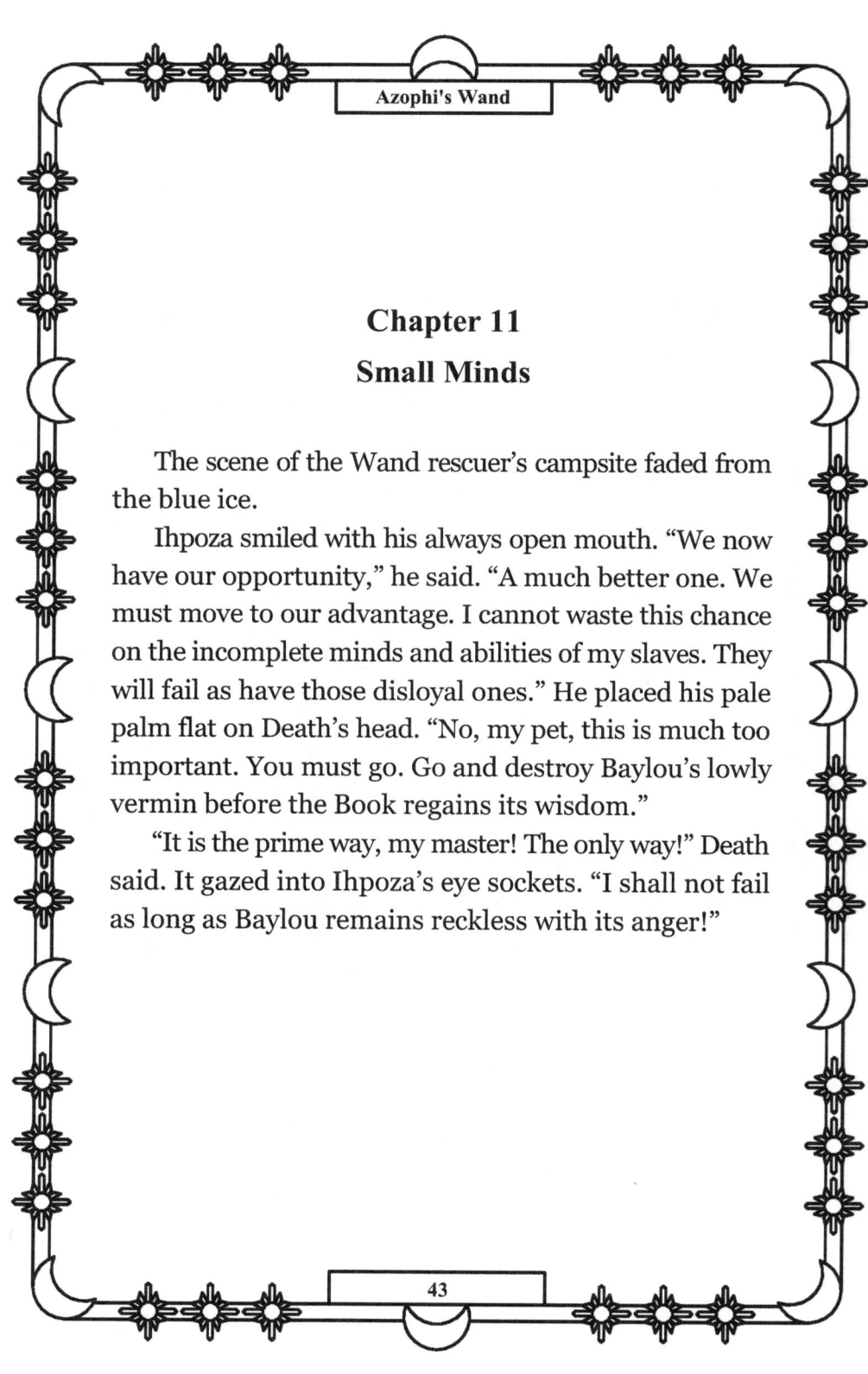

Chapter 11
Small Minds

The scene of the Wand rescuer's campsite faded from the blue ice.

Ihpoza smiled with his always open mouth. "We now have our opportunity," he said. "A much better one. We must move to our advantage. I cannot waste this chance on the incomplete minds and abilities of my slaves. They will fail as have those disloyal ones." He placed his pale palm flat on Death's head. "No, my pet, this is much too important. You must go. Go and destroy Baylou's lowly vermin before the Book regains its wisdom."

"It is the prime way, my master! The only way!" Death said. It gazed into Ihpoza's eye sockets. "I shall not fail as long as Baylou remains reckless with its anger!"

Illustration 12

Ortourian Beast Wrought Iron Window Grillwork

Copyright © 2019 Philip Raymond Sadler

44-A

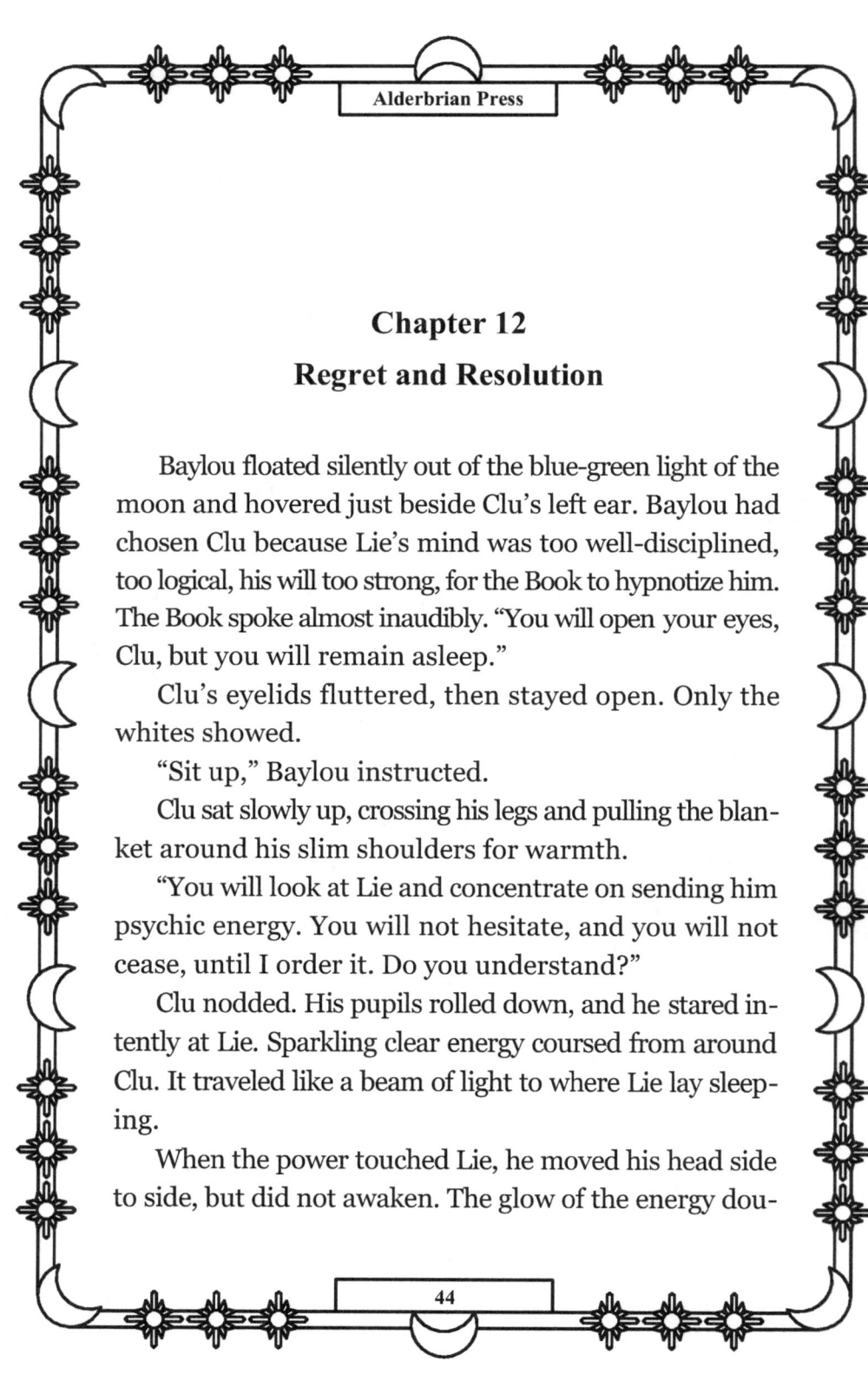

Chapter 12

Regret and Resolution

Baylou floated silently out of the blue-green light of the moon and hovered just beside Clu's left ear. Baylou had chosen Clu because Lie's mind was too well-disciplined, too logical, his will too strong, for the Book to hypnotize him. The Book spoke almost inaudibly. "You will open your eyes, Clu, but you will remain asleep."

Clu's eyelids fluttered, then stayed open. Only the whites showed.

"Sit up," Baylou instructed.

Clu sat slowly up, crossing his legs and pulling the blanket around his slim shoulders for warmth.

"You will look at Lie and concentrate on sending him psychic energy. You will not hesitate, and you will not cease, until I order it. Do you understand?"

Clu nodded. His pupils rolled down, and he stared intently at Lie. Sparkling clear energy coursed from around Clu. It traveled like a beam of light to where Lie lay sleeping.

When the power touched Lie, he moved his head side to side, but did not awaken. The glow of the energy dou-

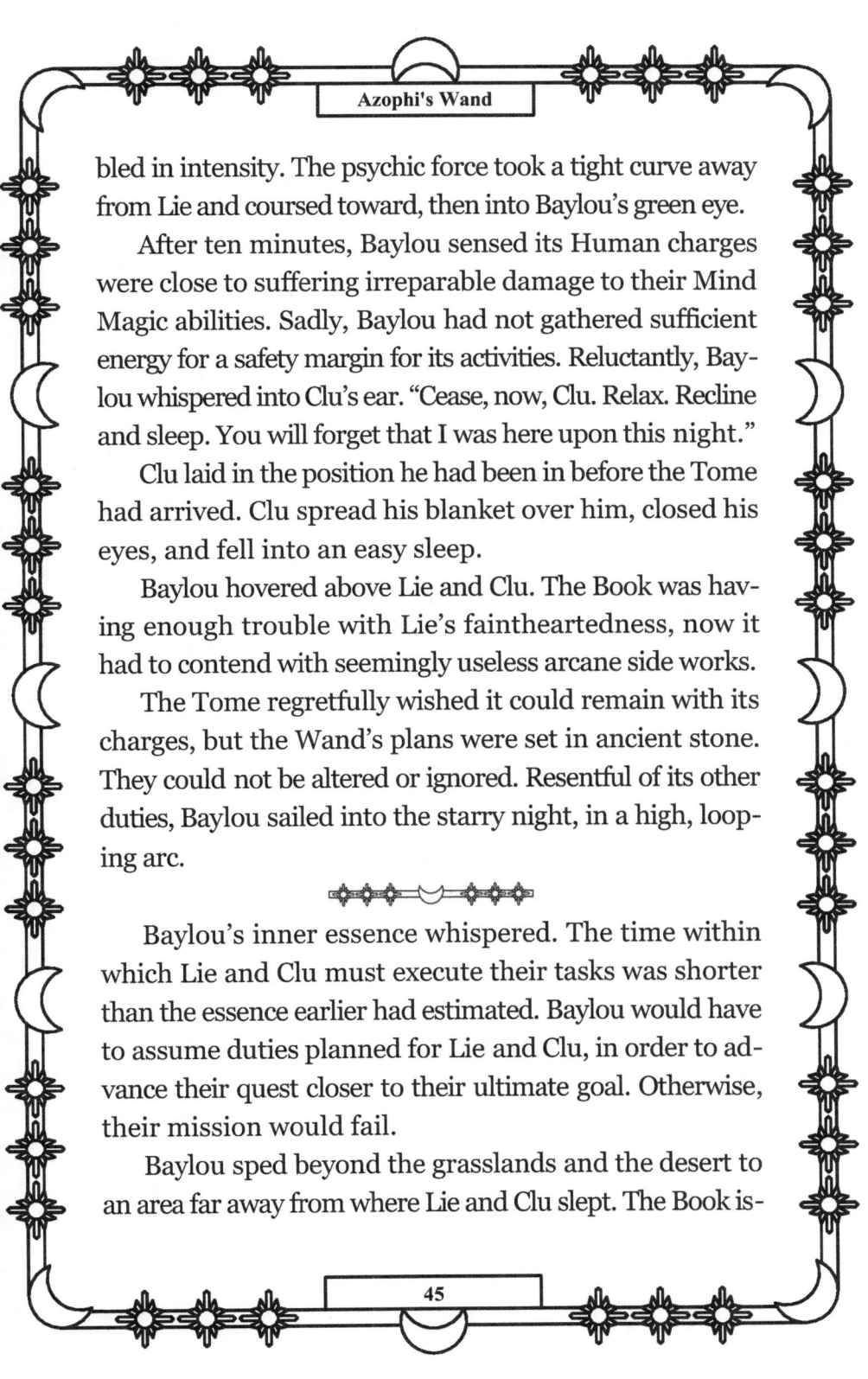

bled in intensity. The psychic force took a tight curve away from Lie and coursed toward, then into Baylou's green eye.

After ten minutes, Baylou sensed its Human charges were close to suffering irreparable damage to their Mind Magic abilities. Sadly, Baylou had not gathered sufficient energy for a safety margin for its activities. Reluctantly, Baylou whispered into Clu's ear. "Cease, now, Clu. Relax. Recline and sleep. You will forget that I was here upon this night."

Clu laid in the position he had been in before the Tome had arrived. Clu spread his blanket over him, closed his eyes, and fell into an easy sleep.

Baylou hovered above Lie and Clu. The Book was having enough trouble with Lie's faintheartedness, now it had to contend with seemingly useless arcane side works.

The Tome regretfully wished it could remain with its charges, but the Wand's plans were set in ancient stone. They could not be altered or ignored. Resentful of its other duties, Baylou sailed into the starry night, in a high, looping arc.

❖❖❖〜❖❖❖

Baylou's inner essence whispered. The time within which Lie and Clu must execute their tasks was shorter than the essence earlier had estimated. Baylou would have to assume duties planned for Lie and Clu, in order to advance their quest closer to their ultimate goal. Otherwise, their mission would fail.

Baylou sped beyond the grasslands and the desert to an area far away from where Lie and Clu slept. The Book is-

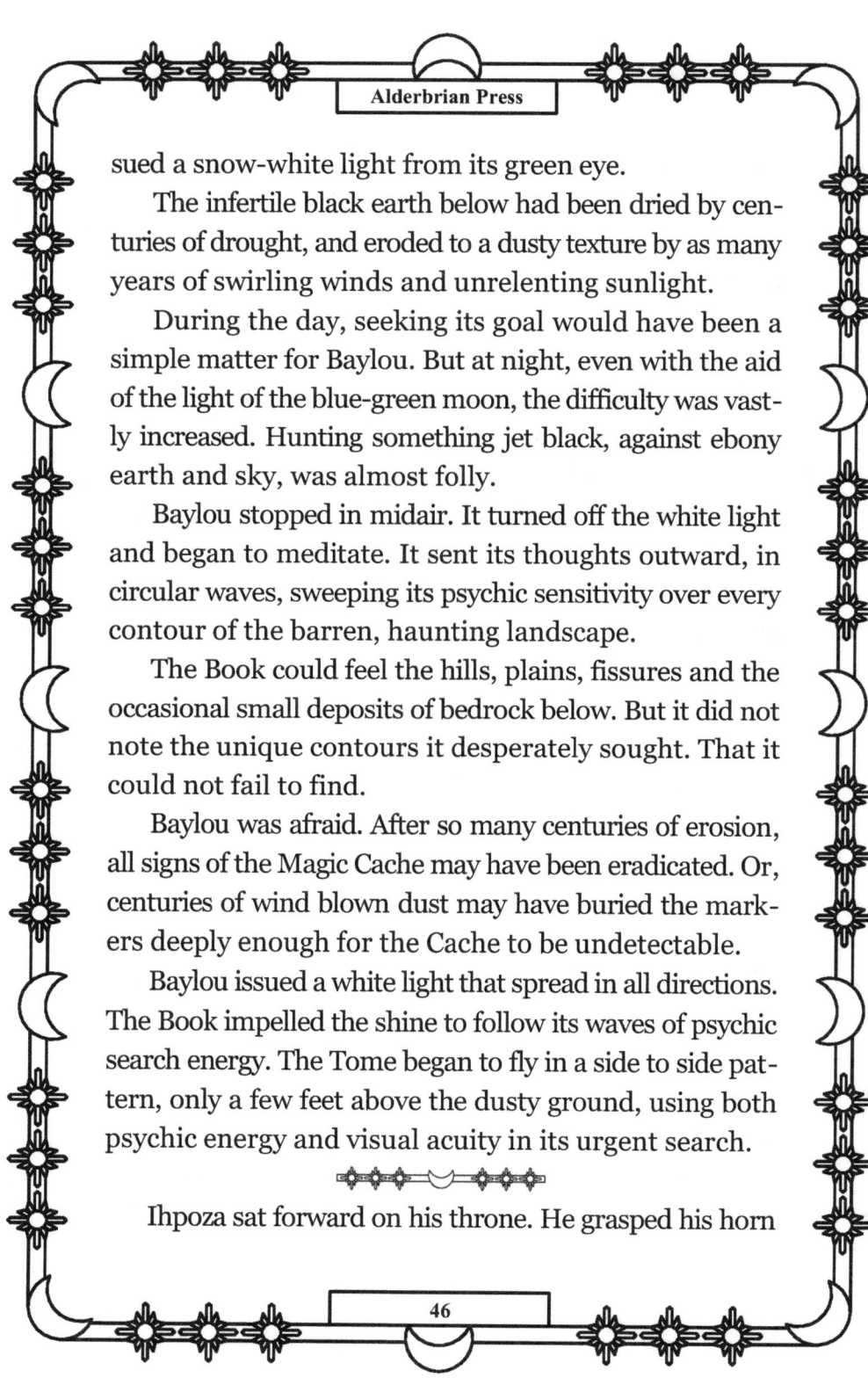

sued a snow-white light from its green eye.

The infertile black earth below had been dried by centuries of drought, and eroded to a dusty texture by as many years of swirling winds and unrelenting sunlight.

During the day, seeking its goal would have been a simple matter for Baylou. But at night, even with the aid of the light of the blue-green moon, the difficulty was vastly increased. Hunting something jet black, against ebony earth and sky, was almost folly.

Baylou stopped in midair. It turned off the white light and began to meditate. It sent its thoughts outward, in circular waves, sweeping its psychic sensitivity over every contour of the barren, haunting landscape.

The Book could feel the hills, plains, fissures and the occasional small deposits of bedrock below. But it did not note the unique contours it desperately sought. That it could not fail to find.

Baylou was afraid. After so many centuries of erosion, all signs of the Magic Cache may have been eradicated. Or, centuries of wind blown dust may have buried the markers deeply enough for the Cache to be undetectable.

Baylou issued a white light that spread in all directions. The Book impelled the shine to follow its waves of psychic search energy. The Tome began to fly in a side to side pattern, only a few feet above the dusty ground, using both psychic energy and visual acuity in its urgent search.

Ihpoza sat forward on his throne. He grasped his horn

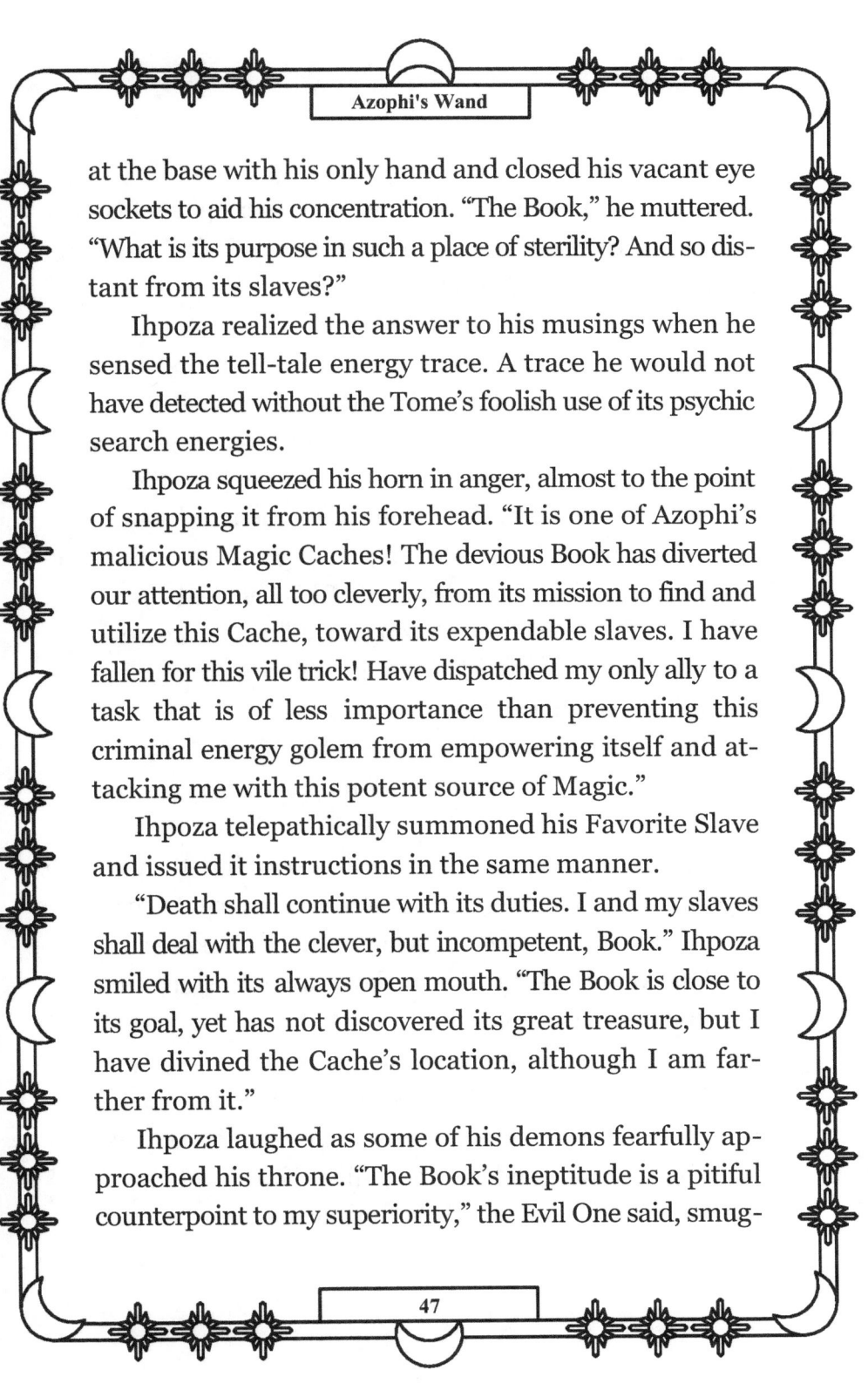

at the base with his only hand and closed his vacant eye sockets to aid his concentration. "The Book," he muttered. "What is its purpose in such a place of sterility? And so distant from its slaves?"

Ihpoza realized the answer to his musings when he sensed the tell-tale energy trace. A trace he would not have detected without the Tome's foolish use of its psychic search energies.

Ihpoza squeezed his horn in anger, almost to the point of snapping it from his forehead. "It is one of Azophi's malicious Magic Caches! The devious Book has diverted our attention, all too cleverly, from its mission to find and utilize this Cache, toward its expendable slaves. I have fallen for this vile trick! Have dispatched my only ally to a task that is of less importance than preventing this criminal energy golem from empowering itself and attacking me with this potent source of Magic."

Ihpoza telepathically summoned his Favorite Slave and issued it instructions in the same manner.

"Death shall continue with its duties. I and my slaves shall deal with the clever, but incompetent, Book." Ihpoza smiled with its always open mouth. "The Book is close to its goal, yet has not discovered its great treasure, but I have divined the Cache's location, although I am farther from it."

Ihpoza laughed as some of his demons fearfully approached his throne. "The Book's ineptitude is a pitiful counterpoint to my superiority," the Evil One said, smug-

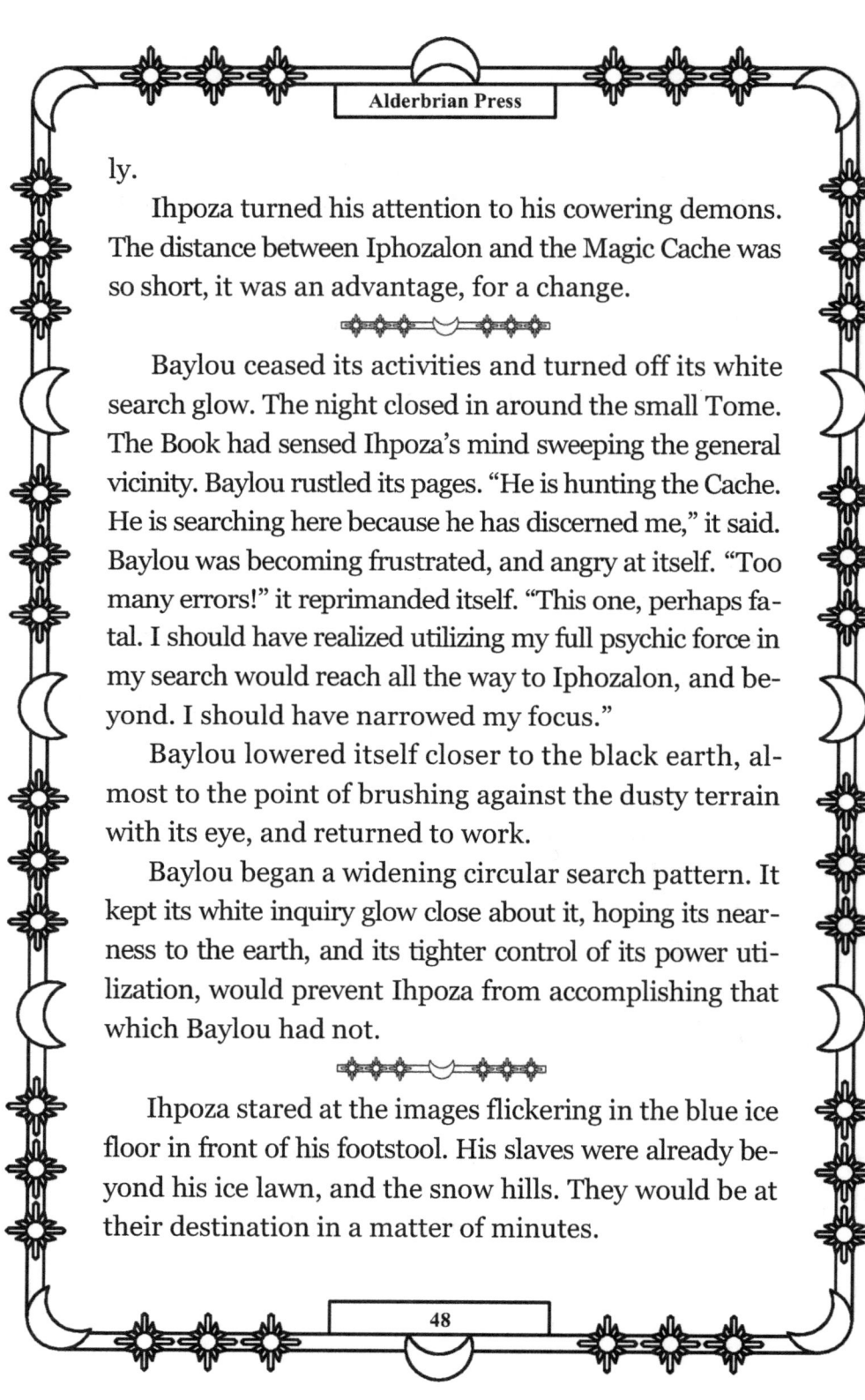

ly.

Ihpoza turned his attention to his cowering demons. The distance between Iphozalon and the Magic Cache was so short, it was an advantage, for a change.

Baylou ceased its activities and turned off its white search glow. The night closed in around the small Tome. The Book had sensed Ihpoza's mind sweeping the general vicinity. Baylou rustled its pages. "He is hunting the Cache. He is searching here because he has discerned me," it said. Baylou was becoming frustrated, and angry at itself. "Too many errors!" it reprimanded itself. "This one, perhaps fatal. I should have realized utilizing my full psychic force in my search would reach all the way to Iphozalon, and beyond. I should have narrowed my focus."

Baylou lowered itself closer to the black earth, almost to the point of brushing against the dusty terrain with its eye, and returned to work.

Baylou began a widening circular search pattern. It kept its white inquiry glow close about it, hoping its nearness to the earth, and its tighter control of its power utilization, would prevent Ihpoza from accomplishing that which Baylou had not.

Ihpoza stared at the images flickering in the blue ice floor in front of his footstool. His slaves were already beyond his ice lawn, and the snow hills. They would be at their destination in a matter of minutes.

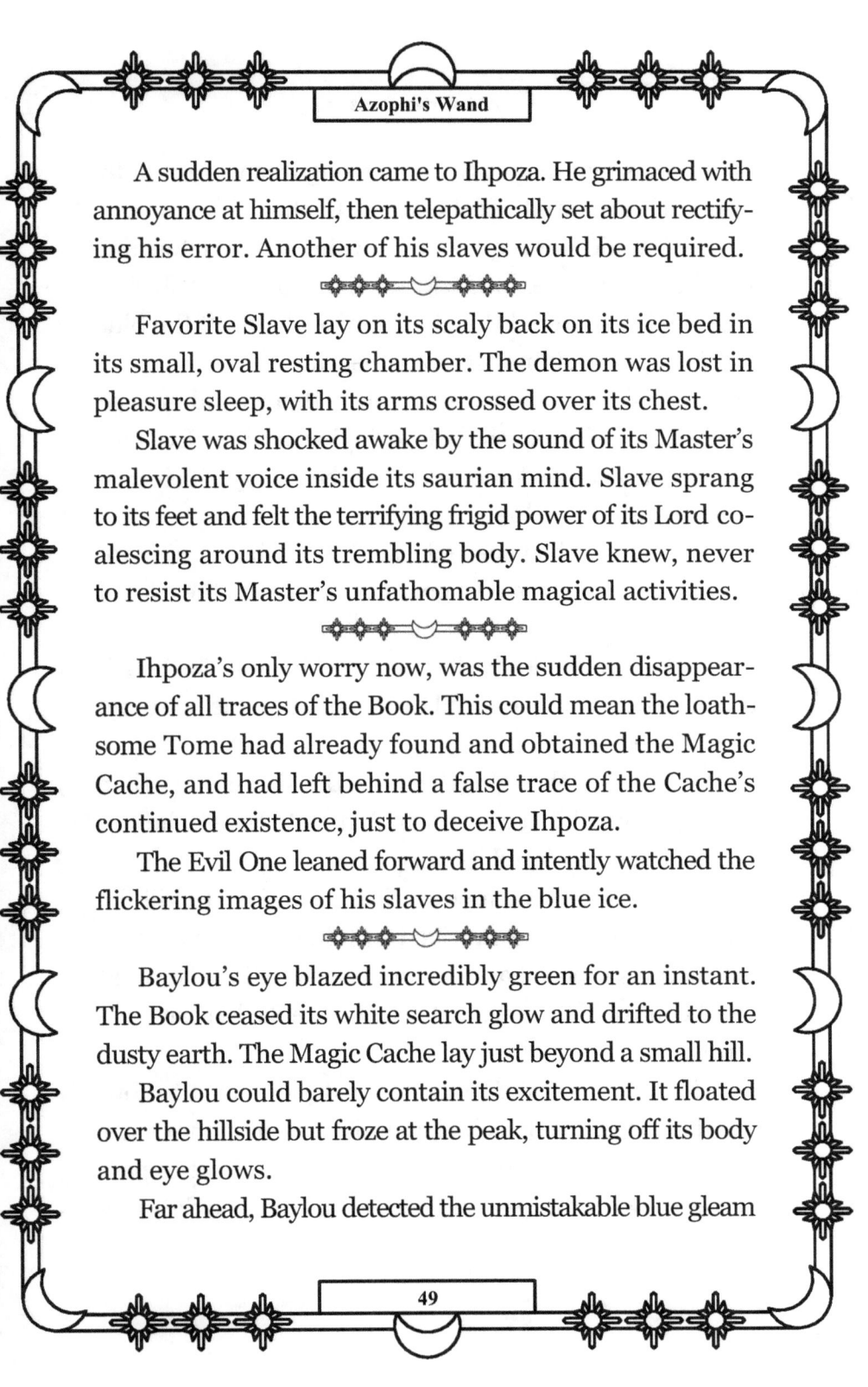

A sudden realization came to Ihpoza. He grimaced with annoyance at himself, then telepathically set about rectifying his error. Another of his slaves would be required.

Favorite Slave lay on its scaly back on its ice bed in its small, oval resting chamber. The demon was lost in pleasure sleep, with its arms crossed over its chest.

Slave was shocked awake by the sound of its Master's malevolent voice inside its saurian mind. Slave sprang to its feet and felt the terrifying frigid power of its Lord coalescing around its trembling body. Slave knew, never to resist its Master's unfathomable magical activities.

Ihpoza's only worry now, was the sudden disappearance of all traces of the Book. This could mean the loathsome Tome had already found and obtained the Magic Cache, and had left behind a false trace of the Cache's continued existence, just to deceive Ihpoza.

The Evil One leaned forward and intently watched the flickering images of his slaves in the blue ice.

Baylou's eye blazed incredibly green for an instant. The Book ceased its white search glow and drifted to the dusty earth. The Magic Cache lay just beyond a small hill.

Baylou could barely contain its excitement. It floated over the hillside but froze at the peak, turning off its body and eye glows.

Far ahead, Baylou detected the unmistakable blue gleam

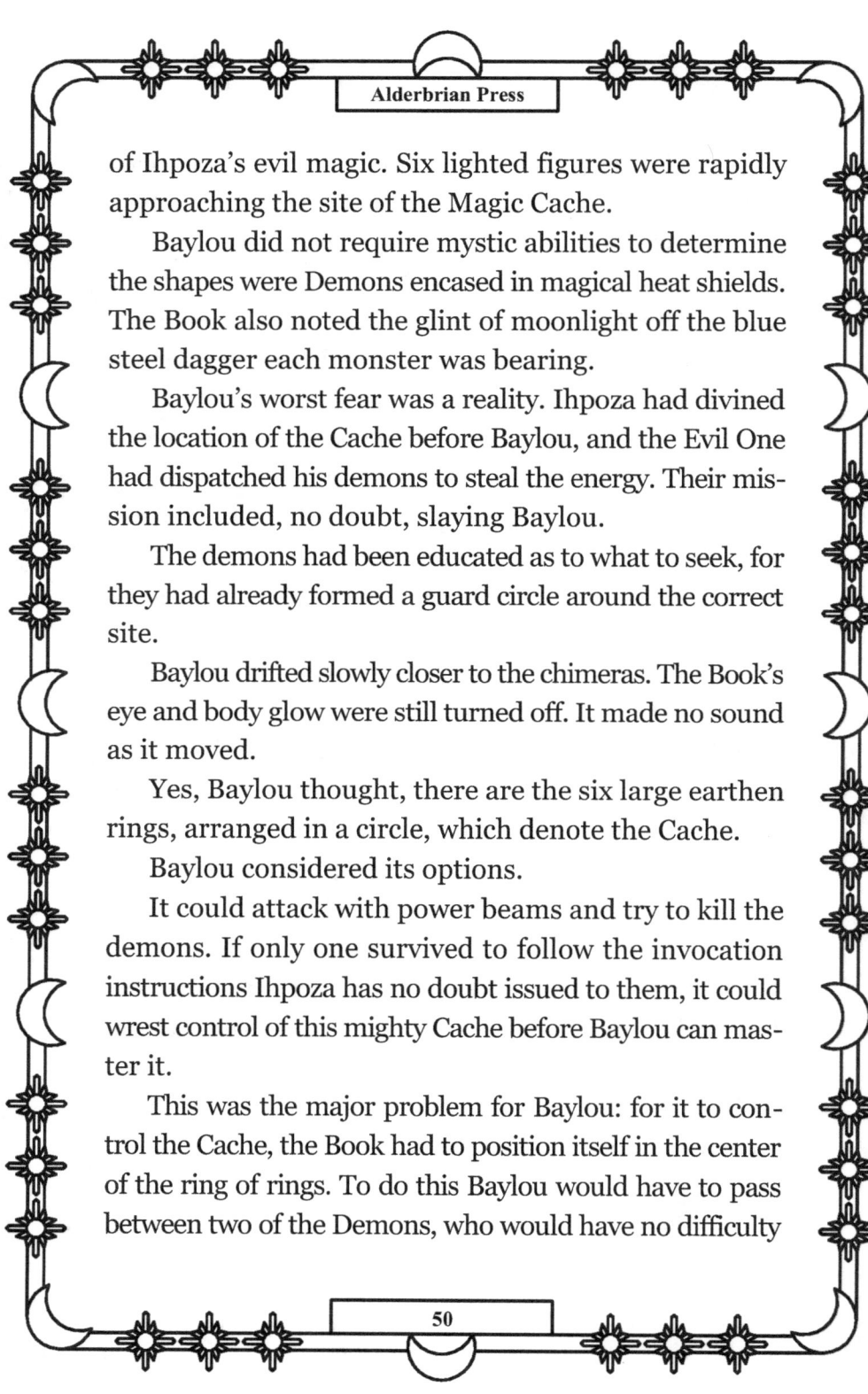

of Ihpoza's evil magic. Six lighted figures were rapidly approaching the site of the Magic Cache.

Baylou did not require mystic abilities to determine the shapes were Demons encased in magical heat shields. The Book also noted the glint of moonlight off the blue steel dagger each monster was bearing.

Baylou's worst fear was a reality. Ihpoza had divined the location of the Cache before Baylou, and the Evil One had dispatched his demons to steal the energy. Their mission included, no doubt, slaying Baylou.

The demons had been educated as to what to seek, for they had already formed a guard circle around the correct site.

Baylou drifted slowly closer to the chimeras. The Book's eye and body glow were still turned off. It made no sound as it moved.

Yes, Baylou thought, there are the six large earthen rings, arranged in a circle, which denote the Cache.

Baylou considered its options.

It could attack with power beams and try to kill the demons. If only one survived to follow the invocation instructions Ihpoza has no doubt issued to them, it could wrest control of this mighty Cache before Baylou can master it.

This was the major problem for Baylou: for it to control the Cache, the Book had to position itself in the center of the ring of rings. To do this Baylou would have to pass between two of the Demons, who would have no difficulty reaching Baylou with their knives. Or, Baylou could drop into the formation from above, and be rushed by six dagger wielding fiends.

Neither prospect appealed to the Book.

Baylou's essence spoke. Baylou was slightly heartened by this, and whispered the question to itself:

"Why has Ihpoza not already absorbed the power of the Cache, and left his demons in wait, to destroy me, with a false trace of the Cache to lure me into the trap?"

There was only one explication. Ihpoza had not yet comprehended how to control the Magic of the Cache.

Baylou could not wait a second longer. "Turn about is fair play," the Book whispered. Then it felt added frustration.

In the distance, and nearing swiftly, was another blue form. It was a seventh demon, protected by Ihpoza's evil magic, and bearing a blue steel dagger.

Favorite Slave grasped its dagger more firmly and ran faster toward its comrades. It grinned fiendishly. It was proud the Master had selected it, out of all its brothers, to actually perform a magical rite. A conjuration that would defeat the Book, and its Humans, and make Favorite Slave more important to the great Evil Master than even the insufferable, egotistical Lizard.

Only a few more yards, and a single, simple phrase, would transform Favorite Slave, from a mere captain of slaves, into the Discipline Lord of all Azon, second

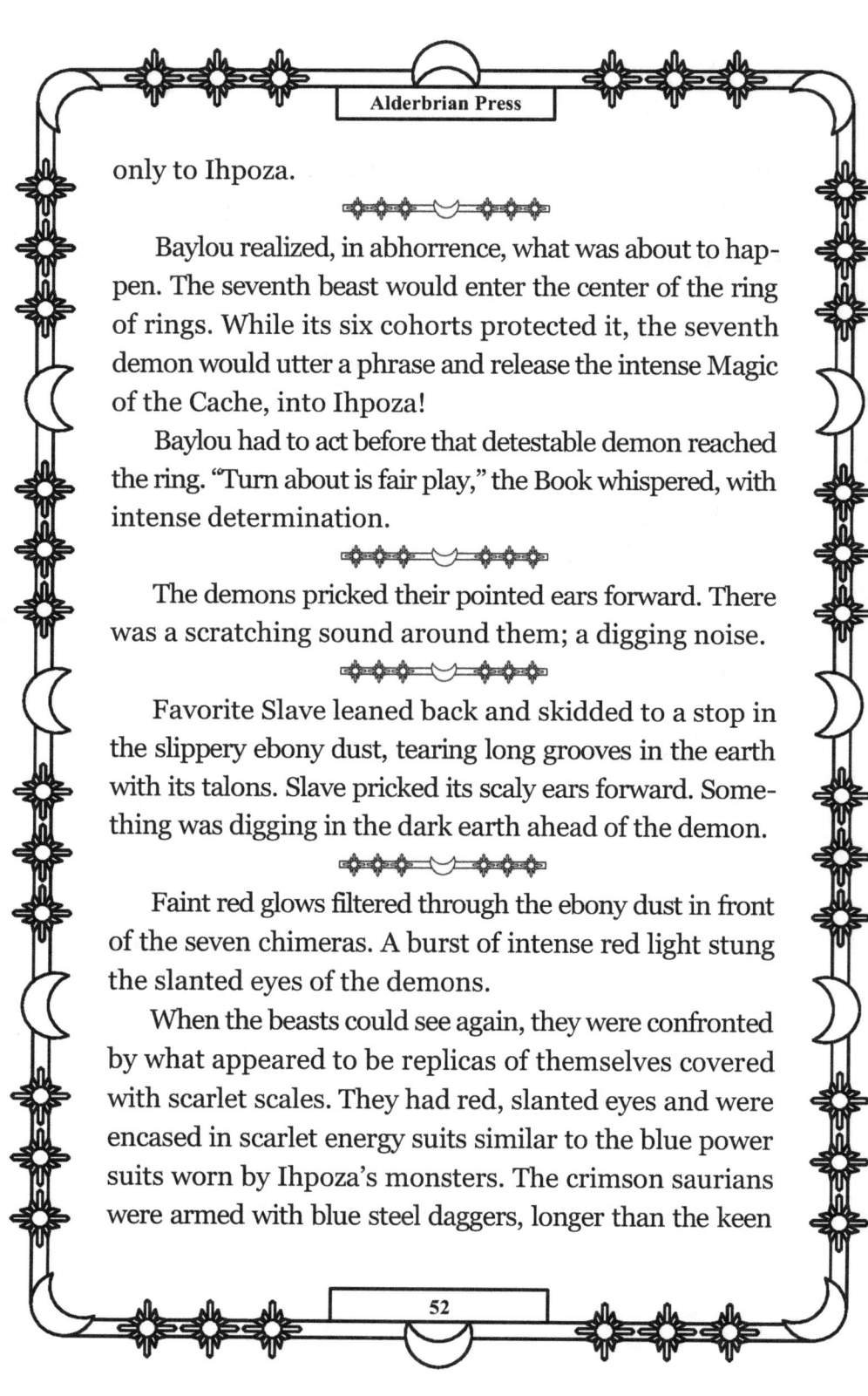

only to Ihpoza.

⬧✦✦〰✦✦⬧

Baylou realized, in abhorrence, what was about to happen. The seventh beast would enter the center of the ring of rings. While its six cohorts protected it, the seventh demon would utter a phrase and release the intense Magic of the Cache, into Ihpoza!

Baylou had to act before that detestable demon reached the ring. "Turn about is fair play," the Book whispered, with intense determination.

⬧✦✦〰✦✦⬧

The demons pricked their pointed ears forward. There was a scratching sound around them; a digging noise.

⬧✦✦〰✦✦⬧

Favorite Slave leaned back and skidded to a stop in the slippery ebony dust, tearing long grooves in the earth with its talons. Slave pricked its scaly ears forward. Something was digging in the dark earth ahead of the demon.

⬧✦✦〰✦✦⬧

Faint red glows filtered through the ebony dust in front of the seven chimeras. A burst of intense red light stung the slanted eyes of the demons.

When the beasts could see again, they were confronted by what appeared to be replicas of themselves covered with scarlet scales. They had red, slanted eyes and were encased in scarlet energy suits similar to the blue power suits worn by Ihpoza's monsters. The crimson saurians were armed with blue steel daggers, longer than the keen knives Ihpoza's demons wielded.

Ihpoza's demons snarled with animal challenge and rushed toward their red impostors.

Ihpoza pounded the arm of his ice throne with his one, taloned fist. "No! Imbeciles!" he roared. "Watch for the Book! Seek only the Book! These are illusions! Ghosts! Nothing! Ignore them and slay only the vile Book!"

The six guard Demons found themselves foiled in every attack technique they tried. They could gain no advantage against the red beasts no matter how mightily, swiftly, or cleverly they struck. And they were slowly being drawn further away from the circle of old earthen rings.

Favorite Slave, snarling, stared at the red beast crouching before it. Something was not right. Something it could not comprehend. Or, perhaps it did.

"Yes!" Favorite Slave said to itself. "It growls challenge exactly as I growl, moves exactly as I move. I see stars through it!"

Baylou noted the seventh demon was not fighting with its red foe. The Book realized it could wait no longer for the distance between the other six demons, and the circle of rings, to increase. Baylou had to take its chance now.

Baylou looped into the moon washed sky and plummeted into the center of the ring of rings. It realized, turning on its eye and body glows would alert the demons to its presence, but it could not operate properly without radiating its energy.

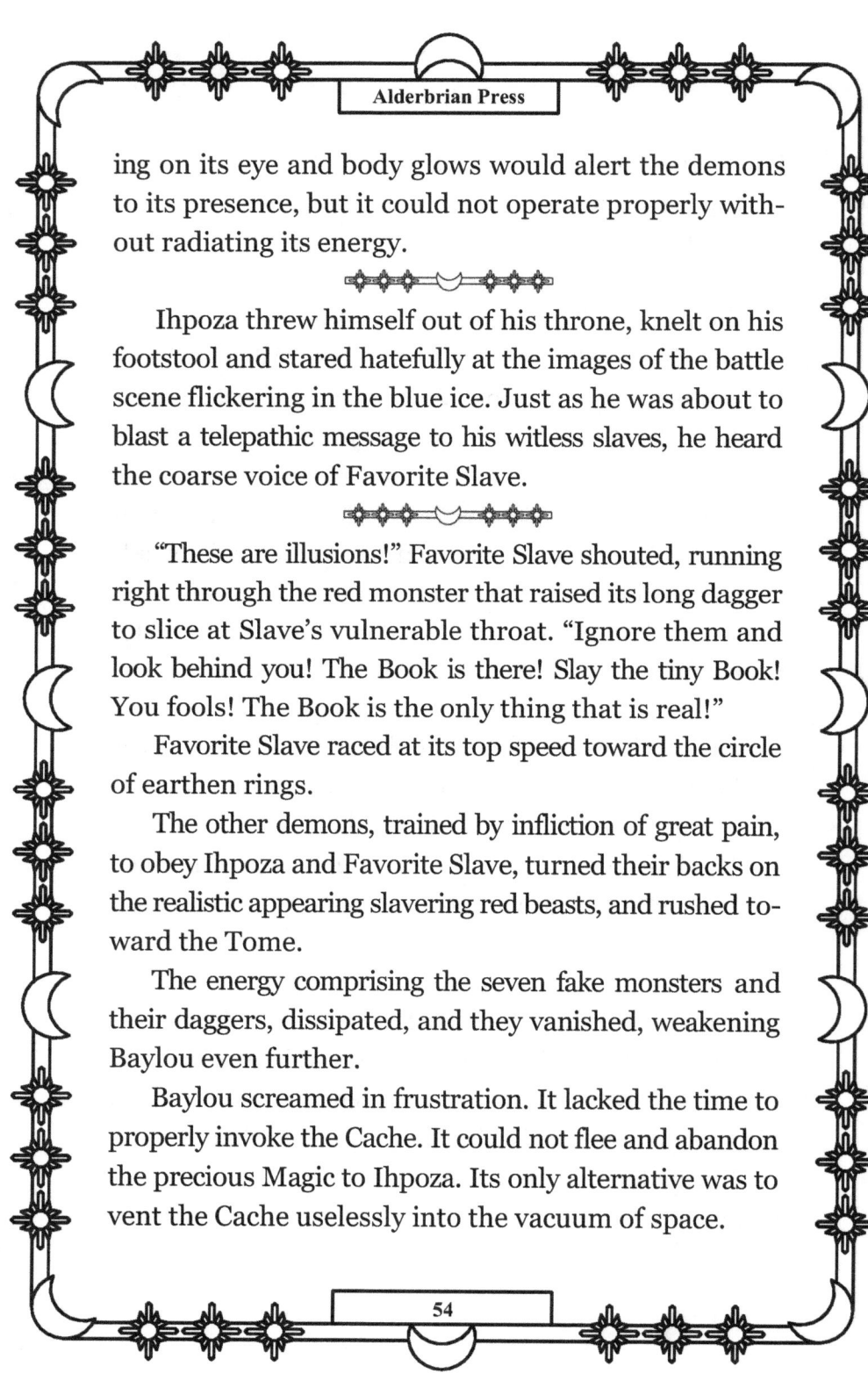

Ihpoza threw himself out of his throne, knelt on his footstool and stared hatefully at the images of the battle scene flickering in the blue ice. Just as he was about to blast a telepathic message to his witless slaves, he heard the coarse voice of Favorite Slave.

"These are illusions!" Favorite Slave shouted, running right through the red monster that raised its long dagger to slice at Slave's vulnerable throat. "Ignore them and look behind you! The Book is there! Slay the tiny Book! You fools! The Book is the only thing that is real!"

Favorite Slave raced at its top speed toward the circle of earthen rings.

The other demons, trained by infliction of great pain, to obey Ihpoza and Favorite Slave, turned their backs on the realistic appearing slavering red beasts, and rushed toward the Tome.

The energy comprising the seven fake monsters and their daggers, dissipated, and they vanished, weakening Baylou even further.

Baylou screamed in frustration. It lacked the time to properly invoke the Cache. It could not flee and abandon the precious Magic to Ihpoza. Its only alternative was to vent the Cache uselessly into the vacuum of space.

The guard demons leaped over the closest edges of the foot high earthen rings. Cylinders of clear energy sprang up around them. The demons collided with the inner walls of the invisible cylinders, rebounding backwards and slamming into the dusty earth on their scaled backs.

Baylou choked off the words of release it was about to hurl at the Cache. Hope surged in the little Book. The demons were trapped within the power rings by the Magic! The Cache was marshaling its might to its own defense!

One demon remained a threat. But, a lone demon, no matter how surprisingly perceptive, was no match for Baylou.

Baylou turned to face the onrushing monster. The Book gathered its energies. Its attack must be unerring and deadly. Time was impossibly short now.

Favorite Slave slammed, head long, into an invisible energy barrier attached to the two power cylinders on the demon's left and right.

Favorite Slave rebounded flat of its green scaly back on the ebony earth, raising a cloud of dust. A look of astonishment was etched into its beastly face.

The other saurians had struggled groggily to their feet. They were howling with fear and jabbing their daggers against the thick walls of the invisible cylinders imprisoning them inside the earthen rings.

Favorite Slave scrambled to his feet and hurled itself, with animal rage, against the transparent barriers between each two of the power cylinders.

The snarling demon completed two circuits of the six, cylinder-filled, earthen rings before exhaustion caused it to fall on its face in the choking ebony dust.

"Damn you to eternity, Azophi!" Ihpoza roared from where he knelt on his icy footstool. "Damn you, Wand!" he screamed, staring hatefully at the silent shimmering symbol of all that eluded him.

There was nothing the Evil One could do except shout in ineffectual rage, and watch a supply of Psychic energy more incredibly vast than he had realized, be released into the control of the hideous Book! To be utilized in malevolent acts against Ihpoza!

Baylou increased its emerald body glow and sent out thin tendrils of energy. They snaked through the chalky ebony dust that surrounded the bases of the six earthen circles.

The earthen rings began to glow green. A humming filled the air and trembled the ground. Dust from around the earthen rings began to rise toward the sky.

The buried power circles flashed up from within the earthen rings, scattering dust and clumps of dirt in all directions. The entrapped demons were incinerated into gray ashes, and their daggers were vaporized.

Favorite Slave howled in horror and rage.

The power circles hovered momentarily at the tops of

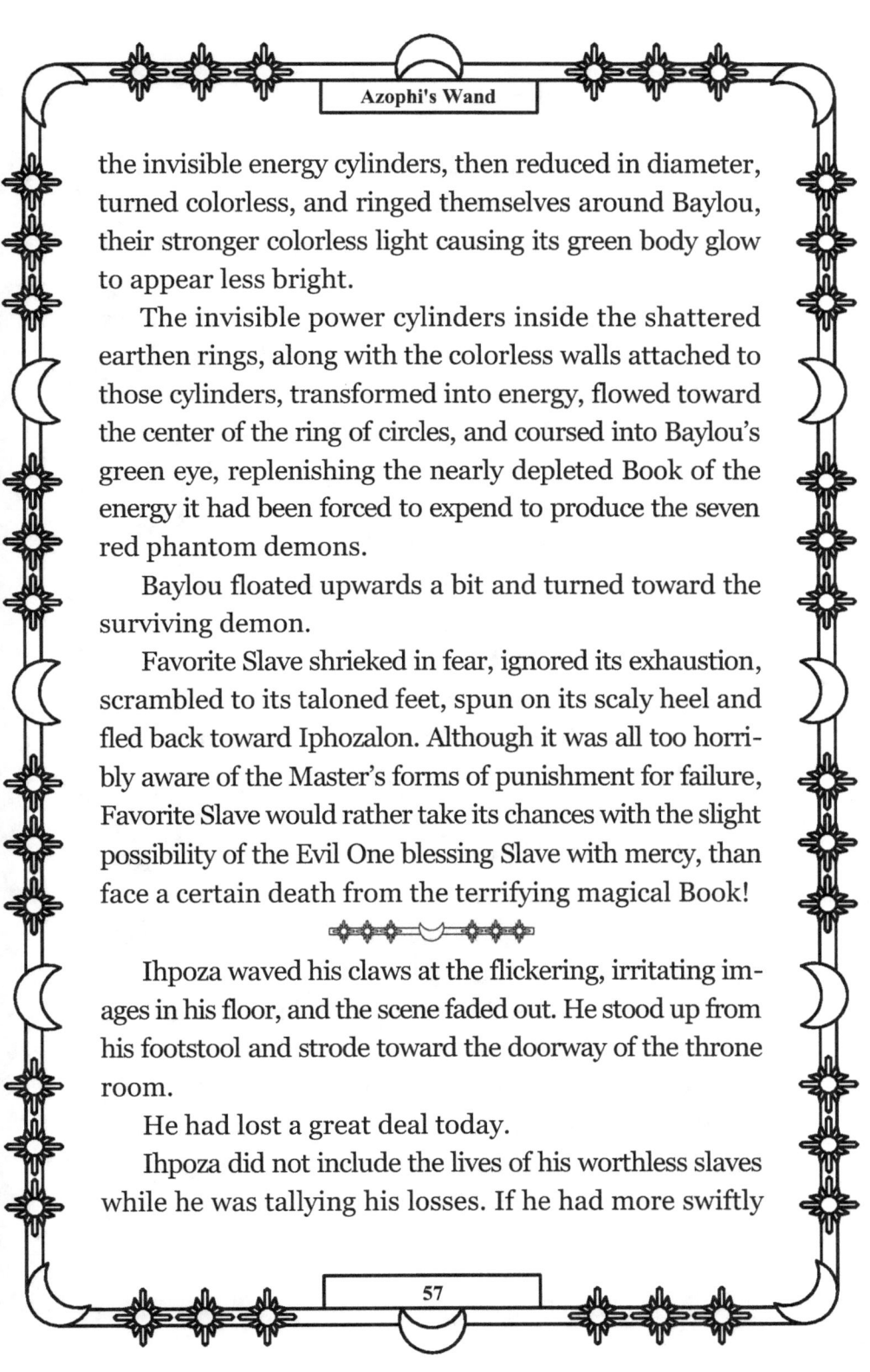

the invisible energy cylinders, then reduced in diameter, turned colorless, and ringed themselves around Baylou, their stronger colorless light causing its green body glow to appear less bright.

The invisible power cylinders inside the shattered earthen rings, along with the colorless walls attached to those cylinders, transformed into energy, flowed toward the center of the ring of circles, and coursed into Baylou's green eye, replenishing the nearly depleted Book of the energy it had been forced to expend to produce the seven red phantom demons.

Baylou floated upwards a bit and turned toward the surviving demon.

Favorite Slave shrieked in fear, ignored its exhaustion, scrambled to its taloned feet, spun on its scaly heel and fled back toward Iphozalon. Although it was all too horribly aware of the Master's forms of punishment for failure, Favorite Slave would rather take its chances with the slight possibility of the Evil One blessing Slave with mercy, than face a certain death from the terrifying magical Book!

Ihpoza waved his claws at the flickering, irritating images in his floor, and the scene faded out. He stood up from his footstool and strode toward the doorway of the throne room.

He had lost a great deal today.

Ihpoza did not include the lives of his worthless slaves while he was tallying his losses. If he had more swiftly

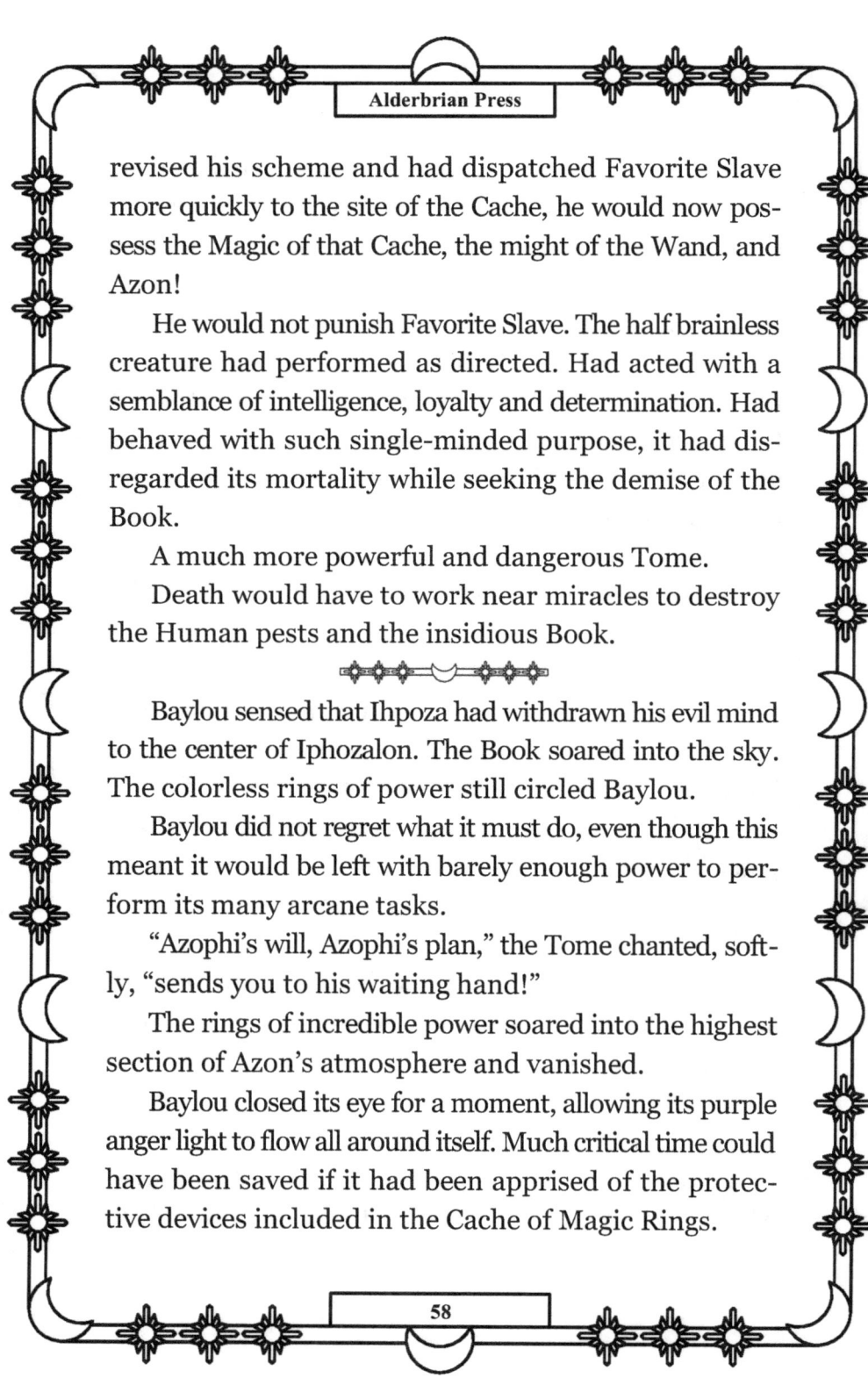

revised his scheme and had dispatched Favorite Slave more quickly to the site of the Cache, he would now possess the Magic of that Cache, the might of the Wand, and Azon!

He would not punish Favorite Slave. The half brainless creature had performed as directed. Had acted with a semblance of intelligence, loyalty and determination. Had behaved with such single-minded purpose, it had disregarded its mortality while seeking the demise of the Book.

A much more powerful and dangerous Tome.

Death would have to work near miracles to destroy the Human pests and the insidious Book.

Baylou sensed that Ihpoza had withdrawn his evil mind to the center of Iphozalon. The Book soared into the sky. The colorless rings of power still circled Baylou.

Baylou did not regret what it must do, even though this meant it would be left with barely enough power to perform its many arcane tasks.

"Azophi's will, Azophi's plan," the Tome chanted, softly, "sends you to his waiting hand!"

The rings of incredible power soared into the highest section of Azon's atmosphere and vanished.

Baylou closed its eye for a moment, allowing its purple anger light to flow all around itself. Much critical time could have been saved if it had been apprised of the protective devices included in the Cache of Magic Rings.

Baylou would have skipped all the uncertainty and the creation of the illusion demons and gone straight to the center of the ring of circles if it had known that it would have been defended by the Cache.

Schemes, time tables and secrets were becoming a threat to the quest for which they had been devised.

"Since I suffered so much difficulty with the Ring Cache," Baylou told itself angrily, "how would Lie and Clu have fared?"

The Book ended its anger light and rustled its pages. Hindsight was useless. Only its next task was important.

In Iphozalon, in Ihpoza's cavernous throne room, the colorless circles of magical might passed soundlessly through the vaulted blue ice ceiling, the flat top of the glittering spell prison, and were absorbed by the Wand as an inseparable part of its unfathomable power.

Ihpoza entered his throne room and shrugged his broad, scaly shoulders. Something seemed different but nothing looked dissonant. He dismissed the matter and reclined on his throne and footstool.

He was already formulating backup plans. Seeking in his mind ways to counter any attack the Book and the Humans might commit against him or his beloved pet. Trying to develop ways to assail his vile enemies before they delivered blows to him.

Illustration 13

Ortourian Beast Wrought Iron Window Grillwork

Copyright © 2019 Philip Raymond Sadler

60-A

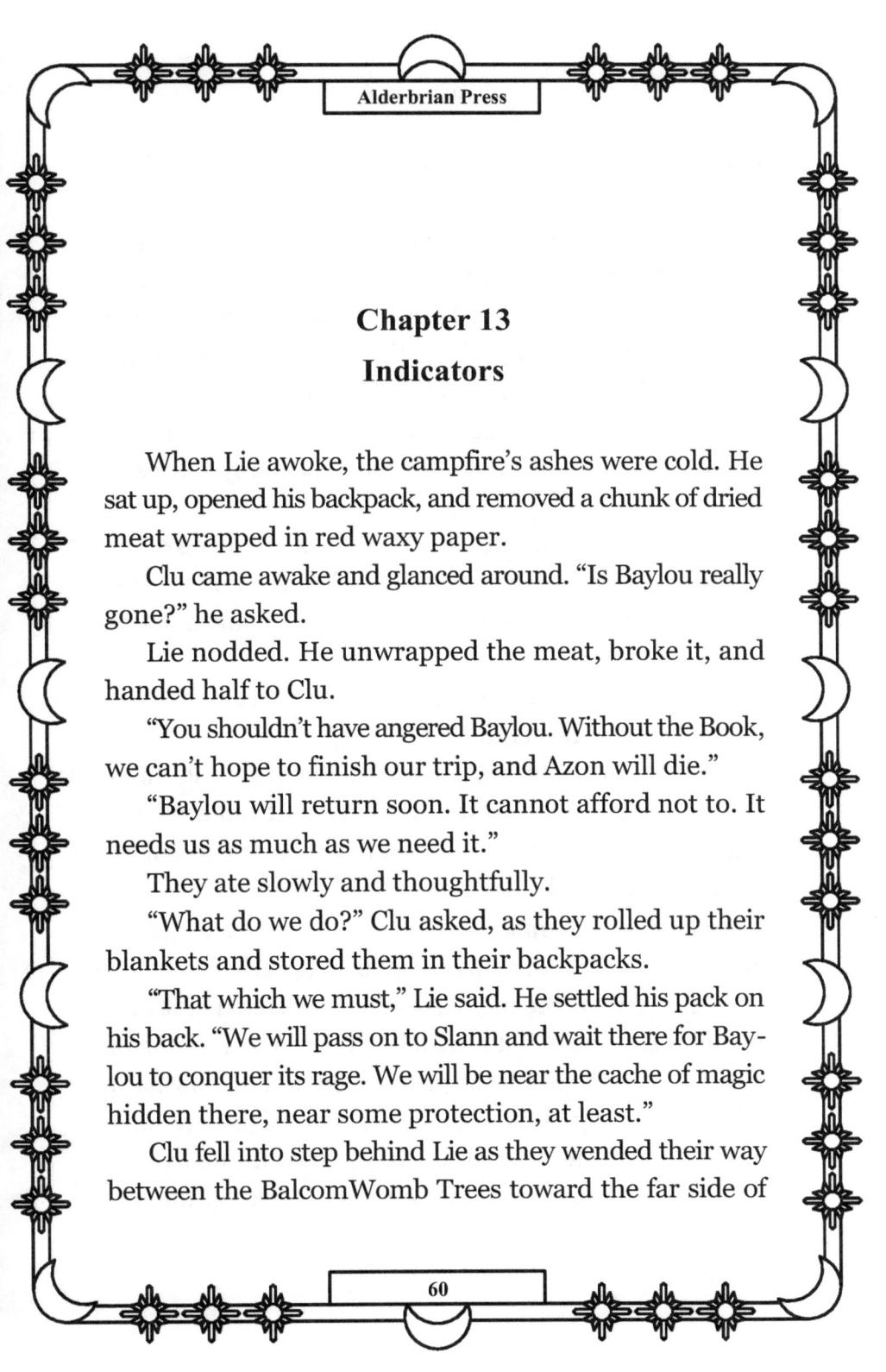

Chapter 13
Indicators

When Lie awoke, the campfire's ashes were cold. He sat up, opened his backpack, and removed a chunk of dried meat wrapped in red waxy paper.

Clu came awake and glanced around. "Is Baylou really gone?" he asked.

Lie nodded. He unwrapped the meat, broke it, and handed half to Clu.

"You shouldn't have angered Baylou. Without the Book, we can't hope to finish our trip, and Azon will die."

"Baylou will return soon. It cannot afford not to. It needs us as much as we need it."

They ate slowly and thoughtfully.

"What do we do?" Clu asked, as they rolled up their blankets and stored them in their backpacks.

"That which we must," Lie said. He settled his pack on his back. "We will pass on to Slann and wait there for Baylou to conquer its rage. We will be near the cache of magic hidden there, near some protection, at least."

Clu fell into step behind Lie as they wended their way between the BalcomWomb Trees toward the far side of

Eelay. "Slann is in the Desert of Aid," he said, "and we have no water to speak of."

"Damn!" Lie said. He gazed beyond the limits of Eelay, at the rolling grassy hillock country awaiting them. "There must be some water near here. Or a farmhouse. We will get extra water and containers there." He scowled. "If we can find a house. Baylou has led us away from the normal trade routes, and most of the farming areas. We must remain vigilant, we can not afford to bypass any source of water."

"What if we can find no water, or farmhouses?"

"We will be in grave trouble, and might not make it across the desert if Slann is at its widest or furthest section."

They passed out of shadowy Eelay Forest, onto the sunny Lesser Grassland.

Lie sat down, staring at the long Eln grass. "Perhaps we should stay here and wait for Baylou. It can probably find us no matter where we are. It might be able to call up the water we need."

"Will Baylou come back to us?" Clu asked, as he sat down. "Or will it continue the quest alone?"

"After gaining the magic Azophi has secreted in Slann, it might. Especially if it thinks I will fight it every step of the way." Lie swiped at the grass. "I did not mean what I said about going home. I was unsettled, frightened, and Baylou made the mistake of trying to calm me by trying to control me; making me rash." He stood up and looked down at Clu. "I thought it was trying to force me to continue this quest. That is why I struck it. Not — Never mind. Let us go on to Slann. Baylou will need us to help it to descry and release the magic."

"Even if we don't find extra water?"

"Yes. But we will discover water, even if we must search for it night and day."

They resumed their, perhaps, hopeless trek. Eelay Forest and the Lesser Grassland fell behind, and they entered the Plain of Hillocks.

Whenever they neared one of the hills, they trudged to the top and looked for farms or sources of water. This intensive searching caused time to pass quickly.

Neither man felt like conversing.

The enormous blue-green moon provided meager illumination.

"I hear water, Mr. Lie!" Clu shouted, excitedly.

It was a faint trickling.

"You have sharp ears, Clu. We go that way, then. And if the water is good, we will make camp and have some much-needed sleep."

"And food! We've walked a terrible long way since breakfast!"

Lie chuckled. "And eat," he agreed.

"What's that light?" Clu said.

"Where?"

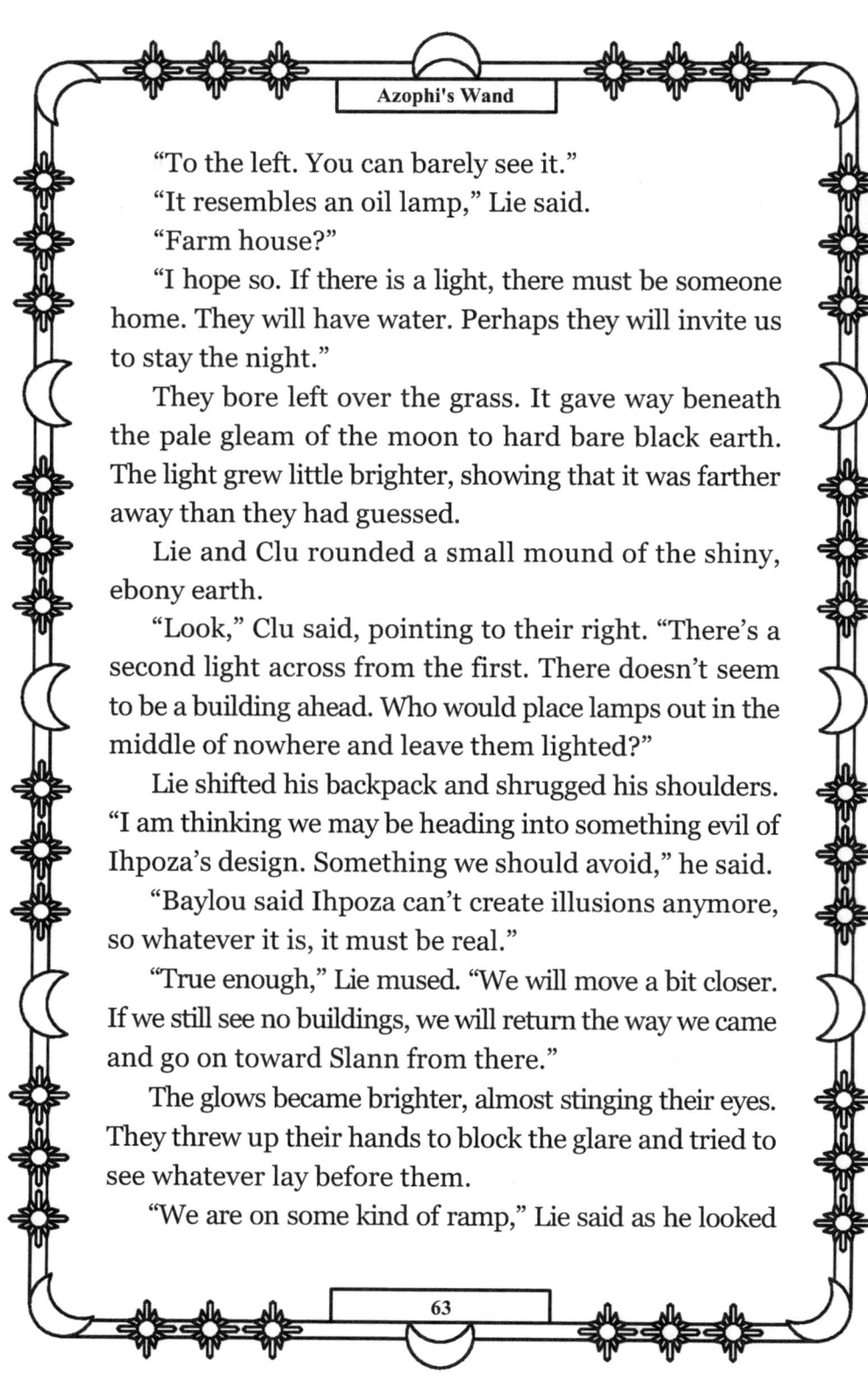

"To the left. You can barely see it."

"It resembles an oil lamp," Lie said.

"Farm house?"

"I hope so. If there is a light, there must be someone home. They will have water. Perhaps they will invite us to stay the night."

They bore left over the grass. It gave way beneath the pale gleam of the moon to hard bare black earth. The light grew little brighter, showing that it was farther away than they had guessed.

Lie and Clu rounded a small mound of the shiny, ebony earth.

"Look," Clu said, pointing to their right. "There's a second light across from the first. There doesn't seem to be a building ahead. Who would place lamps out in the middle of nowhere and leave them lighted?"

Lie shifted his backpack and shrugged his shoulders. "I am thinking we may be heading into something evil of Ihpoza's design. Something we should avoid," he said.

"Baylou said Ihpoza can't create illusions anymore, so whatever it is, it must be real."

"True enough," Lie mused. "We will move a bit closer. If we still see no buildings, we will return the way we came and go on toward Slann from there."

The glows became brighter, almost stinging their eyes. They threw up their hands to block the glare and tried to see whatever lay before them.

"We are on some kind of ramp," Lie said as he looked

at his boots. "I think I see edges on the left and right of us."

They neared the left glow with their hands still in front of their eyes. The light illuminated the ebony earthen ramp as would the sun. The ramp looked as though it had been kiln dried to a glossy shine.

"Is that a pearl?" Clu asked, squinting his eyes.

Lie approached the source of the glow on their left. "It is an orb of clear glass," he said. "There is some liquid inside it which creates this bright light. There must be another similar sphere on our right."

As they passed between the two luminous globes, they could detect, in the distance, two more such lights, and two more beyond those.

"This is some kind of lighted pathway," Lie decided. "Where it might lead, is anyone's guess. It might also lead to a place where we do not wish to go. I have never heard of anything like this on Azon, and it is not likely to be man made."

"Are you saying it's magical?" Clu asked. "Do you think we can turn around before anything bad happens to us?"

"Let us try." Lie led the way back toward the first two light balls.

The globes fell dark. Lie and Clu could see the stars and the blue-green moon, but their comforting light did not reach the ebony ramp, and the pathway was impossible to navigate.

"This must be Ihpoza's magic," Lie muttered angrily.

"Why can't it be Baylou's doing, or Azophi's?" Clu asked. "Maybe it's a cache of magic?"

"Baylou said there were no more caches until Slann."

"I forgot," Clu said. His disappointment was obvious. "What can we do, then."

"We will have to backtrack, by feel, to the end of the ramp, to where we walked onto it, and continue searching for that flowing water, you heard." Lie started forward.

The darkness grew greater. The stars and moon were no longer a cheerful presence in the sky. Lie and Clue lost all reference points and began to feel dizzy and disoriented. It was as if the darkness had reached up from the ebony ramp and joined with the sky, all the way to the horizons.

Lie reached out with his left hand, felt for Clu's arm, and grasped it firmly.

"We must not be separated," Lie said.

Someone took hold of Lie's right arm.

"You can depend on me!" Clu said, from Lie's right side.

Lie jerked his left hand away from whatever he had been grasping, and drew Clu nearer to him. He felt Clu's backpack with his right hand. "Is that you, Clu?" he said. His fright was evident in his voice, although he attempted to hide it.

"Yes, Mr. Lie? Is something wrong?"

"Did you see or hear anything, anyone, passing near us a moment ago?"

"No. I'm so dizzy, I feel like I'm going to be sick. I can't see my hand when I hold it in front of my eyes."

"We will have to crawl our way down the ramp," Lie said. "Once we leave it, I believe the moon light will return, and we will be able to see normally. Keep your hold on my arm, no matter what."

"Let's hurry! I'm getting more dizzy and more nauseated the longer we're in this place!"

Lie knelt, pulling Clu down beside him. They began slowly, cautiously, awkwardly crawling, in what they hoped was a straight line, in the direction from which they had originally walked onto the ebony ramp.

Their eyes were shocked by a bright light on their left and right.

"What!" Lie shouted, in frustration. "We are right back at the first two globes! I was certain we were headed in the opposite direction. I was most careful to pay attention! Damn it!"

Lie tugged Clu about face and they stepped forward. The globes fell into that abominable blackness.

"Well," Clu said, with a tired sigh, "at least we know we're in the correct direction to backtrack. Even if we can't see once more."

Lie said nothing. He pulled Clu into the kneeling position, and they started their awkward crawling.

Their eyes were shocked by a bright light on their left and right.

"Magic be damned!" Lie cursed.

"I honestly doubt we could have crawled in a circle," Clu muttered, angrily, "we didn't, even, go two feet."

"We must have!" Lie said. "Look, I am not prepared to remain in this midnight limbo for eternity. It is risky, but we must run straight to where we think that little mound was. Are you willing?"

"I don't know enough about what is around us to decide if we should," Clu said. "We're on some kind of ramp. What if we veer left or right and fall over an edge? What's down there? How far down, is there?"

"Excellent point, Clu!" Lie commended. He walked to the left light globe.

The orb was about ten inches in circumference. It was pressed against a vertical rectangular column of mirror like ebony stone. There did not seem to be anything to explain why the globe remained in its place. It did not reside in a niche, and there was no stem jutting from the bright globe and piercing into the obelisk.

Lie grabbed the orb angrily, and pulled with all his might. He pitched backwards, and landed on his rump with the shining globe in his trembling hands.

"Should you be messing with magic devices?" Clu said, with a worried expression. "Breaking them?"

"If this belongs to Ihpoza, I delight in breaking it all to hell," Lie said, angrily.

"What if it's Azophi's. Maybe the Wand didn't tell the Book everything there is to know? Azophi might not like you breaking his property."

"Have you ever heard of Azophi popping up at any time, anywhere, in the history of our people?" Lie asked.

"Well, no," Clu said, grudgingly, "but, this could be the final straw."

"I hope so. I very, intensely, hope so," Lie said. "We could use his assistance. Azophi should be here eradicating Ihpoza, not us. Wait here." He stepped around the left obelisk, walked carefully to the edge of the ramp, held the globe out at arms length, and whistled in frightened amazement.

Clu ran over to Lie's left side, looked down, and said: "Impossible!"

The Globe was illuminating a twenty foot drop, and millions of needle sharp projections of ebony rock, that spread as far as their vision could rectify the image.

Lie turned the globe to their left, along the edge of the ramp. The light cut into the incredible darkness, seeming to penetrate to the horizon.

"Even more impossible!" Clu said, irately. "We didn't walk that far up this ramp, even in my wildest nightmare!"

"We must be viewing illusions," Lie said. "There is no other explanation. Baylou must be incorrect. Ihpoza must have retained, or surely, regained, his ability to spin illusions."

"What can we do?"

"We have this light, now," Lie said. "I'll be damned if I am going to play Ihpoza's insane game. We will return to the end of the ramp. We know that it is not physically as

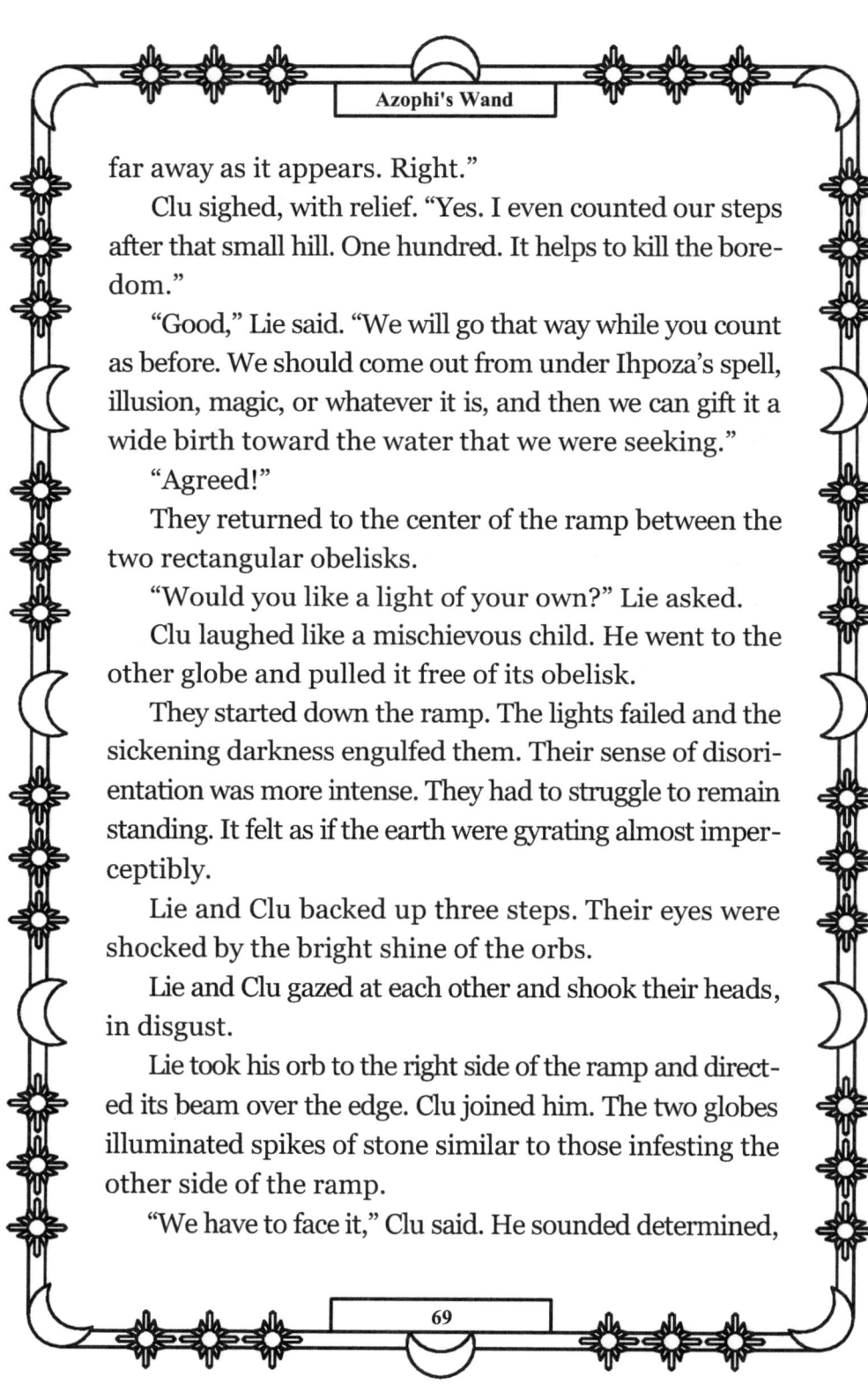

far away as it appears. Right."

Clu sighed, with relief. "Yes. I even counted our steps after that small hill. One hundred. It helps to kill the boredom."

"Good," Lie said. "We will go that way while you count as before. We should come out from under Ihpoza's spell, illusion, magic, or whatever it is, and then we can gift it a wide birth toward the water that we were seeking."

"Agreed!"

They returned to the center of the ramp between the two rectangular obelisks.

"Would you like a light of your own?" Lie asked.

Clu laughed like a mischievous child. He went to the other globe and pulled it free of its obelisk.

They started down the ramp. The lights failed and the sickening darkness engulfed them. Their sense of disorientation was more intense. They had to struggle to remain standing. It felt as if the earth were gyrating almost imperceptibly.

Lie and Clu backed up three steps. Their eyes were shocked by the bright shine of the orbs.

Lie and Clu gazed at each other and shook their heads, in disgust.

Lie took his orb to the right side of the ramp and directed its beam over the edge. Clu joined him. The two globes illuminated spikes of stone similar to those infesting the other side of the ramp.

"We have to face it," Clu said. He sounded determined,

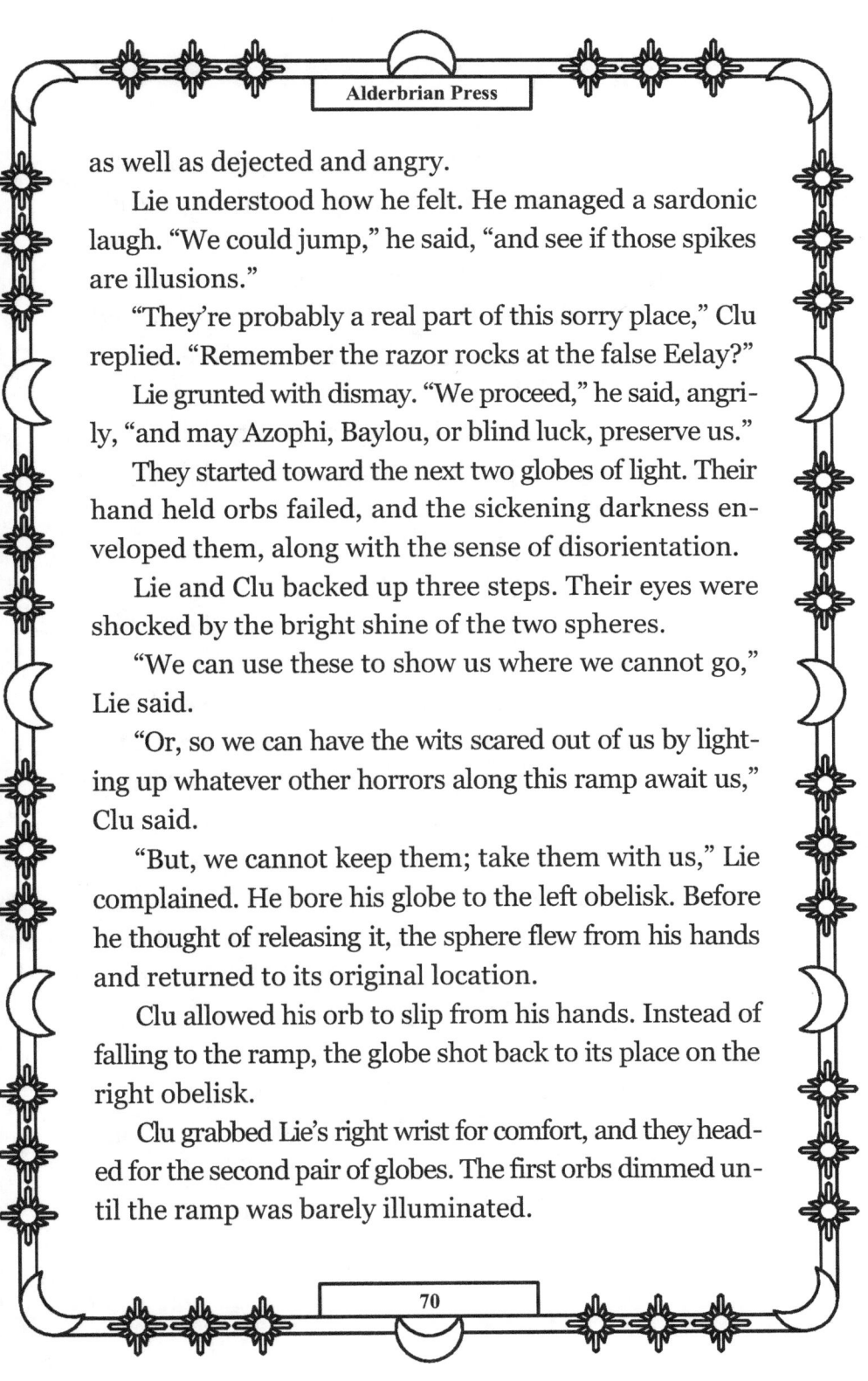

as well as dejected and angry.

Lie understood how he felt. He managed a sardonic laugh. "We could jump," he said, "and see if those spikes are illusions."

"They're probably a real part of this sorry place," Clu replied. "Remember the razor rocks at the false Eelay?"

Lie grunted with dismay. "We proceed," he said, angrily, "and may Azophi, Baylou, or blind luck, preserve us."

They started toward the next two globes of light. Their hand held orbs failed, and the sickening darkness enveloped them, along with the sense of disorientation.

Lie and Clu backed up three steps. Their eyes were shocked by the bright shine of the two spheres.

"We can use these to show us where we cannot go," Lie said.

"Or, so we can have the wits scared out of us by lighting up whatever other horrors along this ramp await us," Clu said.

"But, we cannot keep them; take them with us," Lie complained. He bore his globe to the left obelisk. Before he thought of releasing it, the sphere flew from his hands and returned to its original location.

Clu allowed his orb to slip from his hands. Instead of falling to the ramp, the globe shot back to its place on the right obelisk.

Clu grabbed Lie's right wrist for comfort, and they headed for the second pair of globes. The first orbs dimmed until the ramp was barely illuminated.

Lie and Clu passed through three more sets of obelisks and orbs before they came to a small tunnel. Its facade was composed of the same baked ebony earth as the ramp, and shone like a mirror. The inside was formed of black stone. They could not climb over the tunnel. Nor could they pass around, on either side, because of the twenty foot drop to the rock spikes.

Knowing it would be folly to try to retreat, Lie and Clu entered the tunnel to brave the unknown but certain threat both reasoned must await. The globes on the last two obelisks, faded to a gleam.

Baylou lay on its back cover atop a high hill of baked earth. Its unblinking green eye stared at the giant moon. Something was wrong in connection with Lie and Clu. There was an energy surrounding them that was unfamiliar. It was not the power of Azophi, nor The Wand, nor the might of a cache, nor the evil force of Ihpoza. It was as if this power had created itself around Lie and Clu, out of nothing.

Baylou rustled its pages. If Lie and Clu could not pass from under this mass of power on their own, Baylou would have to find and rescue them. Otherwise, its mission would fail.

Baylou pushed the idea of failure from its confused thoughts and concentrated on Lie and Clu. It sought contact with their minds. Even a tenuous link might allow the Book to aid them in some way. At the least, this would

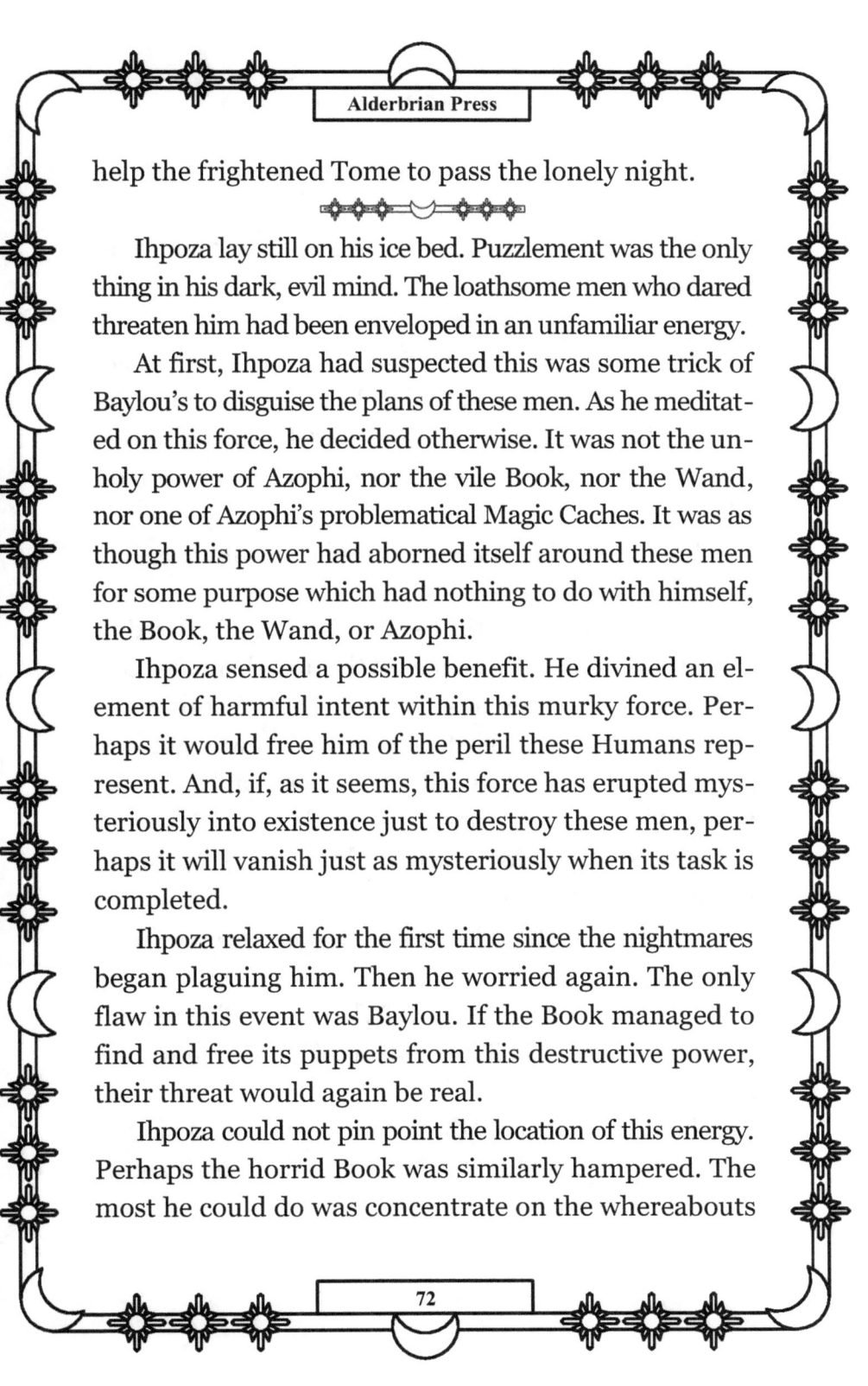

help the frightened Tome to pass the lonely night.

Ihpoza lay still on his ice bed. Puzzlement was the only thing in his dark, evil mind. The loathsome men who dared threaten him had been enveloped in an unfamiliar energy.

At first, Ihpoza had suspected this was some trick of Baylou's to disguise the plans of these men. As he meditated on this force, he decided otherwise. It was not the unholy power of Azophi, nor the vile Book, nor the Wand, nor one of Azophi's problematical Magic Caches. It was as though this power had aborned itself around these men for some purpose which had nothing to do with himself, the Book, the Wand, or Azophi.

Ihpoza sensed a possible benefit. He divined an element of harmful intent within this murky force. Perhaps it would free him of the peril these Humans represent. And, if, as it seems, this force has erupted mysteriously into existence just to destroy these men, perhaps it will vanish just as mysteriously when its task is completed.

Ihpoza relaxed for the first time since the nightmares began plaguing him. Then he worried again. The only flaw in this event was Baylou. If the Book managed to find and free its puppets from this destructive power, their threat would again be real.

Ihpoza could not pin point the location of this energy. Perhaps the horrid Book was similarly hampered. The most he could do was concentrate on the whereabouts

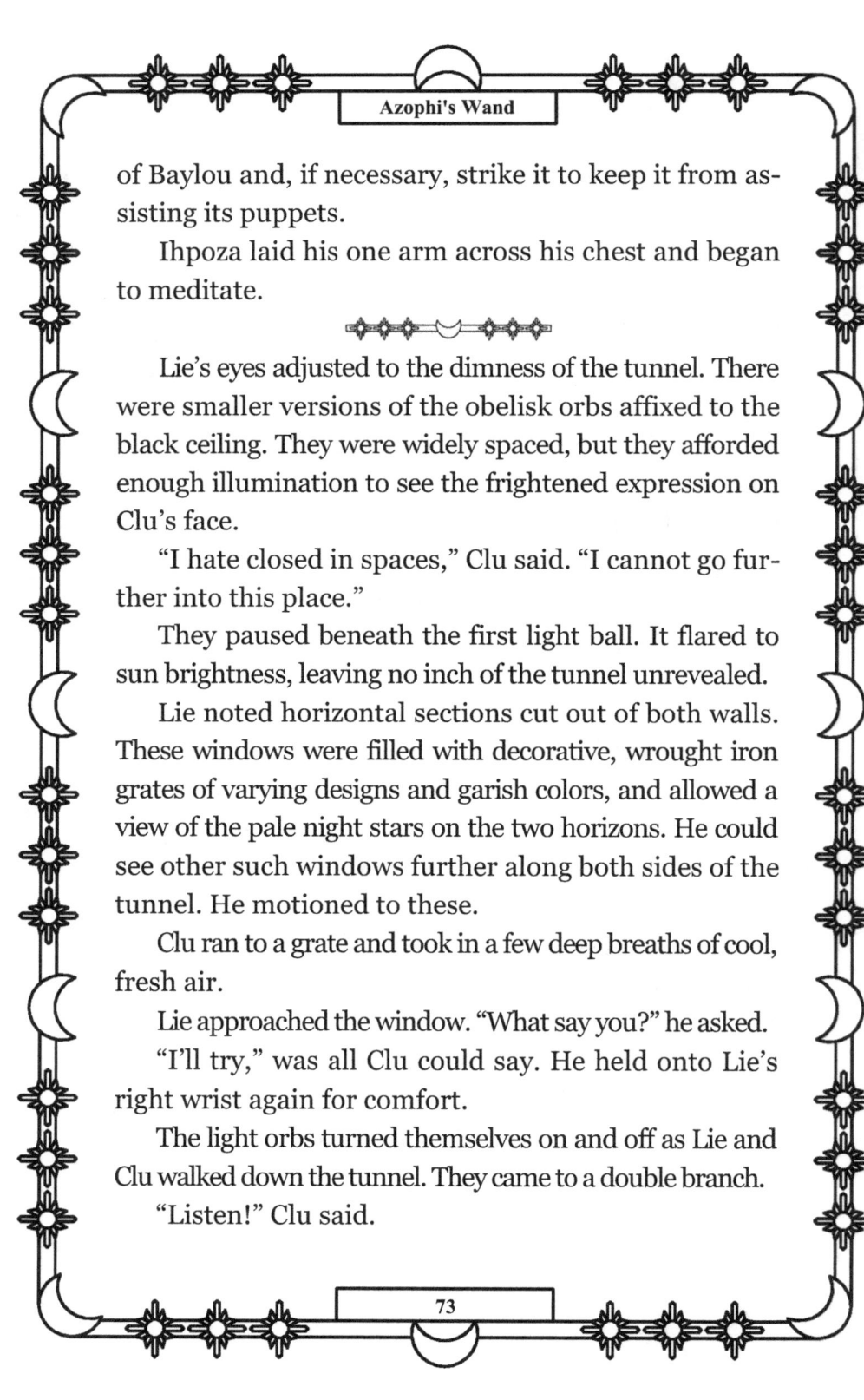

of Baylou and, if necessary, strike it to keep it from assisting its puppets.

Ihpoza laid his one arm across his chest and began to meditate.

Lie's eyes adjusted to the dimness of the tunnel. There were smaller versions of the obelisk orbs affixed to the black ceiling. They were widely spaced, but they afforded enough illumination to see the frightened expression on Clu's face.

"I hate closed in spaces," Clu said. "I cannot go further into this place."

They paused beneath the first light ball. It flared to sun brightness, leaving no inch of the tunnel unrevealed.

Lie noted horizontal sections cut out of both walls. These windows were filled with decorative, wrought iron grates of varying designs and garish colors, and allowed a view of the pale night stars on the two horizons. He could see other such windows further along both sides of the tunnel. He motioned to these.

Clu ran to a grate and took in a few deep breaths of cool, fresh air.

Lie approached the window. "What say you?" he asked.

"I'll try," was all Clu could say. He held onto Lie's right wrist again for comfort.

The light orbs turned themselves on and off as Lie and Clu walked down the tunnel. They came to a double branch.

"Listen!" Clu said.

"Water flowing?" Lie said.

"I forgot we were headed in this general direction, following after the water we heard, before we found the ramp," Clu said. "You don't suppose this is Baylou's heavy-handed way of leading us to some water before we have to enter the desert?"

"The Book is a control freak," Lie said, sounding doubtful. "We had better not let our guard down for a minute, though. This could still be some bizarre scheme created by Ihpoza."

"I'll wager it's Baylou and water," Clu said, optimistically.

Lie led the way toward the left branch.

Winds suctioned the two men in opposite directions, breaking Clu's hold on Lie's right wrist. Try as they might, neither could make headway against the winds. They ceased trying to approach each other, and the winds ended.

"This is not acceptable, Baylou!" Lie screamed, with ire. His words echoed weirdly throughout the three tunnels. "We will not be separated! It is time for you and grand Azophi to stop playing inscrutable games and actually assist us!"

The echoes of Lie's distorted words seemed to be absorbed by the ebony tunnels.

Lie indicted, with a movement of his head, the way they had come.

Clu nodded assent.

They tried to retreat, but the same mysterious winds

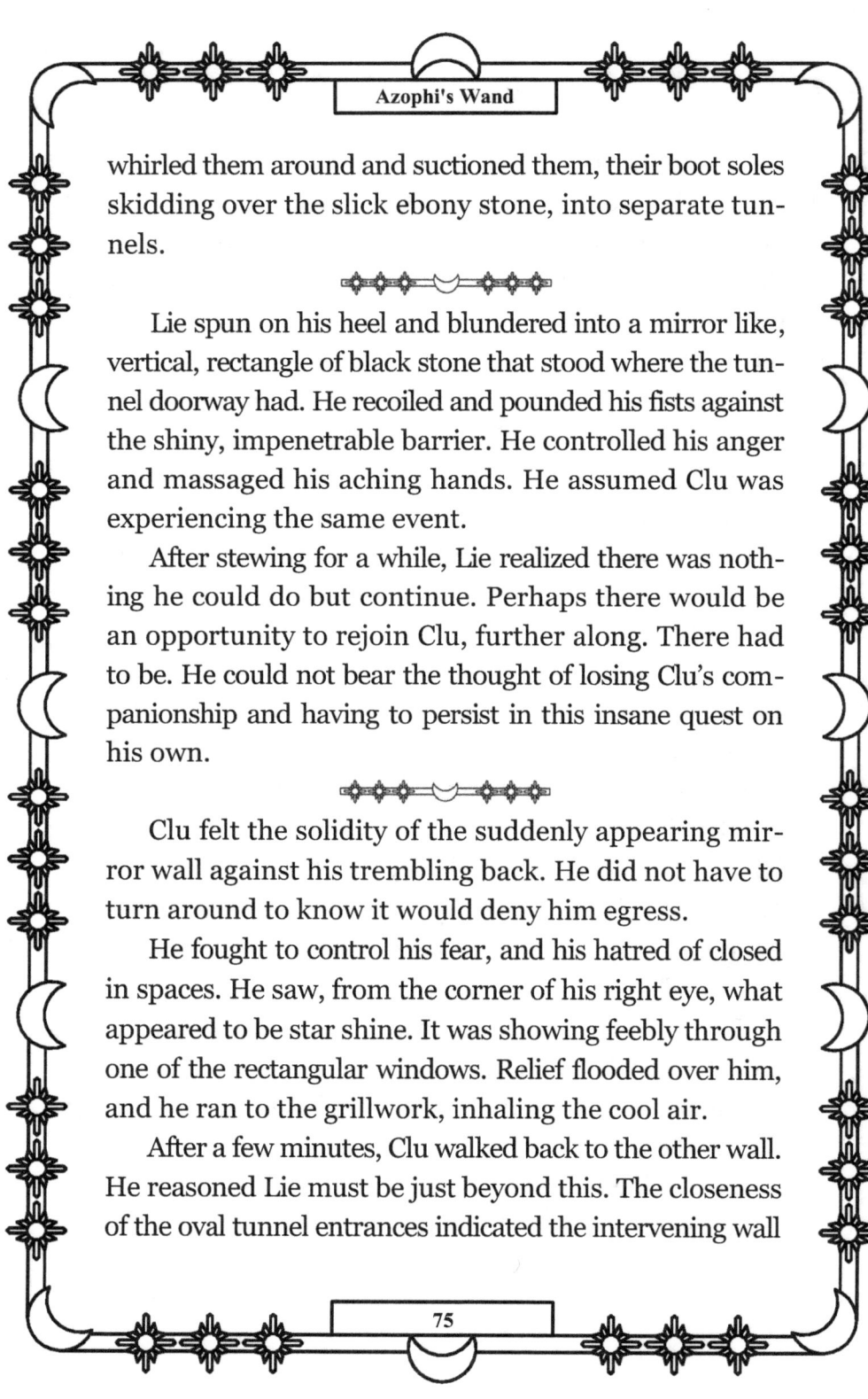

whirled them around and suctioned them, their boot soles skidding over the slick ebony stone, into separate tunnels.

Lie spun on his heel and blundered into a mirror like, vertical, rectangle of black stone that stood where the tunnel doorway had. He recoiled and pounded his fists against the shiny, impenetrable barrier. He controlled his anger and massaged his aching hands. He assumed Clu was experiencing the same event.

After stewing for a while, Lie realized there was nothing he could do but continue. Perhaps there would be an opportunity to rejoin Clu, further along. There had to be. He could not bear the thought of losing Clu's companionship and having to persist in this insane quest on his own.

Clu felt the solidity of the suddenly appearing mirror wall against his trembling back. He did not have to turn around to know it would deny him egress.

He fought to control his fear, and his hatred of closed in spaces. He saw, from the corner of his right eye, what appeared to be star shine. It was showing feebly through one of the rectangular windows. Relief flooded over him, and he ran to the grillwork, inhaling the cool air.

After a few minutes, Clu walked back to the other wall. He reasoned Lie must be just beyond this. The closeness of the oval tunnel entrances indicated the intervening wall should not be so thick as to prevent his communicating with Lie. He cupped his hands against the stone and yelled through them as loudly as he could.

"Mr. Lie? Are you there?" He placed his ear to the cold stone. Nothing.

Clu pounded on the unfeeling stone. He turned around and kicked savagely at the wall with the heel of his boot. The thudding echoed strangely, and there was no response from Lie.

"Maybe he has continued," Clu whispered. "Maybe he expects to meet me further along. Maybe these tunnels will meet again. It is a sure bet Mr. Lie won't just stay here. Neither will I."

Clu banged his heel one last angry time, then crossed the hall and started walking quickly along the windows and their fresh air. Close to the illusion of escape. If not for that desperate illusion, he would collapse.

Lie was walking swiftly along the depressing tunnel. He had no particular problem with closed in spaces, but he would have felt a bit claustrophobic without the starlight and cool fresh air provided by the windows in the left wall.

Lie stopped short. The tunnel had turned into a huge cavern to his left. The far left wall was so distant, it was hazy. Throughout the cavern were other tunnels which ran in the same direction he had been going. Along the walls of these passages he could see vertical, rectangular, mirror-like sections of ebony stone spaced by vertical, rectangular, lamp-

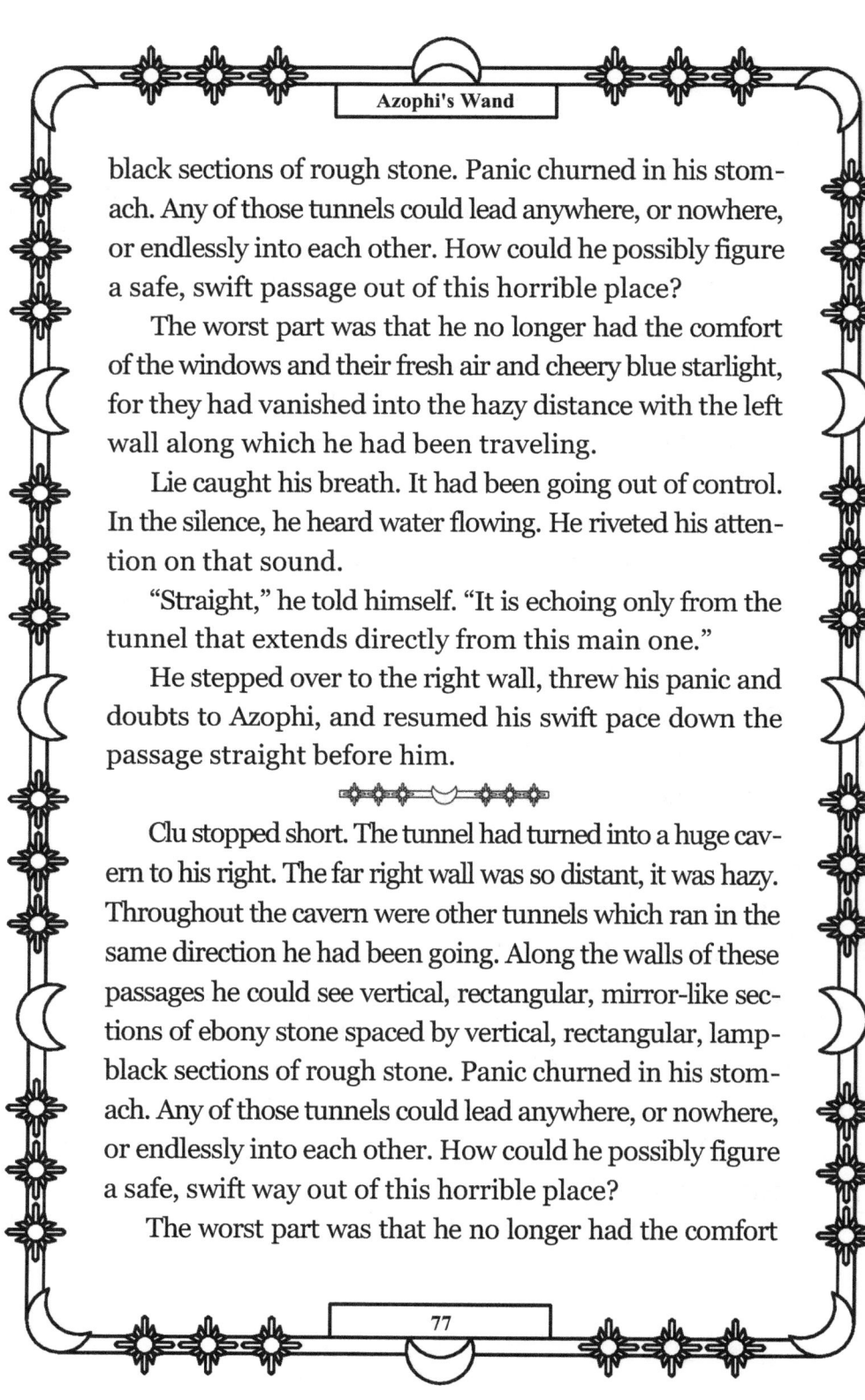

black sections of rough stone. Panic churned in his stomach. Any of those tunnels could lead anywhere, or nowhere, or endlessly into each other. How could he possibly figure a safe, swift passage out of this horrible place?

The worst part was that he no longer had the comfort of the windows and their fresh air and cheery blue starlight, for they had vanished into the hazy distance with the left wall along which he had been traveling.

Lie caught his breath. It had been going out of control. In the silence, he heard water flowing. He riveted his attention on that sound.

"Straight," he told himself. "It is echoing only from the tunnel that extends directly from this main one."

He stepped over to the right wall, threw his panic and doubts to Azophi, and resumed his swift pace down the passage straight before him.

Clu stopped short. The tunnel had turned into a huge cavern to his right. The far right wall was so distant, it was hazy. Throughout the cavern were other tunnels which ran in the same direction he had been going. Along the walls of these passages he could see vertical, rectangular, mirror-like sections of ebony stone spaced by vertical, rectangular, lamp-black sections of rough stone. Panic churned in his stomach. Any of those tunnels could lead anywhere, or nowhere, or endlessly into each other. How could he possibly figure a safe, swift way out of this horrible place?

The worst part was that he no longer had the comfort

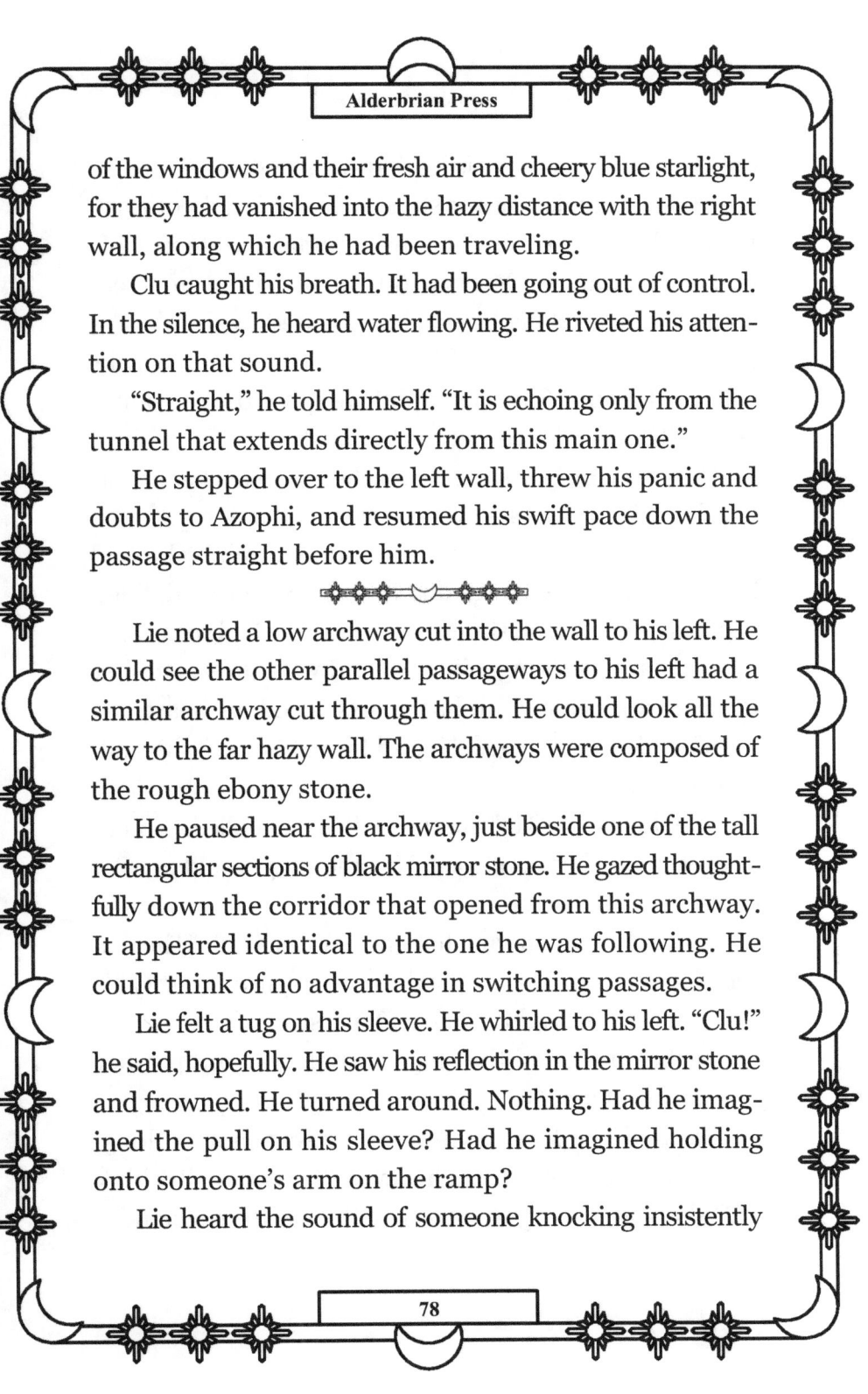

of the windows and their fresh air and cheery blue starlight, for they had vanished into the hazy distance with the right wall, along which he had been traveling.

Clu caught his breath. It had been going out of control. In the silence, he heard water flowing. He riveted his attention on that sound.

"Straight," he told himself. "It is echoing only from the tunnel that extends directly from this main one."

He stepped over to the left wall, threw his panic and doubts to Azophi, and resumed his swift pace down the passage straight before him.

Lie noted a low archway cut into the wall to his left. He could see the other parallel passageways to his left had a similar archway cut through them. He could look all the way to the far hazy wall. The archways were composed of the rough ebony stone.

He paused near the archway, just beside one of the tall rectangular sections of black mirror stone. He gazed thoughtfully down the corridor that opened from this archway. It appeared identical to the one he was following. He could think of no advantage in switching passages.

Lie felt a tug on his sleeve. He whirled to his left. "Clu!" he said, hopefully. He saw his reflection in the mirror stone and frowned. He turned around. Nothing. Had he imagined the pull on his sleeve? Had he imagined holding onto someone's arm on the ramp?

Lie heard the sound of someone knocking insistently

on wood. He spun on his heel and gasped.

The rectangular mirror stone was as if it did not exist. Instead, he was looking at the front portal and steps of his house. His fiancée, MerraLynn, stood on the small cement porch, her long blonde hair colored by the glow of the blue-green moon. White blouse, blue riding slacks and black boots. She was rapidly tapping the toe of her boot with impatience, as was her custom.

"MerraLynn," Lie said. He reached to touch her shoulder, but his fingers struck an invisible barrier.

MerraLynn turned half around as though she had heard Lie. Her green eyes and lovely face were sad, filled with disappointment, showing no signs she had seen Lie.

Lie stared adoringly into MerraLynn's eyes, and her intense expression of unhappiness ached his heart.

MerraLynn shrugged. "Lie still is not home," she said, dejectedly.

"Neither is my Clu," another soft voice replied. "Something very bad has happened. No other way would my Clu vanish."

"No," MerraLynn said, holding her arms out. "There is some business of Lie's with which he required your Clu's aid. They are all right, AarLee, I am sure of this."

AarLee mounted the steps and MerraLynn put her arms around her.

Dressed like MerraLynn, AarLee was shorter: long, lustrous, raven hair, dark blue eyes. "Do you really think so?" she said, wiping at tears with the heel of one hand.

"Absolutely!" MerraLynn avowed. "If harm had befallen Lie, I would know it, feel it, almost like it had befall-
en me. He is safe, and your Clu is safe, since we are sure he
is with my Lie."

"But, what could be vital enough to make them depart
HeyTown without leaving word with anyone?" AarLee insisted. "Clu has never done such a thoughtless thing, and I
have known him since we were born."

MerraLynn could not offer a response. They just stood
there gazing forlornly at Lie.

Lie tried to caress MerraLynn's smooth cheek. Again,
he touched only cold, transparent stone.

"I am here," he said, firmly, lovingly, trying to make
her sense his emotions and presence. "I am safe and yearn
to return to you. You must not cede hope that I will return
to you."

The scene faded to shiny ebony stone: cold, hard and
uncaring.

Lie groaned in despair. He pounded his palms against
the stone, trying to will the scene to return, but to no avail.
Then he flushed with rage.

"Ihpoza!" he shouted. "You shall not torment me any
longer! Do not show these things to me, for I shall not ache
to your scheme! Leave my MerraLynn out of this, or as the
universe exists, even without the magic of Baylou and
Azophi, I will strangle the life out of you to preserve she
whom I cherish! Hear me, demon! Mark my oath, and beware!"

He started running down the corridor, hoping for an archway that would open on his right so he could reunite with Clu and vacate this dark, accursed place.

Clu noted a low archway cut into the wall to his right. He could see the other parallel passageways to his right had a similar archway cut through them. He could look all the way to the far hazy wall. The archways were composed of the rough ebony stone.

He paused near the archway, just beside one of the tall rectangular sections of black mirror stone. He gazed thoughtfully down the corridor that opened from this archway. It appeared identical to the one he was following. He could think of no advantage in switching passages.

Clu felt a tug on his sleeve. He whirled to his right. "Lie!" he said, hopefully. He saw his reflection in the mirror stone and frowned. He turned around. Nothing. Had he imagined that pull on his sleeve? He heard the sound of someone sniffling. He spun on his heel and gasped.

The rectangular mirror stone was as if it did not exist. Instead, he was looking at the front portal and steps of Lie's house. His adored brunet wife, AarLee, stood on the small cement porch, with a taller woman who had blond hair and emerald eyes. She had an arm around AarLee, comforting her. White blouses, blue riding slacks and black boots. They appeared forlorn under the blue-green shine of the great moon.

"AarLee," Clu said. He reached to touch her shoulder,

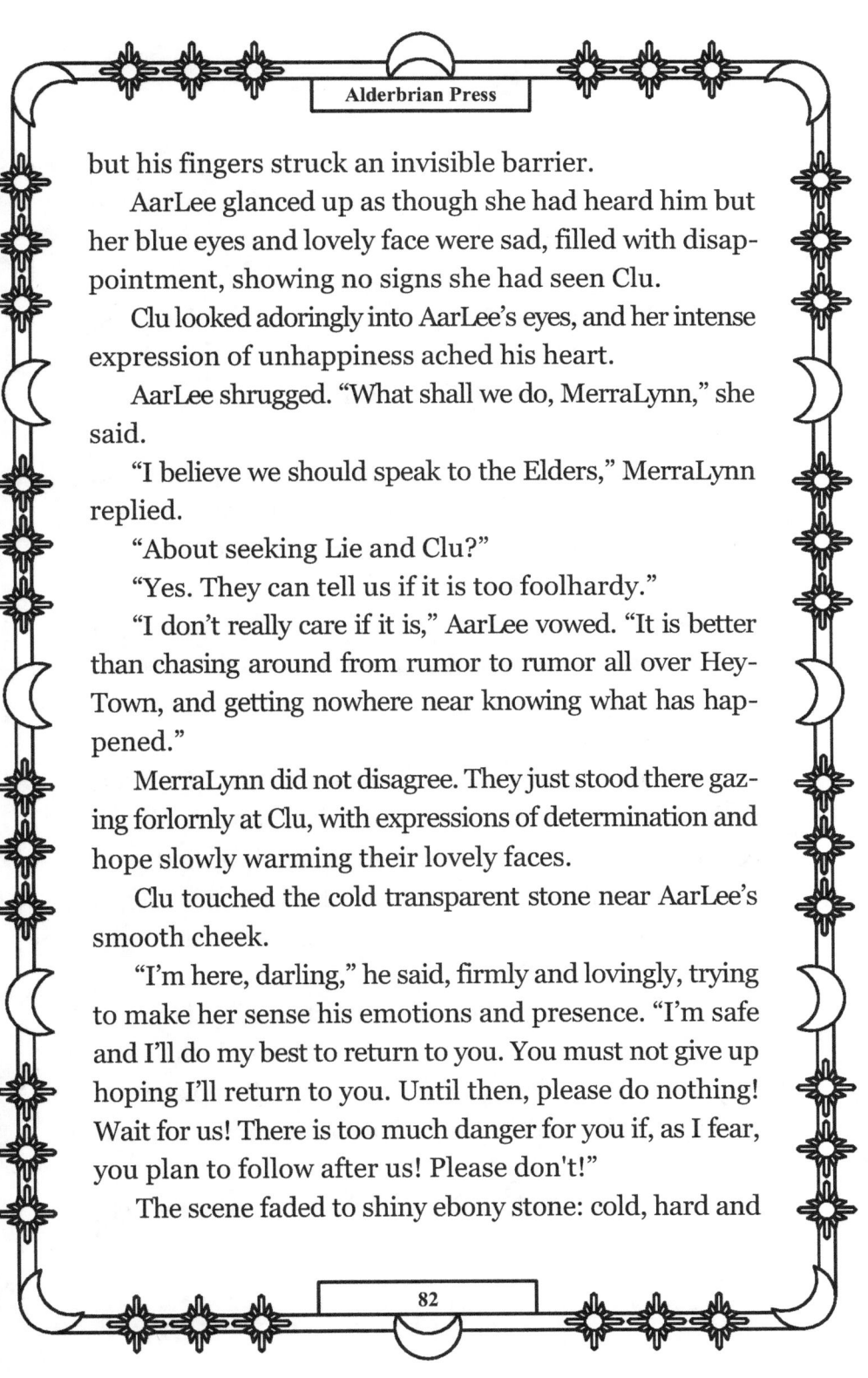

but his fingers struck an invisible barrier.

AarLee glanced up as though she had heard him but her blue eyes and lovely face were sad, filled with disappointment, showing no signs she had seen Clu.

Clu looked adoringly into AarLee's eyes, and her intense expression of unhappiness ached his heart.

AarLee shrugged. "What shall we do, MerraLynn," she said.

"I believe we should speak to the Elders," MerraLynn replied.

"About seeking Lie and Clu?"

"Yes. They can tell us if it is too foolhardy."

"I don't really care if it is," AarLee vowed. "It is better than chasing around from rumor to rumor all over Hey-Town, and getting nowhere near knowing what has happened."

MerraLynn did not disagree. They just stood there gazing forlornly at Clu, with expressions of determination and hope slowly warming their lovely faces.

Clu touched the cold transparent stone near AarLee's smooth cheek.

"I'm here, darling," he said, firmly and lovingly, trying to make her sense his emotions and presence. "I'm safe and I'll do my best to return to you. You must not give up hoping I'll return to you. Until then, please do nothing! Wait for us! There is too much danger for you if, as I fear, you plan to follow after us! Please don't!"

The scene faded to shiny ebony stone: cold, hard and

uncaring.

Clu groaned in despair. He pounded his fists against the rock, trying to will the scene to return, but to no avail. He stood trembling with rage.

"Don't do anything, AarLee!" he shouted. "You must hear me! Do not leave HeyTown! That vile demon will not hesitate to harm you! Mark my warning, AarLee, and beware!"

He started running down the corridor, hoping for an archway that would open on his left so he could reunite with Lie and flee from this vile, haunted place.

Lie skidded to a halt. He leaned forward, struggling to hold his breath and listening. There it was, faint, but understandable.

"Mr. Lie! It's me, Clu! Where are you?"

The voice came from an archway on Lie's left. He stood in the archway, cupped his hands to his mouth and shouted: "This way, Clu! I will count from one until you find me!"

"Mr. Lie! I'm injured! I can't walk! I think my leg is broken! It hurts so badly! Please! Come quickly! Help me!"

Lie felt a tug on his left sleeve. He startled and turned. One of the rectangles of mirror stone was beside the archway. It had turned into a viewing screen. It showed Clu walking resolutely down a corridor. His gait was unhampered by a broken leg.

Lie felt frustrated. Which was true? The cries for help

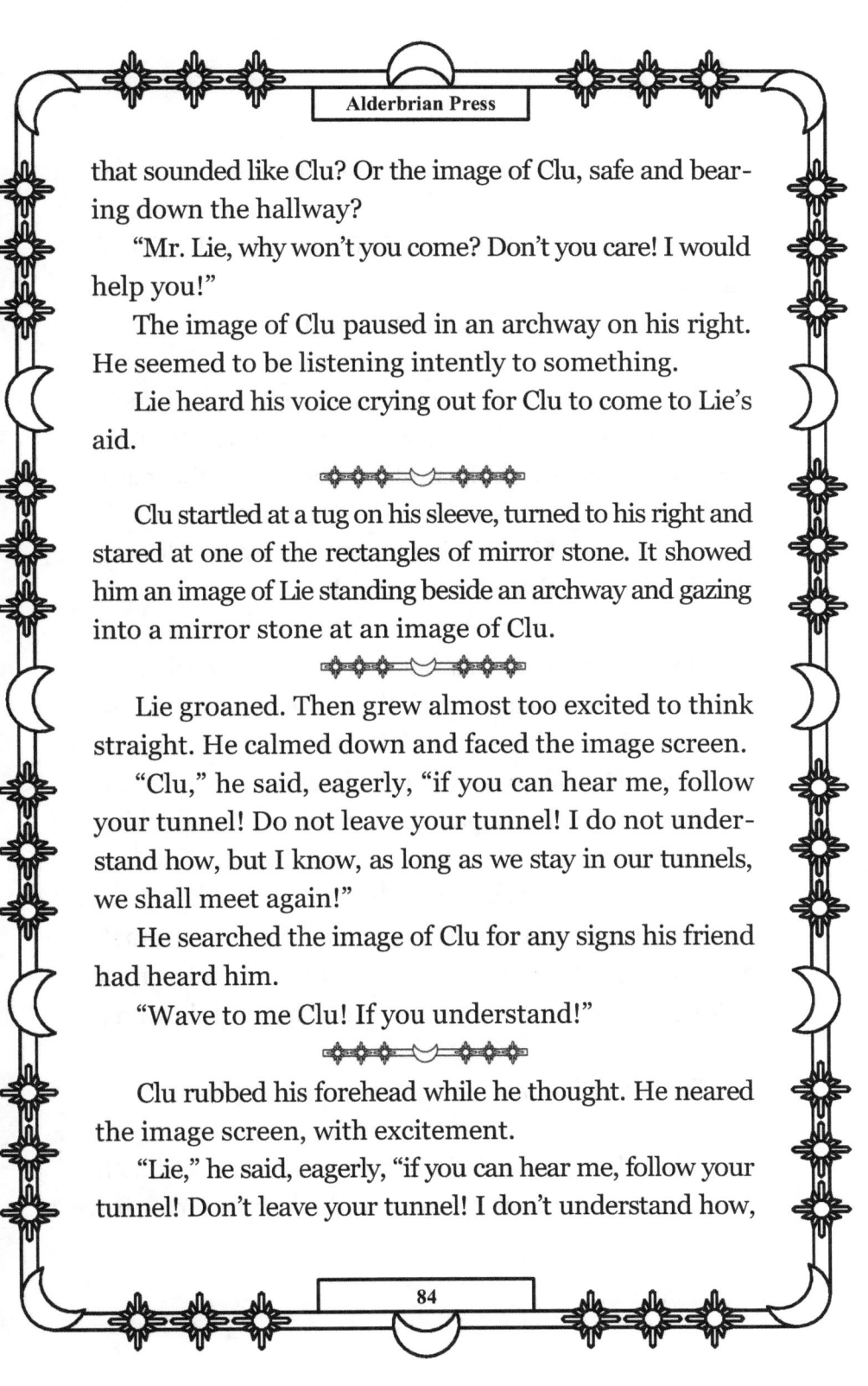

that sounded like Clu? Or the image of Clu, safe and bear-ing down the hallway?

"Mr. Lie, why won't you come? Don't you care! I would help you!"

The image of Clu paused in an archway on his right. He seemed to be listening intently to something.

Lie heard his voice crying out for Clu to come to Lie's aid.

⬥⬥⬥〜⬥⬥⬥

Clu startled at a tug on his sleeve, turned to his right and stared at one of the rectangles of mirror stone. It showed him an image of Lie standing beside an archway and gazing into a mirror stone at an image of Clu.

⬥⬥⬥〜⬥⬥⬥

Lie groaned. Then grew almost too excited to think straight. He calmed down and faced the image screen.

"Clu," he said, eagerly, "if you can hear me, follow your tunnel! Do not leave your tunnel! I do not under-stand how, but I know, as long as we stay in our tunnels, we shall meet again!"

He searched the image of Clu for any signs his friend had heard him.

"Wave to me Clu! If you understand!"

⬥⬥⬥〜⬥⬥⬥

Clu rubbed his forehead while he thought. He neared the image screen, with excitement.

"Lie," he said, eagerly, "if you can hear me, follow your tunnel! Don't leave your tunnel! I don't understand how, but I know, as long as we stay in our tunnels, we'll meet again!"

He searched the image of Lie for any signs his friend had heard him.

"Wave to me Lie! If you understand!"

Lie was confused, frustrated and angry. He could hear the false Clu voice, and through the image mirror, the false Lie voice Clu heard, but he could not hear what the image of Clu said. He had no doubt Clu had not heard a word Lie had said. On a whim, hoping he and Clu were following the same line of thought, he waved.

Clu was confused, frustrated and angry. He could hear the false Lie voice, and through the image mirror, the false Clu voice Lie heard, but he could not hear what the image of Lie said. He had no doubt Lie had not heard a word Clu had said. On a whim, hoping that he and Lie were thinking alike, he waved.

Lie smiled and turned to continue down his tunnel. As he walked, he kept his eyes on the image mirror for as long as he could to be sure Clu was bearing down his tunnel.

The false Clu voice ceased its haunting pleas.

Clu smiled and turned to continue down his tunnel. As he walked, he kept his eyes on the image mirror for as long as he could to be sure Lie was bearing down his tunnel.

The false Lie voice ceased its haunting pleas.

The sound of claws on stone made Clu's skin crawl. A chill breeze swept past him. He slowed his pace, listening fearfully for further evidence he was not alone.

As he cautiously neared one of the mirror rectangles, Clu heard an animal snarl. He shied to his right, away from the mirror.

The ebony stone flashed clear for an instant, and a demon, armed with a blue steel dagger, leaped into the tunnel.

Clu fled in terror. He could hear the demon's claws scratching the stone floor as it pursued. He realized the monster was twice his height, with a gait twice as long. Even so, it was catching up with him unusually swiftly. He sighted an archway ahead. He felt, with certainty, if he left this tunnel, he might not be able to find his way back. To successfully rejoin Lie, he had to remain in this tunnel. With no weapon, he had no option but to dart through that archway.

Clu crossed that tunnel, raced through the next archway and flattened himself fearfully against the rough stone of the wall on the right-hand side of that archway. He smothered his breathing, covering his mouth with both hands.

The demon howled and hurled itself through the archway, across the tunnel, and into the next tunnel.

Clu spun around, through the archway, across that tunnel, and back into his original tunnel. He fled head long down the tunnel, in his original direction. His breathing was labored and loud. His face was pale with fright. As he ran, he glanced over his shoulder as often as he dared.

Lie startled at the harsh, enraged animal howling. A chill wind sweep past him. He paused long enough to glance over his left shoulder, before he took flight at his utmost pace.

The demon emerged through an archway Lie had just passed. It seemed surprised when it sighted Lie, then raised its blue steel dagger and gave chase, moving extraordinarily swiftly.

Lie noted the monster had an unfair advantage in the desperate race. When it passed the mirror stone rectangles, the beast vanished, then reappeared at the next rectangle of rough stone. This meant the monster had to run only the length of the width of the rough sections of rock. During its invisible moments, the chimera coasted the length of the width of the mirror stone rectangles. The demon was nearing its quarry, with mind-numbing speed.

Lie sighted an archway. It was a heart aching gamble, but he had no choice but to leave his tunnel. If he could dupe the demon, he could return to his original path. He veered through the archway, intending to flatten himself against the wall to the left of the archway. His right foot slipped from under him, and he went down on his left knee. He caught himself with his palms against the floor, but it was too late.

The demon reached Lie. Slavering fearsomely, it blundered into his legs and sprawled flat of its green scaled chest on the rough ebony stone. Its dagger slipped from its claws and slid through the next archway, into that tunnel.

Lie threw himself to his right, over onto his back and scrambled up to his feet, shaking in horror. He sucked in a breath and kicked the demon in its scaly rump with his hatred, rage and frustration. The blow sent the ugly monster rolling head over heels through the next archway and tunnel, after its dagger.

Lie felt so weak from fatigue he wanted to sink to his seat against a wall to control his fear, trembling, and labored breathing. He knew this would cost his life. He spun on his heel and hurled himself back through the archways and into his original tunnel, racing in his original direction. He ran with his right shoulder nearly brushing the right-hand wall to put as much space as possible between himself and the archways, in the unhappy event the demon returned. He had no illusions it would fail to resume its pursuit.

Clu heard the demon's affronted howls of rage and frustration before he looked over his right shoulder and saw the monster racing through an archway Clu had just passed.

When it sighted Clu, the demon appeared surprised, then growled and gave pursuit.

Clu cried out in despair. He could run no faster, could not flee for much longer. There was no archway ahead.

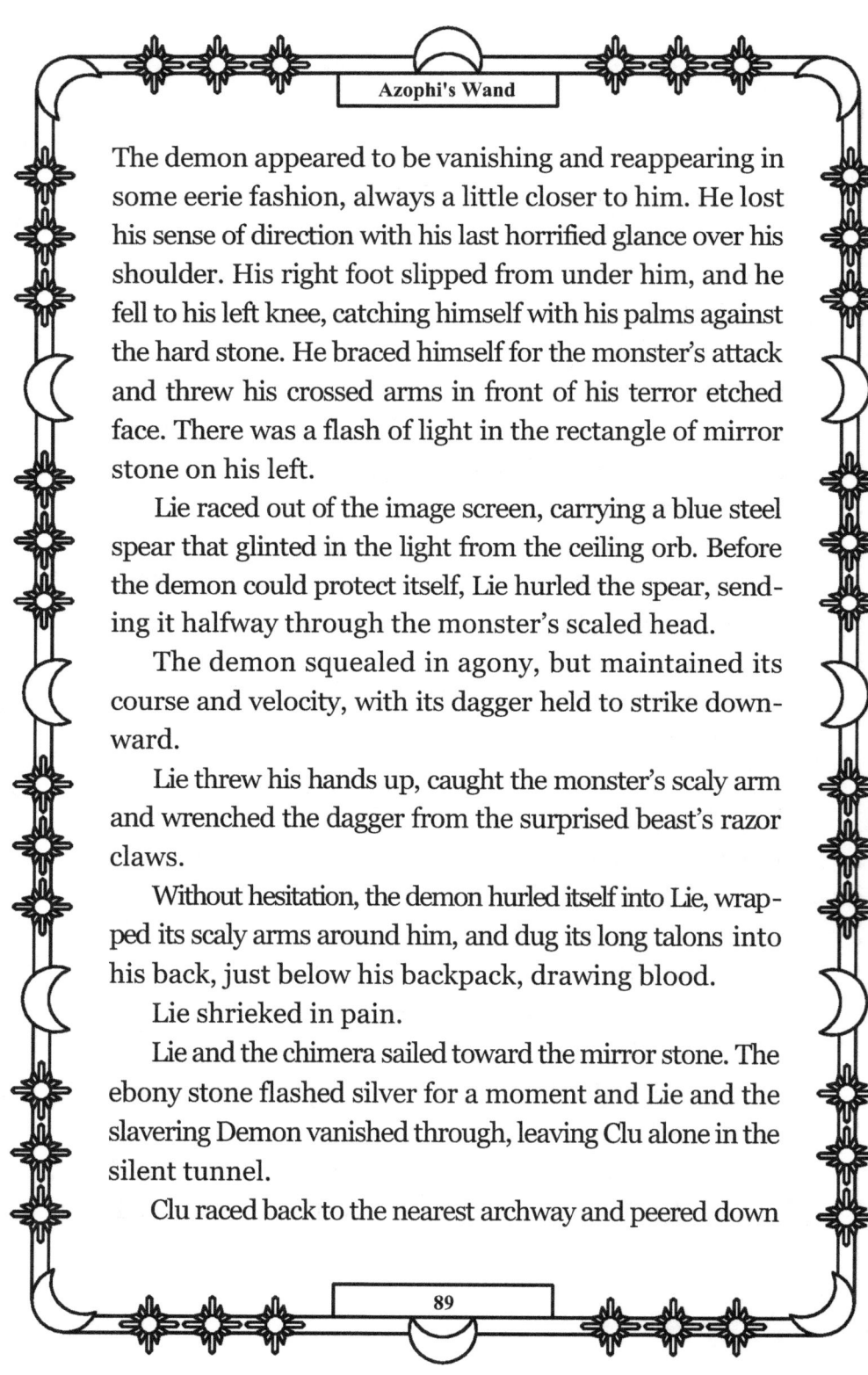

The demon appeared to be vanishing and reappearing in some eerie fashion, always a little closer to him. He lost his sense of direction with his last horrified glance over his shoulder. His right foot slipped from under him, and he fell to his left knee, catching himself with his palms against the hard stone. He braced himself for the monster's attack and threw his crossed arms in front of his terror etched face. There was a flash of light in the rectangle of mirror stone on his left.

Lie raced out of the image screen, carrying a blue steel spear that glinted in the light from the ceiling orb. Before the demon could protect itself, Lie hurled the spear, sending it halfway through the monster's scaled head.

The demon squealed in agony, but maintained its course and velocity, with its dagger held to strike downward.

Lie threw his hands up, caught the monster's scaly arm and wrenched the dagger from the surprised beast's razor claws.

Without hesitation, the demon hurled itself into Lie, wrapped its scaly arms around him, and dug its long talons into his back, just below his backpack, drawing blood.

Lie shrieked in pain.

Lie and the chimera sailed toward the mirror stone. The ebony stone flashed silver for a moment and Lie and the slavering Demon vanished through, leaving Clu alone in the silent tunnel.

Clu raced back to the nearest archway and peered down

that tunnel, hoping, wildly, Lie would be there, so he could assist Lie against the demon.

Semidarkness and desolate silence.

Something tugged on Clu's right sleeve. He startled and stepped to his right to look at the rectangle of mirror stone.

The blackness vanished, revealing an image of Lie running down his tunnel. He was checking over his shoulder and appeared unharmed.

"Which is true, mirror?" Clu whispered, with angry frustration.

"That which is seen is true," the towering bright mirror whispered, using Clu's voice.

Clu leaped back from the image, on the edge of hysteria. "Was the demon real, or illusion?" he asked.

"That it can be seen, is real. That it can be heard, is real. That it can be feared and fled, is real," the mirror said.

"Look," Clu said, "I don't need riddles, I need answers. Could that demon have harmed me?"

The demon appeared in the mirror, seeming to be standing on the other side of the stone, in that tunnel. It reached through the mirror with its razor claws and grinned fiendishly.

Clu became irate with the mirror and himself. Why had he imagined he could receive truth inside Ihpoza's conjured nightmare? He slapped the demon's hand, intending to prove it was a harmless illusion.

The chimera grasped Clu's wrist and drew his arm halfway into the mirror.

Clu screamed in horror, summoned his strength and slugged the demon between its slanted yellow eyes, then in each eye, in rapid succession.

The amazed monster released the human's wrist and drew back from the surface of the mirror. It rubbed at its eyes with the backs of its scaled hands.

"Mirror," Clu screamed, "turn off this image!"

"It must be extinguished at the source," the mirror said, in Clu's voice.

Clu snorted with frustration. Then thought of removing the image of the demon from his thoughts. The mirror went dark. Clu thought of Lie. The mirror stone showed him an image of Lie proceeding down his tunnel.

Clu began to run down his tunnel. He did not want Lie to get too far ahead of him.

Clu felt and smelled a cool breeze of fresh air. He skidded to a stop and stared to his right. "Thank god!" he shouted.

The parallel tunnels and archways, which had yawned on his right, had ended, and he was looking through one of the long, horizontal, rectangular window grates at the pale twinkling stars. He ran to the window and gasped in the invigorating air.

Clu noticed the walls of this section of the tunnel, for as far as he could see, no longer contained the alternating sections of vertical rough and mirror smooth stone rectangles.

He smiled a little. No demons were likely to leap out at him. In fact, with its windows, this section of the tunnel reminded him of the beginning of the tunnels into which he and Lie had been vacuumed by the magic winds. Perhaps he was reaching the end of his tunnel, where it would soon join with a main exit tunnel. He increased his pace along the somber passage.

Lie felt and smelled a cool breeze of fresh air. He skidded to a stop and stared to his left. "Thank god," he said.

The parallel tunnels and archways, which had yawned on his left, had ended, and he was looking through one of the long, horizontal, rectangular window grates at the pale twinkling stars. He ran to the window and tried to refresh himself with the sweet air.

Lie noticed the walls of this section of the tunnel, for as far as he could see, no longer contained the alternating sections of vertical rough and mirror smooth stone rectangles.

He smiled wryly. No dagger wielding demons were likely to leap out at him. In fact, with its windows, this section of the tunnel reminded him of the beginning of the tunnels into which he and Clu had been suctioned by the magic winds. Perhaps he was reaching the end of his tunnel, where it would soon join with a main exit tunnel. He increased his pace along the depressing passage.

Clu slowed because he was feeling uneasy. Soon, he saw the left side of his tunnel had vertical mirror stone rectangles. This time, they were closer together, separated by strips of the rough ebony stone no wider than one foot.

Clu stopped. Although he had no evidence on which to base such a belief, he felt he dare not proceed further. He did not know what to do. He could not retreat, and was too terrified to move forward.

Lie slowed because he was feeling uneasy. Soon, he saw the right side of his tunnel had vertical mirror stone rectangles. This time, they were closer together, separated by strips of the rough ebony stone no wider than one foot.

Lie stopped. Although he had no evidence on which to base such a belief, he felt he dare not proceed further. He did not know what to do. He could not retreat, and was too terrified to move forward.

Lie was so tired he was starting to sway left and right where he stood. Perhaps he could risk a short rest. He frowned. He had no choice. Until he could overcome his fear and proceed along the tunnel, there was little else to do.

Lie sat down against the left-hand wall beneath one of the windows. He leaned forward. The first mirror stone to his left, across the tunnel, was showing him an image of an immense white fowl. It was sleek and beautiful, and flying in a silvery sky. The fowl was soaring left, then right,

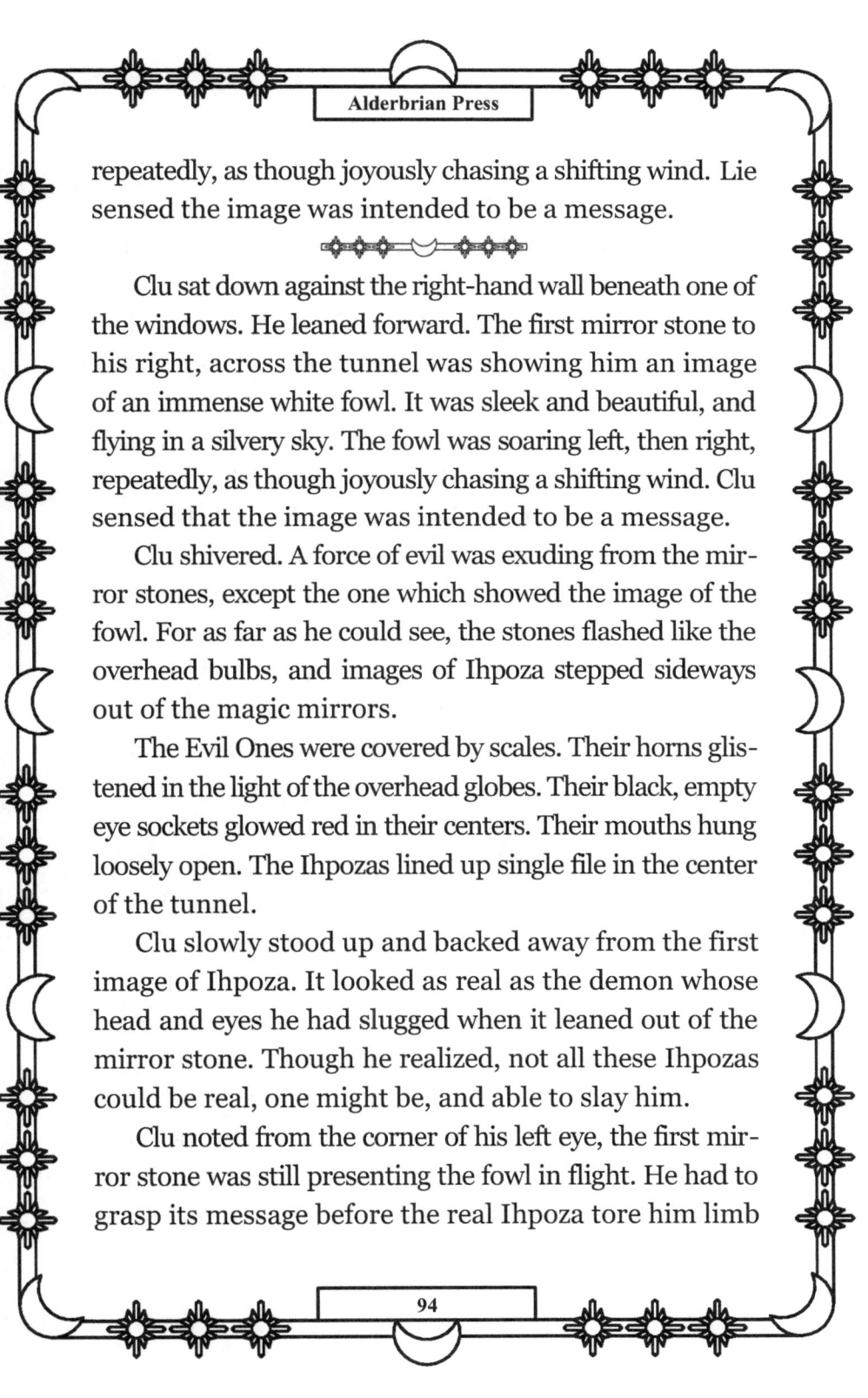

repeatedly, as though joyously chasing a shifting wind. Lie sensed the image was intended to be a message.

Clu sat down against the right-hand wall beneath one of the windows. He leaned forward. The first mirror stone to his right, across the tunnel was showing him an image of an immense white fowl. It was sleek and beautiful, and flying in a silvery sky. The fowl was soaring left, then right, repeatedly, as though joyously chasing a shifting wind. Clu sensed that the image was intended to be a message.

Clu shivered. A force of evil was exuding from the mirror stones, except the one which showed the image of the fowl. For as far as he could see, the stones flashed like the overhead bulbs, and images of Ihpoza stepped sideways out of the magic mirrors.

The Evil Ones were covered by scales. Their horns glistened in the light of the overhead globes. Their black, empty eye sockets glowed red in their centers. Their mouths hung loosely open. The Ihpozas lined up single file in the center of the tunnel.

Clu slowly stood up and backed away from the first image of Ihpoza. It looked as real as the demon whose head and eyes he had slugged when it leaned out of the mirror stone. Though he realized, not all these Ihpozas could be real, one might be, and able to slay him.

Clu noted from the corner of his left eye, the first mirror stone was still presenting the fowl in flight. He had to grasp its message before the real Ihpoza tore him limb from limb.

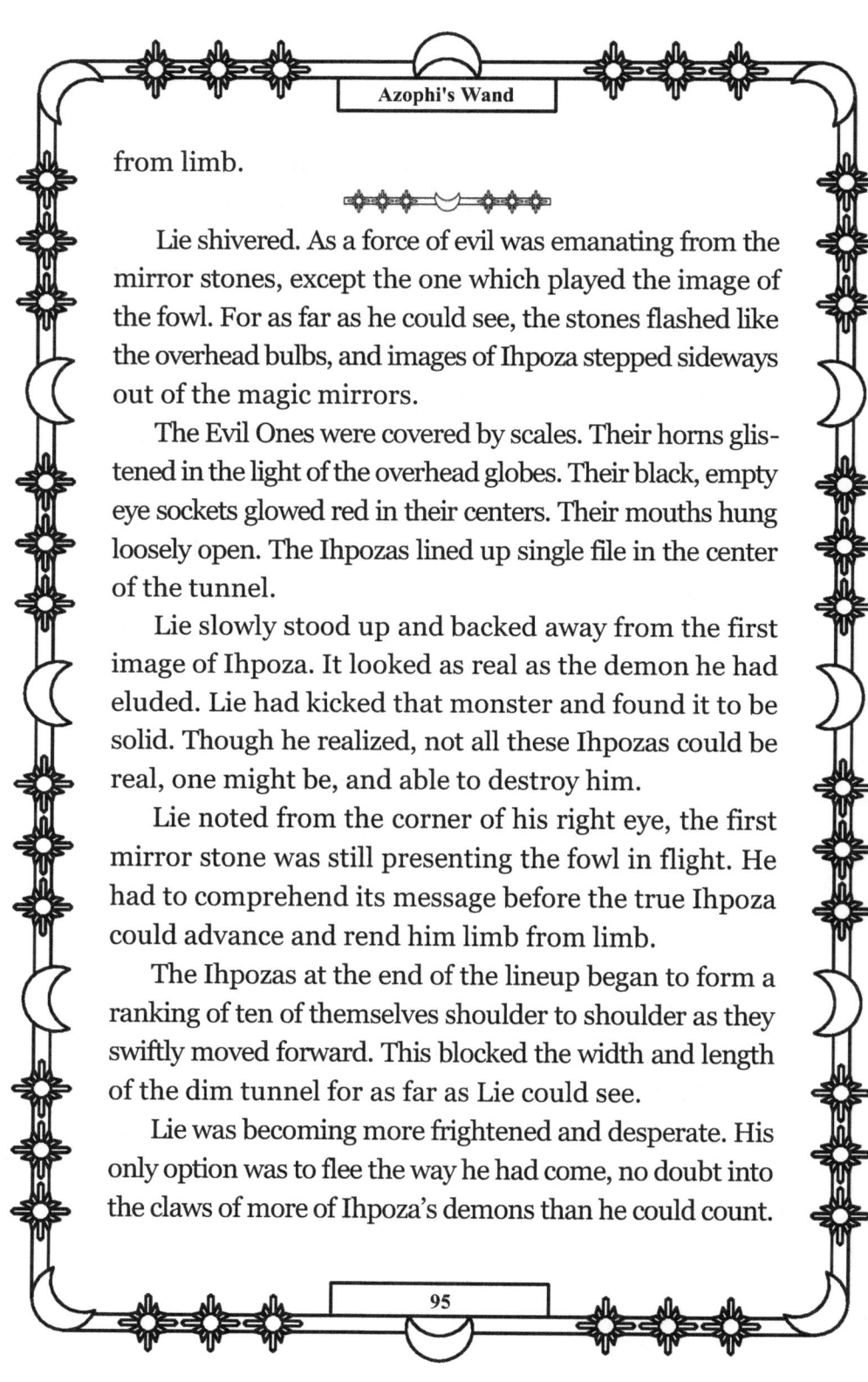

Lie shivered. As a force of evil was emanating from the mirror stones, except the one which played the image of the fowl. For as far as he could see, the stones flashed like the overhead bulbs, and images of Ihpoza stepped sideways out of the magic mirrors.

The Evil Ones were covered by scales. Their horns glistened in the light of the overhead globes. Their black, empty eye sockets glowed red in their centers. Their mouths hung loosely open. The Ihpozas lined up single file in the center of the tunnel.

Lie slowly stood up and backed away from the first image of Ihpoza. It looked as real as the demon he had eluded. Lie had kicked that monster and found it to be solid. Though he realized, not all these Ihpozas could be real, one might be, and able to destroy him.

Lie noted from the corner of his right eye, the first mirror stone was still presenting the fowl in flight. He had to comprehend its message before the true Ihpoza could advance and rend him limb from limb.

The Ihpozas at the end of the lineup began to form a ranking of ten of themselves shoulder to shoulder as they swiftly moved forward. This blocked the width and length of the dim tunnel for as far as Lie could see.

Lie was becoming more frightened and desperate. His only option was to flee the way he had come, no doubt into the claws of more of Ihpoza's demons than he could count.

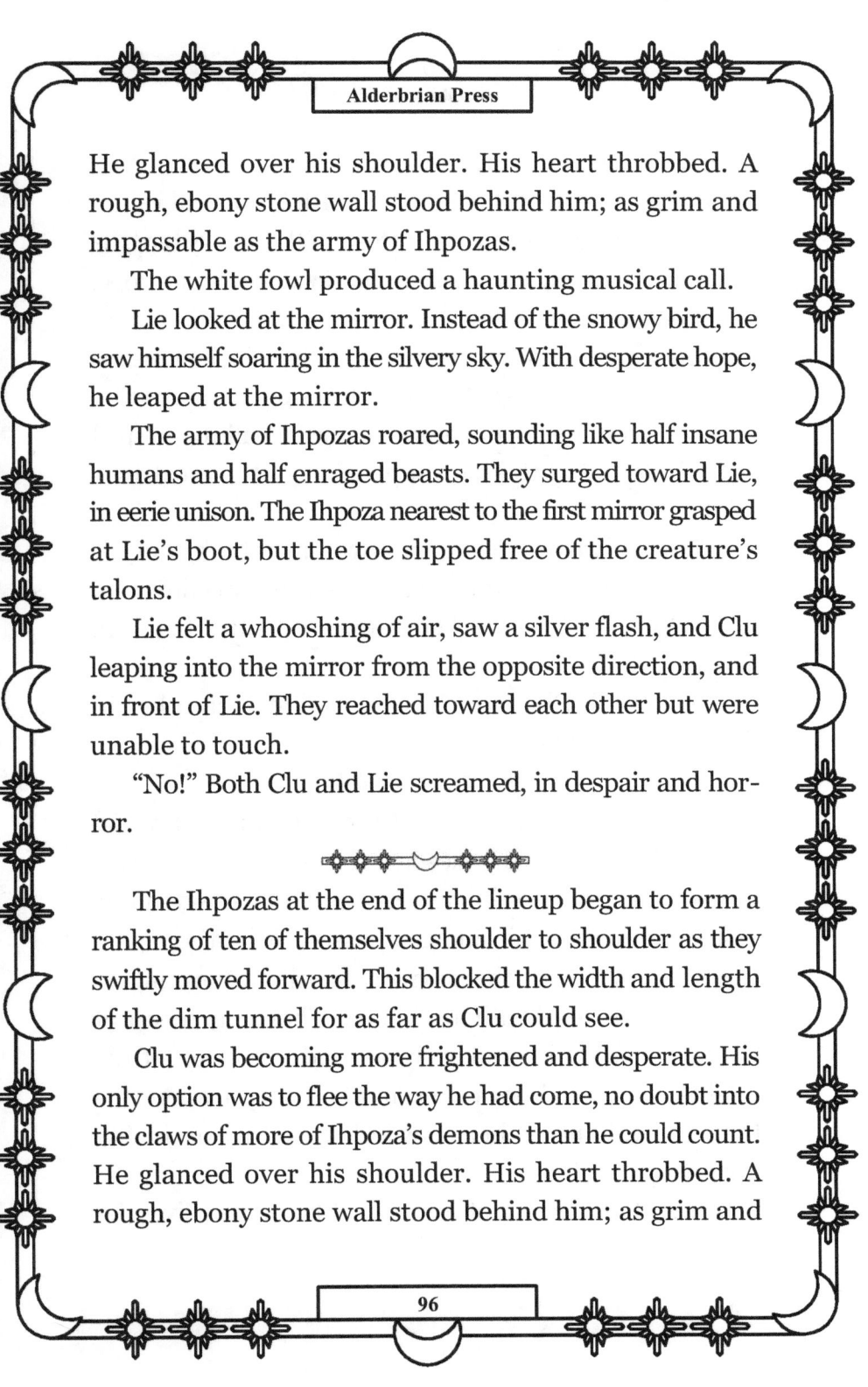

He glanced over his shoulder. His heart throbbed. A rough, ebony stone wall stood behind him; as grim and impassable as the army of Ihpozas.

The white fowl produced a haunting musical call.

Lie looked at the mirror. Instead of the snowy bird, he saw himself soaring in the silvery sky. With desperate hope, he leaped at the mirror.

The army of Ihpozas roared, sounding like half insane humans and half enraged beasts. They surged toward Lie, in eerie unison. The Ihpoza nearest to the first mirror grasped at Lie's boot, but the toe slipped free of the creature's talons.

Lie felt a whooshing of air, saw a silver flash, and Clu leaping into the mirror from the opposite direction, and in front of Lie. They reached toward each other but were unable to touch.

"No!" Both Clu and Lie screamed, in despair and horror.

The Ihpozas at the end of the lineup began to form a ranking of ten of themselves shoulder to shoulder as they swiftly moved forward. This blocked the width and length of the dim tunnel for as far as Clu could see.

Clu was becoming more frightened and desperate. His only option was to flee the way he had come, no doubt into the claws of more of Ihpoza's demons than he could count. He glanced over his shoulder. His heart throbbed. A rough, ebony stone wall stood behind him; as grim and

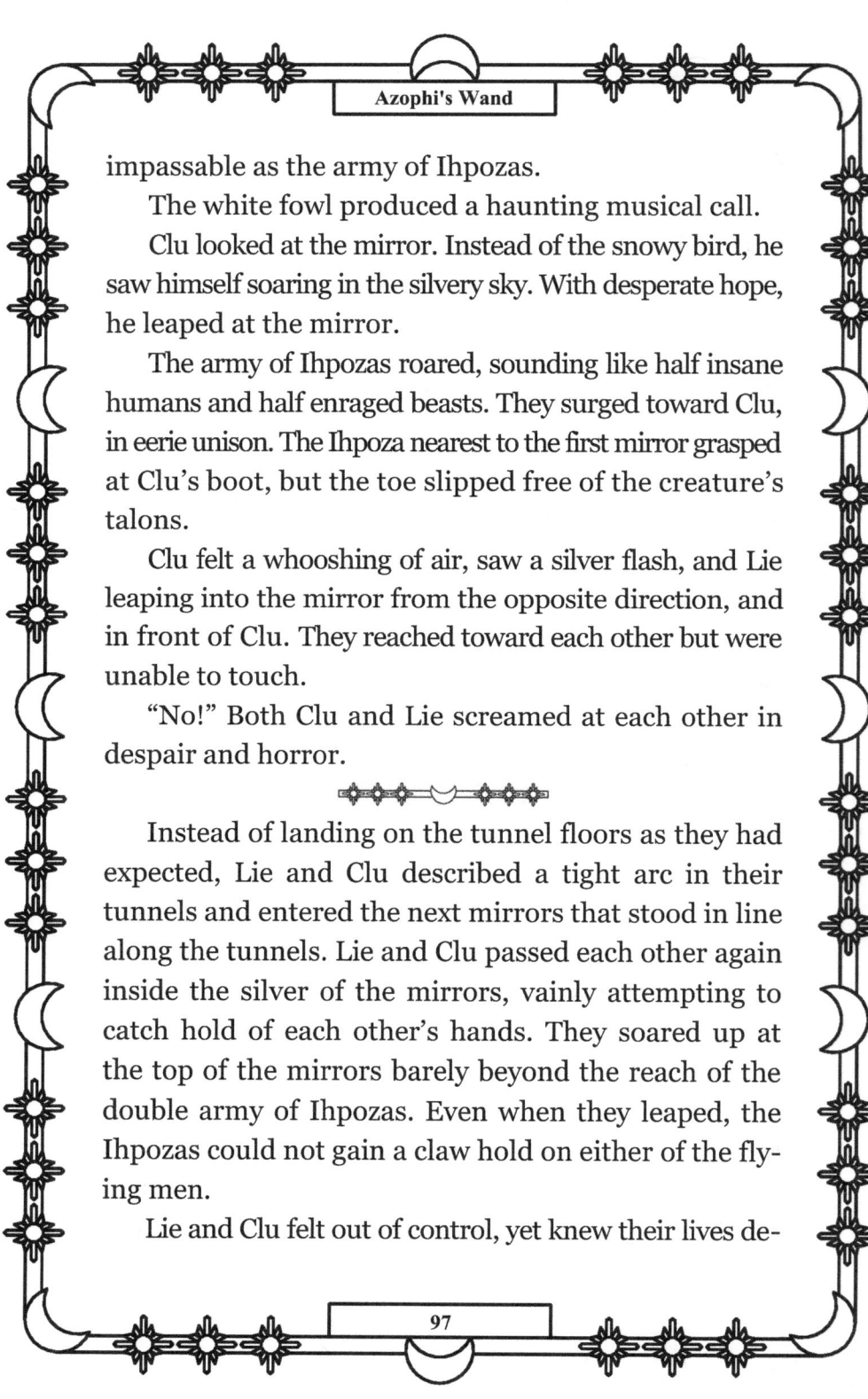

impassable as the army of Ihpozas.

The white fowl produced a haunting musical call.

Clu looked at the mirror. Instead of the snowy bird, he saw himself soaring in the silvery sky. With desperate hope, he leaped at the mirror.

The army of Ihpozas roared, sounding like half insane humans and half enraged beasts. They surged toward Clu, in eerie unison. The Ihpoza nearest to the first mirror grasped at Clu's boot, but the toe slipped free of the creature's talons.

Clu felt a whooshing of air, saw a silver flash, and Lie leaping into the mirror from the opposite direction, and in front of Clu. They reached toward each other but were unable to touch.

"No!" Both Clu and Lie screamed at each other in despair and horror.

Instead of landing on the tunnel floors as they had expected, Lie and Clu described a tight arc in their tunnels and entered the next mirrors that stood in line along the tunnels. Lie and Clu passed each other again inside the silver of the mirrors, vainly attempting to catch hold of each other's hands. They soared up at the top of the mirrors barely beyond the reach of the double army of Ihpozas. Even when they leaped, the Ihpozas could not gain a claw hold on either of the flying men.

Lie and Clu felt out of control, yet knew their lives de-

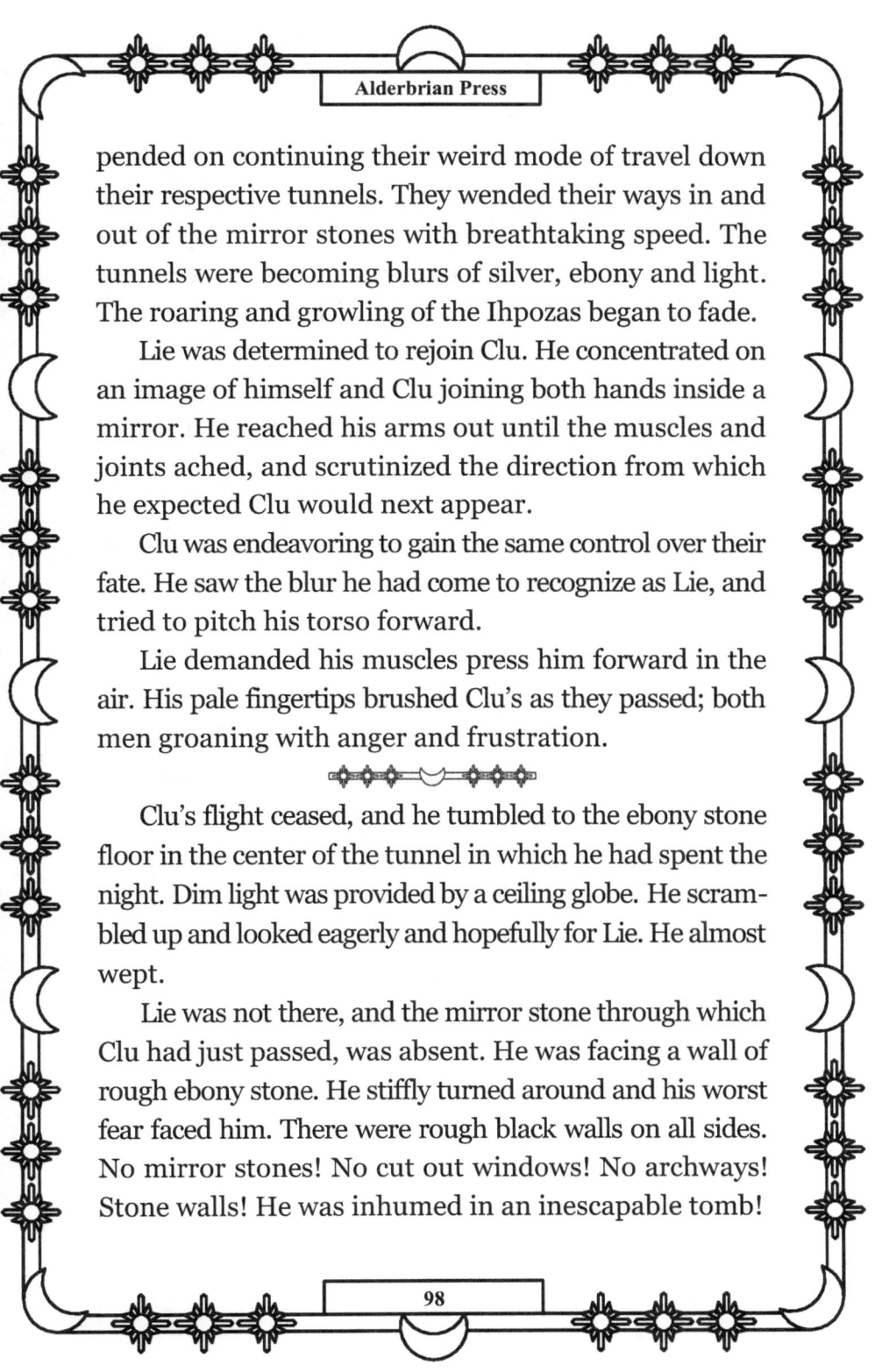

pended on continuing their weird mode of travel down their respective tunnels. They wended their ways in and out of the mirror stones with breathtaking speed. The tunnels were becoming blurs of silver, ebony and light. The roaring and growling of the Ihpozas began to fade.

Lie was determined to rejoin Clu. He concentrated on an image of himself and Clu joining both hands inside a mirror. He reached his arms out until the muscles and joints ached, and scrutinized the direction from which he expected Clu would next appear.

Clu was endeavoring to gain the same control over their fate. He saw the blur he had come to recognize as Lie, and tried to pitch his torso forward.

Lie demanded his muscles press him forward in the air. His pale fingertips brushed Clu's as they passed; both men groaning with anger and frustration.

Clu's flight ceased, and he tumbled to the ebony stone floor in the center of the tunnel in which he had spent the night. Dim light was provided by a ceiling globe. He scrambled up and looked eagerly and hopefully for Lie. He almost wept.

Lie was not there, and the mirror stone through which Clu had just passed, was absent. He was facing a wall of rough ebony stone. He stiffly turned around and his worst fear faced him. There were rough black walls on all sides. No mirror stones! No cut out windows! No archways! Stone walls! He was inhumed in an inescapable tomb!

Lie's flight ceased, and he tumbled to the ebony stone floor in the center of the tunnel in which he had spent the night. Dim light was provided by a ceiling globe. He scrambled up and looked eagerly and hopefully for Clu. His hope died and his stomach knotted.

Clu was not there, and the mirror stone through which Lie had just passed, was absent. He was facing a wall of rough ebony stone. He swiftly turned around and his worst fear assailed him. There were rough black walls on all sides. No mirror stones! No cut out windows! No archways! Stone walls! He was imprisoned inside an inescapable dungeon!

Clu stood with his head in his hands. "AarLee," he whispered, distraught, "I can't bear the thought I'll never be with you again. That I will perish here. So uselessly. So wasted. Our quest lost! AarLee!" he cried out, with despair. "AarLee!"

There was a light from behind Clu. He gathered his thoughts and fearfully turned around. He gasped. One wall had become a mirror stone. It was showing a single large tunnel with windows, identical to the tunnel through which he and Lie had first entered this nightmare of magical rock.

Clu ran to the mirror stone and pressed his palms against the clear barrier. His momentary hope failed. He could not pass through this mirror. He imagined himself as the great white bird, soaring into the larger tunnel, but nothing happened.

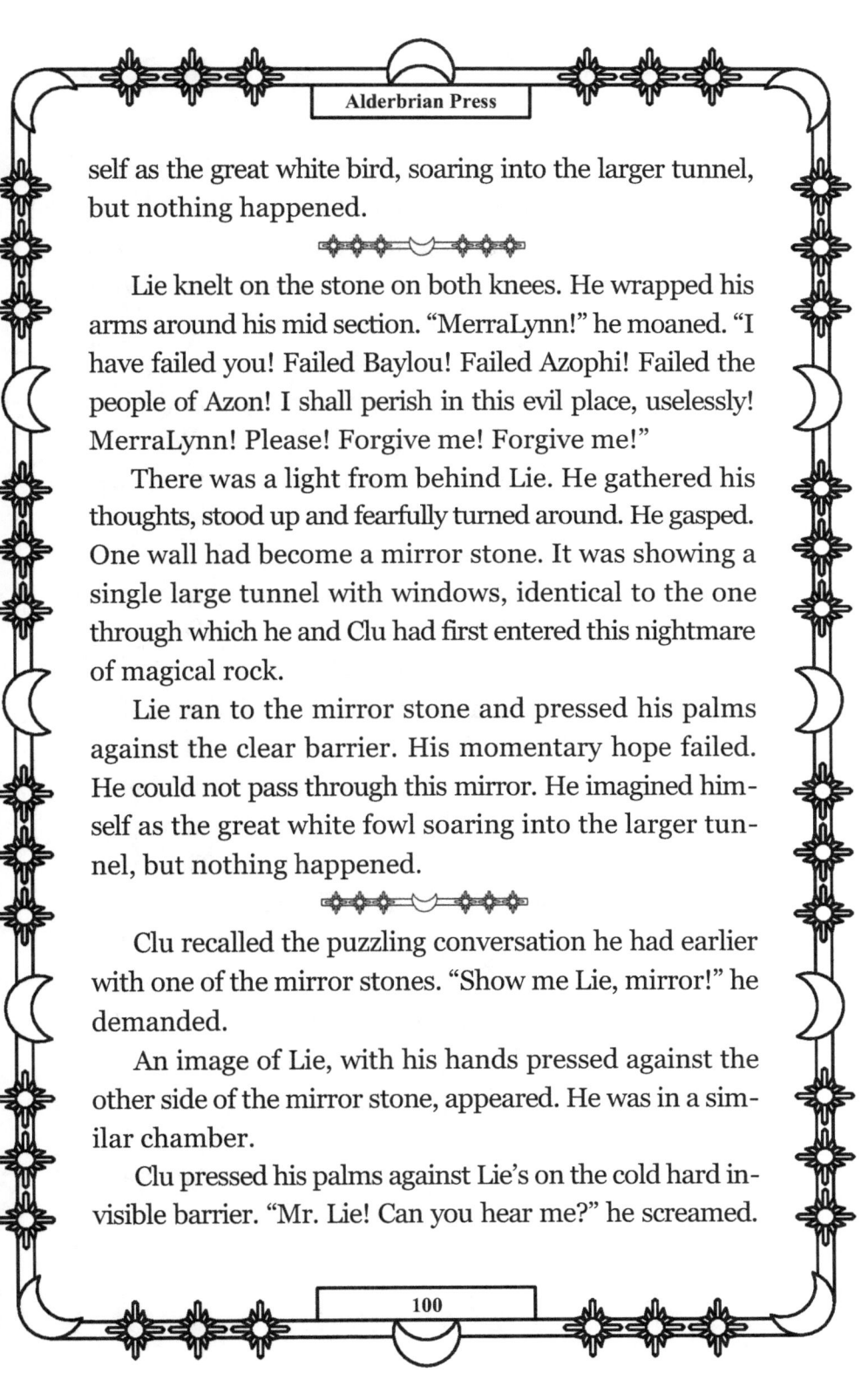

Lie knelt on the stone on both knees. He wrapped his arms around his mid section. "MerraLynn!" he moaned. "I have failed you! Failed Baylou! Failed Azophi! Failed the people of Azon! I shall perish in this evil place, uselessly! MerraLynn! Please! Forgive me! Forgive me!"

There was a light from behind Lie. He gathered his thoughts, stood up and fearfully turned around. He gasped. One wall had become a mirror stone. It was showing a single large tunnel with windows, identical to the one through which he and Clu had first entered this nightmare of magical rock.

Lie ran to the mirror stone and pressed his palms against the clear barrier. His momentary hope failed. He could not pass through this mirror. He imagined himself as the great white fowl soaring into the larger tunnel, but nothing happened.

Clu recalled the puzzling conversation he had earlier with one of the mirror stones. "Show me Lie, mirror!" he demanded.

An image of Lie, with his hands pressed against the other side of the mirror stone, appeared. He was in a similar chamber.

Clu pressed his palms against Lie's on the cold hard invisible barrier. "Mr. Lie! Can you hear me?" he screamed.

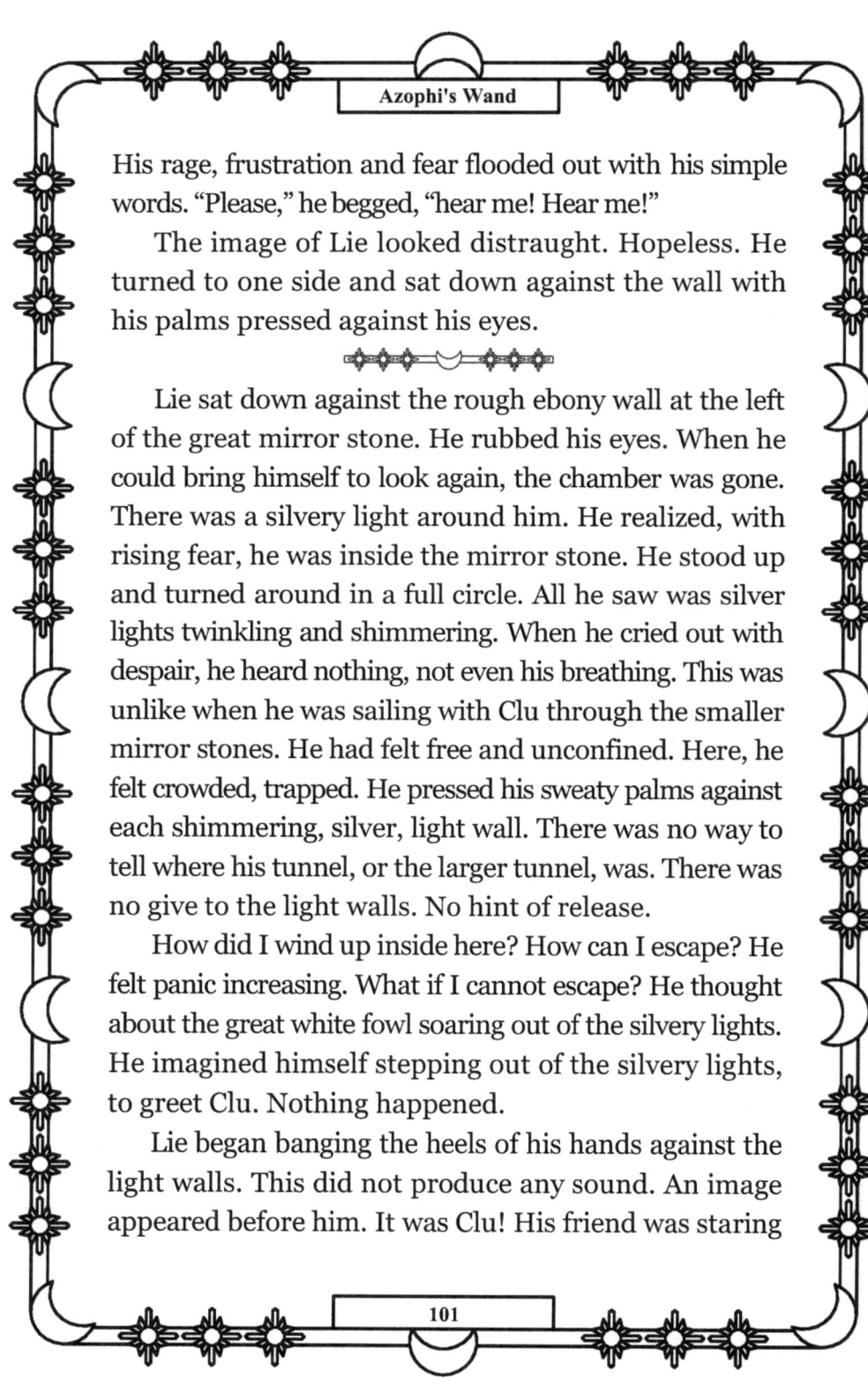

His rage, frustration and fear flooded out with his simple words. "Please," he begged, "hear me! Hear me!"

The image of Lie looked distraught. Hopeless. He turned to one side and sat down against the wall with his palms pressed against his eyes.

◆◆◆ ⌣ ◆◆◆

Lie sat down against the rough ebony wall at the left of the great mirror stone. He rubbed his eyes. When he could bring himself to look again, the chamber was gone. There was a silvery light around him. He realized, with rising fear, he was inside the mirror stone. He stood up and turned around in a full circle. All he saw was silver lights twinkling and shimmering. When he cried out with despair, he heard nothing, not even his breathing. This was unlike when he was sailing with Clu through the smaller mirror stones. He had felt free and unconfined. Here, he felt crowded, trapped. He pressed his sweaty palms against each shimmering, silver, light wall. There was no way to tell where his tunnel, or the larger tunnel, was. There was no give to the light walls. No hint of release.

How did I wind up inside here? How can I escape? He felt panic increasing. What if I cannot escape? He thought about the great white fowl soaring out of the silvery lights. He imagined himself stepping out of the silvery lights, to greet Clu. Nothing happened.

Lie began banging the heels of his hands against the light walls. This did not produce any sound. An image appeared before him. It was Clu! His friend was staring straight at him! Lie pounded harder on the light wall.

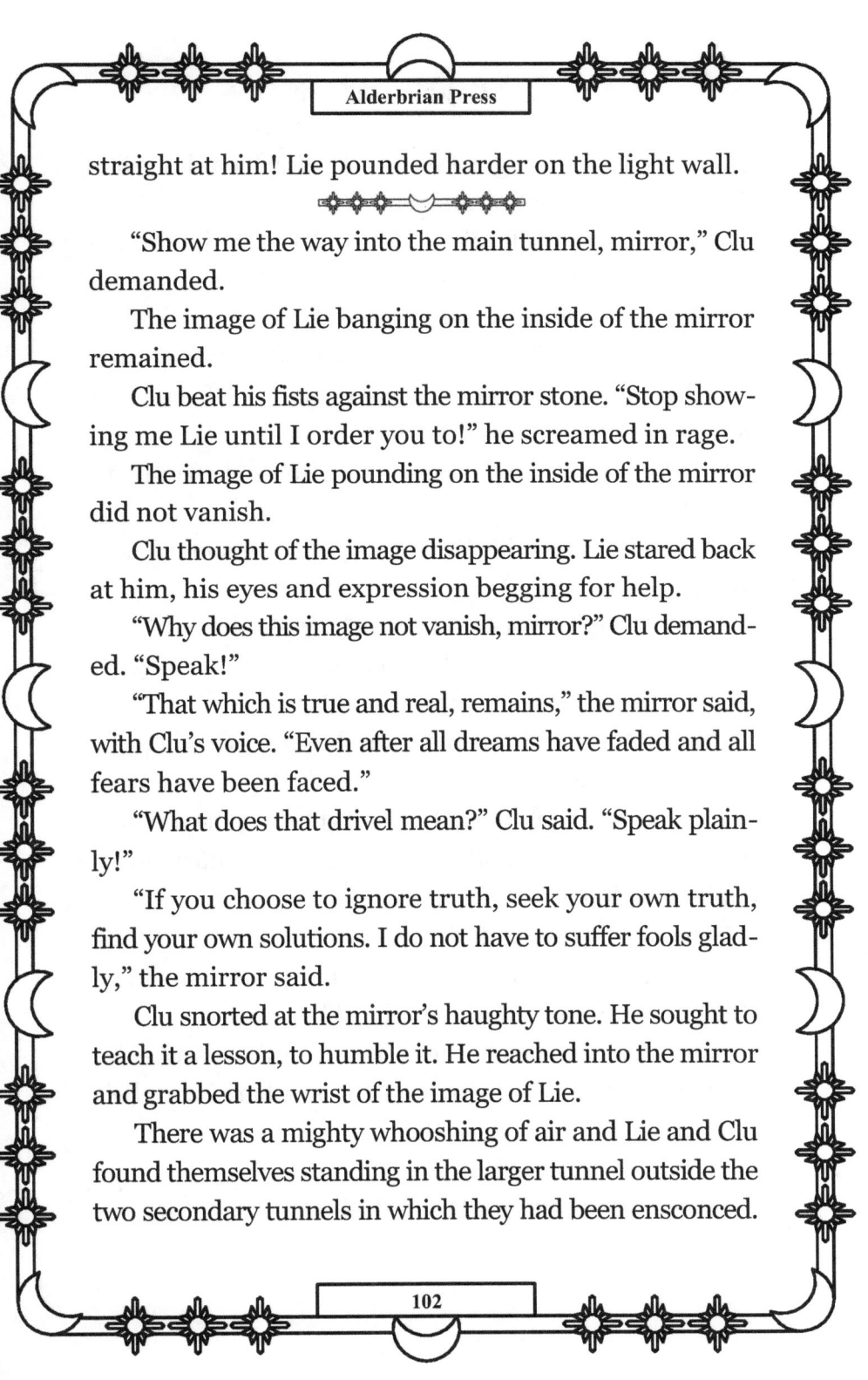

"Show me the way into the main tunnel, mirror," Clu demanded.

The image of Lie banging on the inside of the mirror remained.

Clu beat his fists against the mirror stone. "Stop showing me Lie until I order you to!" he screamed in rage.

The image of Lie pounding on the inside of the mirror did not vanish.

Clu thought of the image disappearing. Lie stared back at him, his eyes and expression begging for help.

"Why does this image not vanish, mirror?" Clu demanded. "Speak!"

"That which is true and real, remains," the mirror said, with Clu's voice. "Even after all dreams have faded and all fears have been faced."

"What does that drivel mean?" Clu said. "Speak plainly!"

"If you choose to ignore truth, seek your own truth, find your own solutions. I do not have to suffer fools gladly," the mirror said.

Clu snorted at the mirror's haughty tone. He sought to teach it a lesson, to humble it. He reached into the mirror and grabbed the wrist of the image of Lie.

There was a mighty whooshing of air and Lie and Clu found themselves standing in the larger tunnel outside the two secondary tunnels in which they had been ensconced.

They were facing two great mirror stones which shone like they were reflecting the sun.

"Thank you for freeing me, Clu," Lie said, with relief warming him. "But, how did you do it?"

Clu stood there, amazed.

"To shame his fine teacher, he sought the truth, though he believed it not," the mirror stone to their left said in a voice like soft winds whispering.

Lie leaped away from the mirror. He reached out and drew Clu away.

"Mr. Lie!" Clu said. "It truly is you! Not some phantom!"

"You thought I was a phantom?" Lie shuddered. "Perhaps, after a while inside this abominable, cruel, magical stone, I would have become a phantom."

"Do not insult that which you do not have a hope of comprehending," the left mirror said.

Lie turned angrily to it. "Then enlighten us," he shouted, "or remain forever silent! We do not have to suffer egotistical fools gladly!"

The mirrors went dark.

Clu felt a rush of excitement. "Mirror!" he demanded. "Show us the way out of this place!"

The mirror stones flashed with silver light, and a demon leaned out of each. Their fangs were bared and their clawed hands reached for the men.

Lie and Clu drew back.

The monsters stepped from the mirror. "You trust me

not, though you seek my help," they growled as one.

"You cannot tell when these are phantoms, or solid enough to inflict harm," Lie whispered to Clu.

"I know," Clu said, remembering his fist fight with a demon.

Lie grabbed the right hand demon by its neck, and threw it to the stone, on its stomach.

The other demon fell flat of its face.

"It felt solid enough to me," Lie said, nervously.

"Let's just leave this place," Clu begged. "Leave these monsters here, and let us exit this place! Please!"

"Can you harm us?" Lie demanded of the demons.

They craned their scaly necks and gazed up at the men with strangely human expressions on their bizarre faces.

"I can inflict only the harm upon you that you can inflict upon yourselves, with your own fears," the demons said, like whispering winds.

Lie relaxed.

Clu noticed this and, though puzzled and still wary of the demons, he calmed down.

"What is this place?" Lie demanded. "Who are you?"

"This is the place of conflict and rectification. I am the Guardian. The guide. The Punisher and Rewarder. The Foreteller of past, future and present events."

"Show your true self, not our fears," Lie demanded.

The demons were suctioned, by drafts of air, onto their feet, and backwards into their mirror stones. The mirrors went black.

"This is your true likeness?" Lie demanded, angrily.

Silence taunted Lie and Clu.

"We have learned an expensive lesson," Lie said. "As long as there are mirror stones along our path, we must think of nothing except exiting from this occult place. I no longer believe this evil construction is of Ihpoza's design. He would not have frightened and toyed with us. He would have slain us, long before now."

"Then, who is responsible for it?" Clu said.

"Listen!" Lie said.

Faintly, there was a trickling echoing through the large tunnel.

"The water!" Clu said.

Lie and Clu turned their backs on the mirror stones. There were windows on both sides of the tunnel. Lie and Clu could see star shine against the inky void of space.

"It is impossible the night should still be upon us because of the time we have remained within these tunnels," Lie said. "Whatever rules this arcane site must still be plying us with illusions. Come, as you wisely suggested, let us continue."

"Congratulations!"

Lie and Clu stopped short and squinted. There was an indistinct shape, almost like a wrinkling in the dim air. It resolved itself into a man. Light gray eyes. Snowy hair, fine and limp, reached his shoulders. Expressionless wrinkled face. White, floor length gown. He leaned on a wooden cane, one wrinkled, trembling hand atop the other. His countenance was not like any, Clu or Lie had encountered on Azon.

"Why do you offer us congratulations?" Lie asked, suspiciously.

"You have survived the gauntlet of the Beast unscathed. Few have fared so well. In fact, none have survived within one thousand years."

Clu couldn't grasp the man's meaning. "Who are you?" he asked.

"We were the Ortourians," the old man said. "This place existed here eons before Azophi and his people. It shall exist here eons after Azophi and his people have ceased to be."

"You were the Ortourians?" Lie said. "What happened to you?"

"Mind War!"

"In these tunnels?" Clu said.

"Indeed. We built the Magic Beast. Keyed it to our racial mental functioning. We rode the Magic Beast into battle and it slew us to the last Ortourian. Not the noble legacy we had wished to bequeath to the Universe."

"If this place is keyed to your minds," Lie asked, "why has it been bedeviling us? We are not Ortourians!"

"You are throwaheads of Azophi's people. You possess Mind Magic abilities. The Beast recognized your impoverished, weak imitation of our great powers. It performed its best with you. How you have outclassed the Beast is a puzzlement. A puzzlement indeed."

"Are you dead?" Clu asked.

"Very," the old man said.

"Are you a ghost?" Lie asked.

"Do not insult me," the old man said, with no hint in his voice or face that he was insulted.

"A spirit, then, a discarnate," Lie said.

"Insult upon insult," the old man said.

"Then," Clu said, with exasperation, "what, in Azophi's name, are you?"

"We were the Ortourians. The essence of all things good, bright, kind and noble. Or so we thought."

"Do not heed the lies of the Great Deceiver," another emotionless voice said, from behind Lie and Clu. "We were the Ortourians, true enough, but we were the essence of all things dark, vile, evil and vicious. Hateful, hated and self hating." This man claimed the likeness of the first, except he wore a black robe.

Clu drew close to Lie. He pulled on Lie's sleeve. Lie bent down.

"They are snaring us like clever spiders nearing flies in a web," Clu whispered, urgently. "Don't you feel it?"

Lie shivered, for Clu had voiced his nagging thoughts. He grabbed Clu by the wrist and swiftly drew him around the white robed man.

Clu glanced over his shoulder as they ran down the tunnel.

The white and black phantoms floated toward each

other with incredible speed. They collided, and there was an explosion that shuddered the tunnel.

"Sweet Lord Azophi!" Clu said, with horror.

Lie looked over his shoulder.

A giant version of the old man stood there. His eyes were like glowing red coals. He wore a gray robe, and held a huge spear composed of blue, crackling energy.

"None can deceive the Beast. None before has survived the Beast. You shall not be the first!" the behemoth roared. His voice was filled with hatred and rage. An emanation of pure evil swept from him to Lie and Clu. He pulled his arm back to hurl his bolt of deadly energy.

Lie hooked his arm around Clu's waist, lifted him off his feet, and raced desperately down the half dark tunnel.

The lights failed and they were in darkness.

Lie did his best not to veer left or right in the tunnel, but came up against the left side and rebounded. Clu fell from his grasp, and both men tumbled to the stone floor.

A blue flash stung their eyes as the bolt of energy seared into the ebony stone floor several feet ahead of them.

Lie used the light of the explosion to reaffirm his hold on Clu. He skirted the four-foot deep scar in the stone floor, and continued his flight.

Behind them, Lie and Clu could hear huge boots slamming into the stone floor of the tunnel. The Ortourian Beast was pursuing. A pale blue glow indicated the Beast had created another power spear.

"Starlight!" Clu cried, with desperate hope.

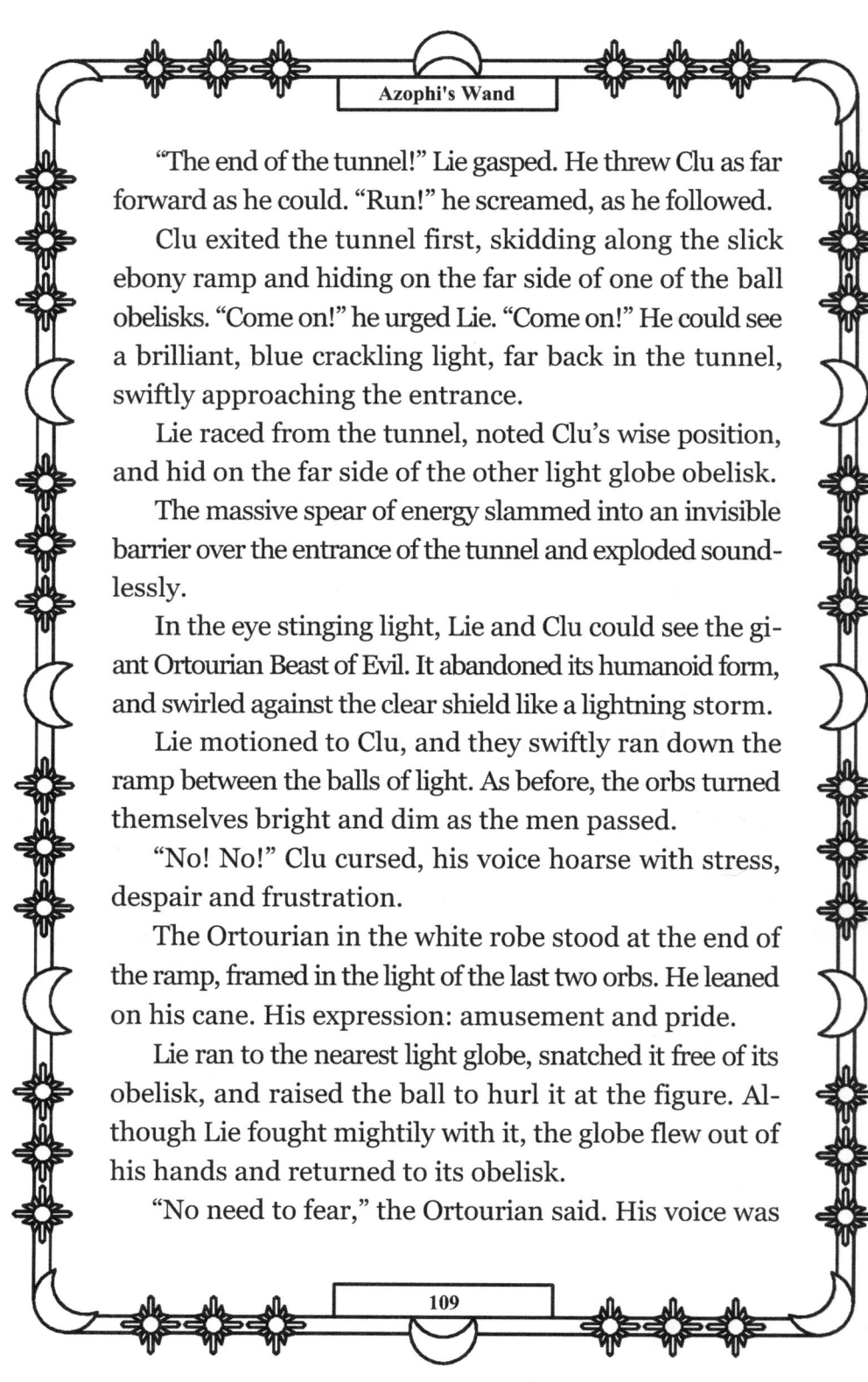

"The end of the tunnel!" Lie gasped. He threw Clu as far forward as he could. "Run!" he screamed, as he followed.

Clu exited the tunnel first, skidding along the slick ebony ramp and hiding on the far side of one of the ball obelisks. "Come on!" he urged Lie. "Come on!" He could see a brilliant, blue crackling light, far back in the tunnel, swiftly approaching the entrance.

Lie raced from the tunnel, noted Clu's wise position, and hid on the far side of the other light globe obelisk.

The massive spear of energy slammed into an invisible barrier over the entrance of the tunnel and exploded soundlessly.

In the eye stinging light, Lie and Clu could see the giant Ortourian Beast of Evil. It abandoned its humanoid form, and swirled against the clear shield like a lightning storm.

Lie motioned to Clu, and they swiftly ran down the ramp between the balls of light. As before, the orbs turned themselves bright and dim as the men passed.

"No! No!" Clu cursed, his voice hoarse with stress, despair and frustration.

The Ortourian in the white robe stood at the end of the ramp, framed in the light of the last two orbs. He leaned on his cane. His expression: amusement and pride.

Lie ran to the nearest light globe, snatched it free of its obelisk, and raised the ball to hurl it at the figure. Although Lie fought mightily with it, the globe flew out of his hands and returned to its obelisk.

"No need to fear," the Ortourian said. His voice was

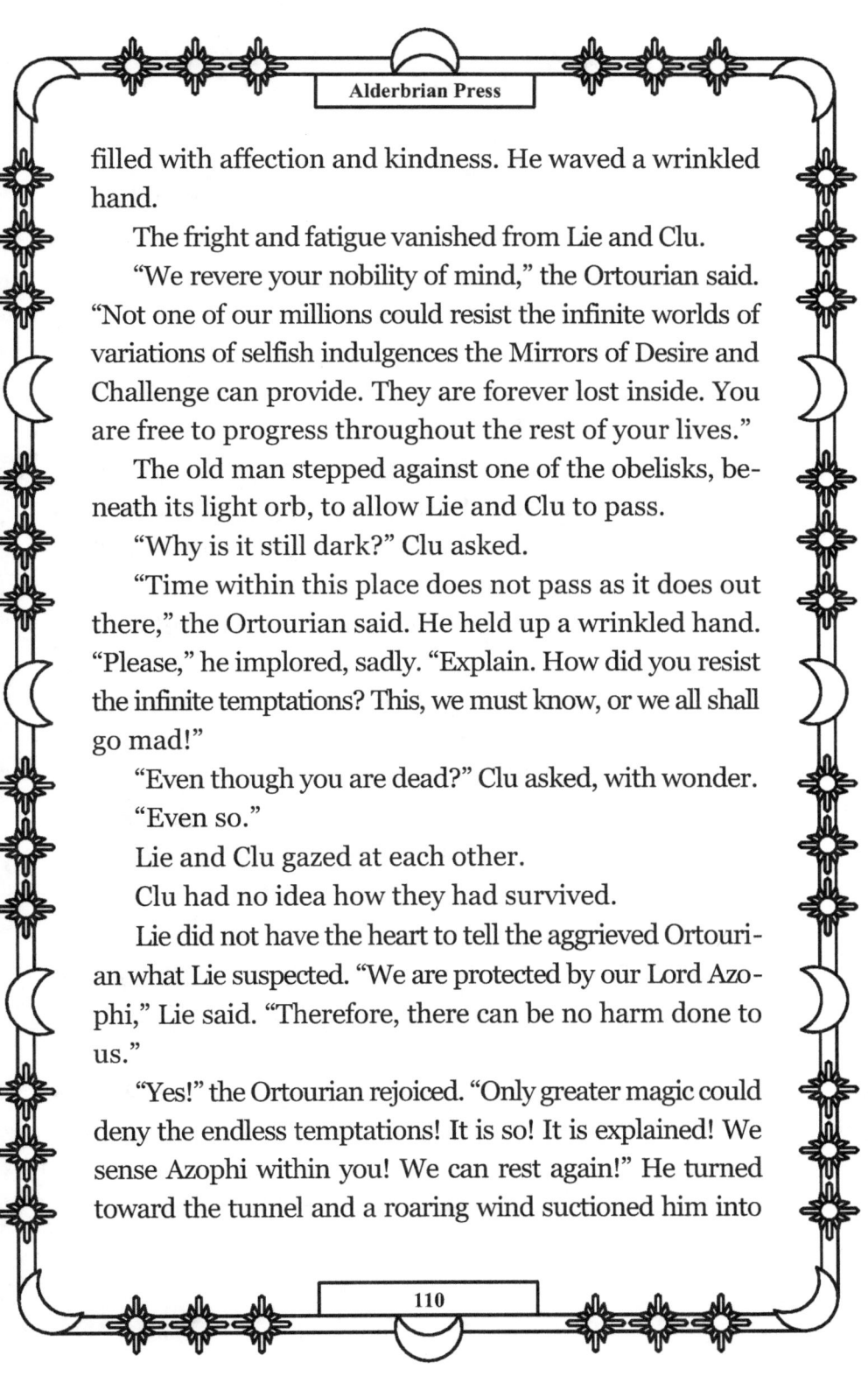

filled with affection and kindness. He waved a wrinkled hand.

The fright and fatigue vanished from Lie and Clu.

"We revere your nobility of mind," the Ortourian said. "Not one of our millions could resist the infinite worlds of variations of selfish indulgences the Mirrors of Desire and Challenge can provide. They are forever lost inside. You are free to progress throughout the rest of your lives."

The old man stepped against one of the obelisks, beneath its light orb, to allow Lie and Clu to pass.

"Why is it still dark?" Clu asked.

"Time within this place does not pass as it does out there," the Ortourian said. He held up a wrinkled hand. "Please," he implored, sadly. "Explain. How did you resist the infinite temptations? This, we must know, or we all shall go mad!"

"Even though you are dead?" Clu asked, with wonder.

"Even so."

Lie and Clu gazed at each other.

Clu had no idea how they had survived.

Lie did not have the heart to tell the aggrieved Ortourian what Lie suspected. "We are protected by our Lord Azophi," Lie said. "Therefore, there can be no harm done to us."

"Yes!" the Ortourian rejoiced. "Only greater magic could deny the endless temptations! It is so! It is explained! We sense Azophi within you! We can rest again!" He turned toward the tunnel and a roaring wind suctioned him into the edifice and out of sight in the semi darkness.

There appeared to be no threat, but Lie and Clu fled down the ramp and into the grassy hills, under the comforting light of the great blue-green moon.

Lie laughed. It was a harsh sound of relief.

Clu sat down on a small mound. "How did we survive?" he said. "Baylou and Azophi had nothing to do with it."

Lie shook his head, with amusement. "Ignorance!" he said. "Blessed ignorance! We knew nothing about the purpose of the tunnels and mirrors, so we couldn't be tempted in any way."

"Except to get the hell out of that awful place!" Clu said.

They laughed, releasing the fear, frustration and anger they had suffered throughout the sorcerous night.

"Listen!" Clu said.

"Water!" Lie said. "This time, it sounds normal, not cruelly enhanced by magical snares. We are still on track!"

"But much closer!" Clu said, cheerfully.

Baylou flipped up to a standing position. Excitement caused its eye to out shine the moon. "Yes!" it rejoiced. "Free!" it affirmed.

The uncanny energy was gone, not just around Lie and Clu, but from the planet. Lie and Clu were stressed, but not injured.

It was just as well, because Baylou had been unable to

establish a link with Lie and Clu, had been powerless to assist them.

Baylou narrowed its eye. Despite the near loss of its Humans, the magic within would not allow Baylou to return to them to offer protection from threats. This puzzled and frustrated Baylou, for it felt as if it were divided within.

"Azophi's wisdom and will," Baylou said, cheerfully. "They are safe. They are on course for Slann. But, when may I join them?"

The Book did not expect an answer. It flew into the night air and resumed the travels and chores planned by the Wand centuries ago.

Ihpoza roared in rage and frustration. He pounded the ice bed at his side with hatred for the Humans and the Wand's accursed Book. The insects were free of the mysterious force!

Ihpoza had sensed the energy attempting to beguile and destroy them, but they had miraculously resisted and survived. A pure abominable puzzlement, and a tragic sin against him.

That strange power had vanished as he had expected, before he was able to devise a magical method of harnessing it. All because of those abhorrent Humans! Ihpoza pounded the ice bed again.

"You will suffer! Make no brainless mistake on this matter! You, and your worrisome Book, will suffer!"

Illustration 14

Ortourian Beast Wrought Iron Window Grillwork

Copyright © 2019 Philip Raymond Sadler

113-A

Chapter 14
Cold and Sweet

As Lie and Clue followed the sound of flowing water, the grassy hills ceded supremacy to an expanse of smooth, snowy-white stone. In the center was a deep cavity. The thirsty travelers knelt at the edge of the rectangular crater, cupped their hands and eagerly dipped them into the pool. The water was cold and tasted sweet.

Lie wiped his hands on his hips and looked for the source of the flow. He gasped.

"What is it?" Clu demanded, dumping a double handful of water.

Lie pointed to a square opening in the far side of the pit. "This is a man made pool, wrought from solid stone. There is probably an opening in the bottom where the water runs back to the artesian source. That is why it is not stagnant and has not overflowed."

Clu watched the flow for a moment. "But, who built it, and why?" he asked.

Lie walked around the pit to the inflow opening and looked down. He motioned for Clu to join him.

Carved into the stone, was an arrow pointing North.

Below this was carved: Slann.

"Our earliest ancestors," Lie thoughtfully said. "Probably intended as a way station or irrigation source."

"We're very near the desert, then!" Clu said.

"Yes. We will see it early tomorrow. We will fill our pack canteens in the morning. They will have to suffice."

"We'd better get some sleep."

"But, not too near to the pool," Lie said. "There are wild animals in these parts; scavengers. We do not want to get between those and the only pure water for a hundred miles."

Baylou floated silently out of the blue-green light of the moon and hovered just beside Clu's left ear. The Book spoke almost inaudibly. "You will open your eyes, Clu, but you will remain asleep."

Clu's eyelids fluttered, then stayed open. Only the whites showed.

"Sit up," Baylou instructed.

Clu sat slowly up, crossing his legs and pulling the blanket around his slim shoulders for warmth.

"You will look at Lie and concentrate on sending him psychic energy. You will not hesitate and you will not cease until I order it. Do you understand?"

Clu nodded. His pupils rolled down, and he stared intently at Lie. Sparkling clear energy coursed from around Clu. It traveled like a beam of light to where Lie lay sleeping.

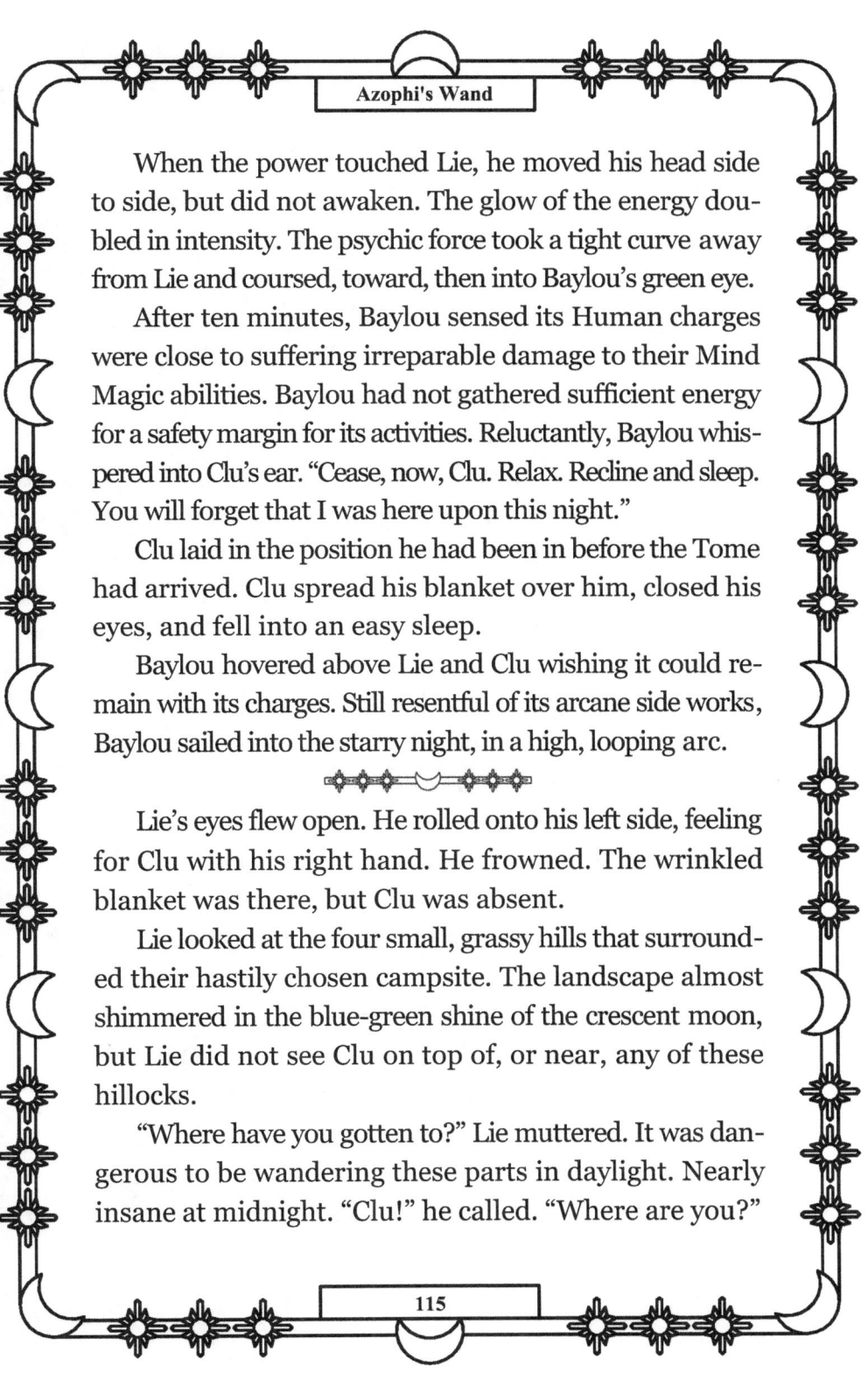

When the power touched Lie, he moved his head side to side, but did not awaken. The glow of the energy doubled in intensity. The psychic force took a tight curve away from Lie and coursed, toward, then into Baylou's green eye.

After ten minutes, Baylou sensed its Human charges were close to suffering irreparable damage to their Mind Magic abilities. Baylou had not gathered sufficient energy for a safety margin for its activities. Reluctantly, Baylou whispered into Clu's ear. "Cease, now, Clu. Relax. Recline and sleep. You will forget that I was here upon this night."

Clu laid in the position he had been in before the Tome had arrived. Clu spread his blanket over him, closed his eyes, and fell into an easy sleep.

Baylou hovered above Lie and Clu wishing it could remain with its charges. Still resentful of its arcane side works, Baylou sailed into the starry night, in a high, looping arc.

Lie's eyes flew open. He rolled onto his left side, feeling for Clu with his right hand. He frowned. The wrinkled blanket was there, but Clu was absent.

Lie looked at the four small, grassy hills that surrounded their hastily chosen campsite. The landscape almost shimmered in the blue-green shine of the crescent moon, but Lie did not see Clu on top of, or near, any of these hillocks.

"Where have you gotten to?" Lie muttered. It was dangerous to be wandering these parts in daylight. Nearly insane at midnight. "Clu!" he called. "Where are you?"

No reply.

Lie checked and found Clu's backpack near his at the heads of their blankets. He had not believed Clu had gone on alone. He just wanted to reassure himself.

Lie searched around the four hills, stopping on the outside of each to peer into the distant gloom. His diligent efforts revealed more grassy hills.

"Mr. Lie!" Clu screamed, his voice sounding muffled, "Help me with haste, or I'm dead!"

Lie's stomach tightened with panic and frustration. He could not tell from which direction Clu's cries had emanated.

"Help me find you!" Lie shouted, through cupped hands. "Count for me!"

"No time, Mr. Lie! I'm all but done for, now!"

Lie startled. This time, Clu's words had sounded to Lie's right and closer than before. Lie raced that way. He curved around a hill, climbed to the top of another, and skidded to a stop, horrified by what he saw below. "A Mayglon!" he oathed.

Mayglons are worm-like beasts as large as the average adult Human male. They see with their bodies, and travel in a vertical position by undulating their bottom layer of flesh. They feed by absorbing prey. Only insanity causes them to leave their RainSoaked Mountains.

Lie shuddered. He could see Clu pressed flat against the Mayglon. His face was turned half away from its tall, red oblong body enabling him to breathe.

Lie's grandfather insisted there was only one way to free someone ensnared by these predators. He prayed his usually savvy grandfather was correct, ran down the hill at a tangent, toward the Mayglon, and slammed his left shoulder into Clu's left shoulder. Instead of dislodging Clu from the Mayglon, Lie rebounded to his side on the long grass.

Lie scrambled to his feet and firmly grasped Clu's shoulders. His hands sank sickeningly into Clu's flesh and became mired. Lie groaned with horror. The Mayglon had fashioned a false image of Clu out of its pliable flesh!

The pseudo Clu melded into the slimy flesh of the red Mayglon and disappeared, drawing Lie's hands further into the body of the creature.

Lie was enraged at failing to recall that deadly Mayglon trick. He dug in his heels and hauled at his hands, but they would not budge from the thick slime-like skin of the Mayglon.

The Mayglon began to undulate backwards.

Lie was certain it intended to drag him to its waiting mate for the kill. Mayglons, even the insane ones, traveled in pairs.

"Clu!" Lie screamed. "Mayglon, Clu! I need you! I need you!"

Clu furrowed his brow as he knelt beside the pool of water. Strange, he could swear he had heard someone calling his name. He stood up and wiped his hands on

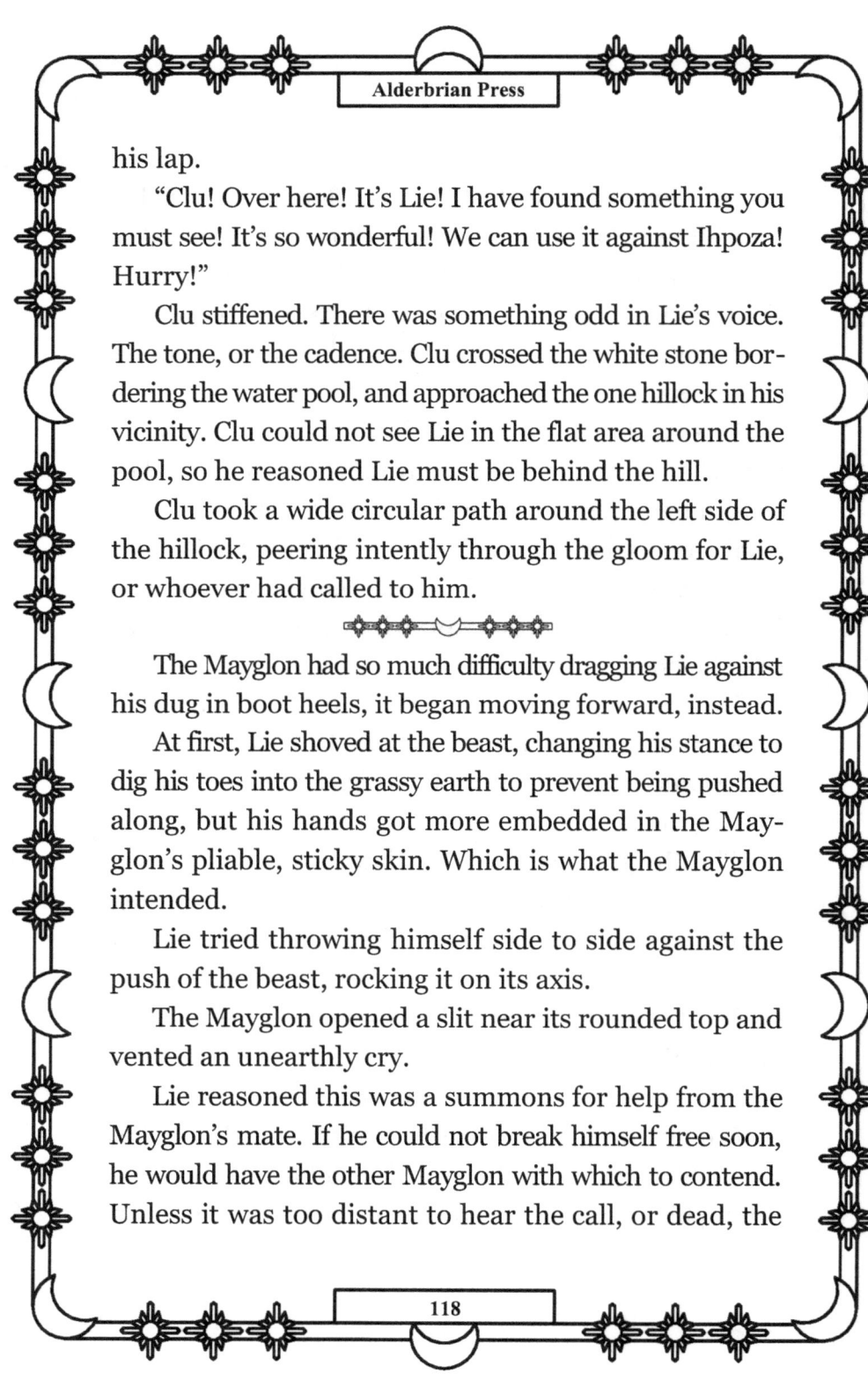

his lap.

"Clu! Over here! It's Lie! I have found something you must see! It's so wonderful! We can use it against Ihpoza! Hurry!"

Clu stiffened. There was something odd in Lie's voice. The tone, or the cadence. Clu crossed the white stone bordering the water pool, and approached the one hillock in his vicinity. Clu could not see Lie in the flat area around the pool, so he reasoned Lie must be behind the hill.

Clu took a wide circular path around the left side of the hillock, peering intently through the gloom for Lie, or whoever had called to him.

The Mayglon had so much difficulty dragging Lie against his dug in boot heels, it began moving forward, instead.

At first, Lie shoved at the beast, changing his stance to dig his toes into the grassy earth to prevent being pushed along, but his hands got more embedded in the Mayglon's pliable, sticky skin. Which is what the Mayglon intended.

Lie tried throwing himself side to side against the push of the beast, rocking it on its axis.

The Mayglon opened a slit near its rounded top and vented an unearthly cry.

Lie reasoned this was a summons for help from the Mayglon's mate. If he could not break himself free soon, he would have the other Mayglon with which to contend. Unless it was too distant to hear the call, or dead, the other Mayglon would not fail to appear. Quickly.

Clu startled at a distant bizarre howl. He was not sure whether it was uttered by an animal or a Human. He made a slow, wide circuit of the small hillock. He sighted nothing to explain the voice or the unnerving cry. Was that a tall form toward his left? He ran that way for a few steps, but saw only grassy hills.

"I had best return to camp and get some rest. Only Azophi knows what is in store for us at Slann, tomorrow."

Clu started a swift walk back to the campsite. He was leery of every shadow and shape. He was damned certain those words, and that weird howl, had not been his imagination. He was fairly sure Mr. Lie was not the type to play scary games. "But Ihpoza is," Clu ruefully muttered. He shuddered and walked more quickly.

"Clu!" Lie said. He stepped from behind an unusually shaped hill. He was bearing a large silver cube. "I thought I saw an animal and hid," he said. "Look at this!"

As Clu approached his friend, he noticed Lie's eyes looked a bit odd: glazed. He saw what appeared to be a rope on the grass behind Lie. The rope had a red cast to it, even under the pale moon light. The odd cadence of Lie's voice and the rope like object caused a memory to speak to Clu. He shrank back.

"What's wrong?" Lie said. "Don't you want to see?" He held the silver cube out. "You can hold it. I won't mind."

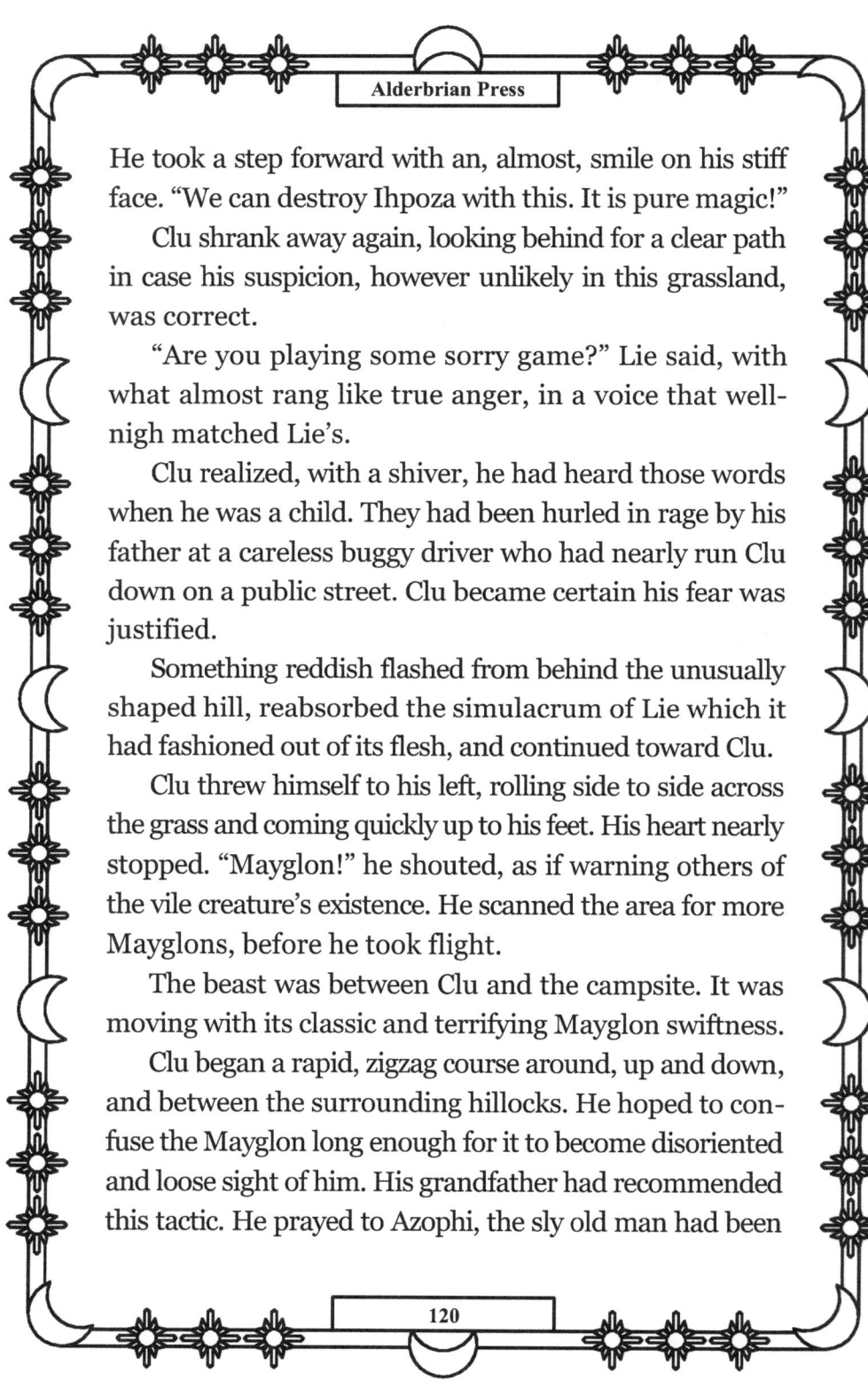

He took a step forward with an, almost, smile on his stiff face. "We can destroy Ihpoza with this. It is pure magic!"

Clu shrank away again, looking behind for a clear path in case his suspicion, however unlikely in this grassland, was correct.

"Are you playing some sorry game?" Lie said, with what almost rang like true anger, in a voice that well-nigh matched Lie's.

Clu realized, with a shiver, he had heard those words when he was a child. They had been hurled in rage by his father at a careless buggy driver who had nearly run Clu down on a public street. Clu became certain his fear was justified.

Something reddish flashed from behind the unusually shaped hill, reabsorbed the simulacrum of Lie which it had fashioned out of its flesh, and continued toward Clu.

Clu threw himself to his left, rolling side to side across the grass and coming quickly up to his feet. His heart nearly stopped. "Mayglon!" he shouted, as if warning others of the vile creature's existence. He scanned the area for more Mayglons, before he took flight.

The beast was between Clu and the campsite. It was moving with its classic and terrifying Mayglon swiftness.

Clu began a rapid, zigzag course around, up and down, and between the surrounding hillocks. He hoped to confuse the Mayglon long enough for it to become disoriented and loose sight of him. His grandfather had recommended this tactic. He prayed to Azophi, the sly old man had been

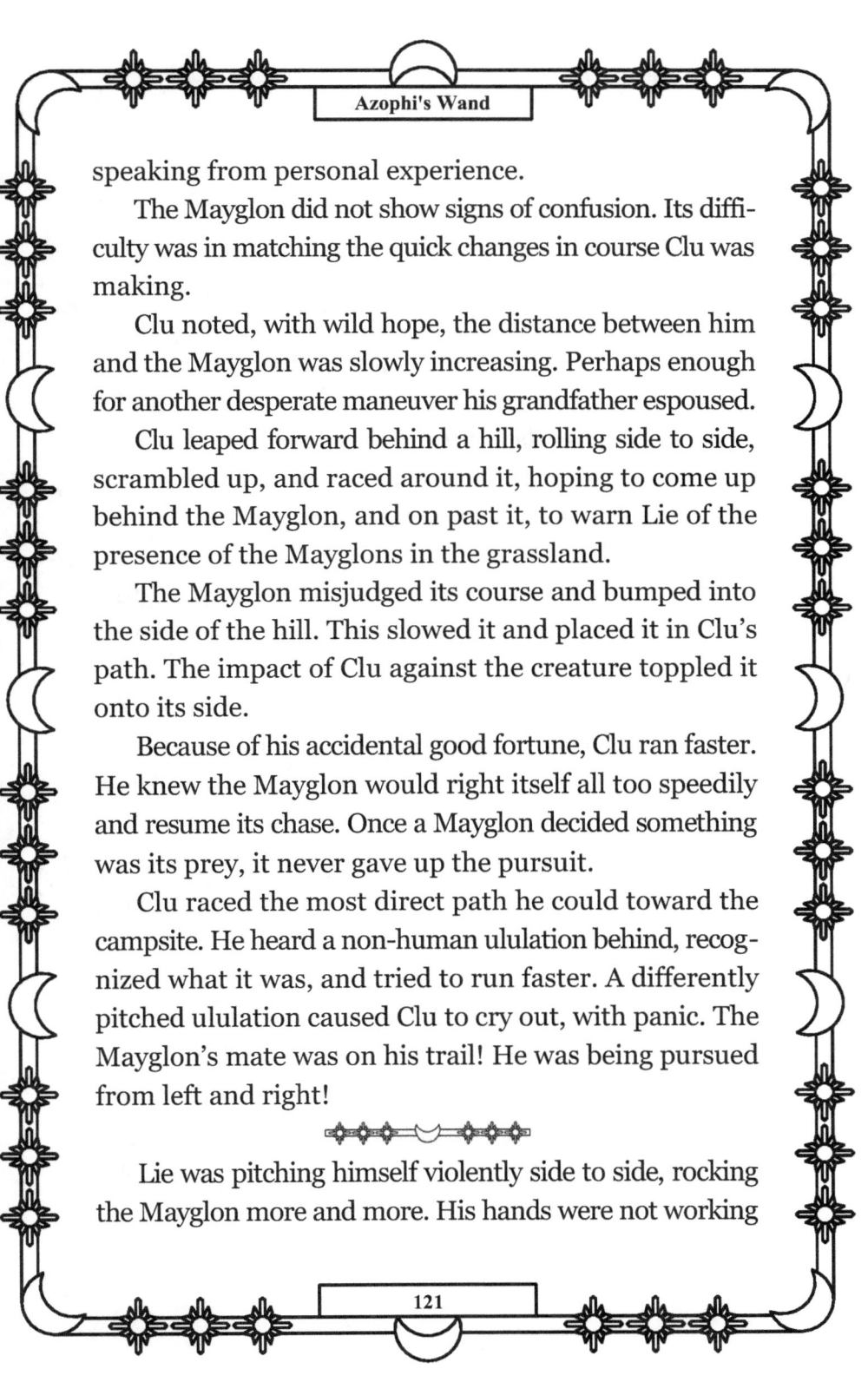

speaking from personal experience.

The Mayglon did not show signs of confusion. Its difficulty was in matching the quick changes in course Clu was making.

Clu noted, with wild hope, the distance between him and the Mayglon was slowly increasing. Perhaps enough for another desperate maneuver his grandfather espoused.

Clu leaped forward behind a hill, rolling side to side, scrambled up, and raced around it, hoping to come up behind the Mayglon, and on past it, to warn Lie of the presence of the Mayglons in the grassland.

The Mayglon misjudged its course and bumped into the side of the hill. This slowed it and placed it in Clu's path. The impact of Clu against the creature toppled it onto its side.

Because of his accidental good fortune, Clu ran faster. He knew the Mayglon would right itself all too speedily and resume its chase. Once a Mayglon decided something was its prey, it never gave up the pursuit.

Clu raced the most direct path he could toward the campsite. He heard a non-human ululation behind, recognized what it was, and tried to run faster. A differently pitched ululation caused Clu to cry out, with panic. The Mayglon's mate was on his trail! He was being pursued from left and right!

Lie was pitching himself violently side to side, rocking the Mayglon more and more. His hands were not working their way out of its red flesh. He despaired that he would not disentangle himself from the beast. "Clu!" he screamed desperately. "Where the hell are you?"

The Mayglon vented its cry. Two more calls answered, not far away.

Lie's heart thudded almost out of control. He had blundered into a family of Mayglons! Clu could not aid him against an entire Clan of the deadly creatures. "Baylou!" he screamed. "Baylou! If you value your damned quest, show yourself, and save me! Save me, you egotistical bastard!"

The Mayglon toppled onto its side, striking with great force. The slit near its top opened and a foul gas was grunted out.

Lie's hands came unstuck. He rolled away from the Mayglon at a furious pace, not stopping until he was several yards distant. When he scrambled to his feet, he groaned with fear.

The Mayglon balled itself up and shot into its normal upright posture. It sent a long tendril of its red flesh snaking toward Lie, then lurched forward.

Lie charged between two hills and returned to the campsite. He climbed the highest hillock and watched the Mayglon pass along the bottom. He was about to flee down the hillock to seek Clu, to warn him, when he recalled an alarum his grandfather had issued concerning Mayglons. A chill shot through him. Mayglons were telepathic! It was imperative to fashion his thoughts to misguide the creatures as to his intentions, or he would surely lose his life!

The Mayglon sped up the hillock on Lie's left side and engulfed Lie's left arm up to his elbow, before he could react.

Lie leaped off the hill head first, pulling the Mayglon after him.

They landed hard.

The Mayglon was not stunned.

Lie lay on his back, gasping for breath.

The Mayglon began to circle itself around Lie.

Clu stumbled and tumbled down the side of a small hill. Before he could regain his bearings and scramble to his feet, a Mayglon was at each side of him, inducting his hands into their flesh. Clu screamed and struggled against the horrid creatures. The Mayglons elongated themselves and lifted him off the ground. "Damn you, Baylou! Damn you, Azophi! Damn you, Ihpoza!" he screamed in fury. "Damn you, Mr. Lie! Have you abandoned me, too!"

After a while, Clu gave up struggling to free himself. He wondered, in a state of shock, why he had not been engulfed. The red Mayglon was male, the pink, female. They usually instantly ingested the prey when they were together. Where, in Azophi's accursed name, could these fiends be bearing him?

Lie managed to catch his breath and struggle to his

feet. He stepped out of the Mayglon's death circle but his arm was still held in a thick tendril of its red flash. He began furiously stomping on the tendril.

The Mayglon shrieked; a definite sound of pain.

Lie was desperately heartened by this. He stomped harder, making sure to use one foot at a time, and instantly withdraw it after each stomp, so as not to get both feet mired in the creature's gluey hide. The suction on his arm began to lessen, and his arm started to slide free, but with torturous slowness. "No!" Lie screamed, tensing his body as the pink flesh of a female Mayglon enveloped his right arm up to his elbow.

The red male reformed itself into a ball, then shot up to its normal vertical posture.

The Mayglons elongated themselves, lifting Lie off the ground. He started kicking savagely at them, landing satisfyingly solid blows to each in turn.

The Mayglons shrilled in pain. Then drew away from Lie, stretching the portion of themselves in which Lie's arms were mired, into thick tendrils.

"That will not prevent me!" Lie screamed. He twisted his body against the tendrils and started double kicking the female Mayglon on its vice-like tentacle.

The female Mayglon shrilled pain. It and the male shot out tendrils from the lower parts of their bodies and engulfed Lie's legs up to his knees before he could avoid it. The Mayglons began a rapid trek across the grassy hill country.

Lie hung from the predators. He had no energy to fight or scream his rage and despair. Though he feared, poor Clu had fallen prey to the cruel Mayglons, "Clu," he whispered, "I Pray to Azophi, you, at least, are safe."

Lie did not know if he was fortunate or cursed because these Mayglons had not instantly engulfed him as was their custom. Now, or later, he thought, numbly, there is little difference.

<hr />

The Mayglons bore Clu to the unusually large, strange appearing hill he had noticed earlier during his flight. They paused on one side of the hillock and remained motionless.

Clu became livid with rage. "What are you waiting for?" he said. "Why must you torment me? May Azophi damn you! And may the Eternal damn Azophi for creating horrors like you!"

After five minutes, there was a rustling of grass and two Mayglons appeared from the murk of the moonlight.

"No!" both Lie and Clu screamed, in despair.

"Mr. Lie!" Clu moaned. "Where is Baylou? You said it watches us from a distance! Surely, Baylou can't be so angry at you that it will not come to our aid, now!"

Lie just slumped.

There was a sound of digging and the side of the great hillock fell away to reveal a hive of infant Mayglons. Perhaps thirty.

Lie and Clu were beyond terror and struggle.

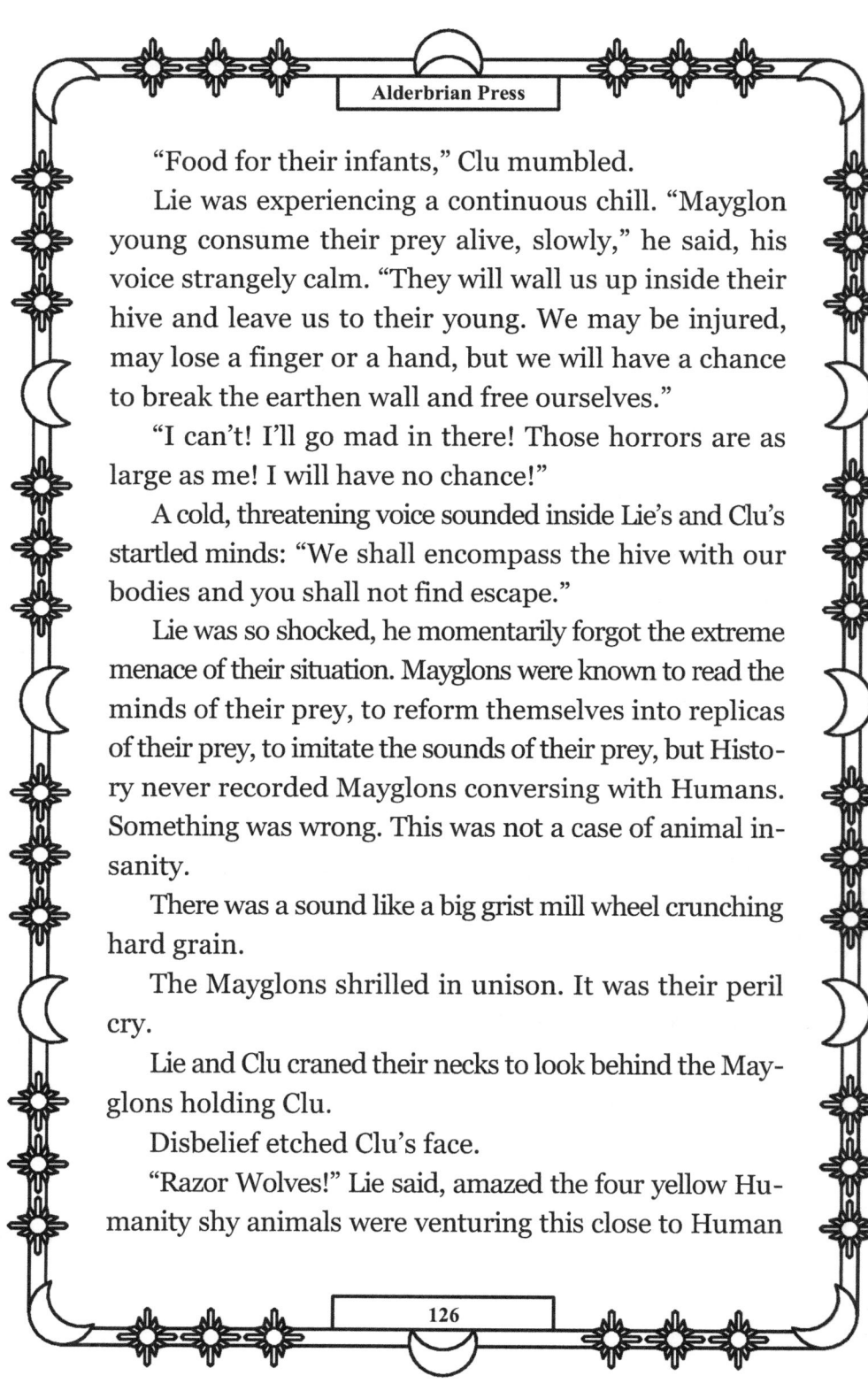

"Food for their infants," Clu mumbled.

Lie was experiencing a continuous chill. "Mayglon young consume their prey alive, slowly," he said, his voice strangely calm. "They will wall us up inside their hive and leave us to their young. We may be injured, may lose a finger or a hand, but we will have a chance to break the earthen wall and free ourselves."

"I can't! I'll go mad in there! Those horrors are as large as me! I will have no chance!"

A cold, threatening voice sounded inside Lie's and Clu's startled minds: "We shall encompass the hive with our bodies and you shall not find escape."

Lie was so shocked, he momentarily forgot the extreme menace of their situation. Mayglons were known to read the minds of their prey, to reform themselves into replicas of their prey, to imitate the sounds of their prey, but History never recorded Mayglons conversing with Humans. Something was wrong. This was not a case of animal insanity.

There was a sound like a big grist mill wheel crunching hard grain.

The Mayglons shrilled in unison. It was their peril cry.

Lie and Clu craned their necks to look behind the Mayglons holding Clu.

Disbelief etched Clu's face.

"Razor Wolves!" Lie said, amazed the four yellow Humanity shy animals were venturing this close to Human inhabited lands.

"For food and the path to water," a sinister sounding voice growled in the men's minds, "we will slay the Mayglons."

"Agreed!" Lie and Clu screamed, without hesitation or doubt as to the wisdom of trusting deadly scavengers.

"The enemy of my enemy is my ally," Lie thought. There was a chorus of growling laughs inside his mind.

Nine Razor Wolves emerged from the grassy Hill Lands to join their Pack. They shook their razor sharp, knife-like horns in a salute to their Leader.

"A wise saying," the Pack Leader said, in Lie's mind. "I shall cherish it, shall pass it on as my own."

Lie felt a glimmer of hope. History recorded many instances where Humans and Razor Wolves had exchanged greetings via the telepathy of the Razor Wolves. Traditionally, Humans, Razor Wolves and Mayglons avoided one another like the plague. Why the Razors were in the Hill Lands was a matter of enigma. Lie feared to consider the answer his mind tried to present.

The Mayglons dropped Lie and Clu to the grass and joined into a single mass, closing off access to their infants in the hive.

The Wolf pack snarled a warning to each other.

"What Human deceit is this?" the Pack Leader growled, in Lie's and Clu's minds. "Once joined, they cannot be defeated."

Lie and Clu struggled to their feet and stood back-to-

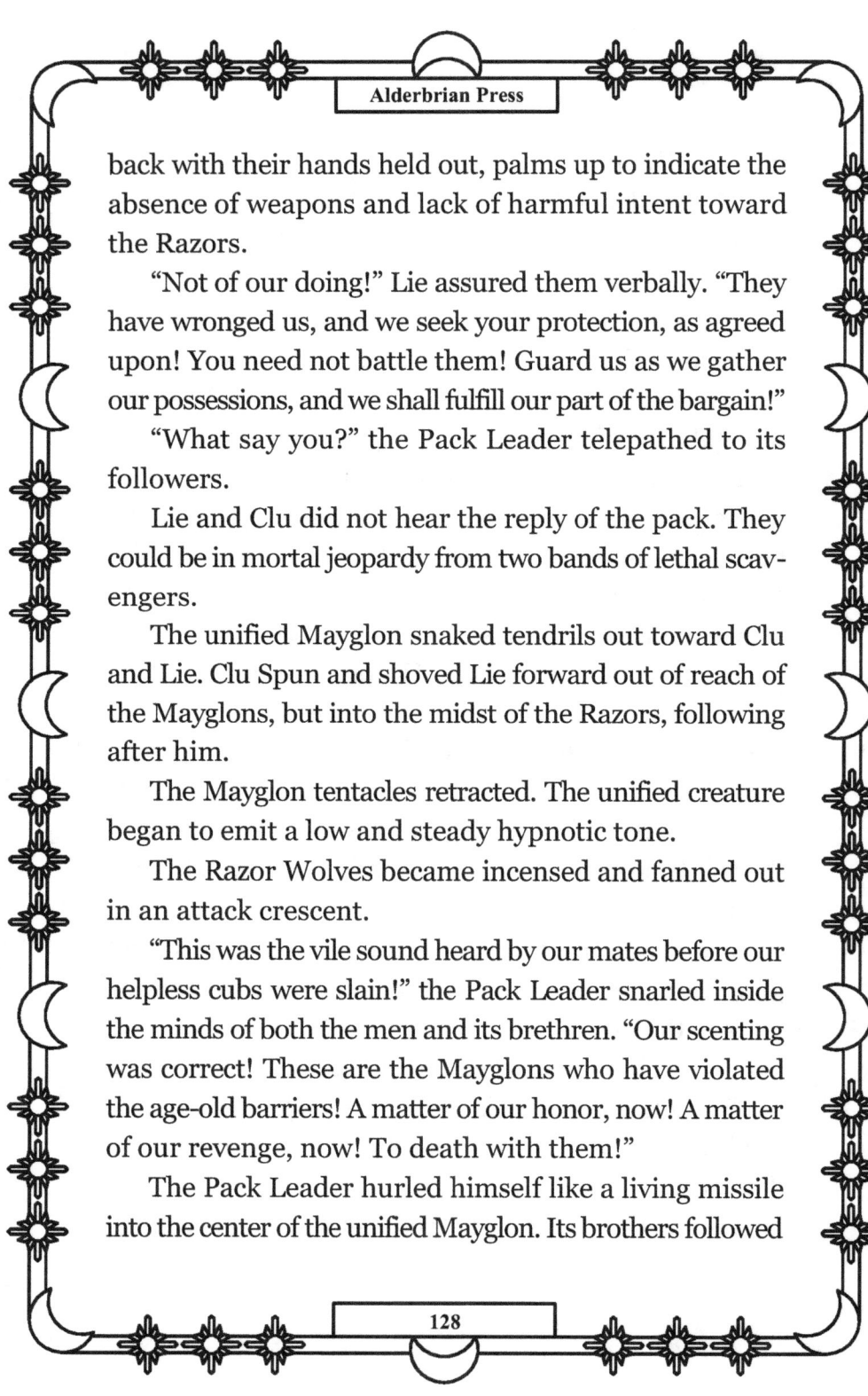

back with their hands held out, palms up to indicate the absence of weapons and lack of harmful intent toward the Razors.

"Not of our doing!" Lie assured them verbally. "They have wronged us, and we seek your protection, as agreed upon! You need not battle them! Guard us as we gather our possessions, and we shall fulfill our part of the bargain!"

"What say you?" the Pack Leader telepathed to its followers.

Lie and Clu did not hear the reply of the pack. They could be in mortal jeopardy from two bands of lethal scavengers.

The unified Mayglon snaked tendrils out toward Clu and Lie. Clu Spun and shoved Lie forward out of reach of the Mayglons, but into the midst of the Razors, following after him.

The Mayglon tentacles retracted. The unified creature began to emit a low and steady hypnotic tone.

The Razor Wolves became incensed and fanned out in an attack crescent.

"This was the vile sound heard by our mates before our helpless cubs were slain!" the Pack Leader snarled inside the minds of both the men and its brethren. "Our scenting was correct! These are the Mayglons who have violated the age-old barriers! A matter of our honor, now! A matter of our revenge, now! To death with them!"

The Pack Leader hurled himself like a living missile into the center of the unified Mayglon. Its brothers followed

suit, an instant behind. Their razor horns and paw claws ripped gashes in the pliable, gluey hide, of the Mayglon Unity. It shrilled in agony, sprouted tendrils that curled around
the Razor Wolves, then hurled them far into the night.

There were yelps of pain as the Razors Wolves struck
the earth.

The savage battle occurred and ended so suddenly,
Lie and Clu were caught unprepared. Until the Mayglon
Unity snaked tendrils toward them.

Lie grabbed Clu's wrist and fled in the direction the
Razor Wolves had been thrown. Before Lie and Clu had
taken five desperate steps, the Razor Wolves were bound-
ing past the men, intent upon their second attack against
the Unity.

Lie and Clu desperately raced toward their campsite.

The sounds of battle grew faint.

Lie and Clu found the four hillocks with relative ease.
They stored their blankets, shouldered their backpacks,
and resumed their course toward the drinking pool, in
utmost haste. They would fill their canteens, wash themselves free of the Mayglon slime, and push on to Slann.

It was nearly daylight and there was no possibility of
sleep or rest as long as the Mayglons and the Razor Wolves
were on the prowl.

Behind Lie and Clu, the battle raged with neither side
gaining advantage.

Not far from the war, inside a natural cave within a hill, and hidden behind thick bushes, something stirred. It slowly emerged from its temporary den, and the feeble blue-green shine of the moon revealed it.

Death flicked its forked tongue in extreme rage, then muttered: "Even without an iota of magic from the accursed Book, these whining insects unwittingly defeat my brilliant planning!"

Death easily mastered the Mayglons through their telepathic traits. Against common sense, Death failed to control the telepathic Razor Wolves.

"I should not have tested my mastery of the Mayglons by directing them to slaughter the wolf pups," Death reprimanded itself, with intense self dislike. "I should have realized their progenitors would never rest until revenge was achieved. Now, must I revert to the Master's canny plan. To the glory of Ihpoza!"

Death took to wing. As it flew, it ceased its telepathic control of the Mayglons.

The Razor Wolves sensed something different about the minds of the Mayglons, paused their assault, and drew back a few feet.

The Unity separated into four Mayglons, formed pouches and tentacles on themselves, gathered their young from the hive, placed them into the pouches, and fled, with impressive speed, back toward the RainSoaked Mountains.

Baylou hovered just high enough above a distant hill to view the confused Razor Wolves.

Blocking Death from controlling the minds of the Razor Wolves, without alerting Death to Baylou's presence, while at the same time exercising Baylou's control of the Razor Wolves, had been a matter of almost impossible magical nuances.

The book ended its telepathic control of the Razor Wolves. Baylou lamented failing to divine Death's activities too late to prevent the murder of the wolf pups. The Tome regretted being forced to manage the adult wolves for the protection of Lie and Clu, because of Death's heartless abuse of the Mayglons.

Baylou could not fathom why it was not allowed to rejoin its Human charges, for trivial arcane matters to which it had to attend.

Baylou sensed Lie's increasing desire to abandon the quest to preserve their lives and return to their loved ones. To avoid what Lie realized would be greater perils as they drew nearer to Iphozalon and Ihpoza.

It might soon be imperative for the Magic to order Baylou to bolster Lie's resolve, or their noble suffering and almost super human effort, would be wasted.

Baylou tingled with anticipation of the time when it could journey with Lie and Clu. The Book soared high into the inky sky to resume its occult duties.

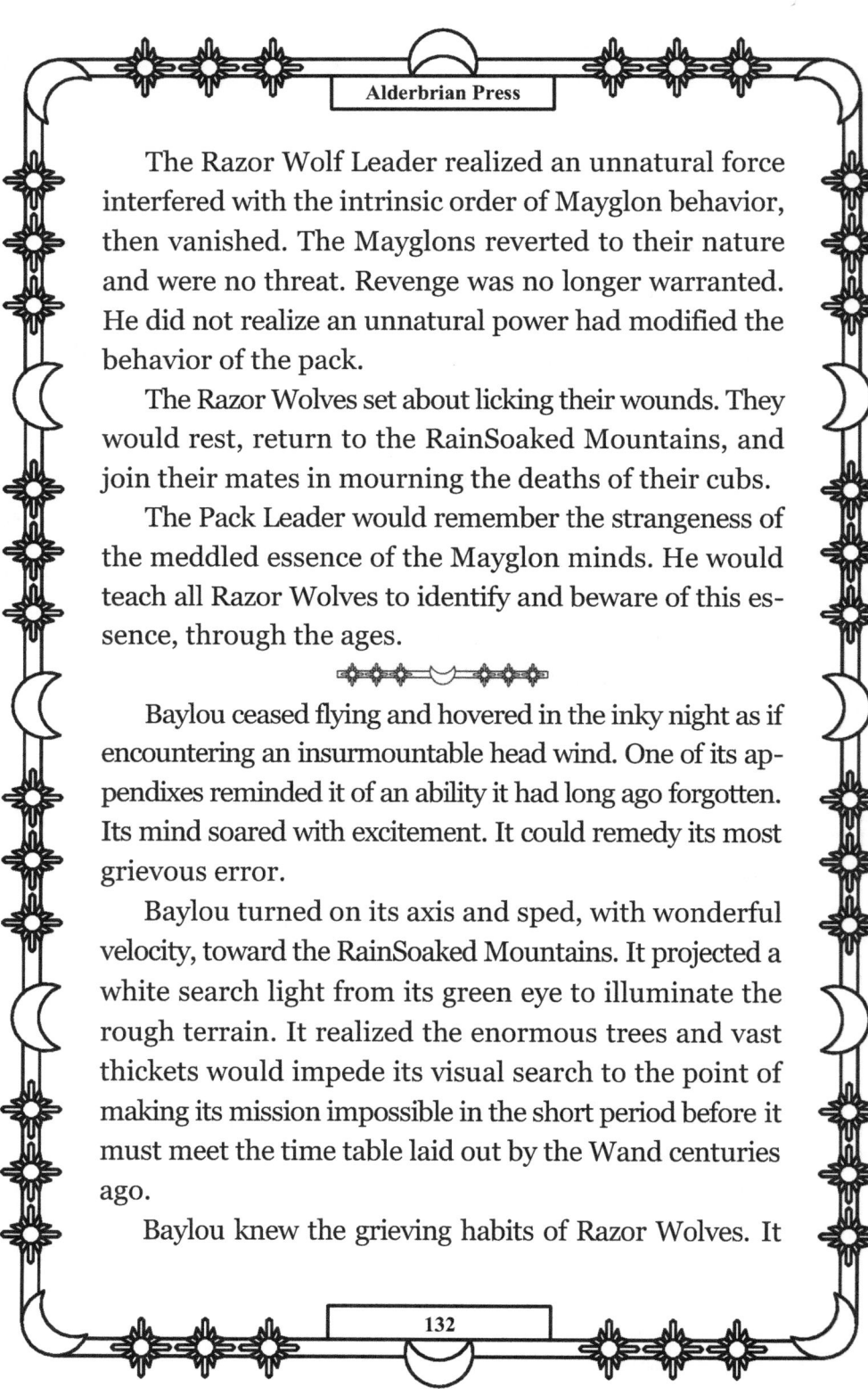

The Razor Wolf Leader realized an unnatural force interfered with the intrinsic order of Mayglon behavior, then vanished. The Mayglons reverted to their nature and were no threat. Revenge was no longer warranted. He did not realize an unnatural power had modified the behavior of the pack.

The Razor Wolves set about licking their wounds. They would rest, return to the RainSoaked Mountains, and join their mates in mourning the deaths of their cubs.

The Pack Leader would remember the strangeness of the meddled essence of the Mayglon minds. He would teach all Razor Wolves to identify and beware of this essence, through the ages.

Baylou ceased flying and hovered in the inky night as if encountering an insurmountable head wind. One of its appendixes reminded it of an ability it had long ago forgotten. Its mind soared with excitement. It could remedy its most grievous error.

Baylou turned on its axis and sped, with wonderful velocity, toward the RainSoaked Mountains. It projected a white search light from its green eye to illuminate the rough terrain. It realized the enormous trees and vast thickets would impede its visual search to the point of making its mission impossible in the short period before it must meet the time table laid out by the Wand centuries ago.

Baylou knew the grieving habits of Razor Wolves. It

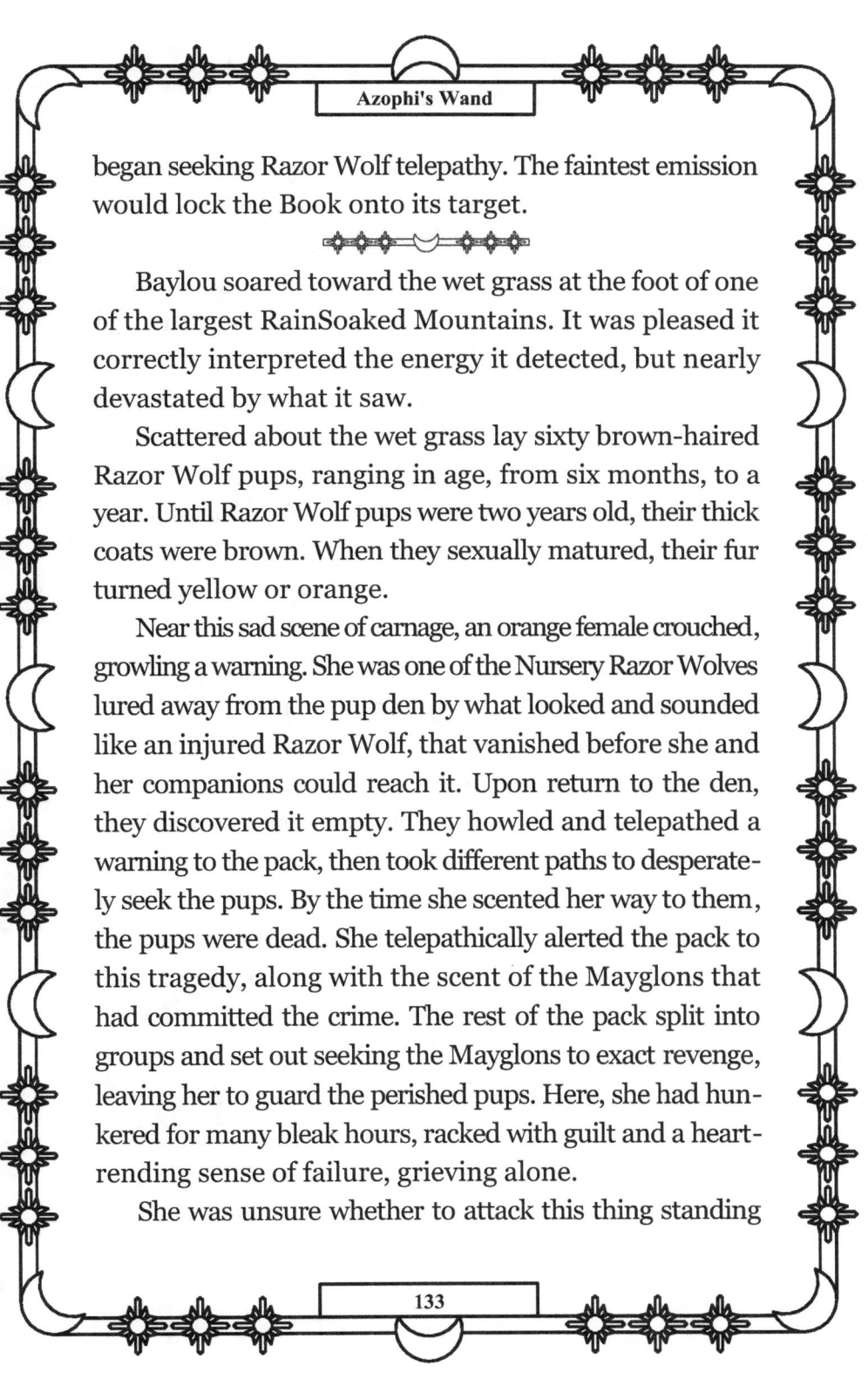

began seeking Razor Wolf telepathy. The faintest emission would lock the Book onto its target.

Baylou soared toward the wet grass at the foot of one of the largest RainSoaked Mountains. It was pleased it correctly interpreted the energy it detected, but nearly devastated by what it saw.

Scattered about the wet grass lay sixty brown-haired Razor Wolf pups, ranging in age, from six months, to a year. Until Razor Wolf pups were two years old, their thick coats were brown. When they sexually matured, their fur turned yellow or orange.

Near this sad scene of carnage, an orange female crouched, growling a warning. She was one of the Nursery Razor Wolves lured away from the pup den by what looked and sounded like an injured Razor Wolf, that vanished before she and her companions could reach it. Upon return to the den, they discovered it empty. They howled and telepathed a warning to the pack, then took different paths to desperately seek the pups. By the time she scented her way to them, the pups were dead. She telepathically alerted the pack to this tragedy, along with the scent of the Mayglons that had committed the crime. The rest of the pack split into groups and set out seeking the Mayglons to exact revenge, leaving her to guard the perished pups. Here, she had hunkered for many bleak hours, racked with guilt and a heart-rending sense of failure, grieving alone.

She was unsure whether to attack this thing standing

before the pups, or flee in terror at something she could not fathom. It was her solemn duty to guard the bodies until the pack returned for the proper burial ceremony. This thing, which was not alive, yet moved as if it was, chilled her. Her choice was to throw back her head and howl a warning to the pack.

She stopped with puzzlement. No sound had escaped her throat. She sensed this odd occurrence was associated with the glowing thing before the pups.

She sent forth a frantic telepathic call to the mothers of the pups. Instead of the comforting words of those females, to her astonishment, a nonliving voice replied to her request for help.

"Do not fear," Baylou telepathed to the She-Wolf. "Although I am not of the flesh world, I am here to remedy the sin committed against your pups, and your pack. I cannot allow you to call your sisters, for in your ignorance and fear, all of you would interfere with my task." It floated closer to the pups.

The She-Wolf went into a pre-attack crouch. "Touch not the wasted seed of the pack!" she warned. Her telepathic voice was filled with threat and resoluteness. If necessary, she would sacrifice her life in an effort to preserve the bodies of the pups.

Baylou realized it had not allayed the She-Wolf's fears. It turned on the Razor Wolf, flashing toward her as if to attack, and flared the glow from its green eye.

The She-Wolf was startled and drew back.

"I shall make them live again!" Baylou said, with exasperation. Its patience was growing thin and its time was waning. "If you will but allow me to work!"

The She-Wolf tilted her head to one side. "How can I trust that which I cannot understand, to be a friend, who will perform a tragically impossible miracle?" she said, telepathically, with hope.

Baylou relaxed. Now it could perform its work without fear the Razor Wolves will snatch up the bodies of the pups in their mouths and scatter in every direction of the compass. It was relieved the abominable Lizard had directed the Mayglons to strangle the pups. If they had inflicted worse damage, there would be no hope of re-animation. It turned to the pups, flew above them, and emitted a brilliant white light tinged with sun-like yellow.

At first, Baylou feared it had misunderstood the information in its appendix, then it felt satisfaction.

One of the smallest pups inhaled, wiggled, and stood up. Swiftly, pup after pup drew breath and got to its feet. They stretched and yawned as if awakening from a deep sleep.

Baylou turned off the yellow-white light, settled tiredly to the grass on the bottom edges of its covers, and watched the pups, with its back to the She-Wolf.

The pups saw the She-Wolf. They barked and yipped with recognition and excitement, but were reluctant to approach her because of Baylou and its shining eye.

The She-Wolf sat in amazement.

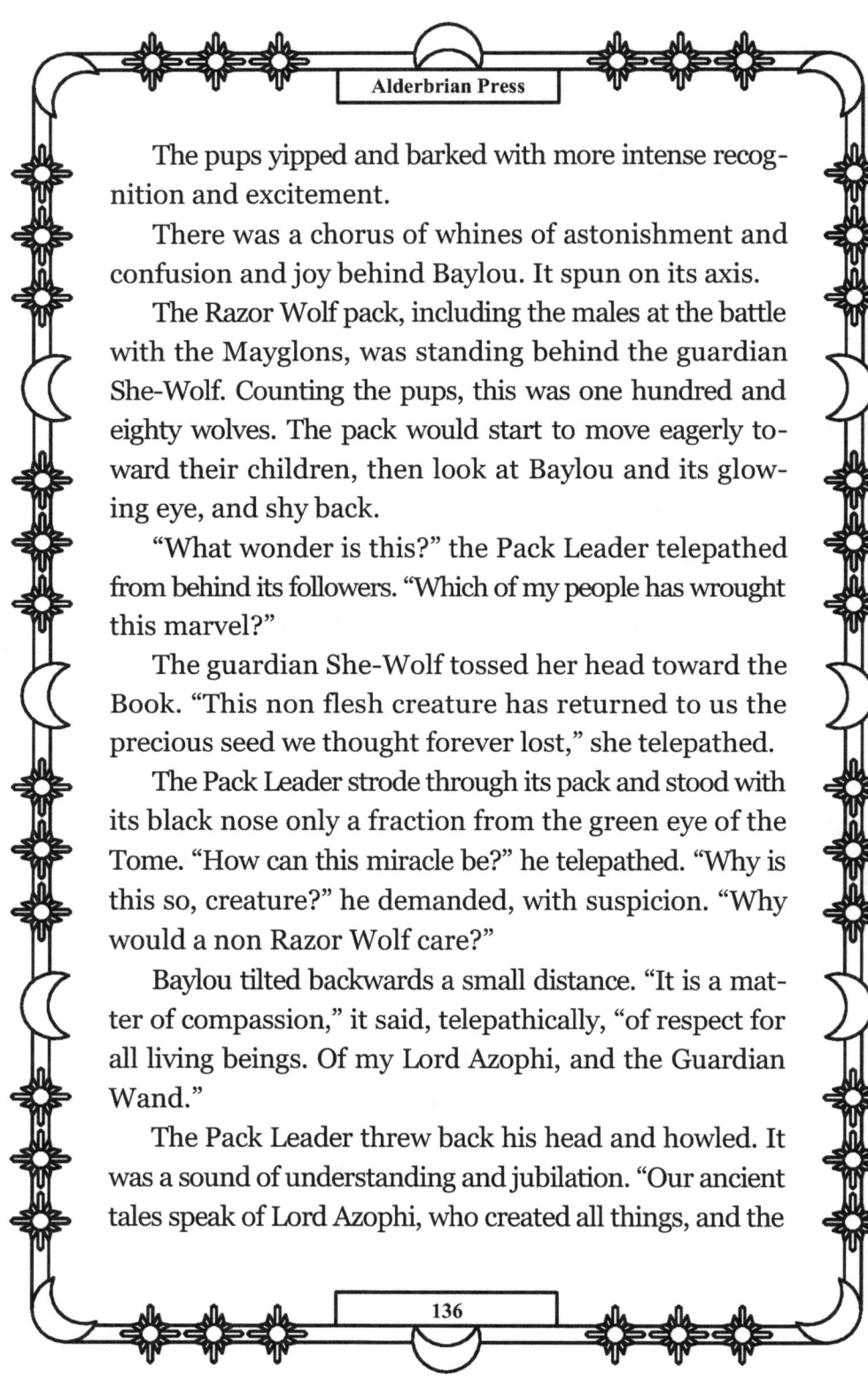

The pups yipped and barked with more intense recognition and excitement.

There was a chorus of whines of astonishment and confusion and joy behind Baylou. It spun on its axis.

The Razor Wolf pack, including the males at the battle with the Mayglons, was standing behind the guardian She-Wolf. Counting the pups, this was one hundred and eighty wolves. The pack would start to move eagerly toward their children, then look at Baylou and its glowing eye, and shy back.

"What wonder is this?" the Pack Leader telepathed from behind its followers. "Which of my people has wrought this marvel?"

The guardian She-Wolf tossed her head toward the Book. "This non flesh creature has returned to us the precious seed we thought forever lost," she telepathed.

The Pack Leader strode through its pack and stood with its black nose only a fraction from the green eye of the Tome. "How can this miracle be?" he telepathed. "Why is this so, creature?" he demanded, with suspicion. "Why would a non Razor Wolf care?"

Baylou tilted backwards a small distance. "It is a matter of compassion," it said, telepathically, "of respect for all living beings. Of my Lord Azophi, and the Guardian Wand."

The Pack Leader threw back his head and howled. It was a sound of understanding and jubilation. "Our ancient tales speak of Lord Azophi, who created all things, and the

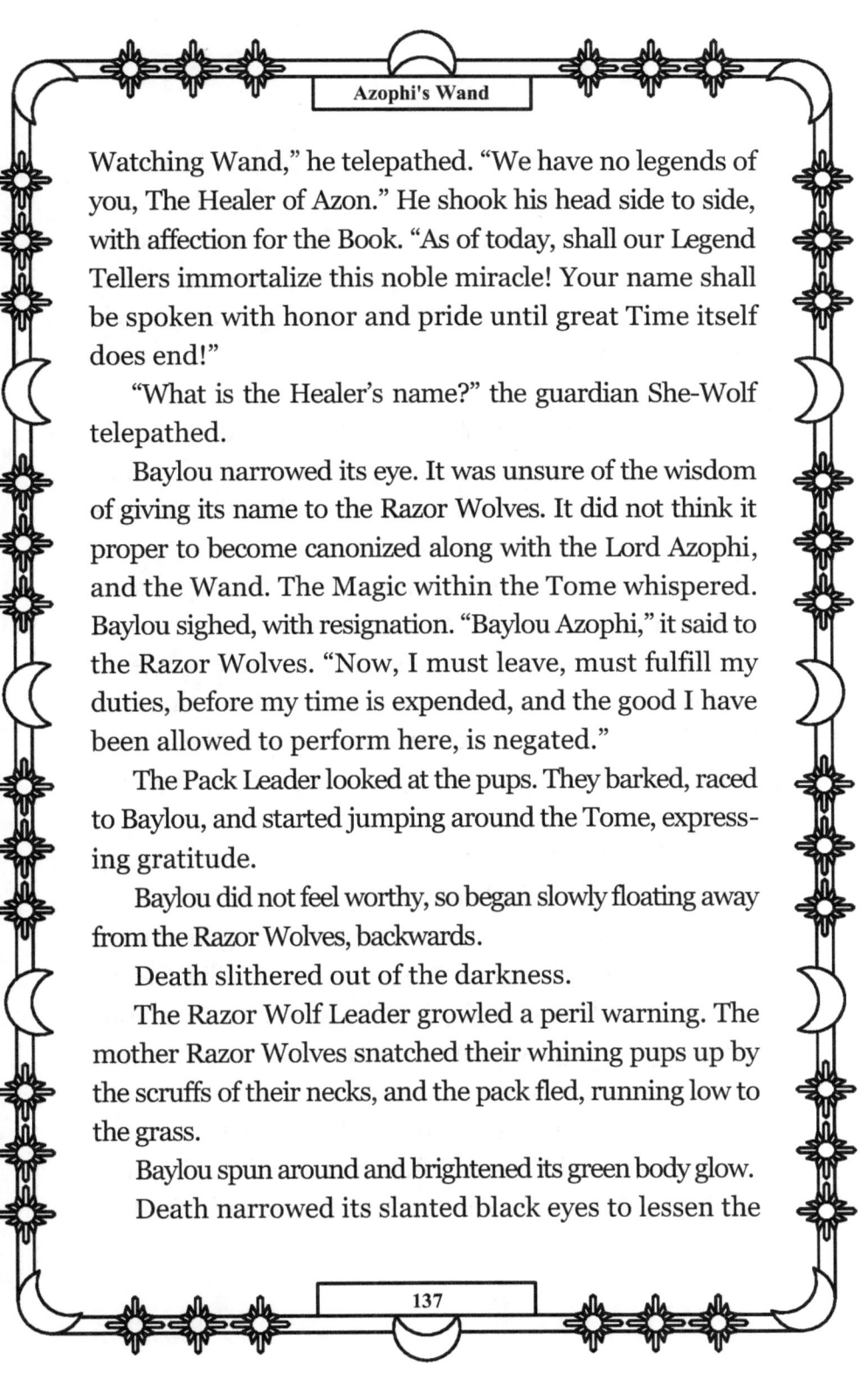

Watching Wand," he telepathed. "We have no legends of you, The Healer of Azon." He shook his head side to side, with affection for the Book. "As of today, shall our Legend Tellers immortalize this noble miracle! Your name shall be spoken with honor and pride until great Time itself does end!"

"What is the Healer's name?" the guardian She-Wolf telepathed.

Baylou narrowed its eye. It was unsure of the wisdom of giving its name to the Razor Wolves. It did not think it proper to become canonized along with the Lord Azophi, and the Wand. The Magic within the Tome whispered. Baylou sighed, with resignation. "Baylou Azophi," it said to the Razor Wolves. "Now, I must leave, must fulfill my duties, before my time is expended, and the good I have been allowed to perform here, is negated."

The Pack Leader looked at the pups. They barked, raced to Baylou, and started jumping around the Tome, expressing gratitude.

Baylou did not feel worthy, so began slowly floating away from the Razor Wolves, backwards.

Death slithered out of the darkness.

The Razor Wolf Leader growled a peril warning. The mother Razor Wolves snatched their whining pups up by the scruffs of their necks, and the pack fled, running low to the grass.

Baylou spun around and brightened its green body glow.

Death narrowed its slanted black eyes to lessen the

glare. "When I detected healing energy, I found you, and realized why I failed to master the Razor Wolves. I was surprised you could play me with such skill," it said, "and realized your weakness, your abject compassion for these hairy parasites, would compel you to stupidly make amends for my actions, bringing you into harms way. Die, now, Book!"

"You truly are the fool!" Baylou said, aloud. "You possess no Magic to harm me, or to protect your weak-minded self, from my Magic. You have brought defeat and demise upon yourself!"

Death laughed smugly, as though it were privy to a secret. It flicked its mighty forked tongue.

Baylou was struck above its eye. The Tome staggered backwards a few feet, surprised by the strength of the blow. There was a double indentation where the lizard's tongue tips had impacted. Baylou seared a green power beam at the saurian.

Death laughed, leaped, with surprising speed and agility, to one side and flicked its tongue.

Baylou was struck below its eye, and staggered backwards further than before. It realized, with chilling astonishment, Death was sapping it of life force with each blow. Baylou beamed again, hitting the wet grass where the saurian had been crouching.

Death unfurled its tongue, striking twice.

Baylou spun half to its left, then half to its right, from the fast mighty blows to each side of its eye. Baylou's Magic calculated and reported: six more draining strikes would cause Baylou to dissipate. Baylou drew itself back beyond the length of the Lizard's forked tongue. It dispatched two green beams at once, cindering the grass and earth at the sides of the Lizard.

Death became frightened. It no longer had a chance of draining the evil Book's life force. It started to leap into the air, to take to its powerful wings.

Baylou laughed sardonically. It formed a thin but un-breakable shield above itself and the saurian, then added four walls. Baylou made certain to remain beyond Death's striking range.

Death backed against the rear wall, kicked its hind paws against it, slashing with its long talons, but wrought no damage. Death flicked its tongue in and out, with rage and fear.

"Thanks to your supreme stupidity, I have neither the time nor the energy," Baylou said, sadly, "to try to salvage you, and I cannot allow you to roam free to imperil Lie and Clu." It gathered its remaining energy, creating a pulsating humming sound.

Death hurled its terrified, spinning thoughts toward Iphozalon.

***

"No! Not my pet!" Ihpoza screamed, with ire. He threw himself off his ice throne, knelt on the icy floor, clenched his one fist against his solar plexus, and marshaled his might.

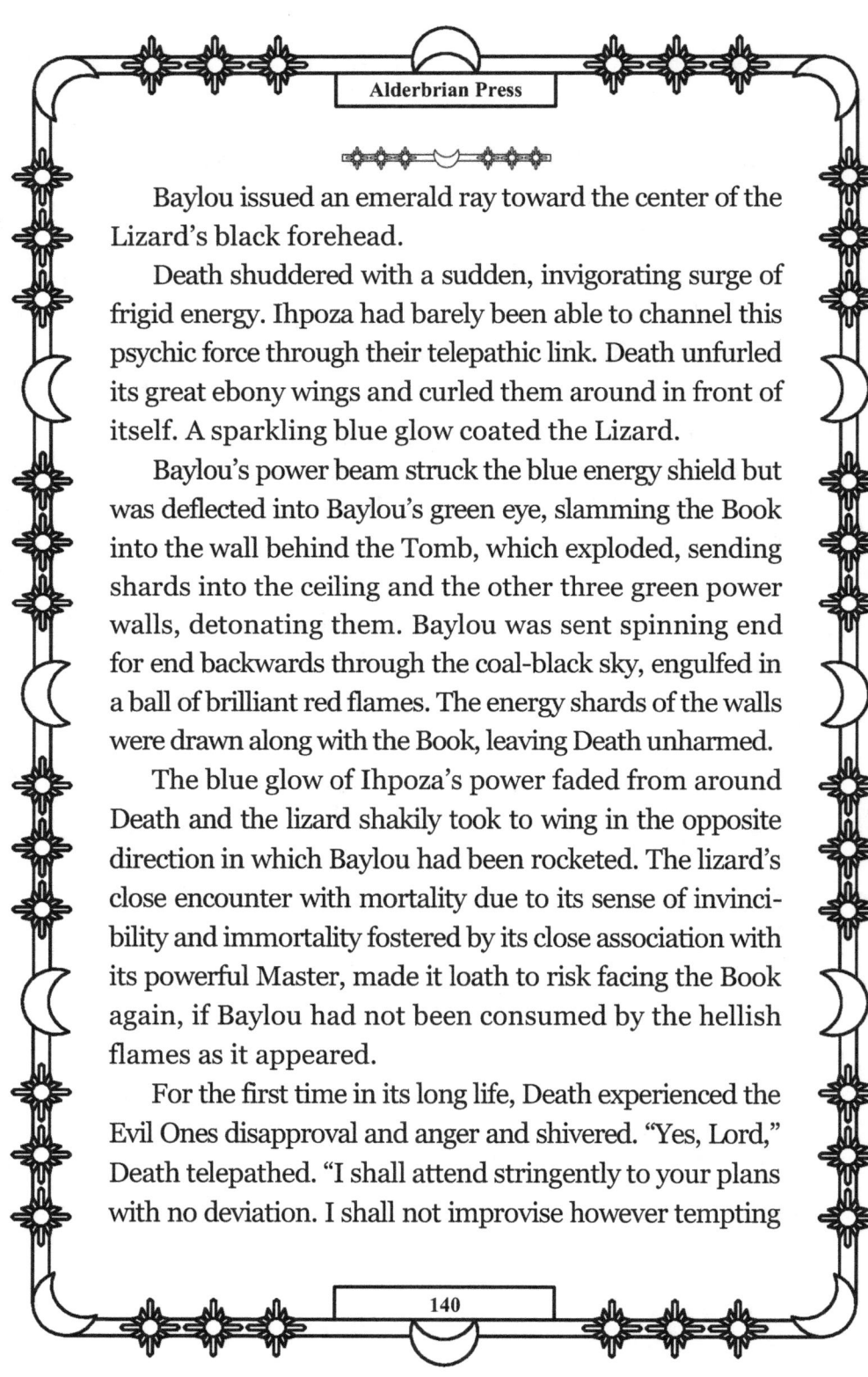

Baylou issued an emerald ray toward the center of the Lizard's black forehead.

Death shuddered with a sudden, invigorating surge of frigid energy. Ihpoza had barely been able to channel this psychic force through their telepathic link. Death unfurled its great ebony wings and curled them around in front of itself. A sparkling blue glow coated the Lizard.

Baylou's power beam struck the blue energy shield but was deflected into Baylou's green eye, slamming the Book into the wall behind the Tomb, which exploded, sending shards into the ceiling and the other three green power walls, detonating them. Baylou was sent spinning end for end backwards through the coal-black sky, engulfed in a ball of brilliant red flames. The energy shards of the walls were drawn along with the Book, leaving Death unharmed.

The blue glow of Ihpoza's power faded from around Death and the lizard shakily took to wing in the opposite direction in which Baylou had been rocketed. The lizard's close encounter with mortality due to its sense of invincibility and immortality fostered by its close association with its powerful Master, made it loath to risk facing the Book again, if Baylou had not been consumed by the hellish flames as it appeared.

For the first time in its long life, Death experienced the Evil Ones disapproval and anger and shivered. "Yes, Lord," Death telepathed. "I shall attend stringently to your plans with no deviation. I shall not improvise however tempting

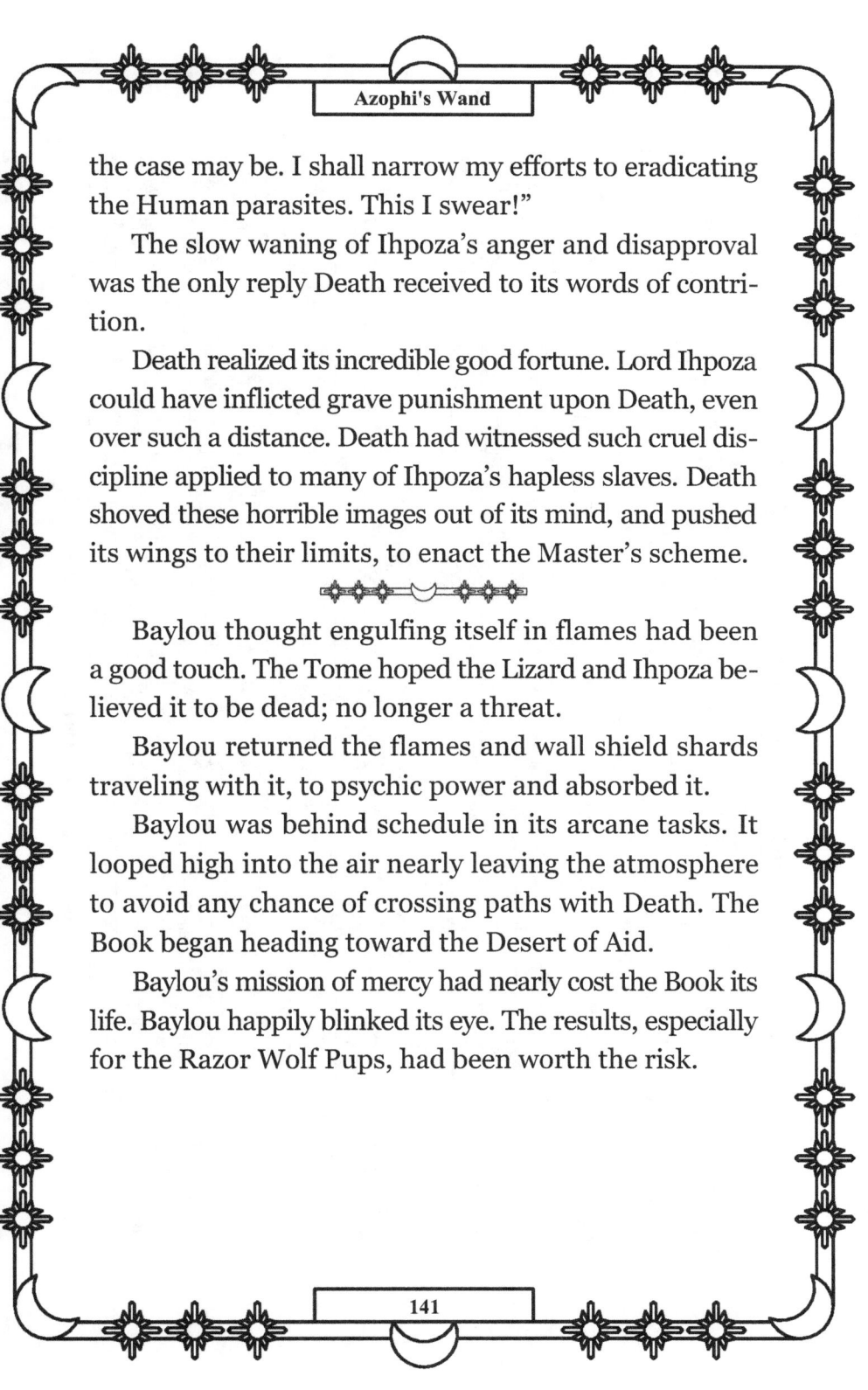

the case may be. I shall narrow my efforts to eradicating the Human parasites. This I swear!"

The slow waning of Ihpoza's anger and disapproval was the only reply Death received to its words of contrition.

Death realized its incredible good fortune. Lord Ihpoza could have inflicted grave punishment upon Death, even over such a distance. Death had witnessed such cruel discipline applied to many of Ihpoza's hapless slaves. Death shoved these horrible images out of its mind, and pushed its wings to their limits, to enact the Master's scheme.

Baylou thought engulfing itself in flames had been a good touch. The Tome hoped the Lizard and Ihpoza believed it to be dead; no longer a threat.

Baylou returned the flames and wall shield shards traveling with it, to psychic power and absorbed it.

Baylou was behind schedule in its arcane tasks. It looped high into the air nearly leaving the atmosphere to avoid any chance of crossing paths with Death. The Book began heading toward the Desert of Aid.

Baylou's mission of mercy had nearly cost the Book its life. Baylou happily blinked its eye. The results, especially for the Razor Wolf Pups, had been worth the risk.

Illustration 15

Ortourian Beast Wrought Iron Window Grillwork

Copyright © 2019 Philip Raymond Sadler

142-A

Chapter 15

Scales on Stone

Slann was ten up side down bowls set in a circle around an exhausted artesian well. The sun reflected from the buildings like faint moonlight from black pearls.

Nomads inhabited it on rare occasion, and almost every genus of animal on the Southern Hemisphere made temporary burrows there.

Solemn, antiquated Slann was considered abandoned.

Haunted.

Perhaps.

They stepped onto the main cobbled street and a welcome breeze played around them. They passed between the nearest bowl buildings and the sunlight was reduced to dusk.

Clu began fidgeting.

Lie grew cautious.

They felt they were being watched.

Something scaly moved across the cobblestones.

Lie and Clu remained motionless, looking around at the weird ancient buildings.

"Monsters!" Clu said, fearfully. "There are hellish mon-

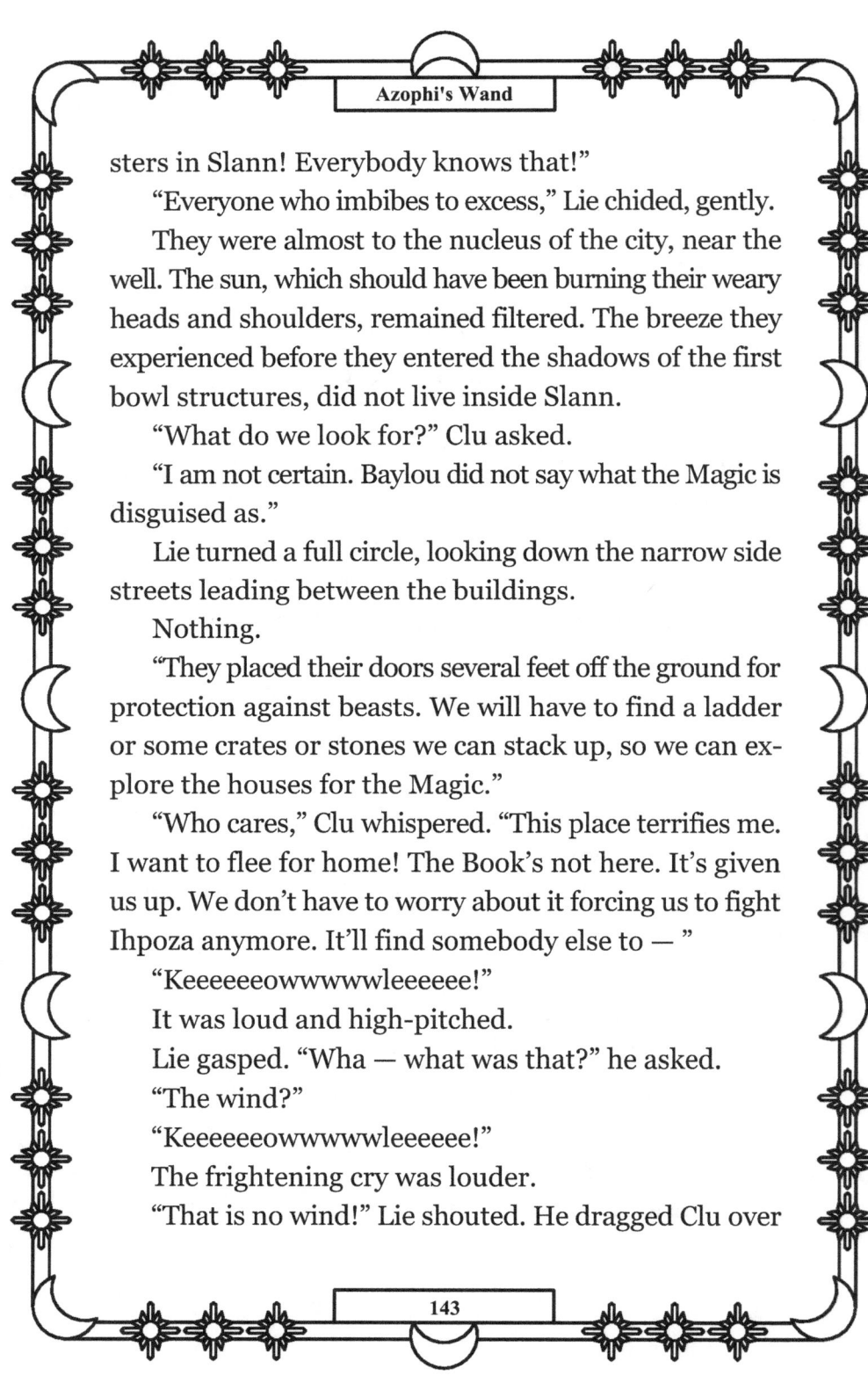

sters in Slann! Everybody knows that!"

"Everyone who imbibes to excess," Lie chided, gently.

They were almost to the nucleus of the city, near the well. The sun, which should have been burning their weary heads and shoulders, remained filtered. The breeze they experienced before they entered the shadows of the first bowl structures, did not live inside Slann.

"What do we look for?" Clu asked.

"I am not certain. Baylou did not say what the Magic is disguised as."

Lie turned a full circle, looking down the narrow side streets leading between the buildings.

Nothing.

"They placed their doors several feet off the ground for protection against beasts. We will have to find a ladder or some crates or stones we can stack up, so we can explore the houses for the Magic."

"Who cares," Clu whispered. "This place terrifies me. I want to flee for home! The Book's not here. It's given us up. We don't have to worry about it forcing us to fight Ihpoza anymore. It'll find somebody else to — "

"Keeeeeeowwwwwleeeeee!"

It was loud and high-pitched.

Lie gasped. "Wha — what was that?" he asked.

"The wind?"

"Keeeeeeowwwwwleeeeee!"

The frightening cry was louder.

"That is no wind!" Lie shouted. He dragged Clu over

against one of the structures. "There is something here with us!" Lie added.

The sound of scales sliding across stones echoed from all directions, as unnerving as unidentifiable sounds in a graveyard at moonless midnight.

Lie oathed under his breath. Baylou had neglected to provide them with arms. Lie had lacked the foresight to purchase them.

"Maybe it's just a ghost, Mr. Lie," Clu said, hopefully. "Ghosts can't hurt us."

Scales scraping stones floated weirdly around, sounding as if the city were under water.

It is a lizard, Lie thought, and lizards, non enchanted ones, grow no larger than two feet. That is half as long as I am tall. A beast like that can easily kill me! Damn you Baylou! Why did we have to anger each other so?

Scales against stones; louder than before.

"Keeeeeeowwwwwleeeeee!"

The terrifying cry was nearer.

Lie's skin crawled. His stomach felt like it was tied in knots, and he was sweating.

Clu was near shock. "I know what it is," he said.

Scales against stones; around, above and below them.

"Keeeeeeowwwwwleeeeee!"

A higher pitch.

It caused their ear drums to jump painfully.

"It was part of a horrible fairy tale my mother told me. A fairy tale no longer!"

The fright in Clu's wild eyes turned Lie colder than the cry of the unseen creature.

Scales against stone.

More volume.

Right beside them.

It felt like the scales were scraping against their faces and hands.

"Keeeeeeowwwwwleeeeee!"

The cry was so loud and high-pitched, the city trembled.

Lie glanced around. From which direction was it approaching? Any way they fled might lead them into its grasp! What was it? Lie shook Clu. "What is it?" Lie shouted. "Tell me!"

Scales against stones issued around the ebony bowl to their left.

"Keeeeeeowwwwwleeeeee!"

Lie's ears ached and a pain seared through his brain as each scale abraded the stones. His eyes began to blur. "What is it, Clu?" he demanded. "What is it?"

Death slithered into sight. The gray light striking its black, red edged, wings and scales, made the lizard look like it was glowing with fire. It flicked its long forked tongue in and out. "Keeeeeeowwwwwleeeeee!"

The terror in Lie died. Ire flooded through him. He spun to his right, pulling Clu along, and fled toward the city limits.

Laughter, then wings, sounded.

Lie stumbled to a stop, holding Clu to his side.

Death alighted heavily before them. It caught Lie on his forehead with its forked tongue.

Lie landed flat of his back. He felt weak and dizzy, like some of his blood had been sucked out of him. He fainted.

Death laughed and reared to trample.

Clu screamed, threw himself to his right, rolled repeatedly away from the huge claws, then scrambled to his feet and ran to Lie.

"Keeeeeeowwwwwleeeeee!"

The pitch and volume of Death's cry shook the sad city, raising dust.

Clu fell to his knees and leaned protectively over Lie. "Azophi!" Clu implored. "Azophi!"

Lie regained consciousness, noted the situation, and pulled Clu flat.

Death's tongue tore through the air where Clu's head had been, making a resounding cracking like a whip. Laughter echoed around the city, cruel and gloating. The ebony predator had its prey at its mercy and took pleasure in taunting and toying with them.

Lie rose unsteadily to his feet. The lizard's tongue caught him on a shoulder, stumbling him against one of the bowl buildings.

Clu lay as though dead.

Lie struggled to remain standing. "Baylou," he gasped, "why will you not help us?"

A soft trilling cleared the dust from the air and a sensation like pins and needles swept over the ancient city.

Death drew back, shivering.

Lie's fatigue vanished. He faced the towering saurian and raised his hands. Invisible energy erupted from his palms and slammed into Death's chest, lifting its front paws from the cobblestones for a few seconds.

"Come, mighty lizard!" he screamed, enraged. "Come to your demise! I shall crush you in my palms!"

Death howled in pain and fright.

"Torture us now, monster! Kill us!" Lie screamed, making trembling fists of fury.

Power crashed into the saurian, sending it skidding backwards a few feet. The lizard's claws tore grooves in the cobblestones.

Death convulsed as though suffering its moment of demise, frantically leaped to wing, and disappeared in the sun washed sky.

Lie felt the energy of the cache vanish.

Clu shakily stood up. "Was — was it Baylou? Or have you powers of your own?" he asked.

"I — I do not know," Lie said.

Clu gasped and pointed.

The bowl structure against which Lie had been knocked, was gone! It was Azophi's Cache, and had supplied Lie with the power to defeat Death. It had provided the light barrier which no longer limited the fire of the sun. Before it was exhausted, the Cache had healed their wounds.

"I cannot imagine what purpose Baylou had in mind

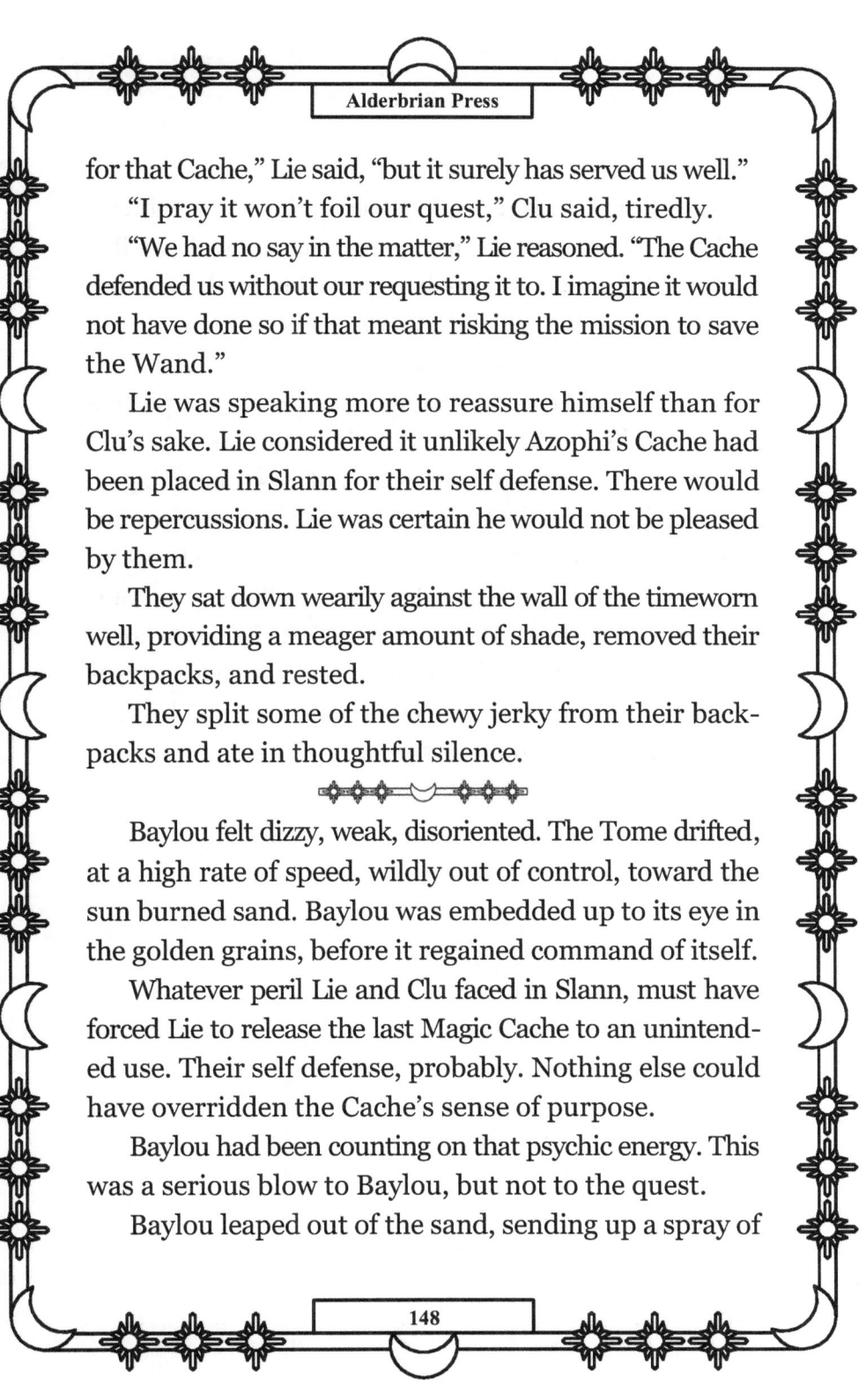

for that Cache," Lie said, "but it surely has served us well."

"I pray it won't foil our quest," Clu said, tiredly.

"We had no say in the matter," Lie reasoned. "The Cache defended us without our requesting it to. I imagine it would not have done so if that meant risking the mission to save the Wand."

Lie was speaking more to reassure himself than for Clu's sake. Lie considered it unlikely Azophi's Cache had been placed in Slann for their self defense. There would be repercussions. Lie was certain he would not be pleased by them.

They sat down wearily against the wall of the timeworn well, providing a meager amount of shade, removed their backpacks, and rested.

They split some of the chewy jerky from their backpacks and ate in thoughtful silence.

Baylou felt dizzy, weak, disoriented. The Tome drifted, at a high rate of speed, wildly out of control, toward the sun burned sand. Baylou was embedded up to its eye in the golden grains, before it regained command of itself.

Whatever peril Lie and Clu faced in Slann, must have forced Lie to release the last Magic Cache to an unintended use. Their self defense, probably. Nothing else could have overridden the Cache's sense of purpose.

Baylou had been counting on that psychic energy. This was a serious blow to Baylou, but not to the quest.

Baylou leaped out of the sand, sending up a spray of

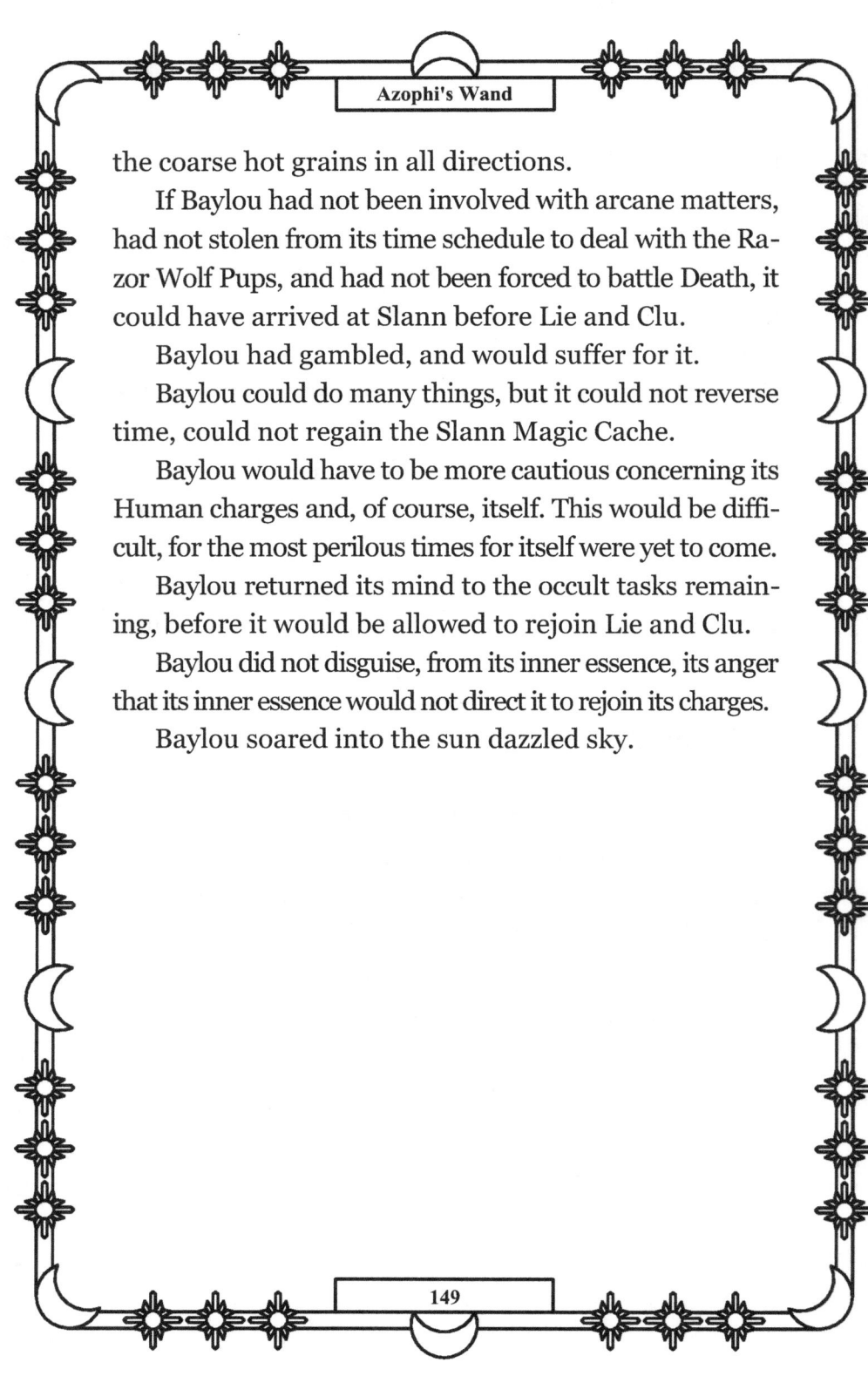

the coarse hot grains in all directions.

If Baylou had not been involved with arcane matters, had not stolen from its time schedule to deal with the Razor Wolf Pups, and had not been forced to battle Death, it could have arrived at Slann before Lie and Clu.

Baylou had gambled, and would suffer for it.

Baylou could do many things, but it could not reverse time, could not regain the Slann Magic Cache.

Baylou would have to be more cautious concerning its Human charges and, of course, itself. This would be difficult, for the most perilous times for itself were yet to come.

Baylou returned its mind to the occult tasks remaining, before it would be allowed to rejoin Lie and Clu.

Baylou did not disguise, from its inner essence, its anger that its inner essence would not direct it to rejoin its charges.

Baylou soared into the sun dazzled sky.

Illustration 16

Ortourian Beast Wrought Iron Window Grillwork

Copyright © 2019 Philip Raymond Sadler

150-A

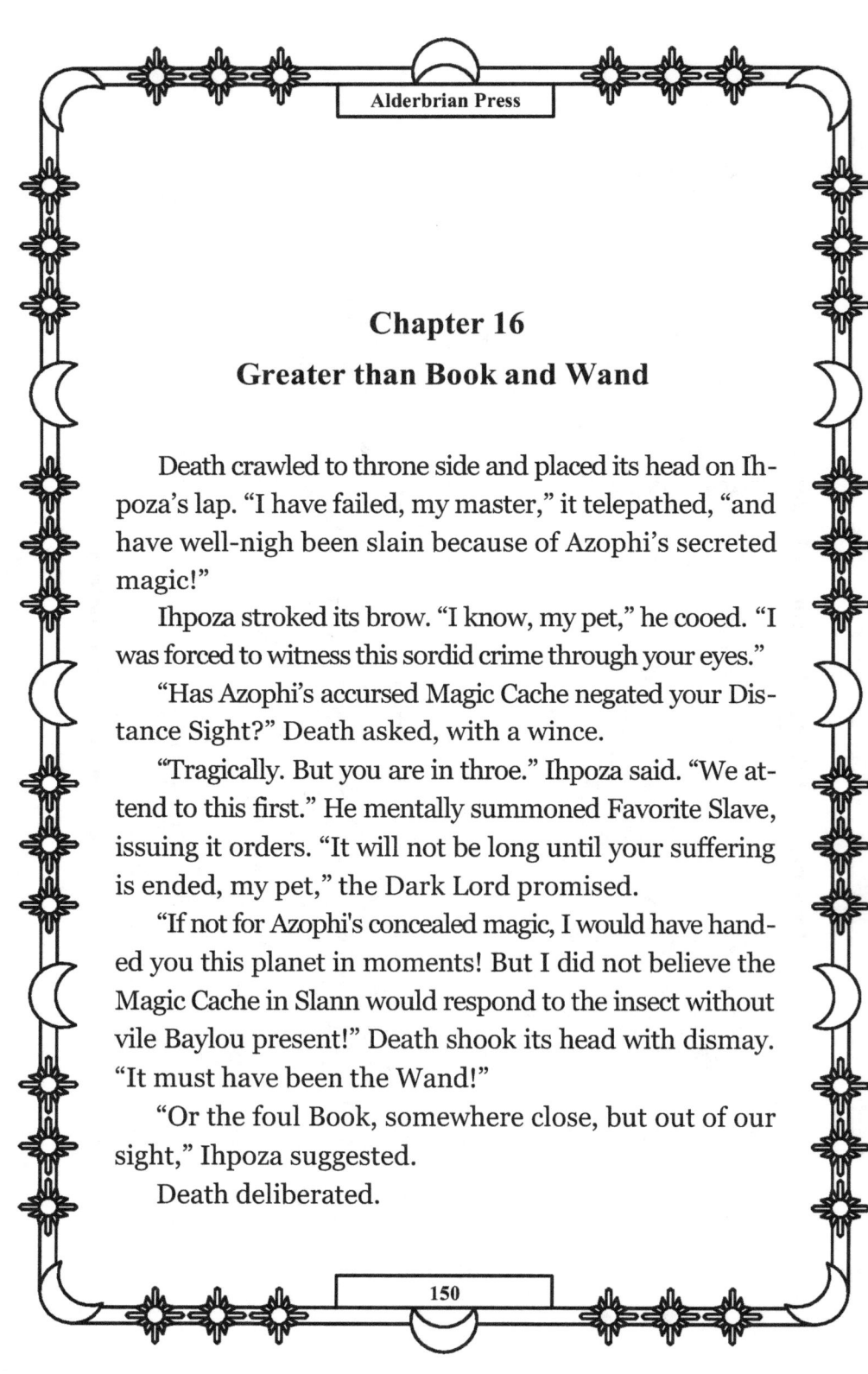

Chapter 16
Greater than Book and Wand

Death crawled to throne side and placed its head on Ihpoza's lap. "I have failed, my master," it telepathed, "and have well-nigh been slain because of Azophi's secreted magic!"

Ihpoza stroked its brow. "I know, my pet," he cooed. "I was forced to witness this sordid crime through your eyes."

"Has Azophi's accursed Magic Cache negated your Distance Sight?" Death asked, with a wince.

"Tragically. But you are in throe." Ihpoza said. "We attend to this first." He mentally summoned Favorite Slave, issuing it orders. "It will not be long until your suffering is ended, my pet," the Dark Lord promised.

"If not for Azophi's concealed magic, I would have handed you this planet in moments! But I did not believe the Magic Cache in Slann would respond to the insect without vile Baylou present!" Death shook its head with dismay. "It must have been the Wand!"

"Or the foul Book, somewhere close, but out of our sight," Ihpoza suggested.

Death deliberated.

"Yes, it was the Book. The Wand is too suitably imprisoned to influence the mind of even an insect. — No! Not the Book! Nor even the magic in Slann!"

"Yes!" Ihpoza said, with astounded understanding. "Something greater than Book and Wand!"

They exchanged looks of fear.

"We must move swiftly!" Death urged.

"Soon," Ihpoza agreed.

Death swayed side to side, with urgency. "Too much energy has been released to this superior force. We cannot, must not, allow the pure magic of the Book and Wand to be combined with it!"

Ihpoza squeezed Death's neck to calm the reptile. "Yes, the true plan unwittingly begins to reveal itself," Ihpoza said. "We will see to it, this scheme never comes to fruition. It will be difficult without my distance sight and my illusion ability, but it shall be done!"

Favorite Slave strode into the room with a blue steel spear held vertically in its claws. Two demons followed, dragging a third.

The restrained demon fought to free itself, but was no match for the guards.

Favorite Slave smiled fiendishly and bowed low. "We are ready, my gracious lord," it announced.

The guards forced the sacrifice to its back on the ice and held it down.

The hapless demon thrashed about wildly, growling and snarling in terror and rage.

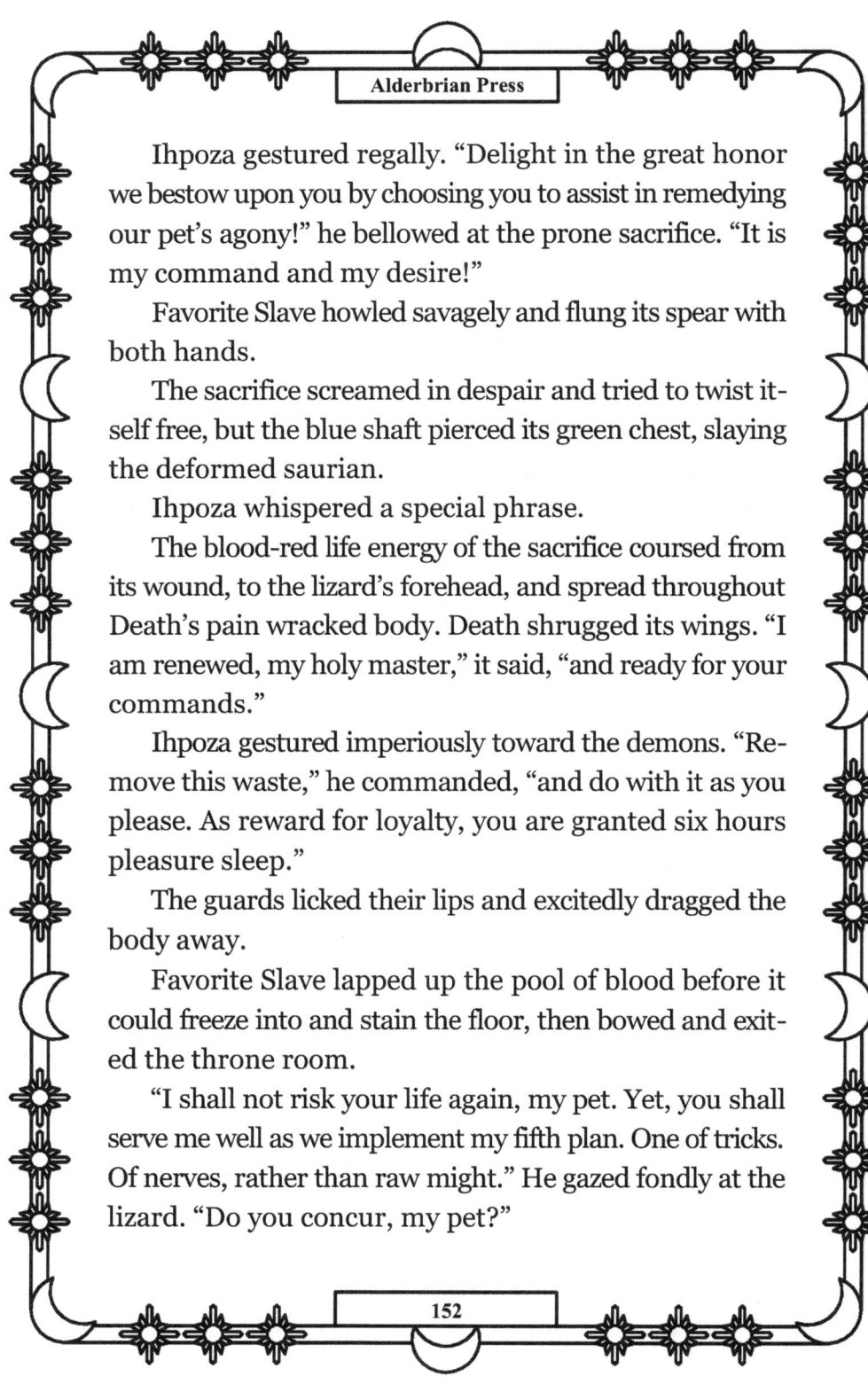

Ihpoza gestured regally. "Delight in the great honor we bestow upon you by choosing you to assist in remedying our pet's agony!" he bellowed at the prone sacrifice. "It is my command and my desire!"

Favorite Slave howled savagely and flung its spear with both hands.

The sacrifice screamed in despair and tried to twist itself free, but the blue shaft pierced its green chest, slaying the deformed saurian.

Ihpoza whispered a special phrase.

The blood-red life energy of the sacrifice coursed from its wound, to the lizard's forehead, and spread throughout Death's pain wracked body. Death shrugged its wings. "I am renewed, my holy master," it said, "and ready for your commands."

Ihpoza gestured imperiously toward the demons. "Remove this waste," he commanded, "and do with it as you please. As reward for loyalty, you are granted six hours pleasure sleep."

The guards licked their lips and excitedly dragged the body away.

Favorite Slave lapped up the pool of blood before it could freeze into and stain the floor, then bowed and exited the throne room.

"I shall not risk your life again, my pet. Yet, you shall serve me well as we implement my fifth plan. One of tricks. Of nerves, rather than raw might." He gazed fondly at the lizard. "Do you concur, my pet?"

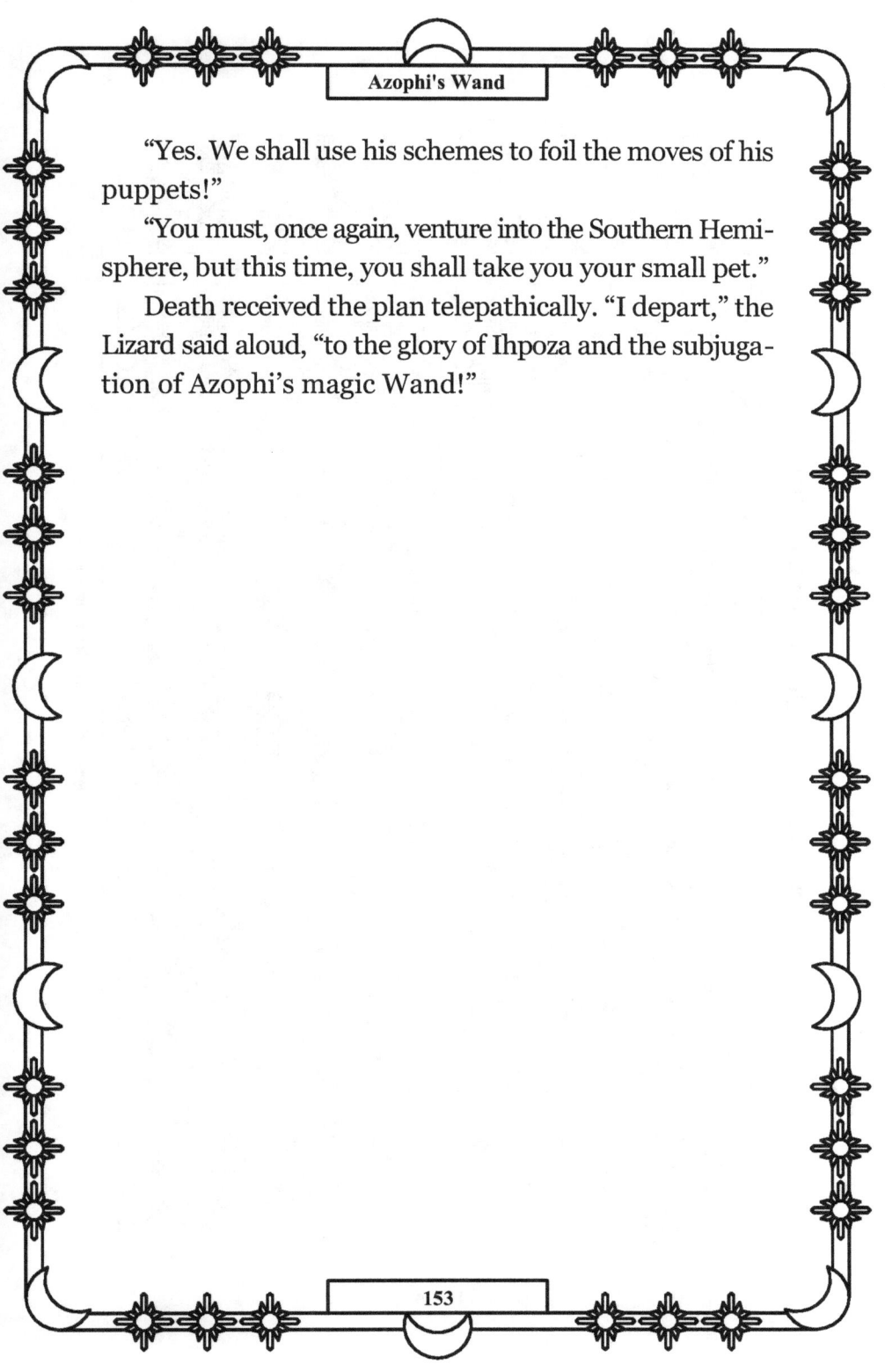

"Yes. We shall use his schemes to foil the moves of his puppets!"

"You must, once again, venture into the Southern Hemisphere, but this time, you shall take you your small pet."

Death received the plan telepathically. "I depart," the Lizard said aloud, "to the glory of Ihpoza and the subjugation of Azophi's magic Wand!"

Illustration 17

Ortourian Beast Wrought Iron Window Grillwork

Copyright © 2019 Philip Raymond Sadler

154-A

Chapter 17
Breach of Promise

From the northern side of Slann Lie and Clu could see a wood. Beyond, stood a towering projection of vivid white stone. The top of the craggy mesa was somewhat indistinct because of its altitude, but appeared flat.

Fearing Death would return before Baylou would deign to reappear, they embarked for the woods. From the brownness of the leaves, there was little water available to the trees, but that did not matter to Lie and Clu.

Lie shook his head, sadly. "Your wife fears that we are dead."

"You saw AarLee in the mirror stone?" Clu said, with surprise.

"Yes. On my front porch, with my fiancée." Lie sighed, wearily. "We were pledged to be wed yesterday. Merra-Lynn probably had all the Elders out searching the streets for me for breach of promise until they determined we left HeyTown. She believes we are alive and are on some secret errand."

"So, it was your intended who was with my AarLee. When I saw them in the mirror stone, they were talking of going to the Elders about a plan your MerraLynn has to follow after us."

"Lord! I dearly hope our families, our friends, or at least, the Elders will talk them out of that!"

"AarLee is headstrong."

"So is MerraLynn. But I feel both have good sense and will request the bailiffs search for us. The bailiffs have experience in such matters of which MerraLynn is aware. This should keep them in HeyTown while the bailiffs perform their duties."

"I surely trust so," Clu said. "Mr. Lie, with all that's happened, it's arduous to believe we are still alive. Azophi must be looking after us."

"Baylou, I would say." Lie kicked at the sand. "It thinks to teach me a lesson, but it only wastes time."

"Can we spare enough time for lunch?"

Lie chuckled, which was what Clu had intended.

"Do you have two hollow legs?" Lie asked.

"Fear makes an unhappy man sweat his food out his lucky pores. Besides, we haven't eaten in — a long time. It must be!"

"All, right, we shall sup in the cool shade of the woods."

Illustration 18

Ortourian Beast Wrought Iron Window Grillwork

Copyright © 2019 Philip Raymond Sadler

156-A

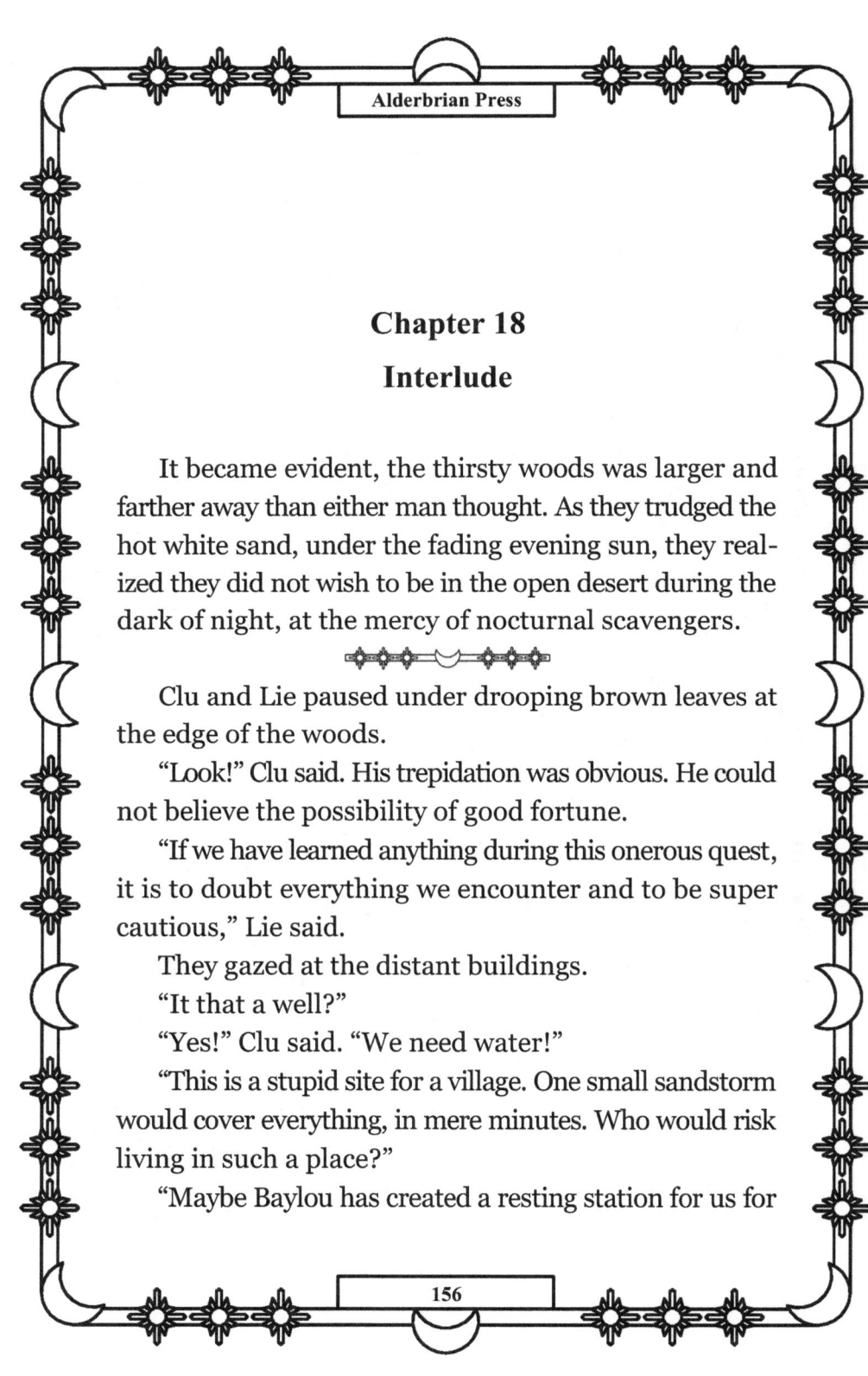

Chapter 18

Interlude

It became evident, the thirsty woods was larger and farther away than either man thought. As they trudged the hot white sand, under the fading evening sun, they realized they did not wish to be in the open desert during the dark of night, at the mercy of nocturnal scavengers.

Clu and Lie paused under drooping brown leaves at the edge of the woods.

"Look!" Clu said. His trepidation was obvious. He could not believe the possibility of good fortune.

"If we have learned anything during this onerous quest, it is to doubt everything we encounter and to be super cautious," Lie said.

They gazed at the distant buildings.

"It that a well?"

"Yes!" Clu said. "We need water!"

"This is a stupid site for a village. One small sandstorm would cover everything, in mere minutes. Who would risk living in such a place?"

"Maybe Baylou has created a resting station for us for

the night," Clu said. "Maybe the Book is waiting for us there."

Lie considered this. "It matters little how this village came to be here," he finally said. "We must have shelter for the night."

"Then, we go into the town?" Clu said.

"Yes."

Lie and Clu were exhausted and sweaty when they reached the first of the four odd, square adobe structures that faced each other at the cardinal points of the compass. They were the same modest size. Three featured the adobe steps, wooden doors, and shuttered windows of regular family domiciles. The fourth had double portals, as well as shuttered windows, but no adobe steps. The shutters and portals had been weathered to a dark gray, and were closed.

A large well, formed of worn adobe blocks, sat in the center of the tiny village.

Lie and Clu strode eagerly to the well.

"Water!" Lie said, with a gasp. He had doubted the well could be active. This explained how the trees were still half alive.

Clu started lowering the bucket with the winch arm, eager for a taste of the cool liquid.

Lie stiffened. "Horses!" he said.

Clu paused and listened. "Yes," he agreed. "Over in that building." He quickly cranked the bucket up from the water and placed it on the edge of the circular wall of the well.

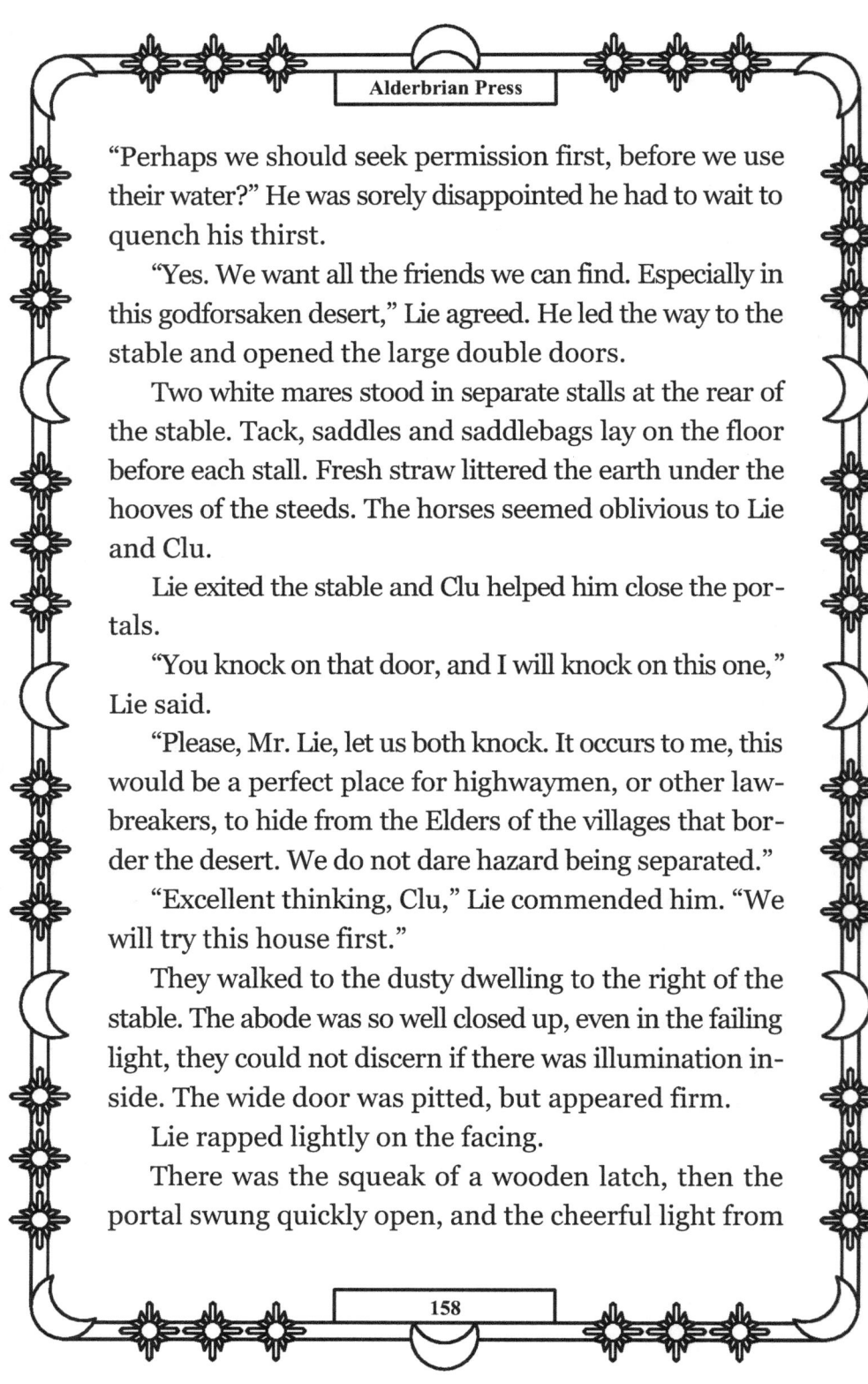

"Perhaps we should seek permission first, before we use their water?" He was sorely disappointed he had to wait to quench his thirst.

"Yes. We want all the friends we can find. Especially in this godforsaken desert," Lie agreed. He led the way to the stable and opened the large double doors.

Two white mares stood in separate stalls at the rear of the stable. Tack, saddles and saddlebags lay on the floor before each stall. Fresh straw littered the earth under the hooves of the steeds. The horses seemed oblivious to Lie and Clu.

Lie exited the stable and Clu helped him close the portals.

"You knock on that door, and I will knock on this one," Lie said.

"Please, Mr. Lie, let us both knock. It occurs to me, this would be a perfect place for highwaymen, or other law-breakers, to hide from the Elders of the villages that border the desert. We do not dare hazard being separated."

"Excellent thinking, Clu," Lie commended him. "We will try this house first."

They walked to the dusty dwelling to the right of the stable. The abode was so well closed up, even in the failing light, they could not discern if there was illumination inside. The wide door was pitted, but appeared firm.

Lie rapped lightly on the facing.

There was the squeak of a wooden latch, then the portal swung quickly open, and the cheerful light from a fireplace greeted them.

"AarLee!" Clu exclaimed with astonishment.

"Clu! Darling!" She rushed down the steps and into his arms, kissing him all over his surprised face.

"What is all the fuss!" someone said, from inside the house.

It was a soft voice intimately familiar to Lie. "Merra-Lynn!" Lie said. "How can this be!"

She stood in the tall doorway, tapping the toe of her boot in pretend annoyance. Her eyes narrowed and she slowly frowned. "Not even a polite hello!" she scolded. "Not even after rudely running off without a word and leaving me at the altar!"

Lie was taken aback. "You are not angry?" he said.

"I have known you too long, my love, to believe you would leave town without upright cause. I just cannot imagine what it was that drew you out into this awful desert." She descended the steps.

Lie took her into his arms, kissing her lovingly. Then placed his hands on her shoulders and pushed her away at arms length.

"What?" she said, with puzzlement.

"How could you have known to meet us here?" Lie asked.

"We had no idea you would be arriving here," Merra-Lynn said. "It is just a lucky coincidence. We were abandoned and lost."

"As abandoned and lost as you can get," AarLee said, stroking the hair out of Clu's eyes.

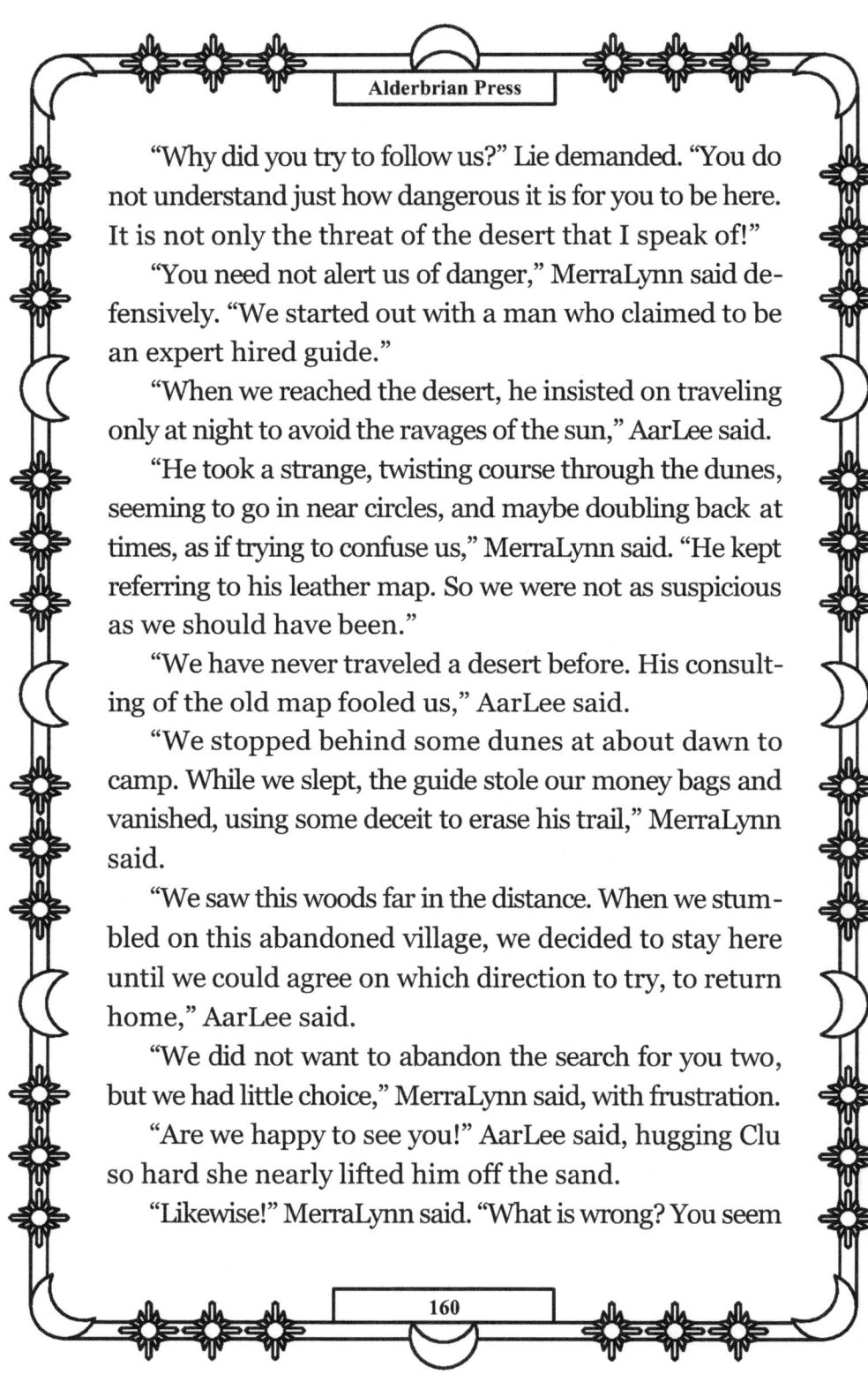

"Why did you try to follow us?" Lie demanded. "You do not understand just how dangerous it is for you to be here. It is not only the threat of the desert that I speak of!"

"You need not alert us of danger," MerraLynn said defensively. "We started out with a man who claimed to be an expert hired guide."

"When we reached the desert, he insisted on traveling only at night to avoid the ravages of the sun," AarLee said.

"He took a strange, twisting course through the dunes, seeming to go in near circles, and maybe doubling back at times, as if trying to confuse us," MerraLynn said. "He kept referring to his leather map. So we were not as suspicious as we should have been."

"We have never traveled a desert before. His consulting of the old map fooled us," AarLee said.

"We stopped behind some dunes at about dawn to camp. While we slept, the guide stole our money bags and vanished, using some deceit to erase his trail," MerraLynn said.

"We saw this woods far in the distance. When we stumbled on this abandoned village, we decided to stay here until we could agree on which direction to try, to return home," AarLee said.

"We did not want to abandon the search for you two, but we had little choice," MerraLynn said, with frustration.

"Are we happy to see you!" AarLee said, hugging Clu so hard she nearly lifted him off the sand.

"Likewise!" MerraLynn said. "What is wrong? You seem

distant?"

Lie shook himself. He gazed intently into MerraLynn's eyes. "Have you seen anything, er — unusual — since you have been here?" he asked.

"Such as?" MerraLynn said.

Clu laughed. "If you had seen it, you would know," he said.

"That is true," Lie said. He pulled his fiancée to him. "Let us go in out of the coming cold. We have much to tell you."

"You will, fixedly, not believe us!" Clu said.

Lie and MerraLynn went up the steps.

Clu led AarLee into the old adobe dwelling and closed the heavy door firmly against the unfriendly night.

Illustration 19

Ortourian Beast Wrought Iron Window Grillwork

Copyright © 2019 Philip Raymond Sadler

162-A

Chapter 19

Traces

Ihpoza stood alone in his frigid audience room, staring at his warped reflection in the mirror-smooth blue, glowing ice wall, as though he were communing with the ghastly image. He was concentrating so intently, he was shaking and drawing deep breaths.

Since he had become aware of the Book and its pawns, he had been able to sense their presence. Now, it seemed as though they had vanished.

The Book, he assumed, was masking its actuality with its Magic. The two men had no such powers. Yet, they could not be divined by any means at his disposal.

What could this betoken?

Was the Book secretly back with them, and was it masking their existence, from him?

Likely. Horribly likely.

This was an increased risk to him and his beloved pet. Without Death, he believed he would never understand the secret of obtaining the power of the Wand.

Despite the great risk, and the pain, he might be forced to sally forth to the Southern Hemisphere to preserve

Death and himself.

He controlled his breathing and placed the tip of his long barbed horn against the frozen wall. He must muster greater concentration and keener sensitivity to their essence traces. He would divine them. He could not afford to fail, especially if the Book were blinding Death and the lizard's small pet to the presence of the Tome and its pawns.

Once he discerned them, he could telepathically disclose their location to Death.

Illustration 20

Ortourian Beast Wrought Iron Window Grillwork

164-A

Chapter 20

Reading Between the Lines

Baylou stood atop the ancient, weathered winch arm of the water-less well in the city of Slann. The sun poured its heat into the Tome's green eye.

The Book was filled with confusion, fear and despair. Nowhere. Their Life Forces were nowhere on the Southern Hemisphere or Iphozalon. Only death could remove the sharp signatures of their Soul Forces from the Living World.

Baylou knew they had not perished. It would have suffered a spasm at the demise of the men so tied to its Life Essence.

The Book could detect Ihpoza's equally desperate psychic probing for Lie and Clu, could sense the Dark Lords panic and fear.

As for Lie and Clu?

If they are not dead, and they live not on the Southern Hemisphere or Iphozalon, where can they be? Without them, Baylou could not hope to succeed in its quest. If they were in danger, how could it assist them if it could not detect them?

For the first time, since its inception at the capture of Azophi's Guardian Wand, the small Tome felt alone. Helpless. Hopeless. The possibility that its noble quest was a failure, engulfed it with despair.

Baylou had searched its pages again and again, but there was no information to explain how the men could be missing and not be dead. No mention of such an eerie, terrifying phenomena.

What could it do?

Baylou closed its sad eye against the sun's merciless light. One thought filled its mind. The only possible answer. No matter how futile, senseless or hopeless it seemed, this was all that ceded hope.

Continue to Iphozalon.

Wreak as much damage as possible. Find a way. There had to be a way to fulfill its quest. It could not, would not, surrender to failure.

Baylou opened its eye and arose from the winch arm. "Azophi," it said aloud, "bless you and guide me, for without your stewardship, I shall not survive, and all that you have wrought is lost!"

Illustration 21

Ortourian Beast Wrought Iron Window Grillwork

Copyright © 2019 Philip Raymond Sadler

166-A

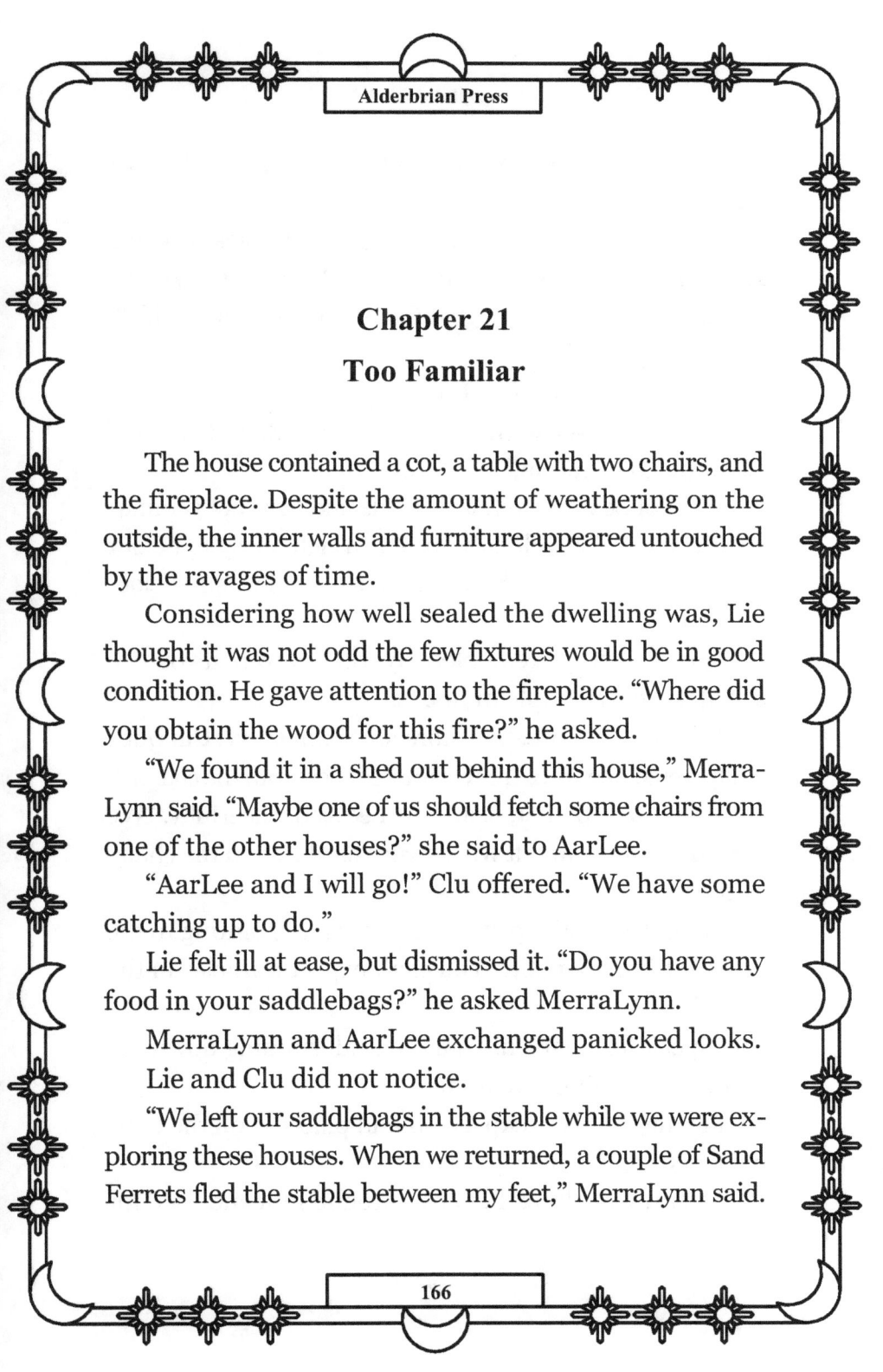

Chapter 21
Too Familiar

The house contained a cot, a table with two chairs, and the fireplace. Despite the amount of weathering on the outside, the inner walls and furniture appeared untouched by the ravages of time.

Considering how well sealed the dwelling was, Lie thought it was not odd the few fixtures would be in good condition. He gave attention to the fireplace. "Where did you obtain the wood for this fire?" he asked.

"We found it in a shed out behind this house," Merra-Lynn said. "Maybe one of us should fetch some chairs from one of the other houses?" she said to AarLee.

"AarLee and I will go!" Clu offered. "We have some catching up to do."

Lie felt ill at ease, but dismissed it. "Do you have any food in your saddlebags?" he asked MerraLynn.

MerraLynn and AarLee exchanged panicked looks. Lie and Clu did not notice.

"We left our saddlebags in the stable while we were exploring these houses. When we returned, a couple of Sand Ferrets fled the stable between my feet," MerraLynn said.

"They raided our supplies. What little food they left, we have already eaten."

"No problem," Clu said, pulling off his backpack and setting it on the wooden table. "Lie and I have lots of jerky."

AarLee laughed. "I'm glad I'm not hungry," she said, "I dislike all jerky!"

"I forgot!" Clu said. "I'm sorry."

"Let's fetch those chairs, Clu, I think MerraLynn and Lie want to be alone!"

"Do not be impolite, AarLee. Lie and I are not yet married. You and Clu will have to return right away to be our chaperons. We must observe the customs. Lie is a stickler for propriety."

"Lie!" Clu implored. "Nobody will be aware if you two are alone for a couple of hours."

Lie felt ill at ease, but more so. "I am sorry, Clu but I really would like you to return immediately with the chairs."

"Don't be a bother, dear," AarLee said, cheerfully. "We can walk slowly, and it will be very hard to find the chairs in the dark."

"Yes," Clu said, opening the door and pointing to the night for Lie's benefit. "You can't expect miracles in the dark."

"Speak for yourself," AarLee said, running down the stairs and pulling Clu along.

Lie tugged his backpack off and placed it on the table next to Clu's.

MerraLynn placed her arms around him and tried for

a kiss.

Lie shied away. "Propriety," he said, forcing a chuckle.

"Poo," she said, "that was just for their benefit. You have never been too stuffy for kissing."

"This is serious. We are in a dangerous situation. Sit down and listen carefully."

MerraLynn became frightened. "I have never known you to be like this," she said. "Sit here beside me, then, and I will not say another word until you are finished."

Illustration 22

Ortourian Beast Wrought Iron Window Grillwork

169-A

Chapter 22
Small Lights

Clu kissed AarLee on the side of her neck, then frowned. "I can barely see you in this moonlight," he said. "I think I saw a small torch in the stable. It will be needed if we go into those other houses."

"Oh, honey, forget those silly chairs. And don't fret about Lie and MerraLynn and their old conventions. They'll survive even if we don't show up in two seconds. I thought something bad had happened to you and I would never see you again. Let's just sit here by the well and watch the stars, like always."

Clu glanced at the house where Lie and MerraLynn waited, then felt AarLee nibbling his earlobe. He laughed and playfully pushed her away. "I want to see your lovely, smiling, face better," he said. "Race me to the stable!"

When Clu yanked the stable doors open, he froze, closed his eyes, rubbed them, and looked.

"What's wrong?" AarLee said, with worry.

"I'd swear your horses weren't in there a moment ago," he said. "But, there they are."

"You aren't carrying ale in that backpack of yours, are

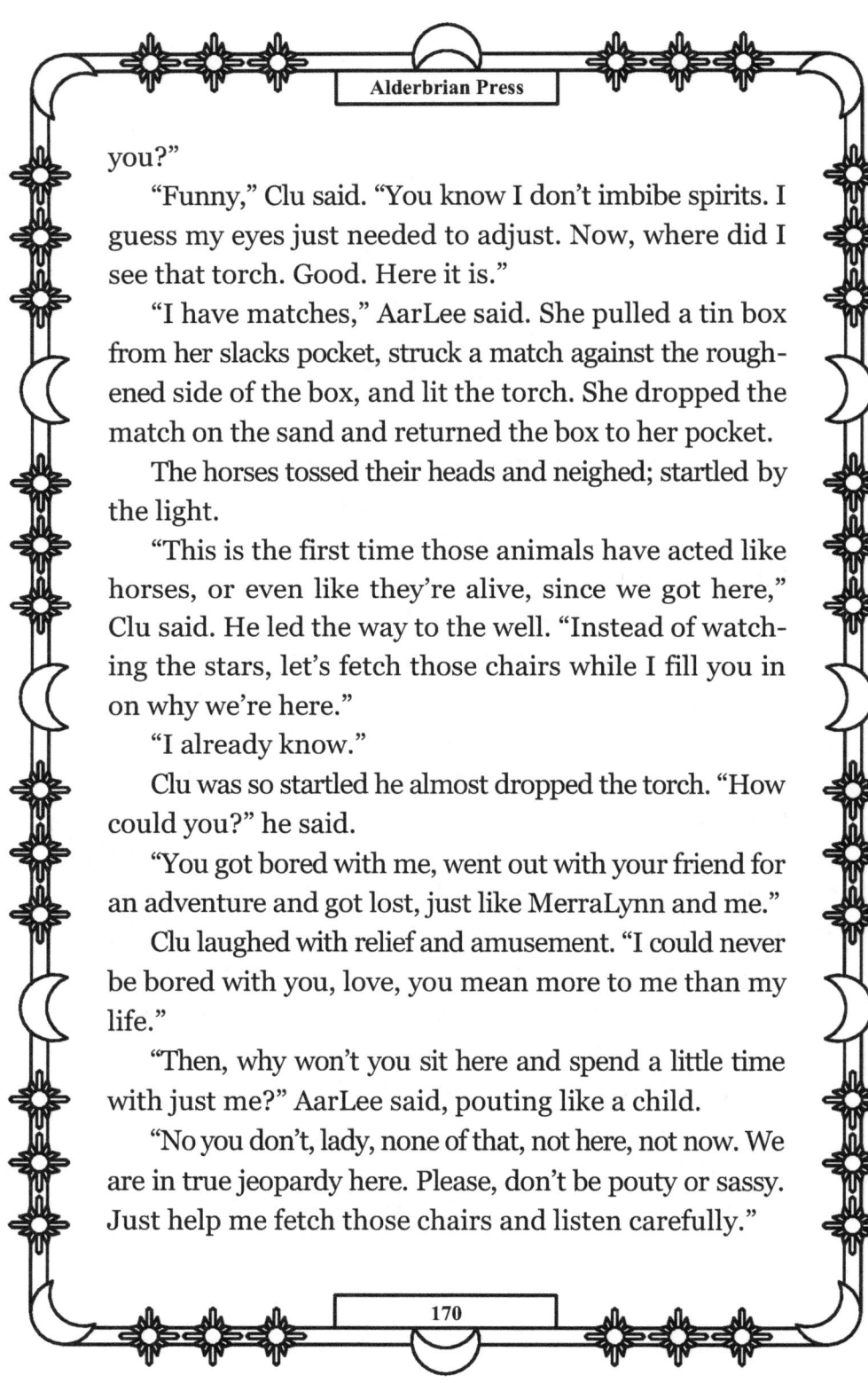

you?"

"Funny," Clu said. "You know I don't imbibe spirits. I guess my eyes just needed to adjust. Now, where did I see that torch. Good. Here it is."

"I have matches," AarLee said. She pulled a tin box from her slacks pocket, struck a match against the roughened side of the box, and lit the torch. She dropped the match on the sand and returned the box to her pocket.

The horses tossed their heads and neighed; startled by the light.

"This is the first time those animals have acted like horses, or even like they're alive, since we got here," Clu said. He led the way to the well. "Instead of watching the stars, let's fetch those chairs while I fill you in on why we're here."

"I already know."

Clu was so startled he almost dropped the torch. "How could you?" he said.

"You got bored with me, went out with your friend for an adventure and got lost, just like MerraLynn and me."

Clu laughed with relief and amusement. "I could never be bored with you, love, you mean more to me than my life."

"Then, why won't you sit here and spend a little time with just me?" AarLee said, pouting like a child.

"No you don't, lady, none of that, not here, not now. We are in true jeopardy here. Please, don't be pouty or sassy. Just help me fetch those chairs and listen carefully."

"You fetch the old chairs, I'm going in with my Mer-raLynn and Mr. Lie, they're bound to be more fun!"

"AarLee!"

She laughed gaily, ran to the house, up the stairs and inside, closing the door softly.

Clu shook his head. Her playfulness was her most irresistible quality, but not here. Better she stays inside with Lie and MerraLynn.

He strode to the nearest house and opened the door. It was so dark within, the fire of the small torch was of little benefit. It was as if the interior soaked up the friendly, reassuring glow.

When he finished searching along the walls of the empty house, he discovered the door had closed. The air was stale and musty, and it was difficult to breathe. He felt like an insect suspended in fossil amber. He shoved the door open wide, and fled from the abode.

Illustration 23

Ortourian Beast Wrought Iron Window Grillwork

Copyright © 2019 Philip Raymond Sadler

172-A

"Maybe she walked around behind the house to fetch firewood as she first intended."

"Let's get inside. That weird music is scary."

"MerraLynn said it is caused by Sand Diggers," Lie said.

"Sand Diggers! Lord, I trust not! My school instructor said Sand Diggers are extinct! When they were alive, they were three feet long, deadly poisonous, and hated Human Beings!"

"Are you certain?" Lie said.

"Yes. Our earliest ancestors eradicated them."

"Maybe they just drove them into the desert." Lie said.

"Then, we'd best get inside, now!"

They hurried to the abode and entered.

Empty.

"Now, where did they go?" Clu said, with exasperation.

"They will not stop playing silly games," Lie complained. "I explained everything to MerraLynn, and she does not seem to comprehend the danger we are facing."

"I never got that far with AarLee."

"Give me the torch. If those Sand Diggers have survived, we must warn — " Lie stopped and stared at Clu.

"What?" Clu said, with fright. He had seen that worried look on Lie's face before.

"Ever since we came here, matters have not been quite correct."

A door beside the fireplace opened.

Had that portal existed, but unnoticed because of the glare from the fireplace? Lie wondered. He found it hard

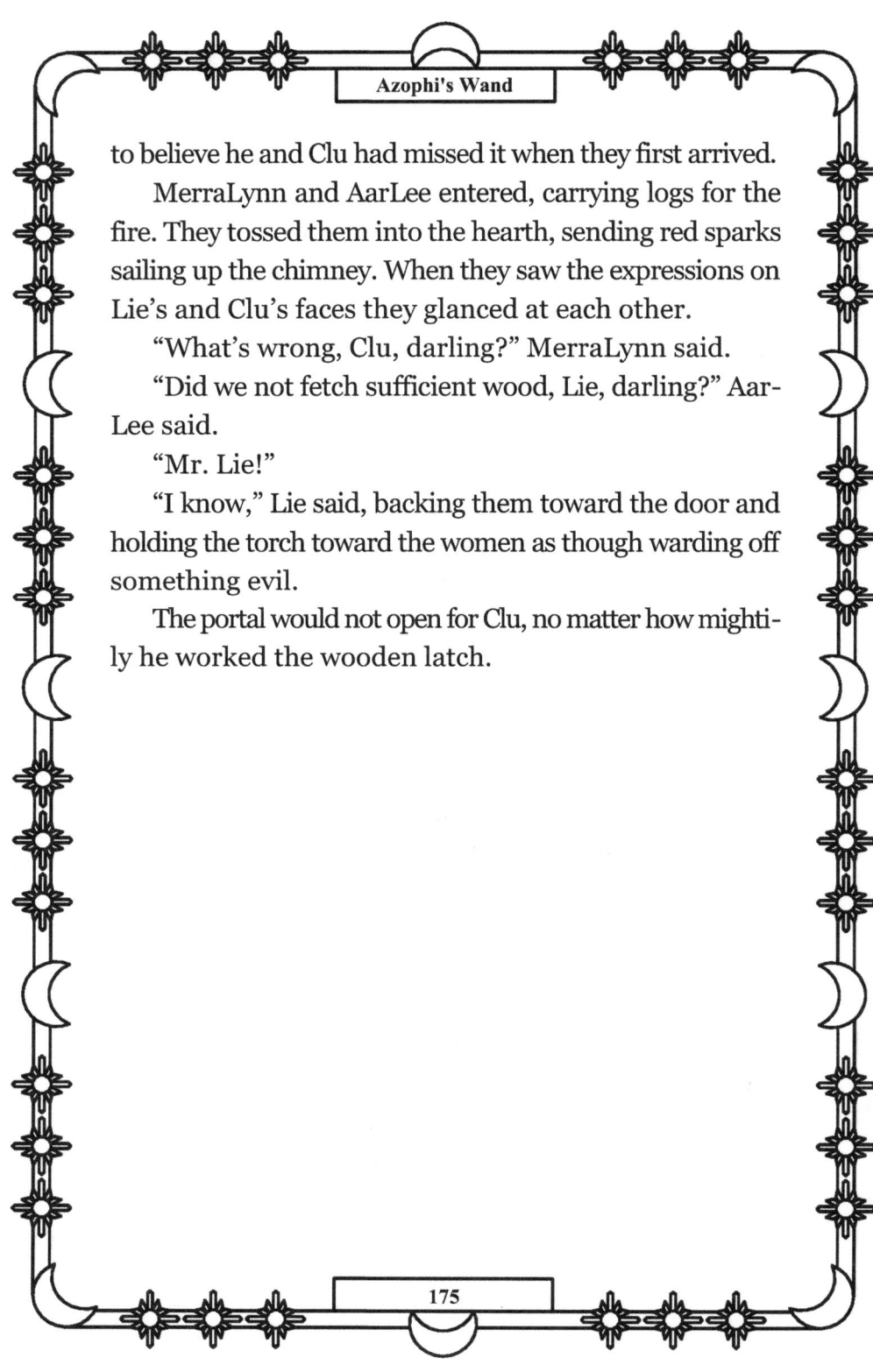

to believe he and Clu had missed it when they first arrived.

MerraLynn and AarLee entered, carrying logs for the fire. They tossed them into the hearth, sending red sparks sailing up the chimney. When they saw the expressions on Lie's and Clu's faces they glanced at each other.

"What's wrong, Clu, darling?" MerraLynn said.

"Did we not fetch sufficient wood, Lie, darling?" Aar-Lee said.

"Mr. Lie!"

"I know," Lie said, backing them toward the door and holding the torch toward the women as though warding off something evil.

The portal would not open for Clu, no matter how mightily he worked the wooden latch.

Illustration 24

176-A

Ortourian Beast Wrought Iron Window Grillwork

Copyright © 2019 Philip Raymond Sadler

Chapter 24
Twisted Trust

MerraLynn pointed a finger at the torch. "We don't need that, we have a cheery fire to warm us."

The torch extinguished as if an angry invisible hand closed its fingers around the flaming top.

Lie clutched the torch more rigidly, ready to strike, to defend them from whatever was with them.

Clu rattled the portal in its frame with his attempts to force it open, then kicked savagely at the latch, to no avail. He turned around with his back pressed against the imprisoning portal.

"Why do you deceive us? Why do you batten us in here?" Lie demanded, mastering his rage as well as he could.

MerraLynn and AarLee exchanged perplexed but delighted glances. They laughed in an eerie, slow, mirthless way. "We only wish to spend time with those we adore, we cherish, we love, we need!" they said, in sync. "Why do you play such strange games? Pretend to be frightened, worried, concerned? Relax. Enjoy the safety for the night. We will ride home to HeyTown, on the morrow." They held up their arms and stepped forward. "Come. Embrace us.

Love us. Stay with us. Yield us your warmth, your affection."

Lie swung the torch at MerraLynn, but it passed through as though she was composed of solid appearing mist.

"Not demons!" Clu shouted, with terror.

"If Ihpoza has regained his illusion ability, if these are illusions, they can not harm us," Lie said nervously.

MerraLynn flicked her fingers.

The torch flew from Lie's hand and speared into the fireplace.

Lie backed up beside Clu. "Please," Lie said, calmly, affectionately, "sit. Let us converse. The night will be long —"

MerraLynn lunged forward and grabbed Lie's wrist.

AarLee did the same to Clu.

The women's hands were as cold as ice. Their eyes were dull and stark.

"Spirits!" Clu shouted, trying to twist free of AarLee. "They can kill us!"

Lie's vexation returned. He grasped MerraLynn's free wrist. "Nonsense, Clu," he said. "There exist no records of spirits harming the living. We have nothing to worry about. We need only wait until daylight ensues. The harsh light of the sun will speed these spirits to where they belong."

MerraLynn and AarLee smiled humorlessly. "You imagine you can just discard us," they said.

Lie yanked and shoved at MerraLynn, but she did not move. "You have no power over me!" he ordered. "Release me! Release me, or I will damn you in the name of the

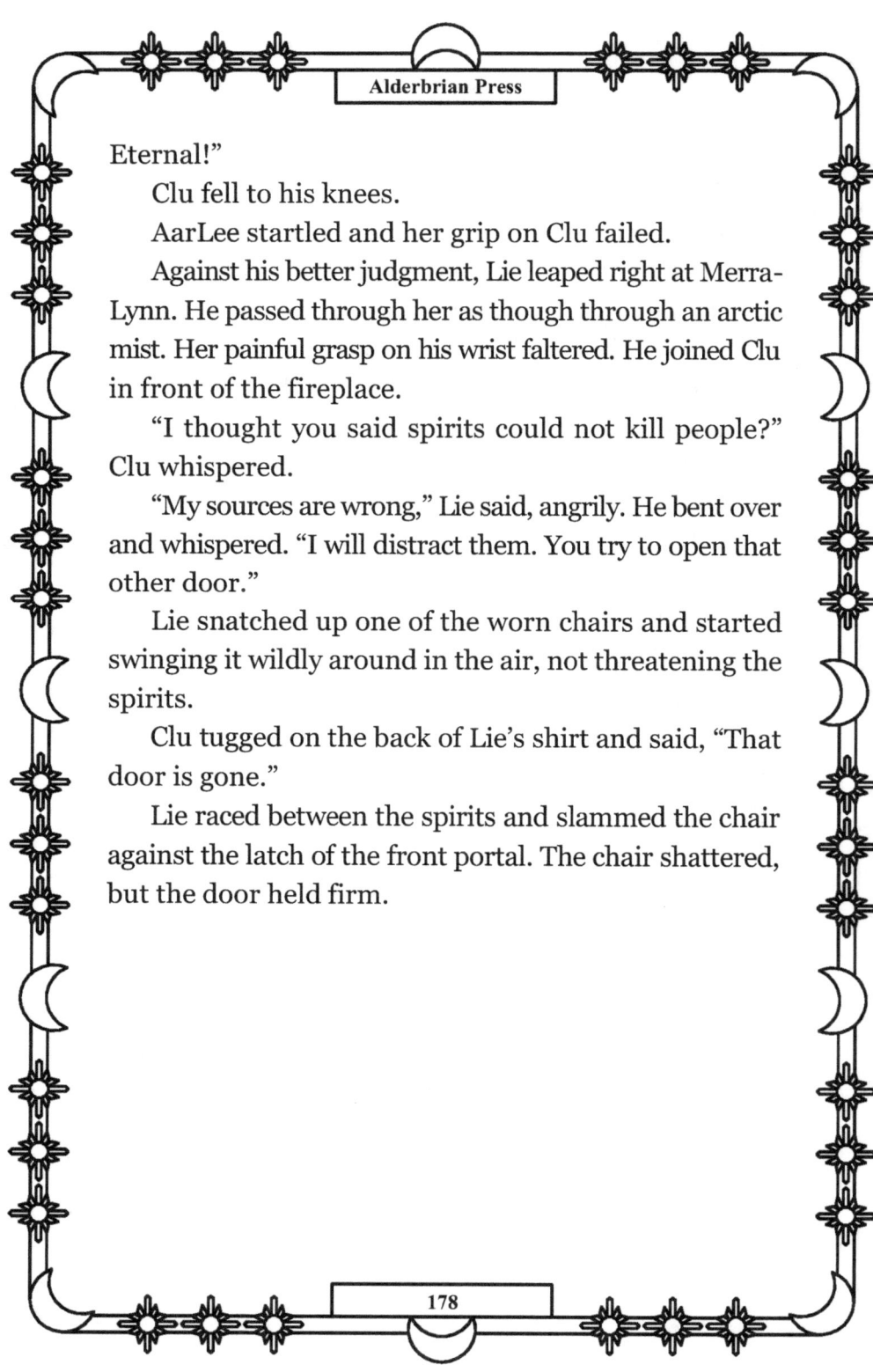

Eternal!"

Clu fell to his knees.

AarLee startled and her grip on Clu failed.

Against his better judgment, Lie leaped right at Merra-Lynn. He passed through her as though through an arctic mist. Her painful grasp on his wrist faltered. He joined Clu in front of the fireplace.

"I thought you said spirits could not kill people?" Clu whispered.

"My sources are wrong," Lie said, angrily. He bent over and whispered. "I will distract them. You try to open that other door."

Lie snatched up one of the worn chairs and started swinging it wildly around in the air, not threatening the spirits.

Clu tugged on the back of Lie's shirt and said, "That door is gone."

Lie raced between the spirits and slammed the chair against the latch of the front portal. The chair shattered, but the door held firm.

Illustration 25

Ortourian Beast Wrought Iron Window Grillwork

Copyright © 2019 Philip Raymond Sadler

179-A

Chapter 25

Dark Questions

"Baylou!" Clu begged. "We need your protection! Please! Baylou! Come and Preserve us! Or all is lost!"

The spirits spun upon Lie.

Lie dove to the floor between them, scrambled up and raced to Clu.

"Why do you wish to do us harm?" Lie demanded, taking up a chair and threatening the wraiths with it.

"Harm you?" MerraLynn said, with great sarcasm and rage. "Harm you. It is not we who harm you! It is the illness! The Sand Fever! Not us!"

"We don't have Sand Fever!" Clu shouted.

"That is what they all say," AarLee screamed. Her face contorted with rage, and she snarled like a rabid animal.

"If you believe them, then you take sick and die as well!" MerraLynn shouted, through clenched teeth.

"The only way to protect yourself, is to lock them up. Abandon them. Turn your back on them. Let the unclean die as the Eternal wills," AarLee screamed.

The apparitions appeared more solid. They stepped away from each other, then slid eerily toward the men.

They watched Lie and Clu like beasts preparing to claw them to death.

Lie slammed the feet the legs of his chair against the floor. "You are not my MerraLynn!" he shouted. "You are not Clu's AarLee! Reveal yourselves! Who are you!"

Clu picked up a chair and began banging the feet of its legs against the floor. "Who are you?" he shouted, in sync with Lie. "Who are you?"

"How dare you?" AarLee screamed, affronted. "You, who betrayed us! You, who murdered us! You know who we are!"

"You know all too well who we are!" MerraLynn shrieked. She dashed forth and clawed at Lie's cheek with pointed finger nails.

Lie ducked and shoved MerraLynn back with one hand. It felt as though he was pushing a lead statue over rough stone. He quickly stepped backwards and resumed banging the feet of the legs of his chair against the wooden floor in unison with Clu.

The thumping sounds appeared to disorient the apparitions.

"You are not my AarLee!" Clu screamed. "You have no right to thieve and foul her appearance! To dishonor her name with your crimes!"

Clu's anger was so intense, Lie felt a chill down his spine. "Reveal yourselves!" Lie shouted. "If you have been wronged, we shall try to rectify the injustice! We cannot do so if we do not know who you are!"

"No more tricks!" MerraLynn screamed. "Just die! Just Die!" She tried to dodge around Lie's chair, but he foiled each attempt. She ululated like a suffering animal and slid over to AarLee. "Join with me, my sister, to destroy these monsters!"

MerraLynn merged with AarLee and the blended spirit doubled its height and girth, retaining the appearance of AarLee.

Clu was trembling with fury and insult that the wraith was using AarLee's likeness. He lunged forward and slammed his chair against the specter's shoulder. The chair shattered.

The spirit lifted Clu into the air, almost pressing Clu's back against the adobe of the ceiling.

"Damn you, Baylou! Damn you, Azophi! If Clu dies, your quest dies!" Lie screamed. He tossed his chair aside and hurled himself at the specter's legs.

The spirit's feet slipped from beneath it, and it fell forward on its face, sounding like solid stone striking the dusty wooden floor. It did not release Clu.

Clu had landed on his feet. He struggled against the iron grasp the spirit had on his shoulders, but to no avail.

Lie straddled the massive specter's back, wrapped his arms around its neck, and yanked its head backward. "If you must kill," he screamed, "then kill me! Kill me! I yield my life to you for wrongs committed against you!"

The spirit went limp.

Clu ran backwards from the ghost's huge hands and

came around beside Lie. "What are you doing?" he shouted. "We have to fight!"

The specter hove upright, like a spring-loaded lever released, throwing Lie against the door.

Clu raced to his side and helped him to his feet.

The apparition rotated toward them. "This you will do to atone for your sins?" it asked, using MerraLynn's soft voice. "Cede to us, your life's essence?"

"Yes!" Lie shouted. "But, not to false images! Only to the true images of those who have been wronged! Only then, shall I yield my life!"

Electricity crept through the room. The apparition wavered and split in half. Two aged women in dirty, tattered dresses and worn sandals, stood before the men. Their skin was blemished with the purplish spots of Sand Fever, which gave them a nightmarish appearance. They were stooped and pain lined their faces. Their eyes were dull and filled with despair. They raised trembling, withered hands toward Lie.

"If we are to correct the injustices committed against you," Lie said, "you must state your full names to be properly recorded. You must list the crimes. The names of those who have wronged you must be written down so that all decent people will hearken."

"Why must we name the accused, who stand before us and denote to them the crimes they know they have committed against us?" The left spirit asked, angrily and impatiently.

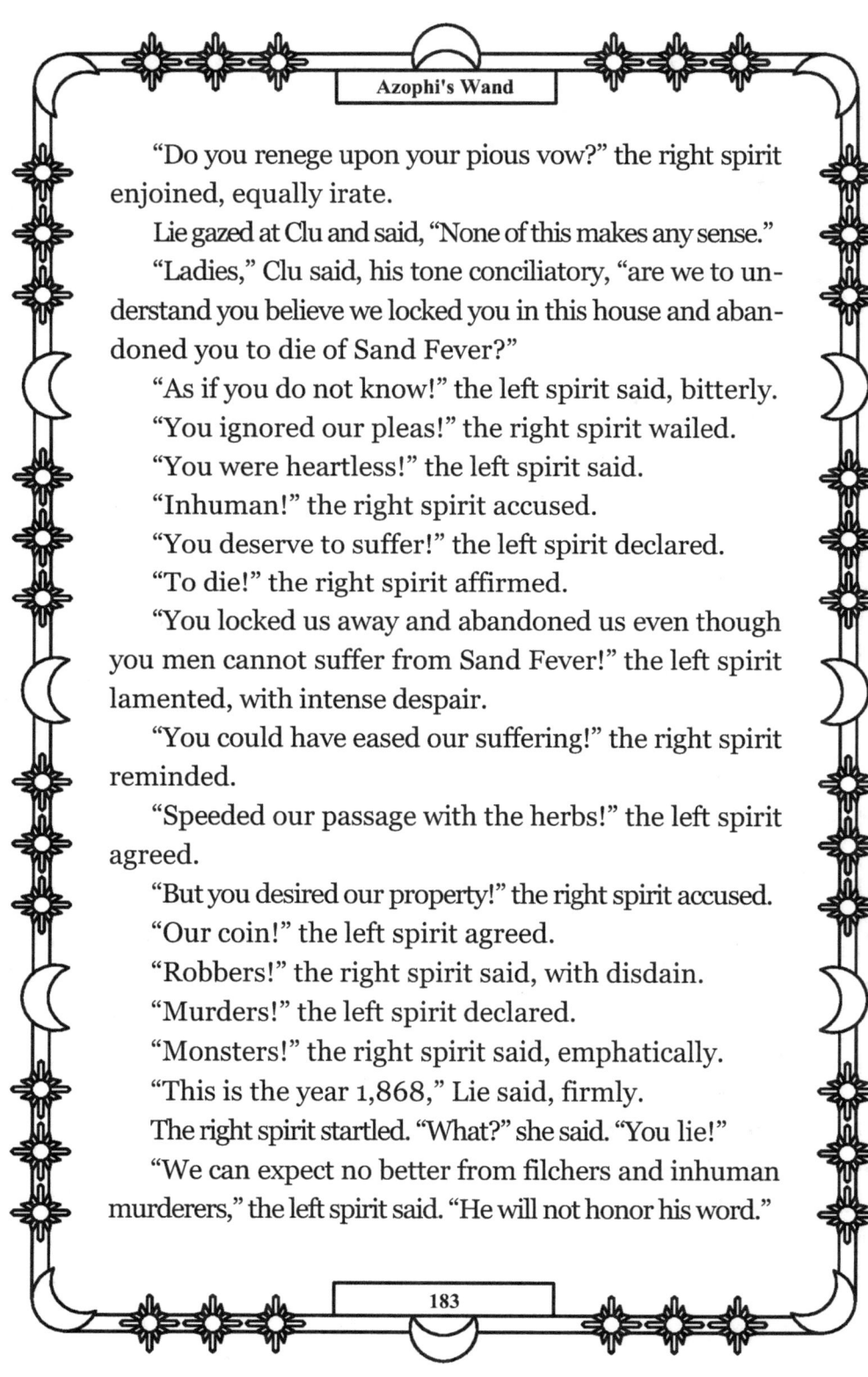

"Do you renege upon your pious vow?" the right spirit enjoined, equally irate.

Lie gazed at Clu and said, "None of this makes any sense."

"Ladies," Clu said, his tone conciliatory, "are we to understand you believe we locked you in this house and abandoned you to die of Sand Fever?"

"As if you do not know!" the left spirit said, bitterly.

"You ignored our pleas!" the right spirit wailed.

"You were heartless!" the left spirit said.

"Inhuman!" the right spirit accused.

"You deserve to suffer!" the left spirit declared.

"To die!" the right spirit affirmed.

"You locked us away and abandoned us even though you men cannot suffer from Sand Fever!" the left spirit lamented, with intense despair.

"You could have eased our suffering!" the right spirit reminded.

"Speeded our passage with the herbs!" the left spirit agreed.

"But you desired our property!" the right spirit accused.

"Our coin!" the left spirit agreed.

"Robbers!" the right spirit said, with disdain.

"Murders!" the left spirit declared.

"Monsters!" the right spirit said, emphatically.

"This is the year 1,868," Lie said, firmly.

The right spirit startled. "What?" she said. "You lie!"

"We can expect no better from filchers and inhuman murderers," the left spirit said. "He will not honor his word."

"Kill him!" the right spirit demanded.

"Slay them both!" the left spirit agreed.

"We are on a quest to rescue the Wand of Azophi, and to destroy the demon Ihpoza," Lie said. "The men who betrayed you have long since died. Just as you are dead."

The spirits stood staring hatefully at the men.

"I am Clu, the Messenger. I hale from HeyTown."

"I am Lie, an author of novels, also from HeyTown. We truly mean you no malice. We — "

"Dead!" the left spirit said, stunned. "Our husbands are dead!"

"Your husbands!" Clu said, with a sick feeling in his stomach.

"When?" the right spirit demanded. "When did they die? How came they to expire? Did you witness this? What proof do you have?"

"Your own husbands robbed and abandoned you to perish?" Clu said, with disgust.

"Yes!" both spirits shrieked, with grief. "We loved them! But they loved only possessions!"

Lie gasped at the breakthrough. They are speaking with us as ourselves, he thought, instead of as their husbands. He carefully listened to Clu.

"Tell us their names," Clu said.

"Barlance of Var," the left spirit said, in a sad whisper. "Strong and handsome. Who would have suspected his heart was dark and pitiless."

"And your husband, matron?" Clu asked, his tone respectful and polite.

"Stence of Var," the right spirit said. "Refined and quiet. Gentle. Kind. A fiend in the guise of an angel."

"You are dead," Lie said, softly. "Your husbands are dead. There is no reason for you to remain in this unhappy place. Go to the Light."

The left spirit startled. "What? What say you?" she asked.

"Look for the Light of Completion," Lie said, firmly. "It hovers before you, guides you, welcomes you away from the tragedy which fetters you to this place, and bears you into the happiness and rest beyond this world."

"Completion," the left spirit said. She shook her sad companion by the shoulders. "Completion! MaLiea!" she said.

"Completion! Ahh, LaVoyal, the brightness warms me, fills me with joy. The joy of before, when love was new and had honor."

LaVoyal held her hands out to her friend. "Come MaLiea. I can see the Elders who hold golden places for us. They beckon! They call!"

MaLiea took her companion's hands, and they walked toward the fireplace. Before they had taken three paces, the spirits misted out of sight.

The fire in the hearth vanished and the house became pitch dark. The front portal swung open, hanging half broken from its hinges. The house started creaking because the adobe was cracking and crumbling around them.

Lie and Clu fled into the night as the house crashed on its floor with a loud, tragic sound.

Lie and Clu paused, turned around, and listened.

Only the strident outcries of the Sand Diggers could be heard in the distance.

Illustration 26

Ortourian Beast Wrought Iron Window Grillwork

Copyright © 2019 Philip Raymond Sadler

187-A

Chapter 26
Recurring DayMare

The sinking sensation in the pit of Lie's stomach was like nothing he had experienced. "I thought the brutal Sand Diggers were part of the Spectral Infestation," he whispered, "and they would vanish when those poor souls passed over."

"Can Sand Diggers climb trees?" Clu asked.

"Regular crickets can. They can also fly, and leap long distances. If all those houses have crumbled like the one we were in, we have no haven anywhere." He noted a slight orange shine in the sand at the toes of his boots. "Danger!" he shouted, dragging Clu back several feet.

Clu stepped behind Lie.

The San Digger's head emerged from the sand. Its antennas undulated wildly.

"They sense movement with their antennas," Clu whispered. "They smell with their feet."

"How do they sting?"

"Their antennas have stingers on the end, and they have one stinger on the rear, like bees," Clu said. "It sensed our footsteps, so it knows we are near. If we move away, it will hone in on us. If it emerges fully from the sand, it will scent

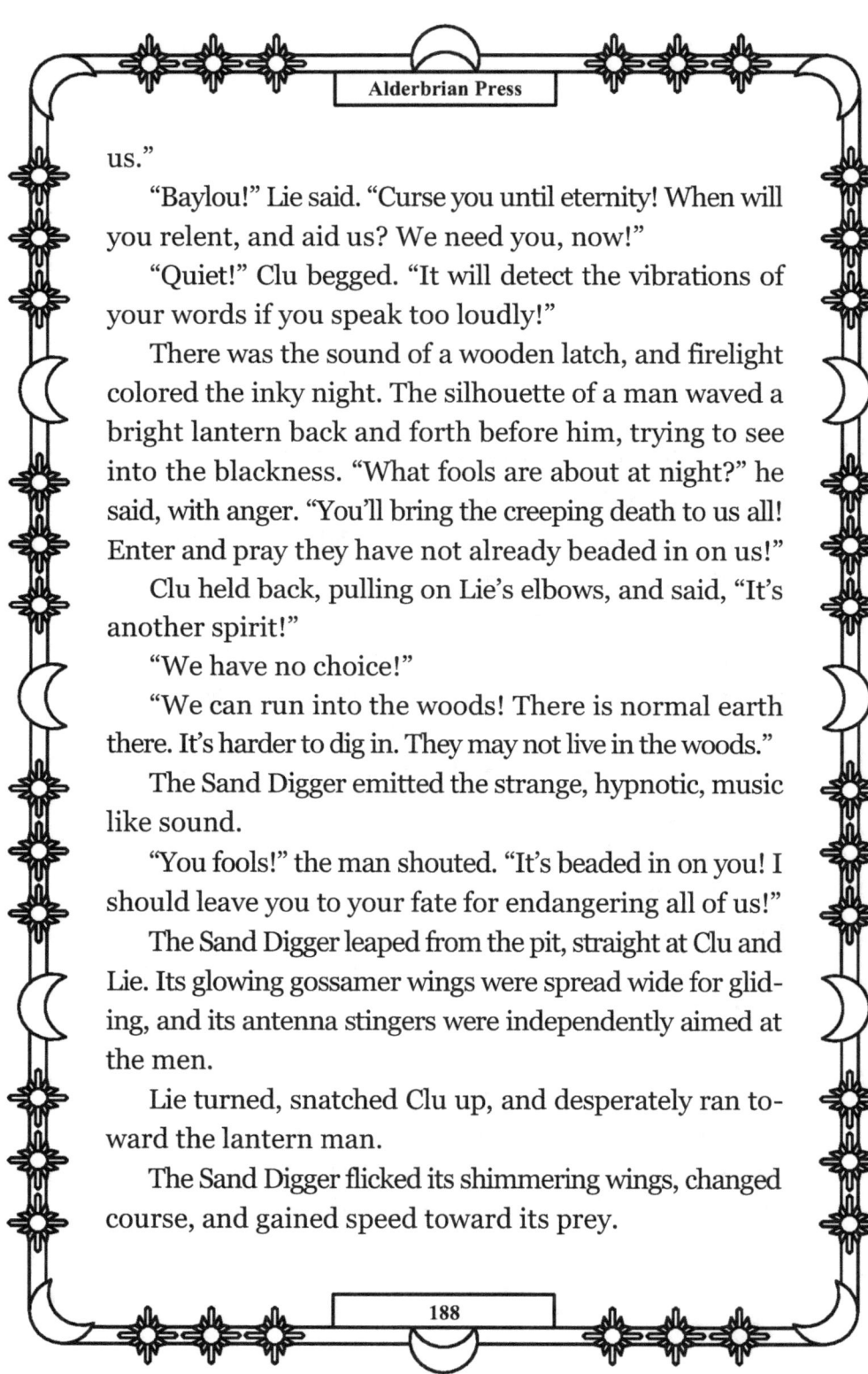

us."

"Baylou!" Lie said. "Curse you until eternity! When will you relent, and aid us? We need you, now!"

"Quiet!" Clu begged. "It will detect the vibrations of your words if you speak too loudly!"

There was the sound of a wooden latch, and firelight colored the inky night. The silhouette of a man waved a bright lantern back and forth before him, trying to see into the blackness. "What fools are about at night?" he said, with anger. "You'll bring the creeping death to us all! Enter and pray they have not already beaded in on us!"

Clu held back, pulling on Lie's elbows, and said, "It's another spirit!"

"We have no choice!"

"We can run into the woods! There is normal earth there. It's harder to dig in. They may not live in the woods."

The Sand Digger emitted the strange, hypnotic, music like sound.

"You fools!" the man shouted. "It's beaded in on you! I should leave you to your fate for endangering all of us!"

The Sand Digger leaped from the pit, straight at Clu and Lie. Its glowing gossamer wings were spread wide for gliding, and its antenna stingers were independently aimed at the men.

Lie turned, snatched Clu up, and desperately ran toward the lantern man.

The Sand Digger flicked its shimmering wings, changed course, and gained speed toward its prey.

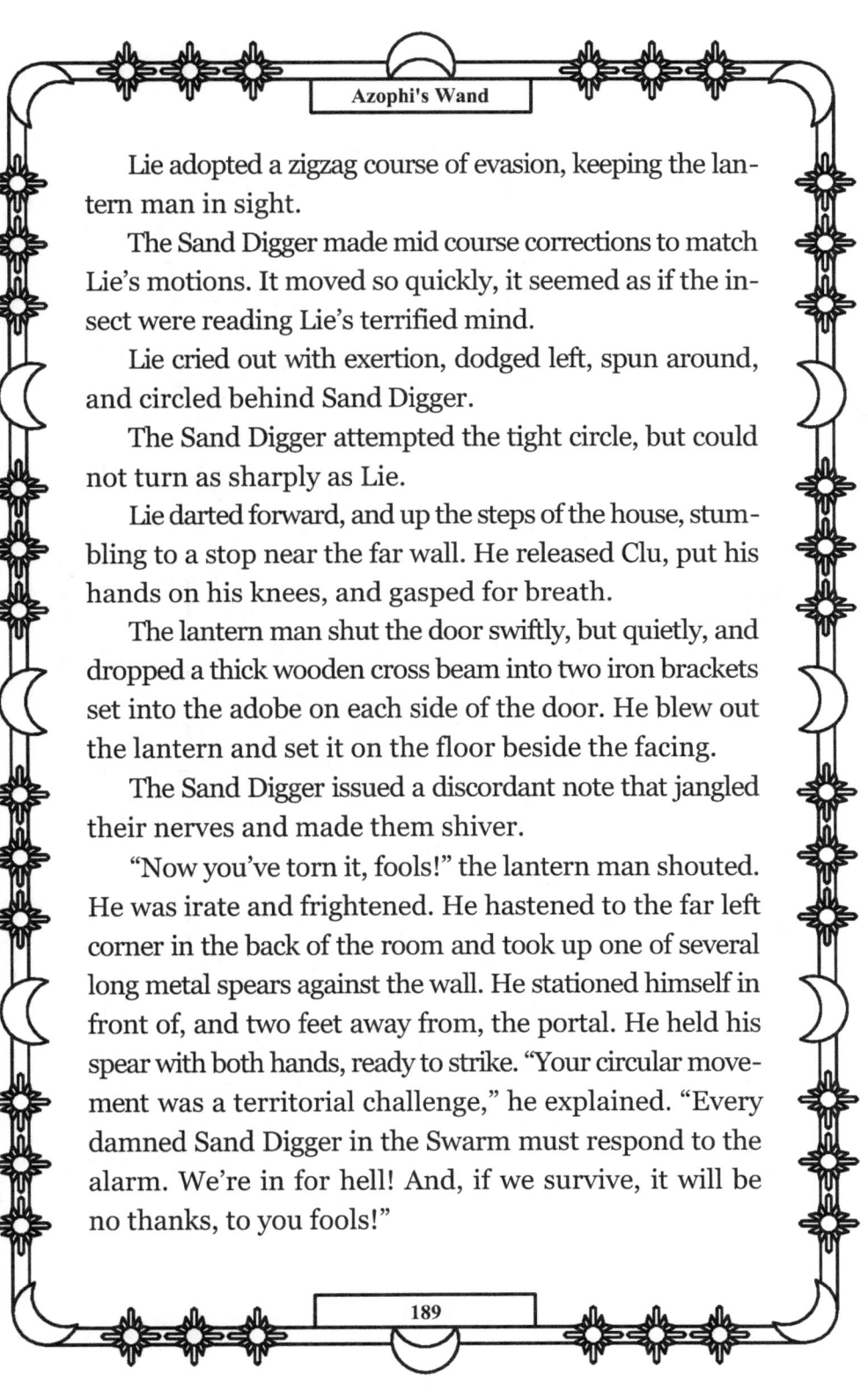

Lie adopted a zigzag course of evasion, keeping the lantern man in sight.

The Sand Digger made mid course corrections to match Lie's motions. It moved so quickly, it seemed as if the insect were reading Lie's terrified mind.

Lie cried out with exertion, dodged left, spun around, and circled behind Sand Digger.

The Sand Digger attempted the tight circle, but could not turn as sharply as Lie.

Lie darted forward, and up the steps of the house, stumbling to a stop near the far wall. He released Clu, put his hands on his knees, and gasped for breath.

The lantern man shut the door swiftly, but quietly, and dropped a thick wooden cross beam into two iron brackets set into the adobe on each side of the door. He blew out the lantern and set it on the floor beside the facing.

The Sand Digger issued a discordant note that jangled their nerves and made them shiver.

"Now you've torn it, fools!" the lantern man shouted. He was irate and frightened. He hastened to the far left corner in the back of the room and took up one of several long metal spears against the wall. He stationed himself in front of, and two feet away from, the portal. He held his spear with both hands, ready to strike. "Your circular movement was a territorial challenge," he explained. "Every damned Sand Digger in the Swarm must respond to the alarm. We're in for hell! And, if we survive, it will be no thanks, to you fools!"

Illustration 27

Ortourian Beast Wrought Iron Window Grillwork

Copyright © 2019 Philip Raymond Sadler

190-A

Chapter 27
To the Point

Lie drew Clu near him and said, "I do not think this is a spirit. He is dealing with us in a normal fashion."

"That man was not in this house when I searched it. Where did he come from so conveniently?"

"Perhaps he was out on business of which we are ignorant, and returned while we were being haunted by the old women?" Lie suggested.

"I hope he is a spirit."

"Why?"

"When dawn comes, he'll vanish, along with the savage Sand Diggers!"

"Don't just laze there! Arm yourselves! Remain vigilant! A moment's hesitation and you'll fry from the inside out from their venom! I don't intend to die because of you!"

Lie and Clu took up javelins and stood on either side of their host.

"What fools do I have to depend upon!" the lantern man implored of the heavens. He gestured left and right with his spear. "Defend the windows in case those fatal fryers breach the shutters! Use your pitiful brains!"

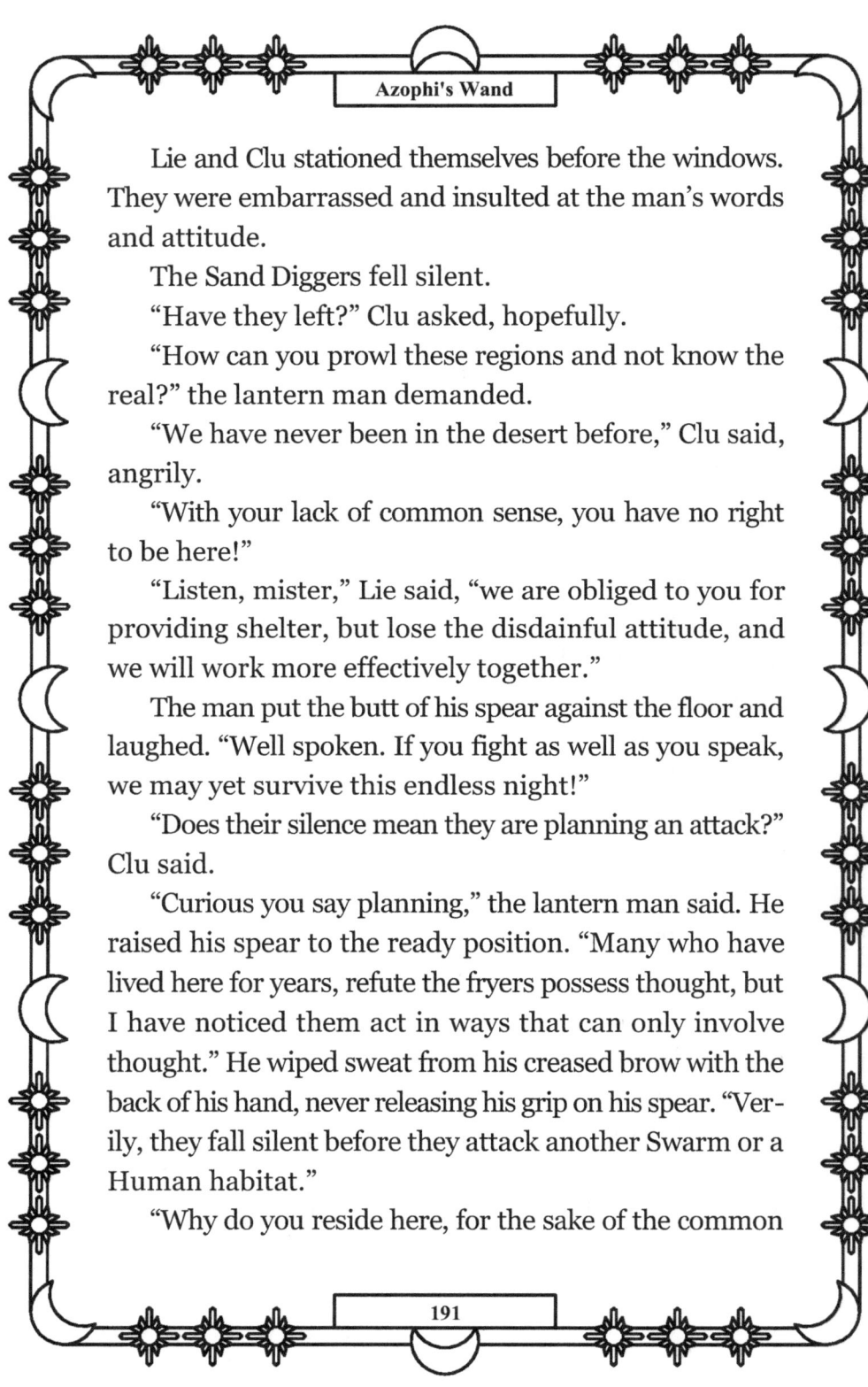

Lie and Clu stationed themselves before the windows. They were embarrassed and insulted at the man's words and attitude.

The Sand Diggers fell silent.

"Have they left?" Clu asked, hopefully.

"How can you prowl these regions and not know the real?" the lantern man demanded.

"We have never been in the desert before," Clu said, angrily.

"With your lack of common sense, you have no right to be here!"

"Listen, mister," Lie said, "we are obliged to you for providing shelter, but lose the disdainful attitude, and we will work more effectively together."

The man put the butt of his spear against the floor and laughed. "Well spoken. If you fight as well as you speak, we may yet survive this endless night!"

"Does their silence mean they are planning an attack?" Clu said.

"Curious you say planning," the lantern man said. He raised his spear to the ready position. "Many who have lived here for years, refute the fryers possess thought, but I have noticed them act in ways that can only involve thought." He wiped sweat from his creased brow with the back of his hand, never releasing his grip on his spear. "Verily, they fall silent before they attack another Swarm or a Human habitat."

"Why do you reside here, for the sake of the common

sense you so value?" Lie asked.

The lantern man stared at Lie as though Lie were insane.

"We are city people," Clu said. "We know nothing of the frontiers."

"Like the others," the lantern man said, "I seek the lavish veins of gold, for the taking, that lie in the rock strata beneath the sands."

"Why do the Sand Diggers live here?" Lie asked.

"The gold."

"What?" both Lie and Clu said.

"Their venom not only slays their competing Swarms, it liquefies the veins of gold, so they can siphon it into their stomachs."

"What a marvel!" Lie said.

"What a waste of good gold!" Clu said, fervently.

"My sentiments, exactly," the lantern man agreed. "Why do you men trek here?" he asked, returning his attention to the door.

Lie and Clu half turned and looked at each other, silently asking one another the same question.

From three hundred sixty degrees, a sound like war trumpets, startled them.

"It begins," the lantern man said, sad and forlorn. "We knew they would tolerate us for only so long. Your blundering has spurred their final assault. Tonight, If they fail to finish us off, they must cede this sector, for twenty miles in all directions, to us. If we fail, we die."

The loud trumpeting re-sounded, coming in waves similar to the rhythms adopted by normal crickets.

"We were taught Sand Diggers were extinct," Clu said, fretfully. "I wonder what else in our teachings is false."

Something thudded into the door, shaking the house.

Lie gasped. "Was that a Sand Digger?" he asked.

"Aye," the lantern man said.

"If we are to die here, on this cold night," Clu said, "may we know your name?"

Two house shuddering thuds struck each pair of shutters, creaking the thick, weathered boards.

The door was impacted again.

"Eerak, of Derin. Now of this godforsaken place," the man said.

"I am Lie, of HeyTown."

"I am Clu, of the same."

Sand Diggers slammed into the windows and door. The men heard claws scratching on the sides of the house, and on the roof.

"This is what I had feared most!" Eerak lamented. "There are more than enough of these brutes to crush the ceiling with their weight. If they have realized this, we have no hope!"

The trumpeting achieved higher octave.

Lie and Clu were startled by someone knocking on the door.

"Not this time, you demonic pests," Eerak said, with a wry smile. "You fooled Eerak once, with that ploy, but not

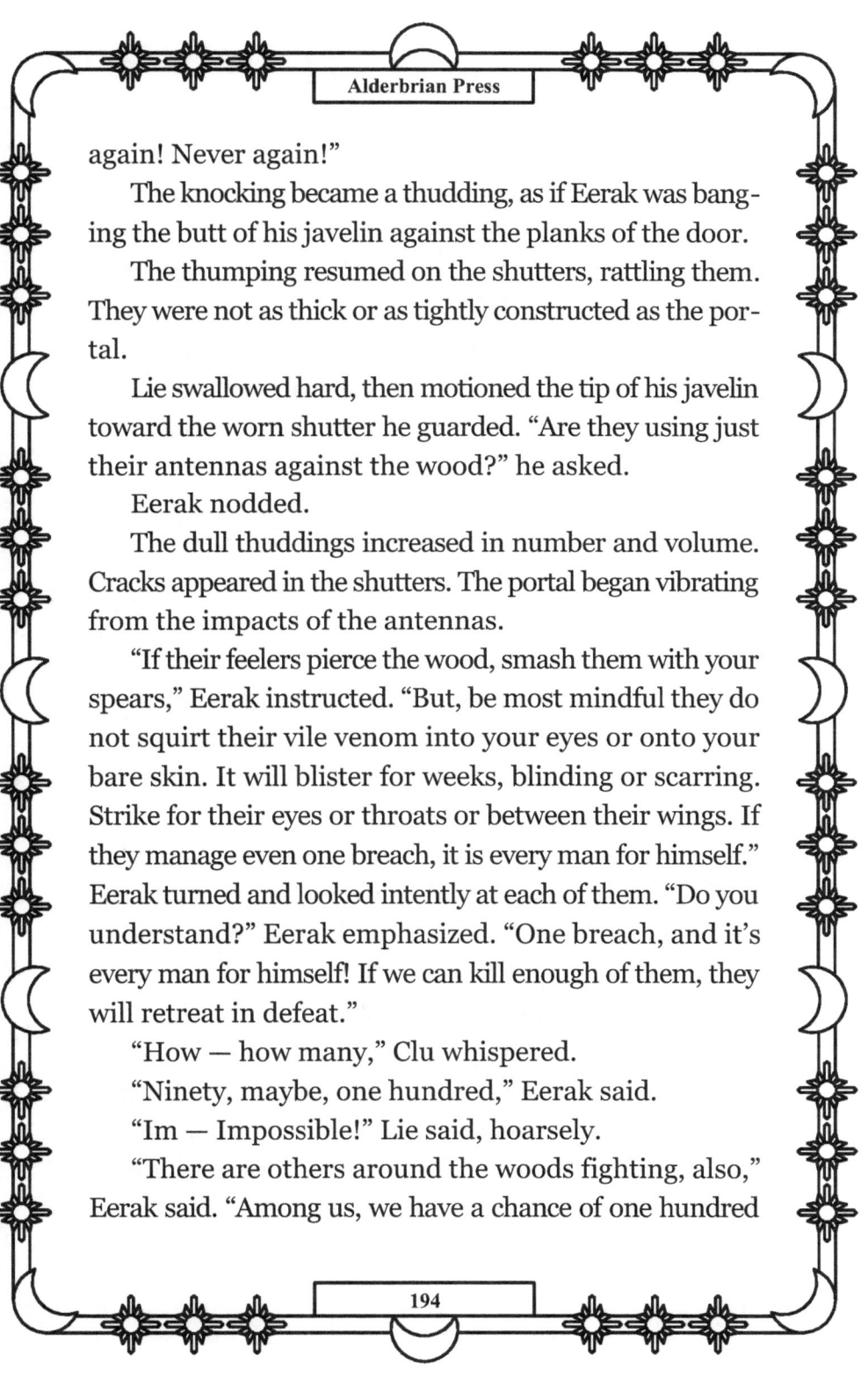

again! Never again!"

The knocking became a thudding, as if Eerak was bang-ing the butt of his javelin against the planks of the door.

The thumping resumed on the shutters, rattling them. They were not as thick or as tightly constructed as the por-tal.

Lie swallowed hard, then motioned the tip of his javelin toward the worn shutter he guarded. "Are they using just their antennas against the wood?" he asked.

Eerak nodded.

The dull thuddings increased in number and volume. Cracks appeared in the shutters. The portal began vibrating from the impacts of the antennas.

"If their feelers pierce the wood, smash them with your spears," Eerak instructed. "But, be most mindful they do not squirt their vile venom into your eyes or onto your bare skin. It will blister for weeks, blinding or scarring. Strike for their eyes or throats or between their wings. If they manage even one breach, it is every man for himself." Eerak turned and looked intently at each of them. "Do you understand?" Eerak emphasized. "One breach, and it's every man for himself! If we can kill enough of them, they will retreat in defeat."

"How — how many," Clu whispered.

"Ninety, maybe, one hundred," Eerak said.

"Im — Impossible!" Lie said, hoarsely.

"There are others around the woods fighting, also," Eerak said. "Among us, we have a chance of one hundred fifty to two hundred. If we are all very lucky!"

The thumpings increased in number and force, and the trumpeting sounded frantic.

Clu shivered. "Are they frightened?" he asked, hesitantly.

Eerak smiled, wryly. "Yes," he said, a small amount of hope entering his trembling voice. "The others are striking killing blows, and morning will soon arrive!"

An antenna speared through a shutter in front of Clu. He twisted sideways and swung his spear down with all his might. The javelin bounced off the antenna without harm. He swung again, putting his weight into the blow. The antenna snapped.

The Sand Digger shrilled pain and rage and jerked the antenna free of the shutter.

The door and the shutters on both windows were pierced by antennas. The men managed to damage four, causing Sand Digger cries of pain and anger, before all the antennas were withdrawn.

A glowing orange glob of venom squirted through a puncture in the door and splattered on Eerak's chest. His shirt smoked for a moment, then the venom plopped to the floor between his feet.

"Damn them! Good Lord Azophi, damn these fiends to extinction!" Eerak screamed. "They have understood to bore holes and glob us with no risk to themselves! Thrust your spears into the holes! Watch for their glows and thrust! Their vile eyes are red, their ugly throats, green. Strike at anything red or green! Without hesitation or

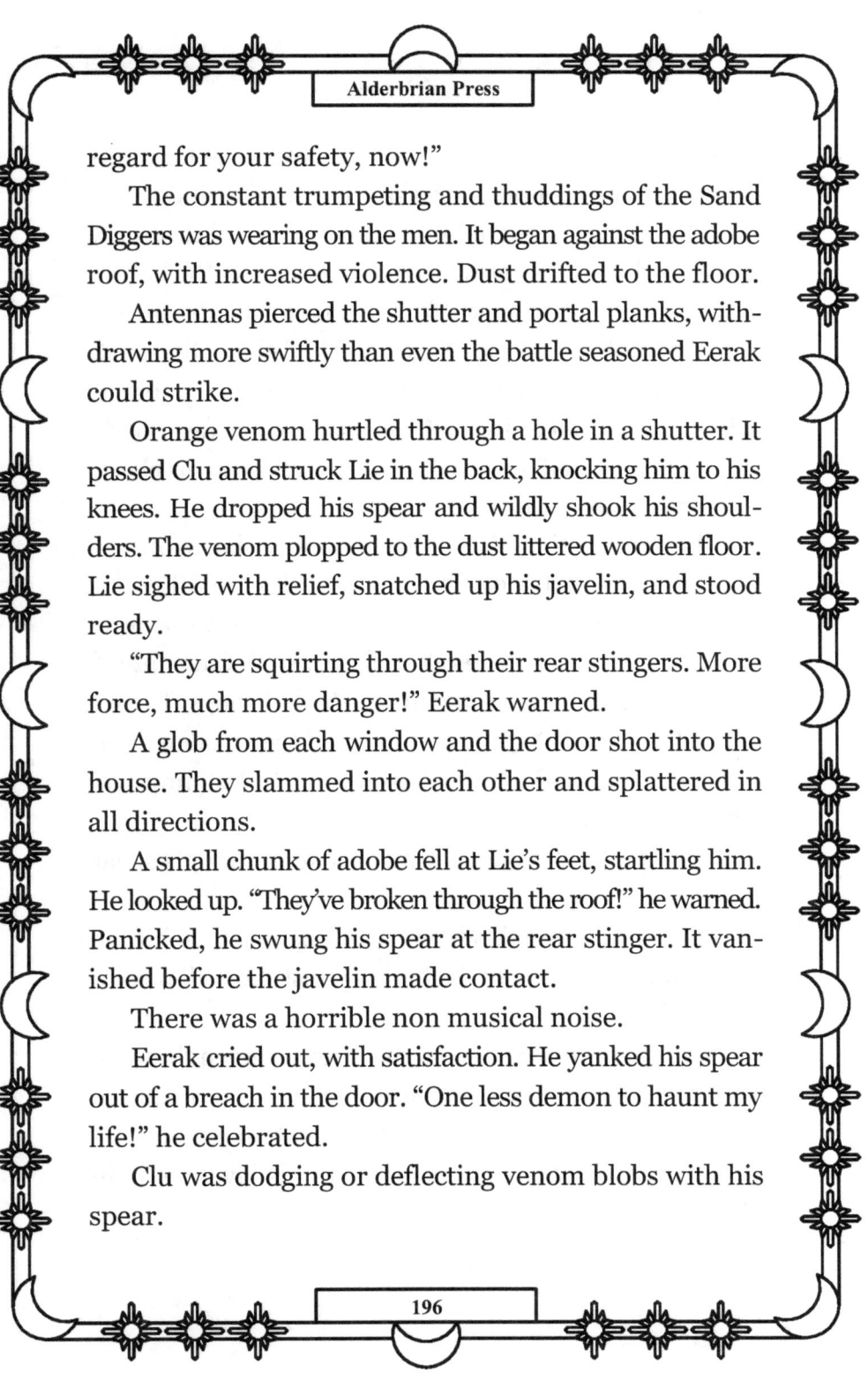

regard for your safety, now!"

The constant trumpeting and thuddings of the Sand Diggers was wearing on the men. It began against the adobe roof, with increased violence. Dust drifted to the floor.

Antennas pierced the shutter and portal planks, withdrawing more swiftly than even the battle seasoned Eerak could strike.

Orange venom hurtled through a hole in a shutter. It passed Clu and struck Lie in the back, knocking him to his knees. He dropped his spear and wildly shook his shoulders. The venom plopped to the dust littered wooden floor. Lie sighed with relief, snatched up his javelin, and stood ready.

"They are squirting through their rear stingers. More force, much more danger!" Eerak warned.

A glob from each window and the door shot into the house. They slammed into each other and splattered in all directions.

A small chunk of adobe fell at Lie's feet, startling him. He looked up. "They've broken through the roof!" he warned. Panicked, he swung his spear at the rear stinger. It vanished before the javelin made contact.

There was a horrible non musical noise.

Eerak cried out, with satisfaction. He yanked his spear out of a breach in the door. "One less demon to haunt my life!" he celebrated.

Clu was dodging or deflecting venom blobs with his spear.

Lie sighted a greenish glow and jabbed the tip of his javelin through a hole in the shutter on his window.

A Sand Digger vented its sad, non musical death cry and fell, with a heavy thud, to the sand outside the house.

Lie's spear was yanked from his hands by the big orange mandibles of a Sand Digger, and pulled into the night. Lie ran to the pile of extra spears and obtained another. Adobe chunks fell at his feet. He snapped his head back, then threw himself toward the door, landing on his chest.

Eerak spun around.

The trumpeting Sand Digger landed hard on the floor and aimed its deadly antennas at Clu and Eerak.

Clu vented a sound of anger and fear and was astride the Sand Digger before Eerak could respond. Clu jammed his spear down between the insects folded wings. The tip pierced the Sand Digger and impacted the wooden floor. The insect emitted a horrible screech and fell limp and dead beneath Clu.

"To your left!" Eerak warned, as he hurled his spear upward.

Clu obeyed Eerak's warning, rolling when he hit the floor, and came up with his back against the wall next to his window.

Eerak's spear was stuck in the lustrous green throat of a Sand Digger that was half-way through the breach in the ceiling. The insect had not been able to cry out.

Lie got unsteadily to his feet with his javelin still in his hands.

Several stingers smashed through the door. Others broke boards in each window. The Sand Diggers were about to invade the house.

Clu retrieved his spear from the insect he had slain.

Eerak grasped his spear. As he pulled, the dead Sand Digger was hauled out of the breach. Two Sand Diggers leaned into the house and fired their antenna stingers at Eerak. Their venom coated his head. Before he could raise his hands to claw at the glowing deadly effluvia, Eerak was dead. He fell onto his back, with his limbs as stiff as a statue's.

"We are lost!" Clu mourned. "No Eerak! No Baylou! No Azophi! We can't win!"

Lie held his spear in one hand, took Clu by the elbow and drew him toward the entry. Lie could see no glows through the holes in the door, and could not hear any sounds of Sand Digger feet on the front wall or in the sand. He threw the door open wide and frantically raced down the steps, tugging Clu behind him. Lie glanced over his shoulder.

The house, including the front wall, was bejeweled by more glowing Sand Digger than could be counted.

Lie fled in the cold darkness until he bumped into a wall. His hand contacted wooden boards. A shutter. He made his way by feel to the corner of the building, then along the next wall until he stumbled into steps.

There was a sound of stone cracking and Lie assumed Eerak's house had collapsed under the frenzied assault and massive weight of the radiant Sand Diggers. He wondered why the Sand Diggers were ignoring this house, but worked the latch, pulled the door open, and tugged Clu in after him.

Lie slammed the heavy door shut and the deafening din of the Sand Diggers ceased as if on command. The blue steel spears both men desperately grasped for comfort, vanished like mist on a windy night.

Lie's skin crawled. The Sand Diggers and Eerak apparently were, after all, a second Spirit Infestation.

Clu pulled his elbow free of Lie's grip. "I remember," he whispered in the eerie silence, with a strange, far away voice, "I was in here before. This is the worst of the four abandoned structures."

"Oh, Azophi," Lie whispered, with despair, "not another Infestation!"

There was a movement of foul, suffocatingly damp air in the rear of the house. A slithering galvanized Lie and Clu to rivet their senses in that direction. One thought shocked through both their fatigued brains: the behemoth lizard Death!

Lie reached behind and wrenched the big wooden latch free. He shoved the creaking old door open so forcefully, it banged against the outer wall, sounding like a firecracker.

Clu leaped from the structure, avoiding the steps. Lie was only a moment behind. He barely managed to clutch Clu's shoulder as they jumped. The questers ran, driven by blind panic, into the cool sands of the hostile desert, under the oppressive and unfriendly night sky.

Illustration 28

Ortourian Beast Wrought Iron Window Grillwork

Copyright © 2019 Philip Raymond Sadler

200-A

Chapter 28
Dark Hopes

Ihpoza ceased his frustrated pacing behind his shining blue frozen throne. His horrid reflection faced him as he focused his senses on the vibrations which touched his mind.

Yes. Once again, Azophi's disgusting puppets were detectable on the planet. A solid, unmistakable presence.

Relief coursed frigidly through Ihpoza. He could not fathom the cause of the irksome men's mysterious absence, nor the etiology of their equally perplexing reappearance, but he showed his bizarre frightening grimace of a smile.

Now, he need not subject himself to the searing jeopardy of the Southern Hemisphere. Now, Death could fulfill their plan!

Illustration 29

Ortourian Beast Wrought Iron Window Grillwork

Copyright © 2019 Philip Raymond Sadler

201-A

Chapter 29
Leap of Faith

Baylou drifted to the cool sand and stood motionless. An ethereal energy sensation swept subtly across the desert. Baylou's iris dilated with astonishment, then returned to normal. There was no doubt! Lie and Clu were discernible presences! Happiness, hope and optimism surged in the Tome, causing its glow to momentarily eradicate the blackness of the cold night.

Baylou could sense Lie and Clu had faced mortal dangers. What those perils had been and how the men had survived them, the Book could not divine. What mattered was, they were present, safe and Baylou still had a chance to prevail upon, or compel, Lie to continue their critical mission.

Baylou twinkled golden with delight. Its magical essence ordered it to resume its indispensable activities so it soared into the ebony sky and sped over the barren sands. Baylou felt strong again! Renewed! Enthusiasm washed away despair. "On with the Quest!" Baylou rejoiced, aloud. "To the rescue of the Wand and the glory of Azophi!"

Illustration 30

202-A

Ortourian Beast Wrought Iron Window Grillwork

Copyright © 2019 Philip Raymond Sadler

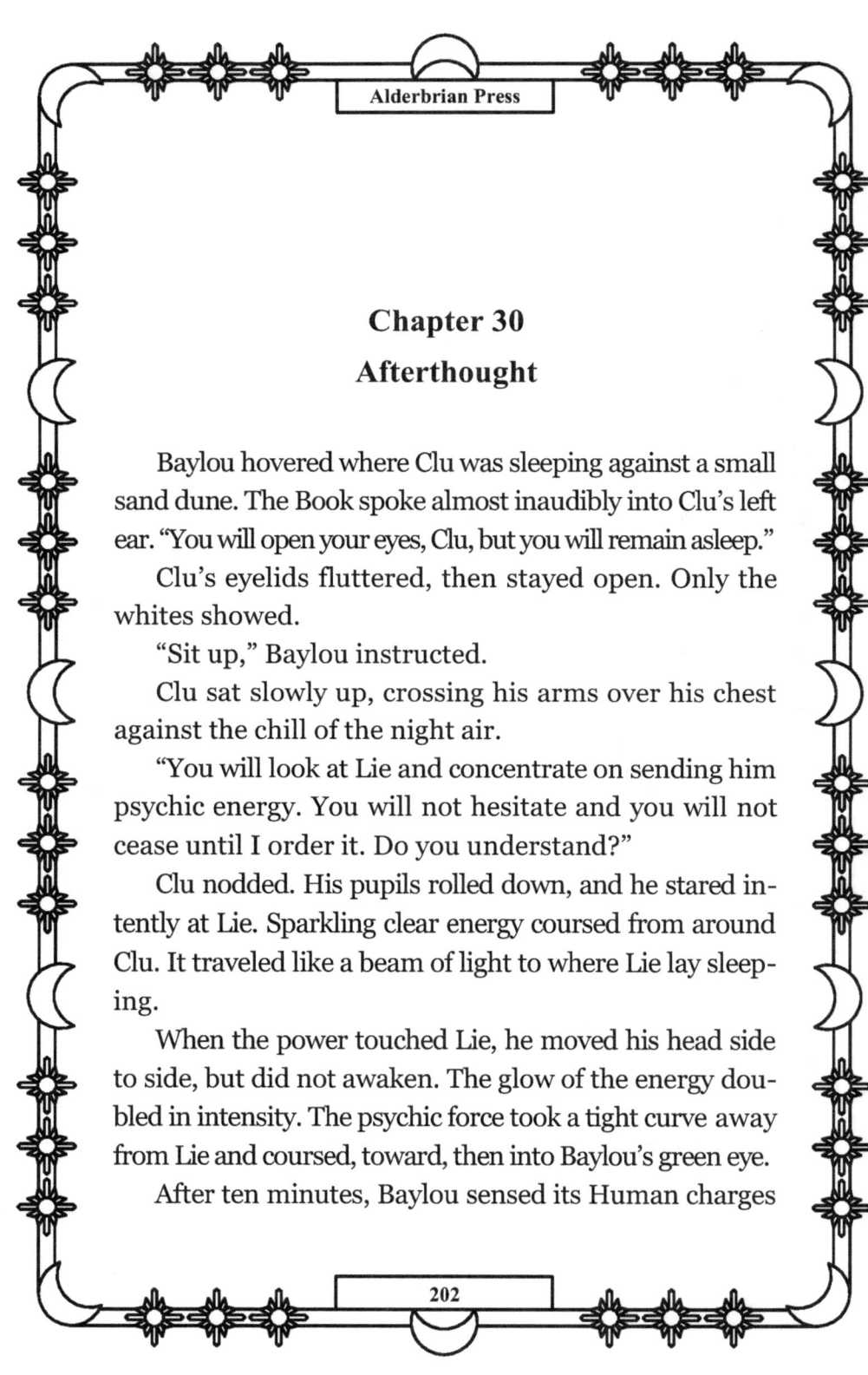

Chapter 30

Afterthought

Baylou hovered where Clu was sleeping against a small sand dune. The Book spoke almost inaudibly into Clu's left ear. "You will open your eyes, Clu, but you will remain asleep."

Clu's eyelids fluttered, then stayed open. Only the whites showed.

"Sit up," Baylou instructed.

Clu sat slowly up, crossing his arms over his chest against the chill of the night air.

"You will look at Lie and concentrate on sending him psychic energy. You will not hesitate and you will not cease until I order it. Do you understand?"

Clu nodded. His pupils rolled down, and he stared intently at Lie. Sparkling clear energy coursed from around Clu. It traveled like a beam of light to where Lie lay sleeping.

When the power touched Lie, he moved his head side to side, but did not awaken. The glow of the energy doubled in intensity. The psychic force took a tight curve away from Lie and coursed, toward, then into Baylou's green eye.

After ten minutes, Baylou sensed its Human charges

were close to suffering irreparable damage to their Mind Magic abilities. Baylou had not gathered sufficient energy for a safety margin for its activities. Reluctantly, Baylou whispered into Clu's ear. "Cease, now, Clu. Relax. Recline and sleep. You will forget that I was here upon this night."

Clu laid against the sand dune in the position he had been in before the Tome had arrived. Clu closed his eyes and fell into an easy sleep. His arms dropped to his sides.

Baylou hovered above Lie and Clu wishing it could remain with its charges. Still resentful of its arcane side works, Baylou sailed into the starry night, in a high, looping arc.

⚬⚬⚬⚬⌣⚬⚬⚬⚬

The pink of dawn enticed Lie out of his sleep of exhaustion. He sat up quickly and fearfully glanced around. His wild heart calmed when he saw Clu slumbering against a small dune.

Clu awoke when he heard the crunching of Lie's boots against the super dry sand.

"I am sorry to say this, but we must return to the village."

"Why?" Clu said, with apprehension and annoyance.

"Our packs, food and water, are there."

Clu hung his head with resigned exasperation. "I thought hauntings occurred only at night," he said. "But those poor women beguiled us by day."

"There are a few recorded claims of daylight apparitions, but nothing approaching what we suffered through."

They reluctantly began retracing their terrified tracks.

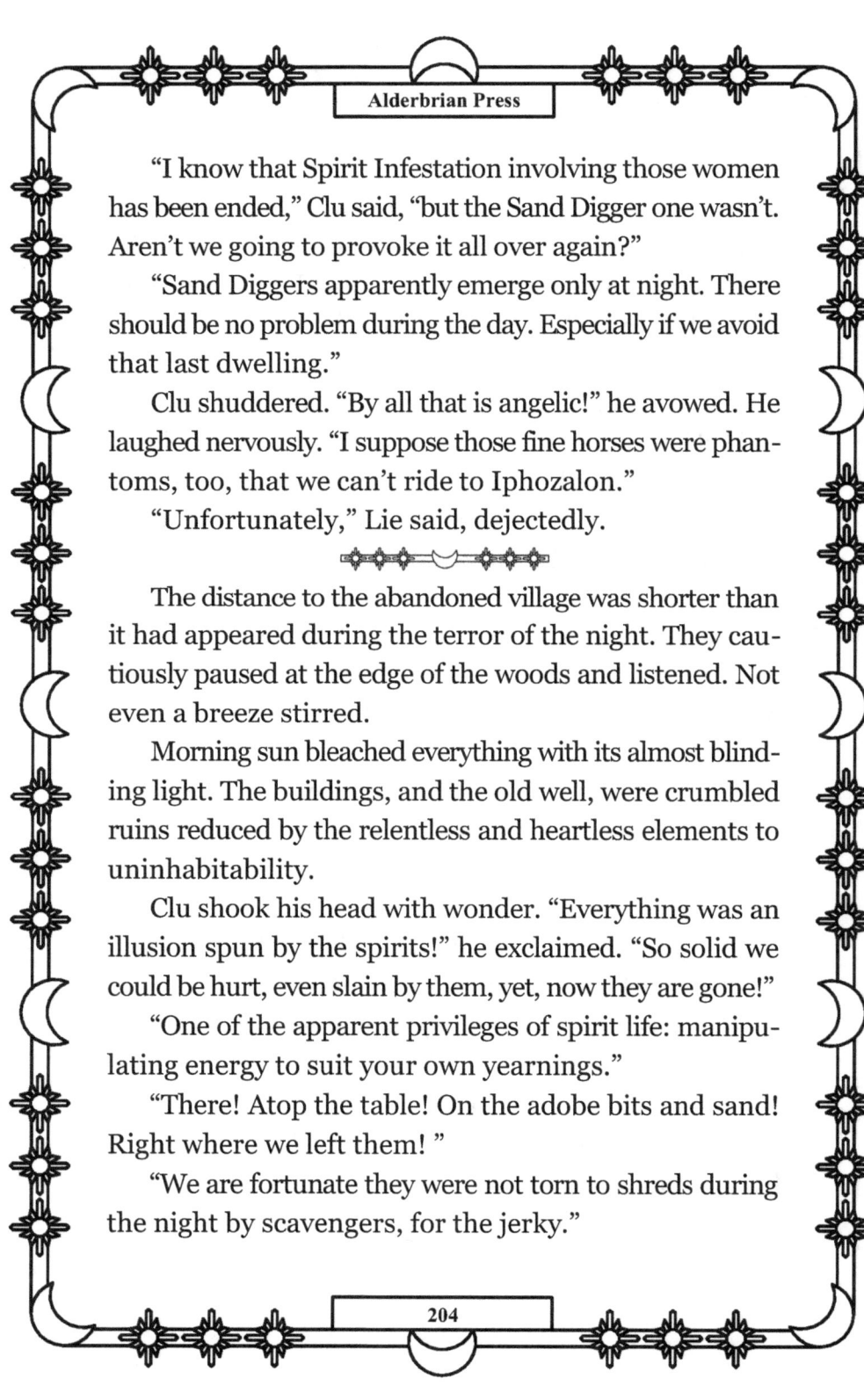

"I know that Spirit Infestation involving those women has been ended," Clu said, "but the Sand Digger one wasn't. Aren't we going to provoke it all over again?"

"Sand Diggers apparently emerge only at night. There should be no problem during the day. Especially if we avoid that last dwelling."

Clu shuddered. "By all that is angelic!" he avowed. He laughed nervously. "I suppose those fine horses were phantoms, too, that we can't ride to Iphozalon."

"Unfortunately," Lie said, dejectedly.

The distance to the abandoned village was shorter than it had appeared during the terror of the night. They cautiously paused at the edge of the woods and listened. Not even a breeze stirred.

Morning sun bleached everything with its almost blinding light. The buildings, and the old well, were crumbled ruins reduced by the relentless and heartless elements to uninhabitability.

Clu shook his head with wonder. "Everything was an illusion spun by the spirits!" he exclaimed. "So solid we could be hurt, even slain by them, yet, now they are gone!"

"One of the apparent privileges of spirit life: manipulating energy to suit your own yearnings."

"There! Atop the table! On the adobe bits and sand! Right where we left them! "

"We are fortunate they were not torn to shreds during the night by scavengers, for the jerky."

"I'm sure happy our gold starved ancestors hunted the Sand Diggers to extinction!"

"Amen!" Lie said.

They warily retrieved their backpacks and returned to the heart of the sickly woods. They were thankful for the shade the drooping leaves provided. The further they traveled from the dusty haunted village, the less uneasy they felt.

Illustration 31

Ortourian Beast Wrought Iron Window Grillwork

Copyright © 2019 Philip Raymond Sadler

206-A

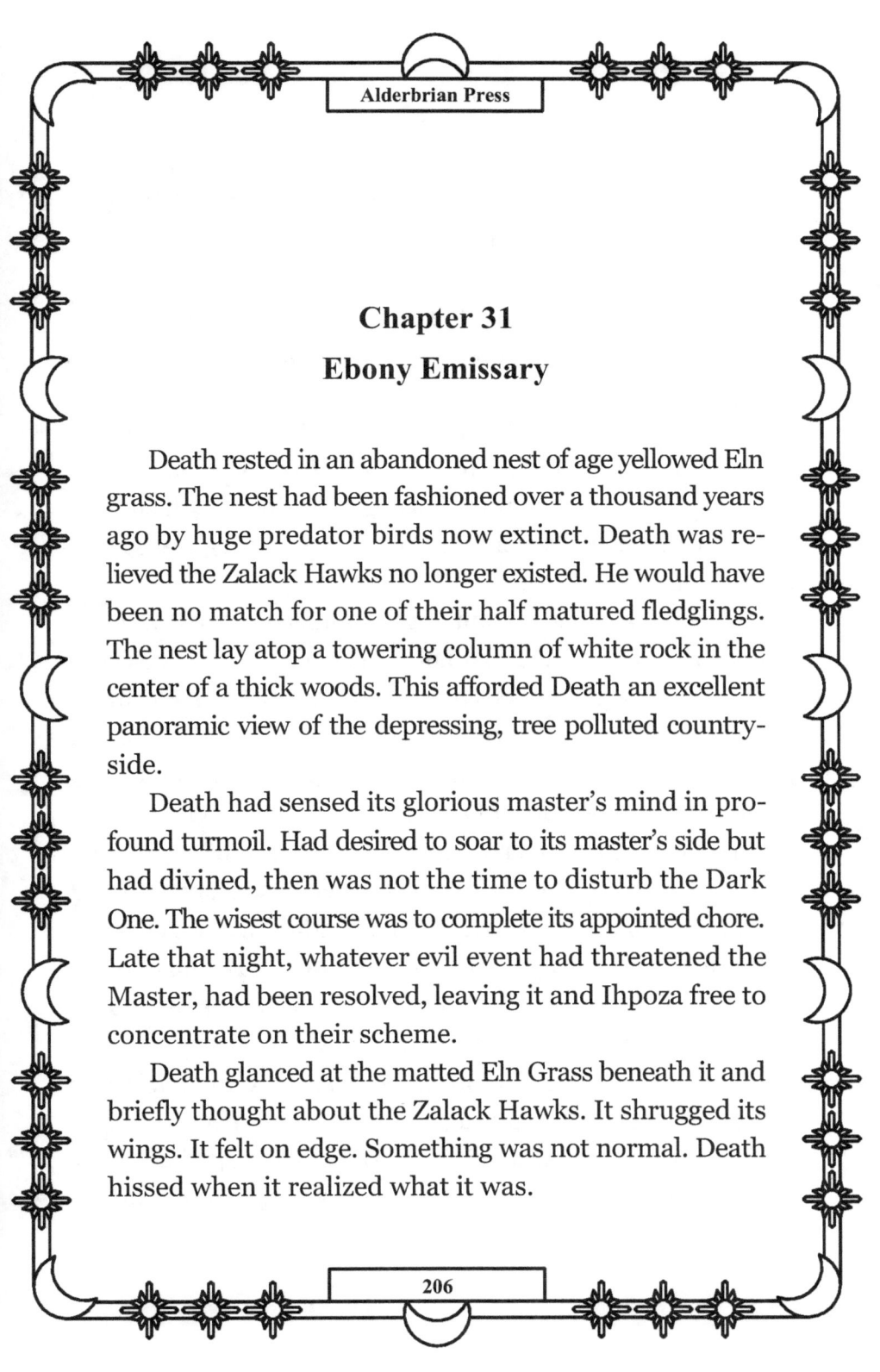

Chapter 31
Ebony Emissary

Death rested in an abandoned nest of age yellowed Eln grass. The nest had been fashioned over a thousand years ago by huge predator birds now extinct. Death was relieved the Zalack Hawks no longer existed. He would have been no match for one of their half matured fledglings. The nest lay atop a towering column of white rock in the center of a thick woods. This afforded Death an excellent panoramic view of the depressing, tree polluted countryside.

Death had sensed its glorious master's mind in profound turmoil. Had desired to soar to its master's side but had divined, then was not the time to disturb the Dark One. The wisest course was to complete its appointed chore. Late that night, whatever evil event had threatened the Master, had been resolved, leaving it and Ihpoza free to concentrate on their scheme.

Death glanced at the matted Eln Grass beneath it and briefly thought about the Zalack Hawks. It shrugged its wings. It felt on edge. Something was not normal. Death hissed when it realized what it was.

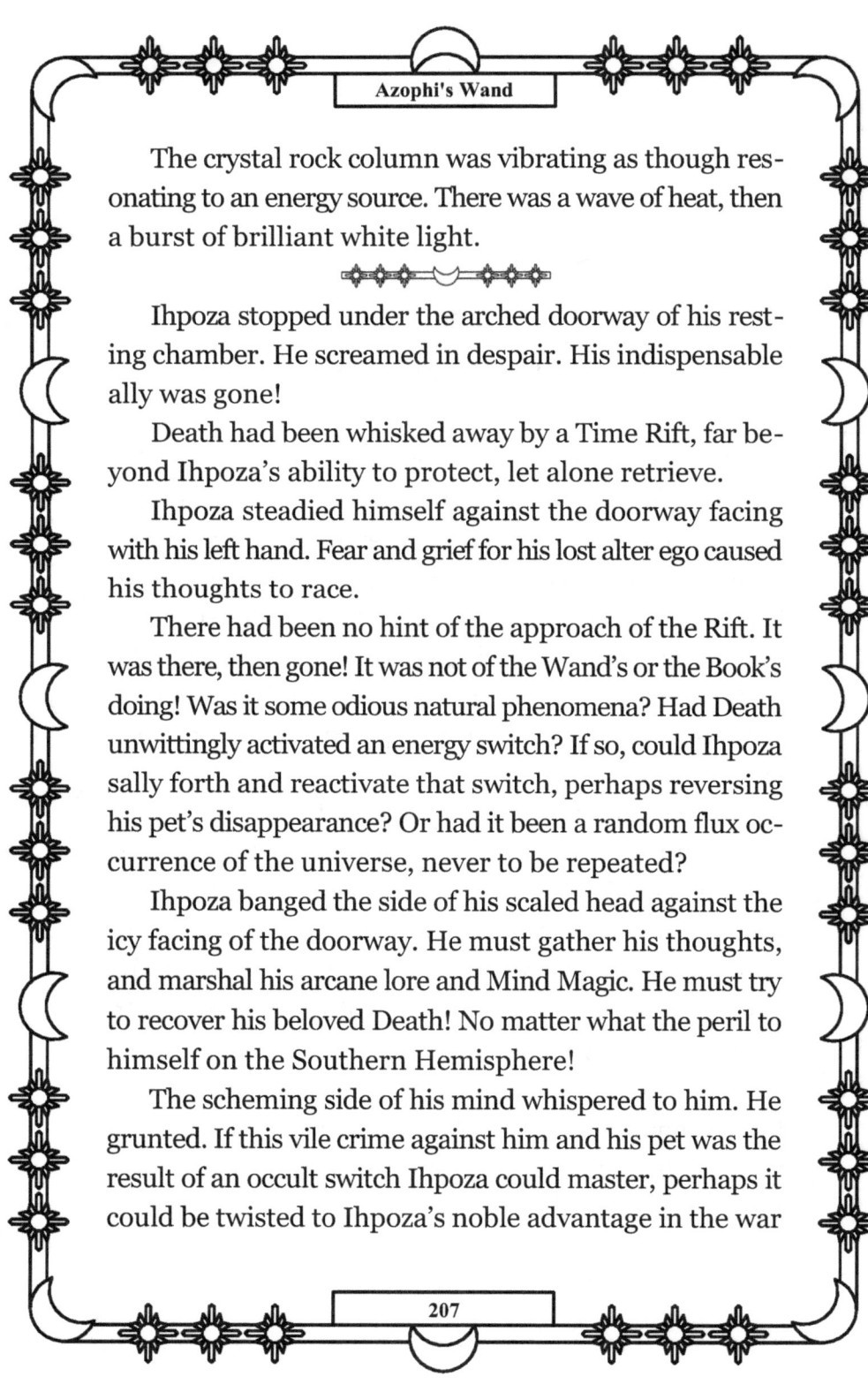

The crystal rock column was vibrating as though resonating to an energy source. There was a wave of heat, then a burst of brilliant white light.

Ihpoza stopped under the arched doorway of his resting chamber. He screamed in despair. His indispensable ally was gone!

Death had been whisked away by a Time Rift, far beyond Ihpoza's ability to protect, let alone retrieve.

Ihpoza steadied himself against the doorway facing with his left hand. Fear and grief for his lost alter ego caused his thoughts to race.

There had been no hint of the approach of the Rift. It was there, then gone! It was not of the Wand's or the Book's doing! Was it some odious natural phenomena? Had Death unwittingly activated an energy switch? If so, could Ihpoza sally forth and reactivate that switch, perhaps reversing his pet's disappearance? Or had it been a random flux occurrence of the universe, never to be repeated?

Ihpoza banged the side of his scaled head against the icy facing of the doorway. He must gather his thoughts, and marshal his arcane lore and Mind Magic. He must try to recover his beloved Death! No matter what the peril to himself on the Southern Hemisphere!

The scheming side of his mind whispered to him. He grunted. If this vile crime against him and his pet was the result of an occult switch Ihpoza could master, perhaps it could be twisted to Ihpoza's noble advantage in the war against detestable Baylou! Perhaps Ihpoza might regain his ally and an inexhaustible new mystical power with which to destroy Azophi's puppets!

Death's slanted eyes recovered from the flash blindness. Its heart throbbed so mightily, the Lizard feared it would burst. Death stared, horrified, into the fierce, golden eyes of a Zalack male. It was a beautiful, but massive and terrifying fowl.

As Death's mind attempted to understand how it could be facing a creature extinct for a thousand years, it recalled a brief conversation it enjoyed with the Evil One. The subject had been Time Rifts.

Ihpoza explained the concept and said, with sufficient Mind Magic, one could create and master Time Rifts. With the might of the Wand, such a feat would still be difficult even for Ihpoza.

Somehow, a Rift had occurred, and drawn Death into a time when the undefeatable Zalack Hawks still thrived. A time of possible sudden death.

Death shuddered and returned its mind to its surroundings. Two huge, gray eggs were to its left. The golden Zalack towered to the right, with its wings half spread.

Death recognized this as the typical pre-attack posture of a predator fowl. The Lizard desperately thought of racing forward, toward the rim of the nest, to hurl itself into flight.

The Zalack was on top of the Lizard, with Death's thick neck in its mighty, sharp beak, before Death had man-

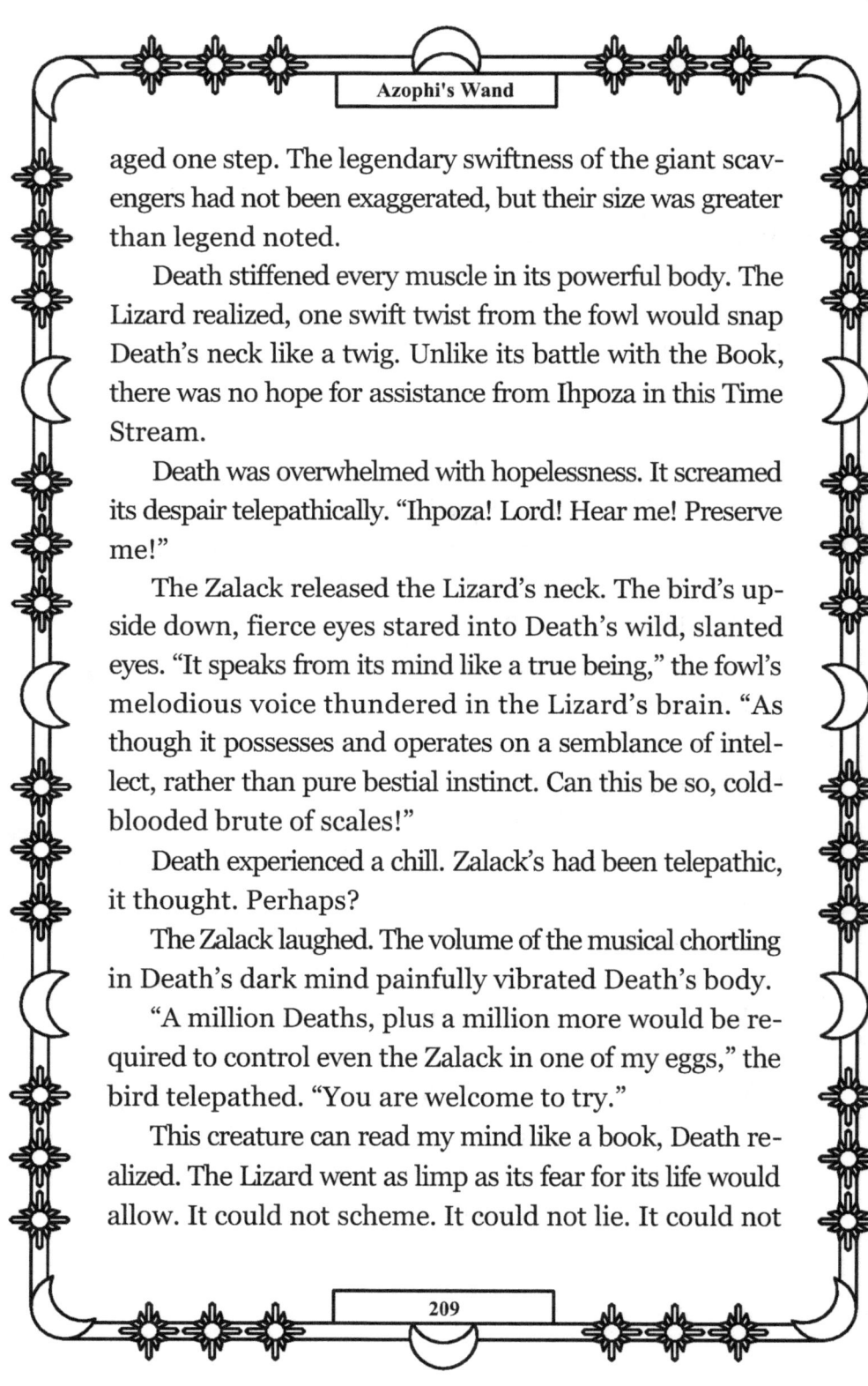

aged one step. The legendary swiftness of the giant scavengers had not been exaggerated, but their size was greater than legend noted.

Death stiffened every muscle in its powerful body. The Lizard realized, one swift twist from the fowl would snap Death's neck like a twig. Unlike its battle with the Book, there was no hope for assistance from Ihpoza in this Time Stream.

Death was overwhelmed with hopelessness. It screamed its despair telepathically. "Ihpoza! Lord! Hear me! Preserve me!"

The Zalack released the Lizard's neck. The bird's upside down, fierce eyes stared into Death's wild, slanted eyes. "It speaks from its mind like a true being," the fowl's melodious voice thundered in the Lizard's brain. "As though it possesses and operates on a semblance of intellect, rather than pure bestial instinct. Can this be so, cold-blooded brute of scales!"

Death experienced a chill. Zalack's had been telepathic, it thought. Perhaps?

The Zalack laughed. The volume of the musical chortling in Death's dark mind painfully vibrated Death's body.

"A million Deaths, plus a million more would be required to control even the Zalack in one of my eggs," the bird telepathed. "You are welcome to try."

This creature can read my mind like a book, Death realized. The Lizard went as limp as its fear for its life would allow. It could not scheme. It could not lie. It could not

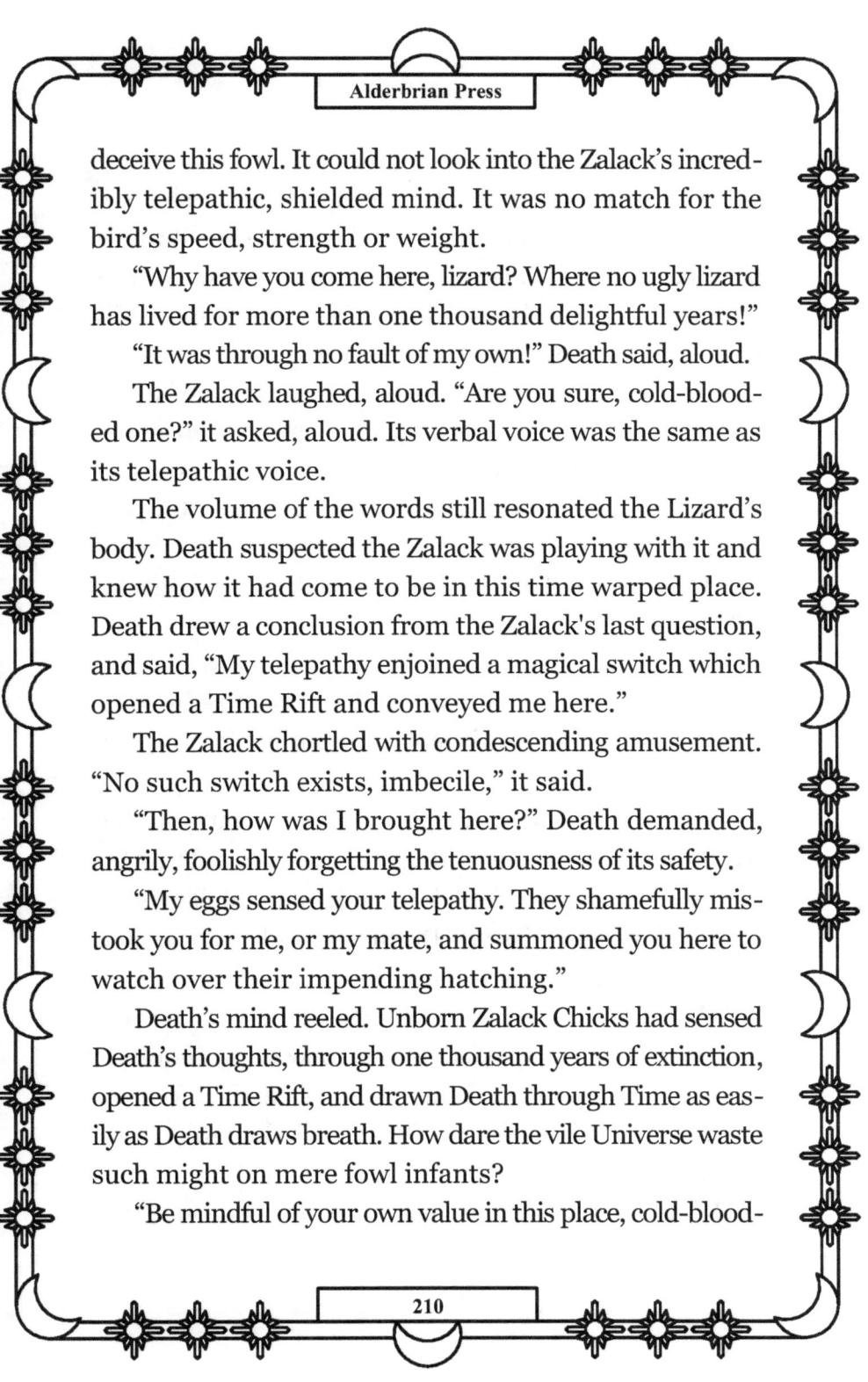

deceive this fowl. It could not look into the Zalack's incredibly telepathic, shielded mind. It was no match for the bird's speed, strength or weight.

"Why have you come here, lizard? Where no ugly lizard has lived for more than one thousand delightful years!"

"It was through no fault of my own!" Death said, aloud.

The Zalack laughed, aloud. "Are you sure, cold-blooded one?" it asked, aloud. Its verbal voice was the same as its telepathic voice.

The volume of the words still resonated the Lizard's body. Death suspected the Zalack was playing with it and knew how it had come to be in this time warped place. Death drew a conclusion from the Zalack's last question, and said, "My telepathy enjoined a magical switch which opened a Time Rift and conveyed me here."

The Zalack chortled with condescending amusement. "No such switch exists, imbecile," it said.

"Then, how was I brought here?" Death demanded, angrily, foolishly forgetting the tenuousness of its safety.

"My eggs sensed your telepathy. They shamefully mistook you for me, or my mate, and summoned you here to watch over their impending hatching."

Death's mind reeled. Unborn Zalack Chicks had sensed Death's thoughts, through one thousand years of extinction, opened a Time Rift, and drawn Death through Time as easily as Death draws breath. How dare the vile Universe waste such might on mere fowl infants?

"Be mindful of your own value in this place, cold-blooded!" the Zalack said, sounding insulted.

Death hunkered down. The weight of the massive bird was creating a constant ache in the Lizard's spine. It would become intolerable. Death had to regain mastery of its emotions and mind and deal carefully and respectfully with this obviously superior creature.

The Zalack issued a flute like song and stepped to the floor of the nest. "Since you can go nowhere but to an instant death, I shall release you, for now," the bird said.

Death wiggled side to side in an effort to ease the pain in its spine.

"Why, then, did you say that Zalack's had been telepathic?"

Death rolled its eyes. It was engaging in conversation with an extinct animal that could end Death's life on a whim. How could Death reply without instigating that feared fatal attack.

"Speak only truth, though I can see within you that truth is a mostly unnatural concept to you and this Ihpoza. As is honor, wisdom, knowledge and intelligence."

"Mock not my Master!" Death said, its love for Ihpoza overcoming its fear of its situation.

The Zalack clucked reproachfully. "At least you possess basic loyalty, as misguided as it is. Answer my inquiry!"

"Upon Azon, Zalack Birds have been extinct for over one thousand short years!" Death said, defiantly.

"Ignorance."

Death's anger began to tense its ebony body to spring

upon the bird.

The Zalack was on top of the Lizard more quickly than Death could believe, twisting Death's thick scaly neck, just short of snapping the vertebra.

"For your information and enlightenment, cold-blooded fool, here, where we stand, is Azon!" the Zalack roared, within Death's pain racked brain. "A different time! A better time! We are not now, nor have we ever been, extinct!"

Death trembled with terror, but forced its muscles to relax again. "If you release me, I pledge to master my anger and not labor to attack or flee!"

The Zalack stepped off the Lizard's back.

Death's inner mind spoke. Death tilted its head, in wonder. "Your unhatched young can control Time Rifts," Death said. "Therefore, you possess enviable mastery of Time. This is how you have managed to travel to this place. You vacated our Azon Time Stream for here. Why?"

"Finally!" the Zalack shouted, with a musical sound of wonder. "It evidences actual intellect!" The bird positioned itself so it faced the lizard, and stared into Death's wary, red, slanted eyes. "We could no longer withstand the chaotic din of the minds of the lesser creatures on your Azon. The smaller fowl, and the prowling four footers, were disharmonious enough, but the Humans were intolerable! Their minds were so loud! So coarse! So incessant! Waking, sleeping, working, playing! Always beaming undisciplined, illogical, nonsensical thought in every direction! We had to leave! Though it violated our purpose as regards our

Lord Azophi, we had to flee the hellishness of their primitive, grunting minds!" The Zalack pushed its massive head closer to the Lizard.

Death flinched, involuntarily.

"We shall never return!" the Zalack said. "Is this why you were in our nest? Why you were sweeping out your telepathy? To convoke us back to Lord Azophi's control and his design for our existence!"

In spite of its situation, Death was forced to hiss with hatred.

The Zalack telepathically emitted grudging admiration for the Lizard, for a moment.

"Never would I be involved in cursed Azophi's nefarious works!" Death vowed. "He has been dead for over a thousand years! If I and my Lord Ihpoza had known of the Zalack Time Rift Powers and that our telepathy could enable contact with you, we would long ago have requested your noble assistance against Azophi, his accursed Wand and the vile Magical Book which now threatens to destroy My Master and I!"

The Zalack snorted. "We care not about who rules old Azon!" it said. "We would turn deaf minds to your pleas for help in your piteous war!"

Death's hatred changed from being directed toward Azophi, the Wand and Baylou, to the Zalack. "Why do you keep me here, then?" the Lizard demanded.

The Zalack's golden eyes seemed to shoot fire.

Death cringed.

"To ascertain the actuality of your presence here."

"You already know your embryos drew me here!"

"But I did not know if you had intended for them to do so!" the Zalack roared. "I did not know whether you old Azonians had developed telepathic control of our young! To utilize them for your free passage back and forth through time! To threaten our harmony here! We are aware of your Ihpoza's Negative Mind Magic! Aware of his obsession with controlling all things that come into his purview! We need him and you not upon our Azon!" The leviathan bird had been inching forward in his rage.

Death had been inching backwards in fear. The ebony Lizard bumped against one of the huge eggs. "Mighty intellect!" Death roared, its fear and anger overcoming its better judgment. "Your rage threatens your own precious eggs! Beware, or I shall rend them with my talons before even you can break my neck!"

"Now that I know you and your weakling Lord Ihpoza are not even a misty semblance of a threat," the Zalack thundered, in Death's aching, reeling brain, "be gone with you!"

There was a wave of heat, then a burst of brilliant white light.

Ihpoza sat forward in his throne, ignoring the twenty terrified demons cowering before him. He smiled with his always open mouth. His mind experienced joy for the first time in his incredibly long life.

"Returned!" Ihpoza shouted, his harsh rejoicing voice echoing eerily throughout the frozen palace. "Alive! Unharmed! I feel your shiny essence within my mind again, my pet! You shall explain! We shall explore this odd journey you have made! Master the unique forces that have allowed it, if possible! But, for now, the war resumes!" Ihpoza waved his hand at his slaves. "Vanish!" he commanded. "Be silent and sleep. Your Lord requires his solitude!"

The demons fled to their cramped frigid sleeping chambers. They cried with relief because their macabre master had not forced them to throw their miserable lives away on one of his insane schemes. Too many of their hapless brethren had already suffered that fate.

When Death's flash blindness vanished, it found itself alone in the nest of age yellowed Eln Grass.

The rock tower ceased vibrating.

Intense relief washed over Death, but it could not control its trembling for several minutes.

When Death finally calmed itself, it thought about its near expiration experience. "I cannot muster the necessary mental skills needed to surmount the haughty Zalack Hawks telepathically to gain control of their Time Rift Abilities, but Lord Ihpoza may be able to do so. Especially when he has gained control of the Wand! Then, shall we see who is the master and who is the prey!"

"Shall I show you who is the master? Who is superior?" the sinister voice of the Zalack thundered in Death's astonished mind. "Shall I pluck your mighty Ihpoza from his icy throne and feed him, alive and screaming in cowardly fear, to my hatchlings?"

Death hissed in rage and clamped down on its telepathic abilities, with all its horrified being. In Death's stunned mind, the snide musical laughter of the Zalack Hawk gradually faded to charitable silence.

"If I disallow myself to meditate upon certain matters, I shall not be discomforted by them," Death advised itself.

When no further essence of the Zalack was evidenced, Death relaxed and turned its mind to the realities of this Azon. The only Azon, from this point forward, Death would allow into its thoughts or worst nightmares.

A tiny black speck soared out of the distant trees directly before, and far below the massive saurian. The dot rapidly grew larger as it neared. With a loud flapping of its small, glistening wings, a crow alighted on the rim of the nest.

"Have you discovered them?" Death demanded.

Crow shook its head.

"Not yet!" Death flicked its forked tongue in and out. "Find them, my small, puny, insignificant slave, or you shall die very slowly!"

Crow cawed with fear and took to wing.

Death watched the blackbird vanish toward Slann. There was no doubt Crow would locate the men this time, and swiftly.

Illustration 32

Ortourian Beast Wrought Iron Window Grillwork

Copyright © 2019 Philip Raymond Sadler

217-A

Chapter 32

Wings of Pain

Clu cocked his head at the crow.

The blackbird cawed once, as if in disbelief.

Clu laughed. "I'm a real man," he said. "Small, perhaps, but still real." He adjusted his backpack for comfort.

Crow pecked Clu on the forehead.

"All right, you are a real bird. I harbored no doubts about that."

Crow eyed Clu more closely, cawed vaguely, then flapped away.

Clu reminded himself why he was perched precariously in the Fug Tree and surveyed the surrounding countryside: more trees everywhere.

Crow landed beside Clu and dropped an earthworm into Clu's lap.

"Thank you," Clu said, politely, "one will be just enough. You look mighty hungry, yourself. Why don't you find yourself something to gobble up?"

Crow peered at Clu with one eye, then the other, then took to wing.

"I'd better climb down from here before he brings me

more worms!" Clu muttered. He paused. "Next time, he might wonder why I didn't devour his first nauseating gift and stick around to watch me gobble it and whatever else he might bring." He started descending again, but more swiftly.

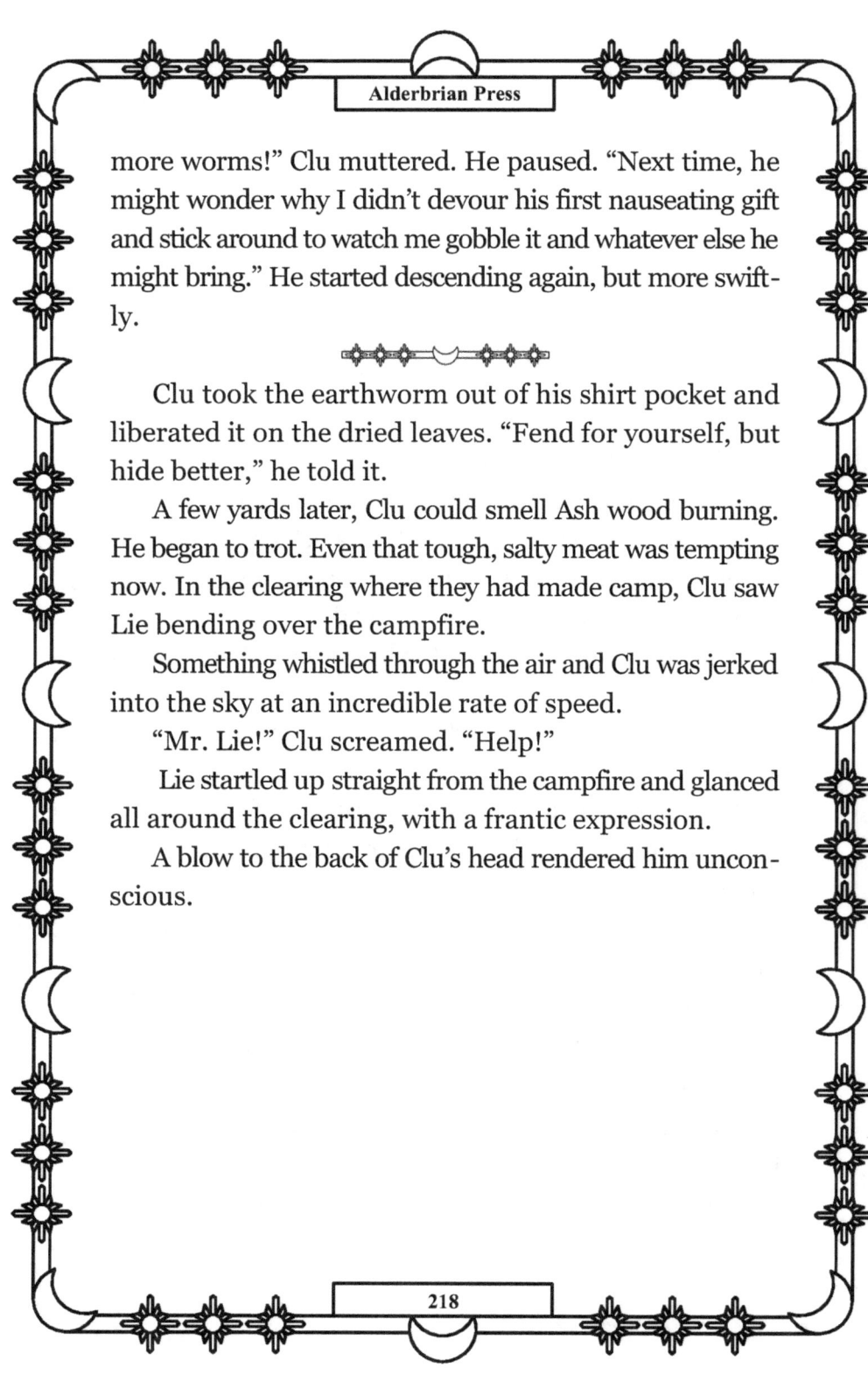

Clu took the earthworm out of his shirt pocket and liberated it on the dried leaves. "Fend for yourself, but hide better," he told it.

A few yards later, Clu could smell Ash wood burning. He began to trot. Even that tough, salty meat was tempting now. In the clearing where they had made camp, Clu saw Lie bending over the campfire.

Something whistled through the air and Clu was jerked into the sky at an incredible rate of speed.

"Mr. Lie!" Clu screamed. "Help!"

Lie startled up straight from the campfire and glanced all around the clearing, with a frantic expression.

A blow to the back of Clu's head rendered him unconscious.

Illustration 33

Ortourian Beast Wrought Iron Window Grillwork

219-A

Chapter 33

Circles of Confusion

Lie raced around through the trees calling for Clu and frantically searching the immediate area. Clu did not respond and Lie sighted nothing to explain his friends outcry, or his disappearance!

Lie forlornly sat down on a log by the campfire. Baylou, he thought angrily, why do you not return and help?

No response.

Lie kicked the flames out and shouldered his backpack. Clu could have been frightened away by an unfamiliar animal. Or he could have been hurt in a fall and rendered unconscious. He might yet be close by. Lie refused to think of the worst possibility.

Cursing himself, the Book, and Azophi, Lie began walking around a Fug tree in an ever widening circle, calling urgently for Clu and searching.

Illustration 34

Ortourian Beast Wrought Iron Window Grillwork

220-A

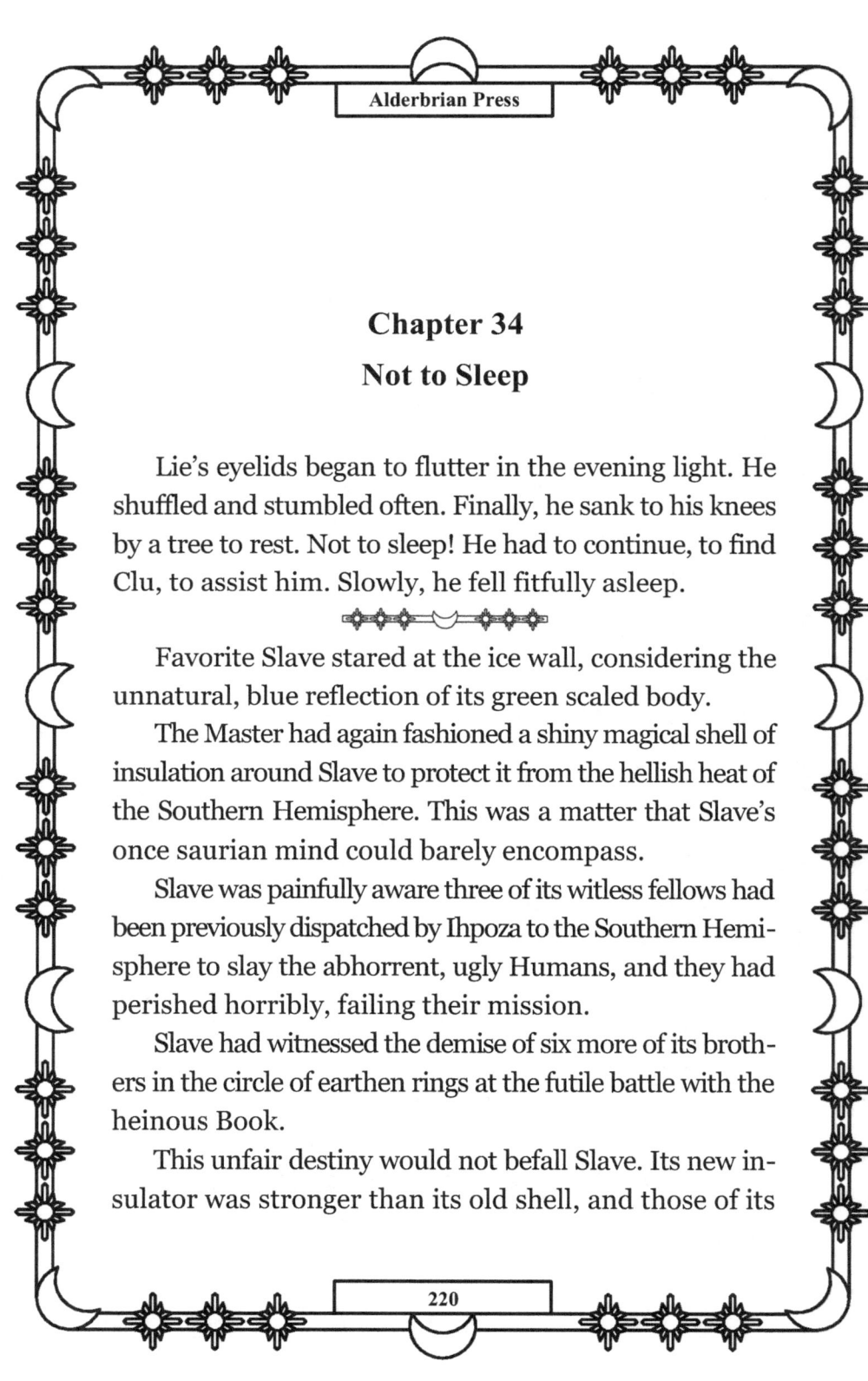

Chapter 34
Not to Sleep

Lie's eyelids began to flutter in the evening light. He shuffled and stumbled often. Finally, he sank to his knees by a tree to rest. Not to sleep! He had to continue, to find Clu, to assist him. Slowly, he fell fitfully asleep.

Favorite Slave stared at the ice wall, considering the unnatural, blue reflection of its green scaled body.

The Master had again fashioned a shiny magical shell of insulation around Slave to protect it from the hellish heat of the Southern Hemisphere. This was a matter that Slave's once saurian mind could barely encompass.

Slave was painfully aware three of its witless fellows had been previously dispatched by Ihpoza to the Southern Hemisphere to slay the abhorrent, ugly Humans, and they had perished horribly, failing their mission.

Slave had witnessed the demise of six more of its brothers in the circle of earthen rings at the futile battle with the heinous Book.

This unfair destiny would not befall Slave. Its new insulator was stronger than its old shell, and those of its hapless cohorts.

Slave's was a superior mind. Slave's beast cunning was greater. Most importantly, the good Master had gracefully transferred into Slave's small reptilian brain, a minute but potent piece of the Master's mighty Magic.

The good Master had also wisely, telepathically burned the Master's wondrous, vital scheme into Slave's brain. Slave would ardently follow this grand plan verbatim and could not fail. The consequences of failure were more horrible than an explosive heat death on the torrid Southern Hemisphere.

Slave's muscles convulsed, propelled by the irresistible force in the insulation shell, drawing Slave tightly and uncomfortably erect.

The magic embedded in Slave's feeble mind whispered harshly to the demon. Slave ran stiffly, but incredibly swiftly, from its tiny oval resting chamber, along the great wide entrance hall of the hoary gleaming palace, and out across the sparkling ice lawn. The landscape was a frightening blur. This made poor Slave dizzy and nauseated. At this amazing magic speed, Slave's trip to the oppressive Southern Hemisphere would be mercifully short. Not that Slave's comfort was a matter of concern to Ihpoza.

Slave was jerked to a stop. It stared at the dull russet vegetation around it. Slave had a vague memory of such homely flora being familiar and comforting. Now the fronds were frightening and irritating. The shapes of the plants, and the faint sounds and slight movements of the vegetation caused by the winds, kept Slave on edge.

The shell turned Slave quickly to its left and moved Slave slowly and carefully through some tall gray fronds. Before Slave had adjusted its slanted eyes to the increasing darkness caused by passing among the lush plants, the insulator yanked Slave to a kneeling position and aimed Slave's head to its right. Slave gasped. The Human whose ugly hated image had been so deeply and painfully burned into Slave's brain by the merciful Master, sat sleeping against an old weathered tree.

The magic in Slave's cerebrum spoke angrily.

Slave grew excited. Now, could Slave do its Master proud. Now, would Slave perform exactly and in minutiae its Master's brilliance. Slave crawled, with classic lizard slowness, up behind Lie.

Illustration 35

Ortourian Beast Wrought Iron Window Grillwork

Copyright © 2019 Philip Raymond Sadler

223-A

Chapter 35

Sleep of Menace

Quiet.

Soft.

Warm.

Clu lay slumbering in a nest of time yellowed Eln grass. His dream unfolded in scary slow motion. He turned onto his side and his head bumped against something curved, hard and smooth. This brought him close to awakening, and he felt he was swaying slightly back and forth like a baby in a cradle.

Clu and Lie awoke at the same time.

The comforting campfire had burned itself out of its fiery life, leaving sad ashes.

Lie and Clu rolled up their sleeping blankets and stuffed them into their backpacks. They shared some of their jerky and took a small drink of water from their canteens.

"Which way do we go now?" Clu asked.

Lie looked through the trees, to where the towering projection of vivid white stone stood. The top of the craggy, shining mesa was indistinct and appeared to be flat.

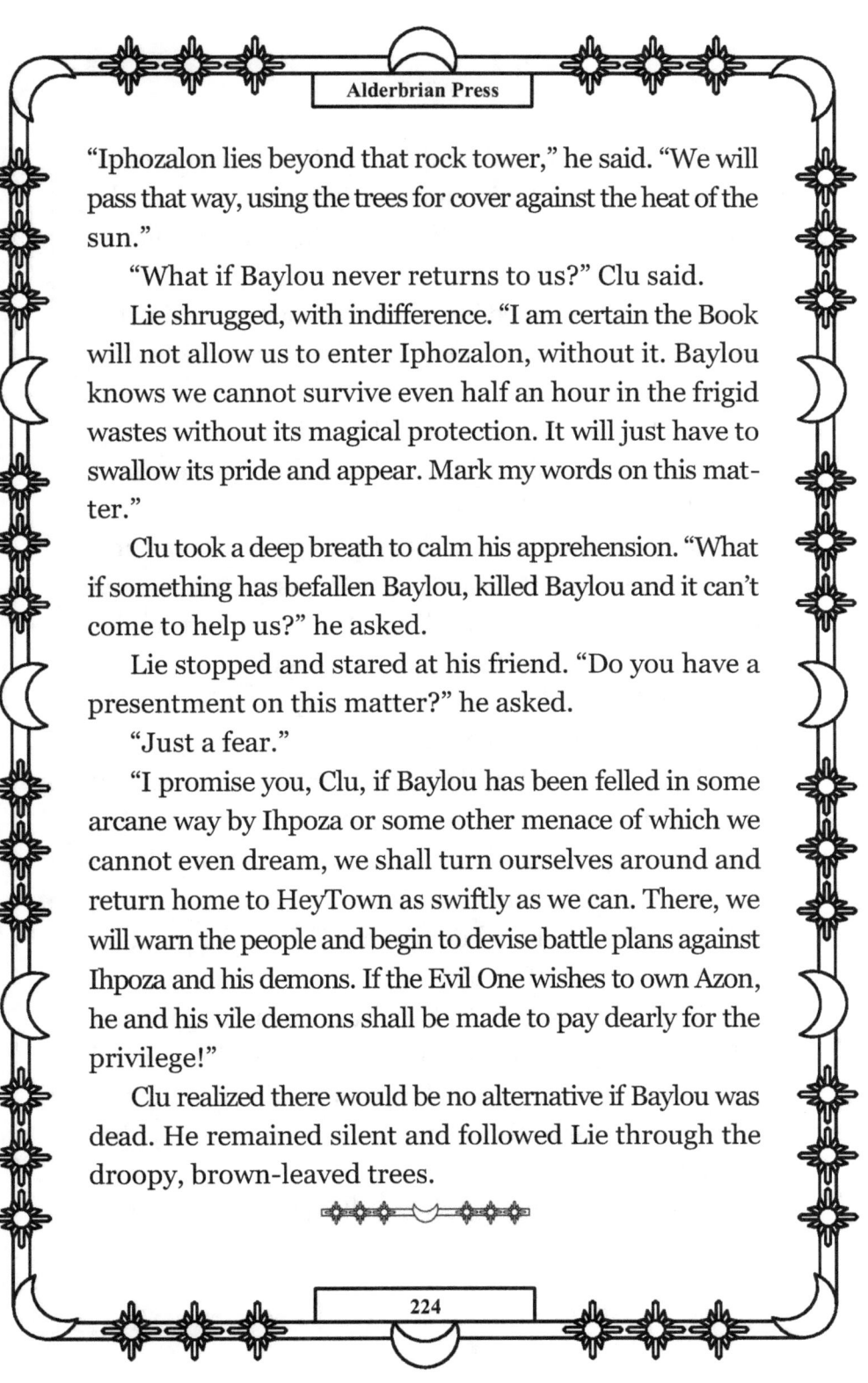

"Iphozalon lies beyond that rock tower," he said. "We will pass that way, using the trees for cover against the heat of the sun."

"What if Baylou never returns to us?" Clu said.

Lie shrugged, with indifference. "I am certain the Book will not allow us to enter Iphozalon, without it. Baylou knows we cannot survive even half an hour in the frigid wastes without its magical protection. It will just have to swallow its pride and appear. Mark my words on this matter."

Clu took a deep breath to calm his apprehension. "What if something has befallen Baylou, killed Baylou and it can't come to help us?" he asked.

Lie stopped and stared at his friend. "Do you have a presentment on this matter?" he asked.

"Just a fear."

"I promise you, Clu, if Baylou has been felled in some arcane way by Ihpoza or some other menace of which we cannot even dream, we shall turn ourselves around and return home to HeyTown as swiftly as we can. There, we will warn the people and begin to devise battle plans against Ihpoza and his demons. If the Evil One wishes to own Azon, he and his vile demons shall be made to pay dearly for the privilege!"

Clu realized there would be no alternative if Baylou was dead. He remained silent and followed Lie through the droopy, brown-leaved trees.

The trees were further apart and the earth was more sandy than loamy. Their path lead up at a steep angle. The sand surrendered to beautiful, sparkling, marble hills, as black as coal.

Lie and Clu crossed into the hills. There were tiny fissures in the marble. This made it easier to walk on the otherwise slick stone.

Clu stopped and tugged on Lie's sleeve.

Lie looked at him, his question in his countenance.

"Ortourians," Clu said.

Lie sucked in a breath. The possibility they had stumbled into another Ortourian Magical Construction startled him with fear. He stared in all directions. "I do not see any of their obelisks and light globes," he said.

"True," Clu said, "but, maybe they appear only at night? Maybe they vanish when the sun rises."

Lie grimaced. "We will go a little further," he said, "and if we see anything that resembles an Ortourian tunnel or might be an Ortourian building, we will retreat and try to circle this rocky plain."

"I feel like we should do that now," Clu said. "Caution is the better part of victory."

Lie started forward. Clu hung back, then shrugged and followed. They reached the top of the steep incline and gasped. Towering, needle sharp spires of ebony marble fanned out as far as they could see. Smooth pathways between the spires, led in all directions.

Lie and Clu thought of the smaller ebony spires lining

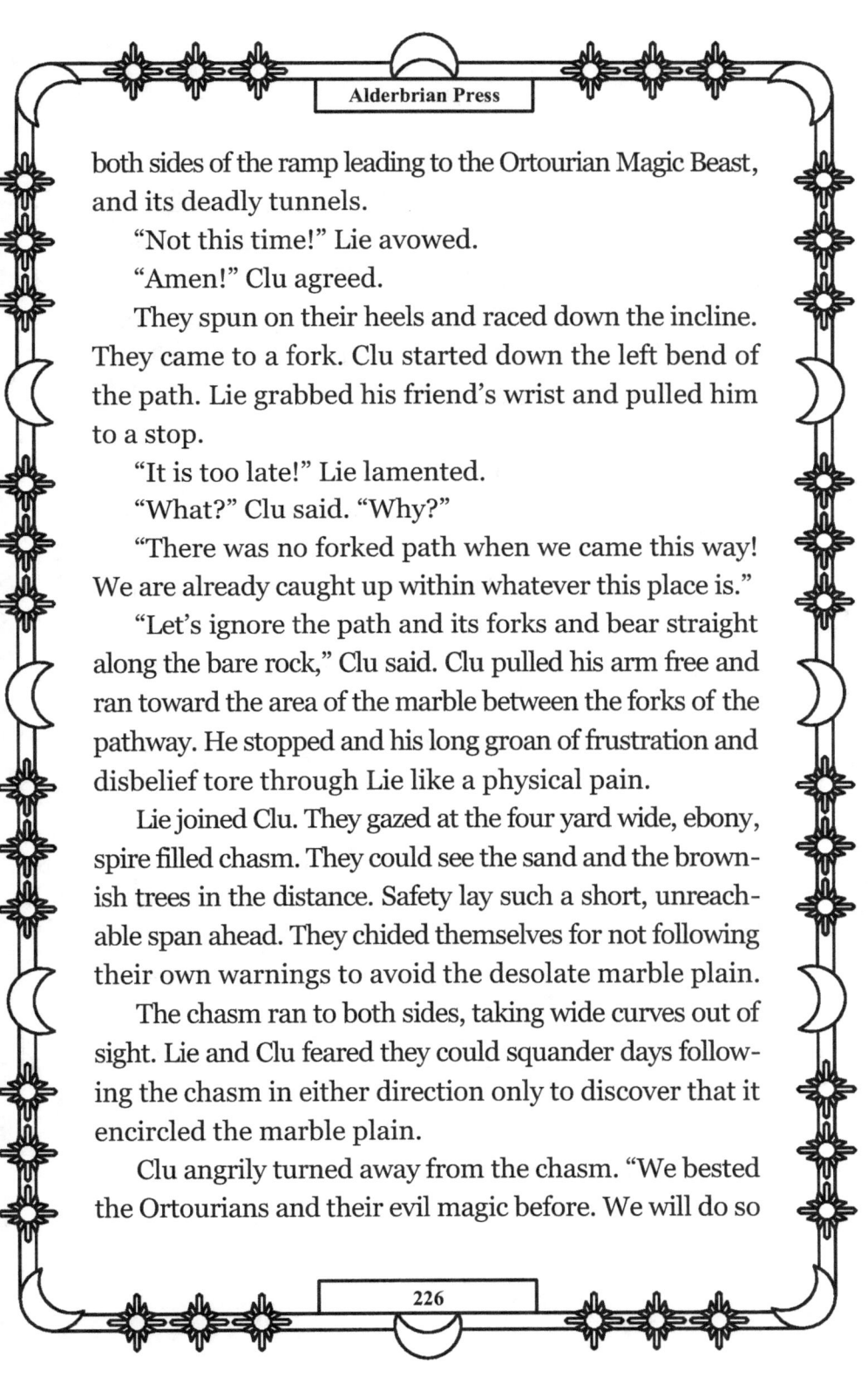

both sides of the ramp leading to the Ortourian Magic Beast, and its deadly tunnels.

"Not this time!" Lie avowed.

"Amen!" Clu agreed.

They spun on their heels and raced down the incline. They came to a fork. Clu started down the left bend of the path. Lie grabbed his friend's wrist and pulled him to a stop.

"It is too late!" Lie lamented.

"What?" Clu said. "Why?"

"There was no forked path when we came this way! We are already caught up within whatever this place is."

"Let's ignore the path and its forks and bear straight along the bare rock," Clu said. Clu pulled his arm free and ran toward the area of the marble between the forks of the pathway. He stopped and his long groan of frustration and disbelief tore through Lie like a physical pain.

Lie joined Clu. They gazed at the four yard wide, ebony, spire filled chasm. They could see the sand and the brownish trees in the distance. Safety lay such a short, unreachable span ahead. They chided themselves for not following their own warnings to avoid the desolate marble plain.

The chasm ran to both sides, taking wide curves out of sight. Lie and Clu feared they could squander days following the chasm in either direction only to discover that it encircled the marble plain.

Clu angrily turned away from the chasm. "We bested the Ortourians and their evil magic before. We will do so again!"

Lie smiled wryly. He admired Clu's determination, but doubted their chances of passing though a second enchanted death machine, alive. "Wait, Clu," he said. "Let us follow one of these forks in the path, first. They are here for a purpose. Perhaps, if we choose wisely, we may be allowed to pass around this place without harm. Rather than bee lining into the heart of the spires and up against whatever arcane horror lurks among them."

Clu raised his eyebrows, with an expression of hope. "It's worth a try!" he agreed.

They returned to the path and faced the fork. They stepped forward.

Lie was unable to walk in any direction except down the right-hand fork.

Clu was unable to walk any direction except down the left-hand fork.

Both stopped.

"We should have known!" Lie shouted, anger reddening his face. "We suspected this was Ortourian! We should have known their first act would be to separate us!"

Clu tried to return to the main pathway. His eyes widened with wonder. There had been no resistance.

Lie was heartened by this. He back tracked and joined Clu without interference.

"Allow me to try one thing," Lie said, "before we do what I believe we will be forced to do."

"Anything," Clu said.

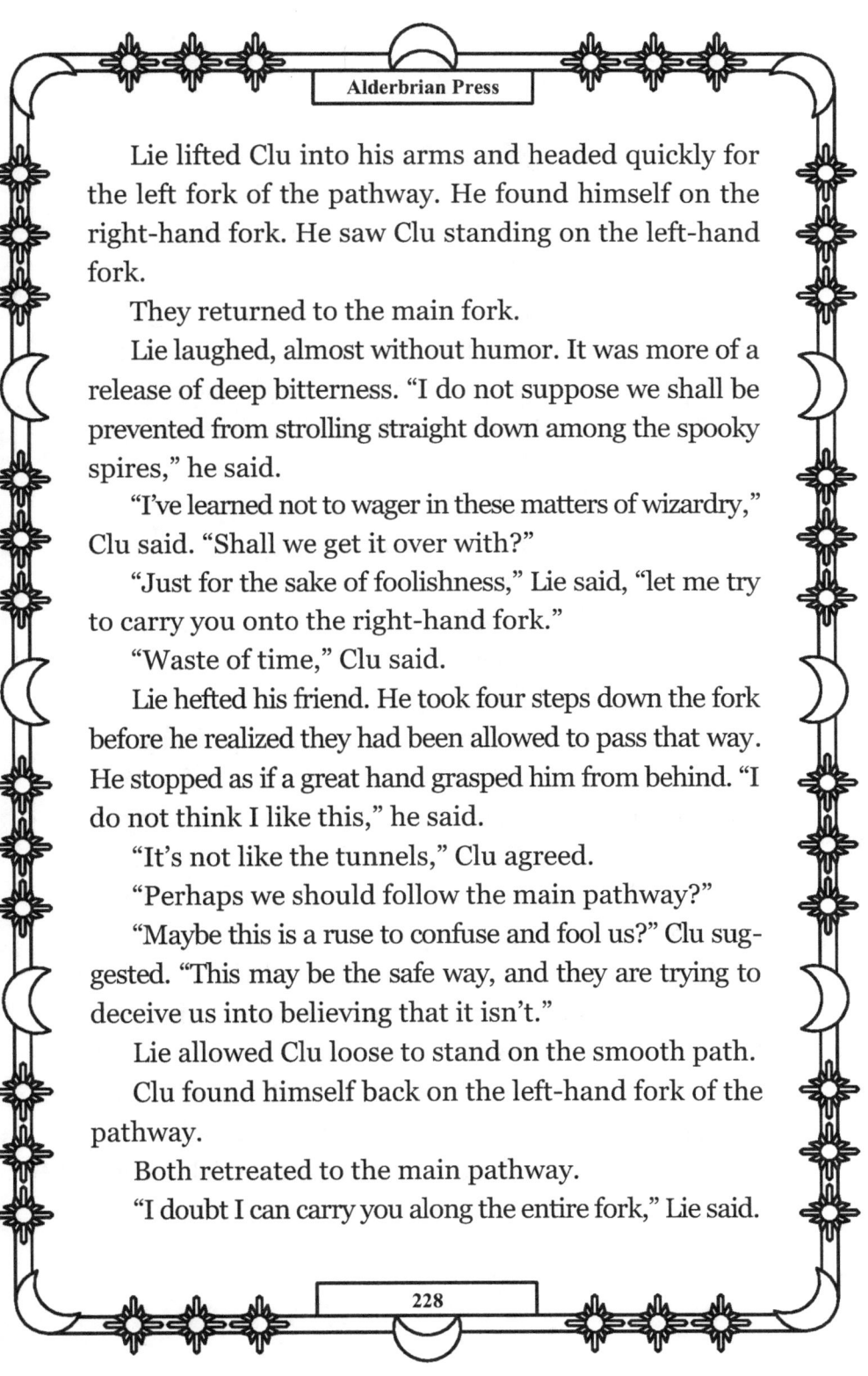

Lie lifted Clu into his arms and headed quickly for the left fork of the pathway. He found himself on the right-hand fork. He saw Clu standing on the left-hand fork.

They returned to the main fork.

Lie laughed, almost without humor. It was more of a release of deep bitterness. "I do not suppose we shall be prevented from strolling straight down among the spooky spires," he said.

"I've learned not to wager in these matters of wizardry," Clu said. "Shall we get it over with?"

"Just for the sake of foolishness," Lie said, "let me try to carry you onto the right-hand fork."

"Waste of time," Clu said.

Lie hefted his friend. He took four steps down the fork before he realized they had been allowed to pass that way. He stopped as if a great hand grasped him from behind. "I do not think I like this," he said.

"It's not like the tunnels," Clu agreed.

"Perhaps we should follow the main pathway?"

"Maybe this is a ruse to confuse and fool us?" Clu suggested. "This may be the safe way, and they are trying to deceive us into believing that it isn't."

Lie allowed Clu loose to stand on the smooth path.

Clu found himself back on the left-hand fork of the pathway.

Both retreated to the main pathway.

"I doubt I can carry you along the entire fork," Lie said.

"How about piggy back?"

"Do you want to try that fork, then?" Lie asked.

"They seem to be making it hard for us to go that route, so I'll say it's the right way."

Lie scowled. "If we go along the main path, we might be blocked from returning to the forks. We might miss our only opportunity to pass safely down the right-hand fork."

Clu ran forward to the lip of the incline and over it out of sight.

Lie raced after his friend. When he topped the rise, he saw only giant ominous spires and pathways. Lie fearfully backed up. He did not want to endure this new threat alone. He needed to think.

"This makes to sense!" Clu said.

Lie whirled around.

Clu was standing at the fork in the main pathway. He was breathing hard as though he had run a long distance. "I was almost down to the first two spires when I just popped up here!" Clu said. "I was there! Then I was here!"

"Does this mean we must follow the right-hand fork?" Lie said as he walked over to Clu.

"See if you can make it to the spires," Clu said.

Lie felt a pang of apprehension. He shook his head, firmly. "I will not risk separating from you. We might not be as lucky here as we were within the Ortourian Tunnel. We might never rejoin each other in this place."

Clu gritted his teeth in anger at himself. "I didn't think of that!" he said.

They stared at each other for a long while. The sun poured its heat on them without mercy.

"Into the breech and the unknown menace," Lie whispered, "or into the unknown of the fork."

Clu nodded. "We can't stand here forever," he said, with sadness. "We can't live forever."

"The fork, then," Lie decided. He knelt on the pathway and Clu mounted his back. Lie strode briskly down the right-hand fork of the obsidian pathway.

Ten resolute paces later, they found themselves standing at the top of the original pathway, bearing toward the first two of the massive needle sharp spires.

Lie allowed Clu to slide off his back, and they continued walking. Their annoyance at the obvious, non humorous game someone was playing, was so intense, neither man could bring himself to speak.

When they passed between the first two spires, the heat of the sun, but not its light, was cut in half, bringing a chill.

Clu pointed to round spots at the bases of each of the ebony spires that lined both sides of the pathway.

Lie shuddered with apprehension. "Caves," he said.

"To be avoided!" Clu avowed.

"It occurs to me, we should run as swiftly as possible, in as straight a path as we can, until we have vacated this place," Lie said.

Clu grasped Lie's right wrist, and they ran along the main pathway. The needle sharp ebony marble spires grew closer together on both side of them. There was a loud scratching behind.

"Do not even think of looking behind us!" Lie ordered. He ran faster, pulling Clu after him.

The scraping sound made them think of Death.

With a cry of despair, Clu drew back against Lie's forward movement. Lie stopped and followed Clu's horrified stare.

On both sides of the pathway, in front of the perfectly circular caves in the bases of the spires, stood large spider like creatures. They were gray, with four, long, jointed legs. Bodies twice the size of Lie. Heads bore the horrendous visage of Ihpoza, including his barbed horn! Rear stingers were longer than Lie's leg. Forty arachnids raptly watched Lie and Clu.

"Ihpoza!" Clu said, his voice trembling with fear, "Not Ortourians!"

"I hope so!" Lie avowed. "We cannot be harmed by illusions!"

"Unless they hide crevices or cliffs from us!"

"We must utilize our Mind Magic to descry any threats masked by Ihpoza's illusions!" Lie urged. "Concentrate! Think of seeing through all illusions! Finding the real lay of the land! Baylou said we are resistant to the Mind Magic of others! Let us utilize this defense to our advantage, for once!"

They stood back-to-back.

"Why haven't the spiders attacked?" Clu said.

"It would be useless for harmless illusions to attack," Lie said. He was staring at the stone surface around them.

"Not if a real demon is behind an illusion!" Clu warned.

"Then, we must see through the illusions to any threat that might walk behind them!"

No matter how intensely he concentrated on viewing through the illusions, Lie achieved no success. He began to doubt they were being threatened by Ihpoza.

The spider nearest Lie raced toward him for several feet, spun around in an unearthly fashion, and fired a white object from its rear protuberance.

Lie put his arms back and threw himself and Clu to the right, sprawling them on the hard, smooth, ebony marble.

The white object was a thick strand of spider silk. The protrusions on the spiders were not stingers.

Clu saw the silk strand being drawn, with wild speed, back into the spider. "They are going to web us in and kill us!" he shouted. He thrilled with sudden understanding. "We must run around behind the spires, to escape!"

Clu and Lie scrambled to his feet.

"How do you know this?" Lie demanded.

"I just do!" Clu assured him.

Lie hoped Clu was profiting from their resistance to Mind Magic in some fashion.

Clu grabbed Lie's wrist, and they started toward one row of the creepy spires.

Spiders were climbing up the spires. Spiders were crawling toward both ends of the files of spires along both sides of the walkway. Spiders were emerging from the circular caves. Soon, there would be hundreds of spiders spinning silk.

Lie and Clu neared the two closest spires, and several spiders raced down them, toward the men. It was obvious, neither man could reach the breech between the spires before the arachnids would.

"Checkmated!" Clu said.

Lie was puzzled. The spiders had been incredibly busy. Strands of sticky silk were strung from the tips of each needle sharp spire to all the other spires on both sides of the pathway, crisscrossed in an almost mesmerizing, beautiful way, creating a roof above the pathway. Lie yanked Clu back to the main pathway, and they began running toward the far end of the lines of spires. They could hear silk strands whizzing through the air above.

Spiders, seeming oblivious to the men, were standing motionless on each side of the pathway at the base of each spire.

The motionless spiders, Clu realized, are awaiting the command from whatever controls this accursed place, to rush in for the kill. They have the end and top of this part of the pathway silked solid, so they must have done the same to the section we are running toward. Where does Lie imagine he is going? Why doesn't Lie realize we have no hope?

The path widened to a large circle, with the lampblack spires describing an arc on both sides.

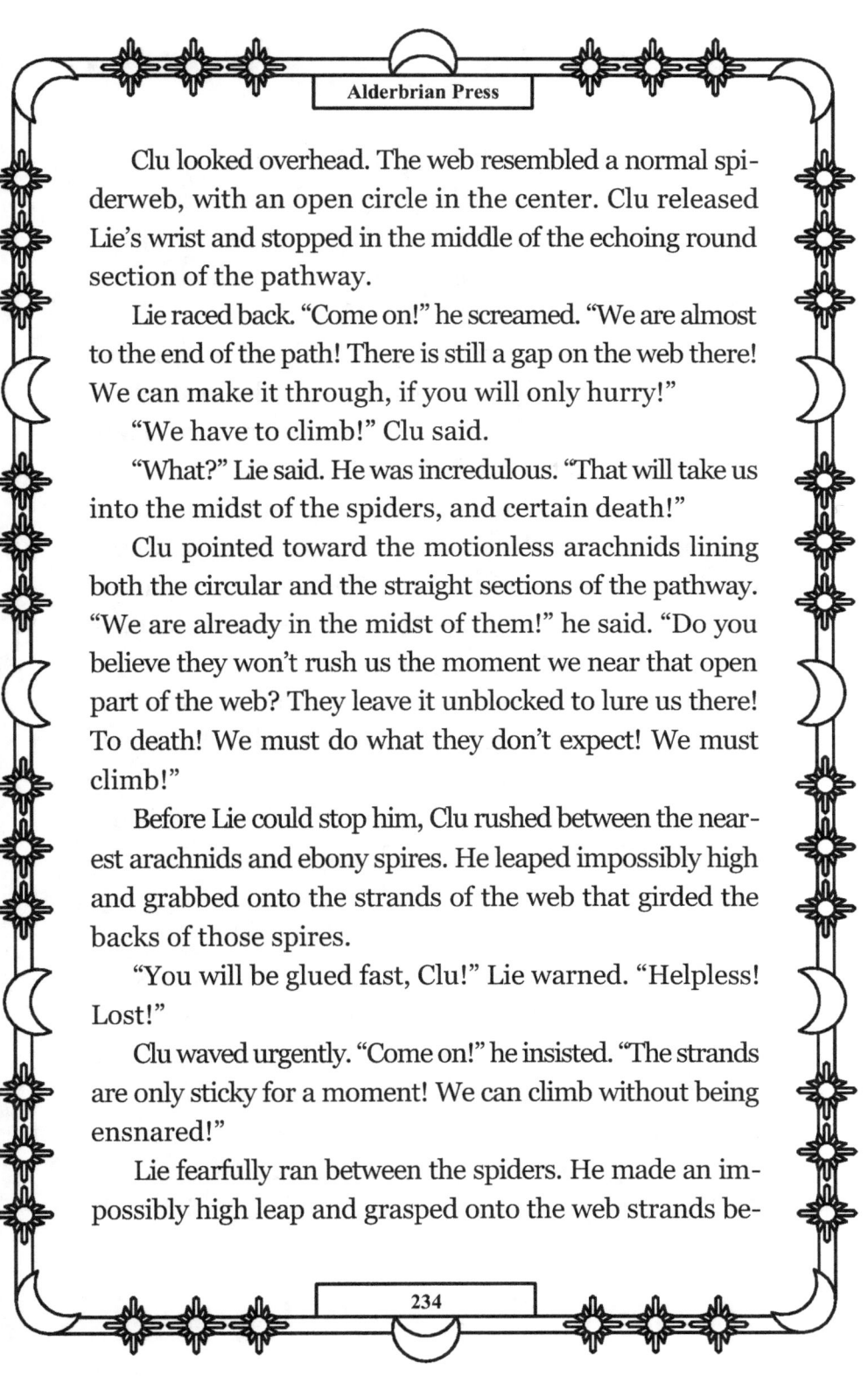

Clu looked overhead. The web resembled a normal spiderweb, with an open circle in the center. Clu released Lie's wrist and stopped in the middle of the echoing round section of the pathway.

Lie raced back. "Come on!" he screamed. "We are almost to the end of the path! There is still a gap on the web there! We can make it through, if you will only hurry!"

"We have to climb!" Clu said.

"What?" Lie said. He was incredulous. "That will take us into the midst of the spiders, and certain death!"

Clu pointed toward the motionless arachnids lining both the circular and the straight sections of the pathway. "We are already in the midst of them!" he said. "Do you believe they won't rush us the moment we near that open part of the web? They leave it unblocked to lure us there! To death! We must do what they don't expect! We must climb!"

Before Lie could stop him, Clu rushed between the nearest arachnids and ebony spires. He leaped impossibly high and grabbed onto the strands of the web that girded the backs of those spires.

"You will be glued fast, Clu!" Lie warned. "Helpless! Lost!"

Clu waved urgently. "Come on!" he insisted. "The strands are only sticky for a moment! We can climb without being ensnared!"

Lie fearfully ran between the spiders. He made an impossibly high leap and grasped onto the web strands be-

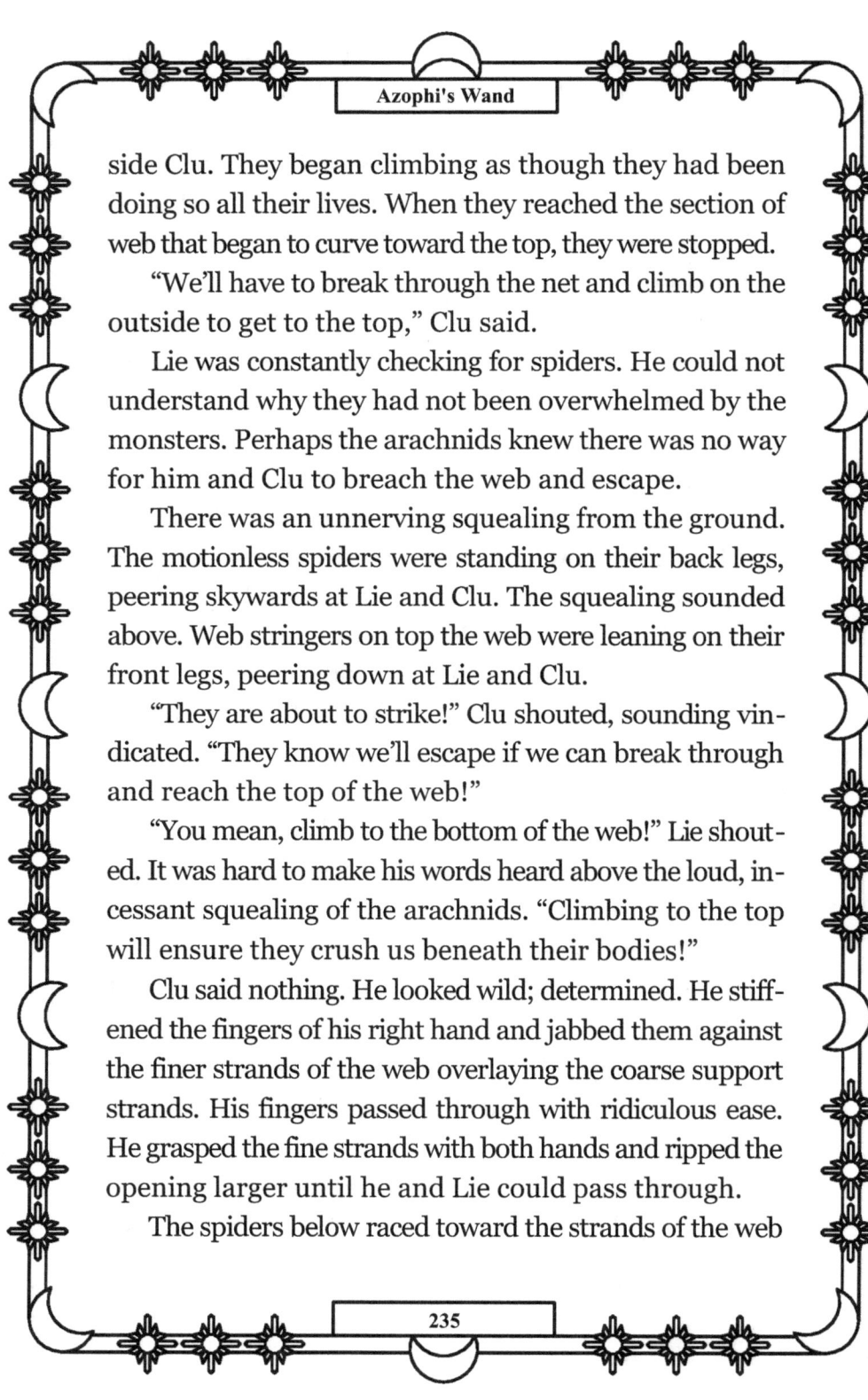

side Clu. They began climbing as though they had been doing so all their lives. When they reached the section of web that began to curve toward the top, they were stopped.

"We'll have to break through the net and climb on the outside to get to the top," Clu said.

Lie was constantly checking for spiders. He could not understand why they had not been overwhelmed by the monsters. Perhaps the arachnids knew there was no way for him and Clu to breach the web and escape.

There was an unnerving squealing from the ground. The motionless spiders were standing on their back legs, peering skywards at Lie and Clu. The squealing sounded above. Web stringers on top the web were leaning on their front legs, peering down at Lie and Clu.

"They are about to strike!" Clu shouted, sounding vindicated. "They know we'll escape if we can break through and reach the top of the web!"

"You mean, climb to the bottom of the web!" Lie shouted. It was hard to make his words heard above the loud, incessant squealing of the arachnids. "Climbing to the top will ensure they crush us beneath their bodies!"

Clu said nothing. He looked wild; determined. He stiffened the fingers of his right hand and jabbed them against the finer strands of the web overlaying the coarse support strands. His fingers passed through with ridiculous ease. He grasped the fine strands with both hands and ripped the opening larger until he and Lie could pass through.

The spiders below raced toward the strands of the web

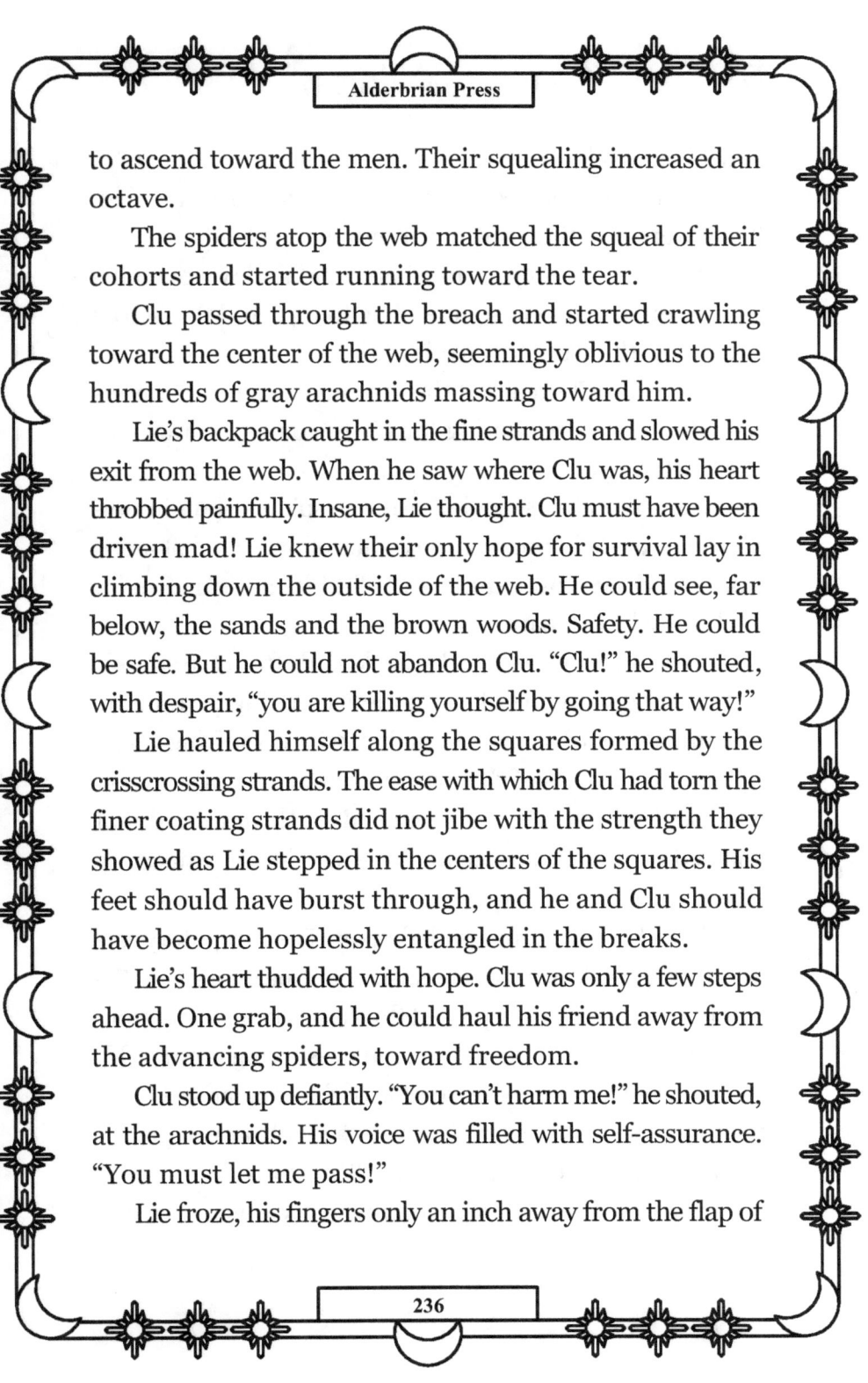

to ascend toward the men. Their squealing increased an octave.

The spiders atop the web matched the squeal of their cohorts and started running toward the tear.

Clu passed through the breach and started crawling toward the center of the web, seemingly oblivious to the hundreds of gray arachnids massing toward him.

Lie's backpack caught in the fine strands and slowed his exit from the web. When he saw where Clu was, his heart throbbed painfully. Insane, Lie thought. Clu must have been driven mad! Lie knew their only hope for survival lay in climbing down the outside of the web. He could see, far below, the sands and the brown woods. Safety. He could be safe. But he could not abandon Clu. "Clu!" he shouted, with despair, "you are killing yourself by going that way!"

Lie hauled himself along the squares formed by the crisscrossing strands. The ease with which Clu had torn the finer coating strands did not jibe with the strength they showed as Lie stepped in the centers of the squares. His feet should have burst through, and he and Clu should have become hopelessly entangled in the breaks.

Lie's heart thudded with hope. Clu was only a few steps ahead. One grab, and he could haul his friend away from the advancing spiders, toward freedom.

Clu stood up defiantly. "You can't harm me!" he shouted, at the arachnids. His voice was filled with self-assurance. "You must let me pass!"

Lie froze, his fingers only an inch away from the flap of

Clu's backpack.

The spiders formed a tight semi circle in front of Clu. They were howling, but not moving any closer.

Lie crept one step nearer his friend and wrapped his arms around Clu's chest, intending to turn and flee across the top of the web, toward its side.

In horror, Clu realized the arachnids went motionless because they were waiting for Lie to come into range of their attack plan.

Like a macabre school of fish, the spiders spun in unison and expelled hundreds of strands of fine silk that arced up, then down toward Lie and Clu like a semi circular flight of white spears.

Lie desperately tried to flee backwards from the strands but collided with one of the spiders creeping up on him. The impact sent Lie and Clu sailing, with mystifying velocity, over the heads of the startled semi circle of spiders.

The deadly sticky strands rained on the arachnid that collided with Lie, covering it in a lethal glob of suffocating silk.

Lie and Clu screamed with despair. Their trajectory carried them, helplessly, hopelessly toward the opening in the center of the web. They passed through, too far away from its rim to manage a desperate, life preserving hand hold.

Clu watched the ebony marble of the circular section of the pathway speed toward him with a nightmarish quality. "I'm sorry!" he screamed to Lie. "I'm sorry!"

Lie could not respond. Their velocity was increasing

incredibly, forcing the air by them so quickly, it was almost impossible to breathe.

Clu noted it was taking an unnaturally long time at this inconceivable speed to cover the distance from the top of the web to the heartless ebony stone.

A moment before they were sure of impact and death, their wild descent ceased, and they gently settled to the lampblack marble, on their unsteady feet.

"Quickly," Baylou commanded. "Without thought, do as I say!" It hovered into Clu's hands. "Place Clu, standing, on your shoulders!"

Lie knelt and complied. When he stood up, Clu raised Baylou over his head toward the center of the web.

Hundreds of spiders were descending on strands of silk from the opening above. Hundreds were issuing from the circular caves that led into the evil spires. All were racing toward the men, toward the kill.

Baylou emanated forty beams of green light toward the tips of the black spires. Lightening crackled all over the spires, then crawled down them, and along the marble pathways. Lightning caught the spiders on the ground, with explosive force. They were hurled up against the underside of the web where they desperately clung to the strands.

The descending arachnids wildly reversed their direction of travel. There was a different squealing from them; a cry of fear.

Baylou's lightning set fire to the web at both ends of

the walkway, and flowed along the two silk pathway roofs, spreading to the main web. Baylou ceased its forty beams of power and the lightning ended.

The roaring green fire flowed upwards in a circle around the spires and circular pathway, engulfing the web.

Lie knelt, and Clu jumped to the marble. Through the top of the web, they watched the shadows of the frenzied arachnids rushing about in insane patterns of desperation, trying to flee when there was no haven available.

The advancing flames forced the arachnids toward the central opening. The spiders realized this was their only escape route. They rushed to the opening and hurled themselves through, looking like a circular flow of gray water, with their climbing strands forming a tunnel behind them.

Lie and Clu raced backwards from under the huge circular opening to avoid being inundated by the enraged spiders.

When the arachnids touched the ebony marble, Baylou's magic fire overwhelmed the web, roared down the climbing strands, engulfed the squealing spiders and became a huge column of psychic force.

The light of the sun struck Lie and Clu, but was pale compared to the flickering tower of energy.

Baylou flew out of Clu's hands and turned to Lie. "Do that which you must!" it said. "Or all of this, indeed, all things, are lost!"

Against fear and better judgment, Lie tilted his wrists back, ran forward, and pushed his palms against the humming tower of power. To his horror, he flashed into its center. His skin prickled from the force dancing around him. The light hurt his eyes. It was difficult to breathe. "Azophi's will! Azophi's needs, you shall fulfill!" Lie intoned. He desperately wanted to be free of the itchy feel of the energy crawling all over him.

The emerald tower speared into the sun gilded sky. As it flew, it compressed until it was two feet long and two inches around. It suppressed its light until it was almost invisible, then vanished due to distance.

Clu and Baylou went to Lie.

Baylou was beaming bright green.

Clu was smiling with satisfaction and pride for Lie.

Lie stood with his hands on his knees, gasping for breath and waiting for the tingling fade away.

The colorless shaft of power soared through the sun yellowed sky, entered Iphozalon, passed through the roof of the ice palace and the ceiling of the throne room, pierced the top of the shimmering spell prison, and became part of the Wand. To look at the Wand, one would be unable to discern any difference. This was as it had to be.

Ihpoza psychically rotated himself off his ornate ice bed, into a standing position, and stalked out of his sleeping chamber. Something had awakened him. Something was different. For an instant, there had been a sense of alteration in his vicinity. He was almost sure it had not been a dream, or his imagination. One thought coursed through his mind: the Wand. He hesitantly paused in the arched doorway of his throne room. He saw the Wand in its spell prison, and relief flooded through him. Perhaps it had been a nightmare, after all. He returned to his sleeping chamber, glowering at himself for not better controlling his sleep state and dreams.

***

Baylou opened its green eye so wide it wrinkled its front cover above and below. Its astonishment at what its senses reported, was so intense, it had to regain control of its flight through the night air to avoid colliding with trees. It hovered inches above the ground.

Someone had released a mighty Cache of magic from within a dream, of all places! How Azophi could place a Cache inside a dream that had not been dreamt until tonight, was beyond the Book's knowledge and ability to comprehend. The psychic power had gone to the Wand. Again, secrets surprised and annoyed it. Baylou raised itself into the night sky and resumed its travels.

***

Quiet.

Soft.

Warm.

Clu fell deeper asleep with his hand resting on the object against which he had rolled his head.

Something bent over Clu and whispered in his ear.

Clu stirred uneasily, but did not awaken.

Illustration 36

Ortourian Beast Wrought Iron Window Grillwork

Copyright © 2019 Philip Raymond Sadler

242-A

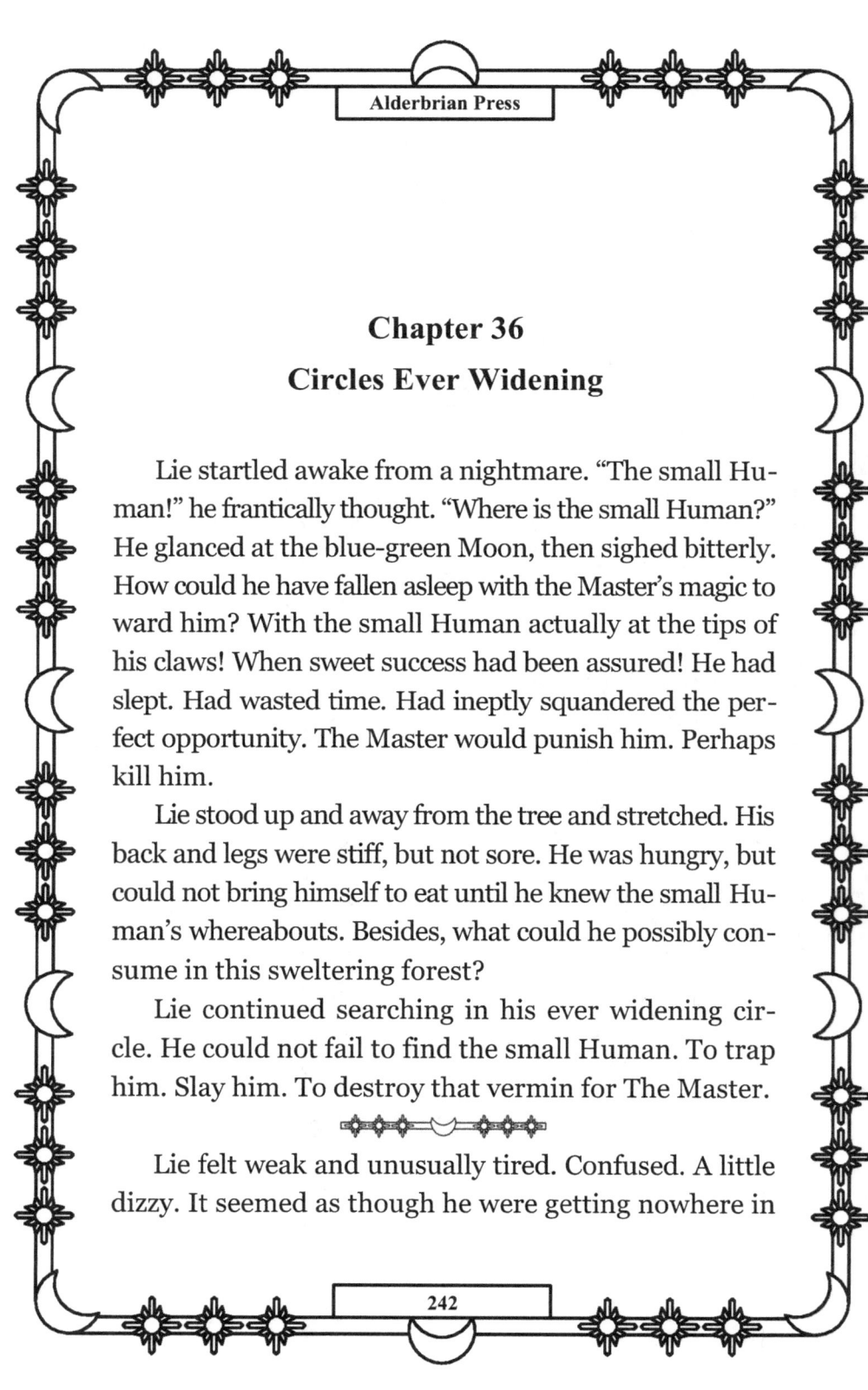

Chapter 36

Circles Ever Widening

Lie startled awake from a nightmare. "The small Human!" he frantically thought. "Where is the small Human?" He glanced at the blue-green Moon, then sighed bitterly. How could he have fallen asleep with the Master's magic to ward him? With the small Human actually at the tips of his claws! When sweet success had been assured! He had slept. Had wasted time. Had ineptly squandered the perfect opportunity. The Master would punish him. Perhaps kill him.

Lie stood up and away from the tree and stretched. His back and legs were stiff, but not sore. He was hungry, but could not bring himself to eat until he knew the small Human's whereabouts. Besides, what could he possibly consume in this sweltering forest?

Lie continued searching in his ever widening circle. He could not fail to find the small Human. To trap him. Slay him. To destroy that vermin for The Master.

Lie felt weak and unusually tired. Confused. A little dizzy. It seemed as though he were getting nowhere in

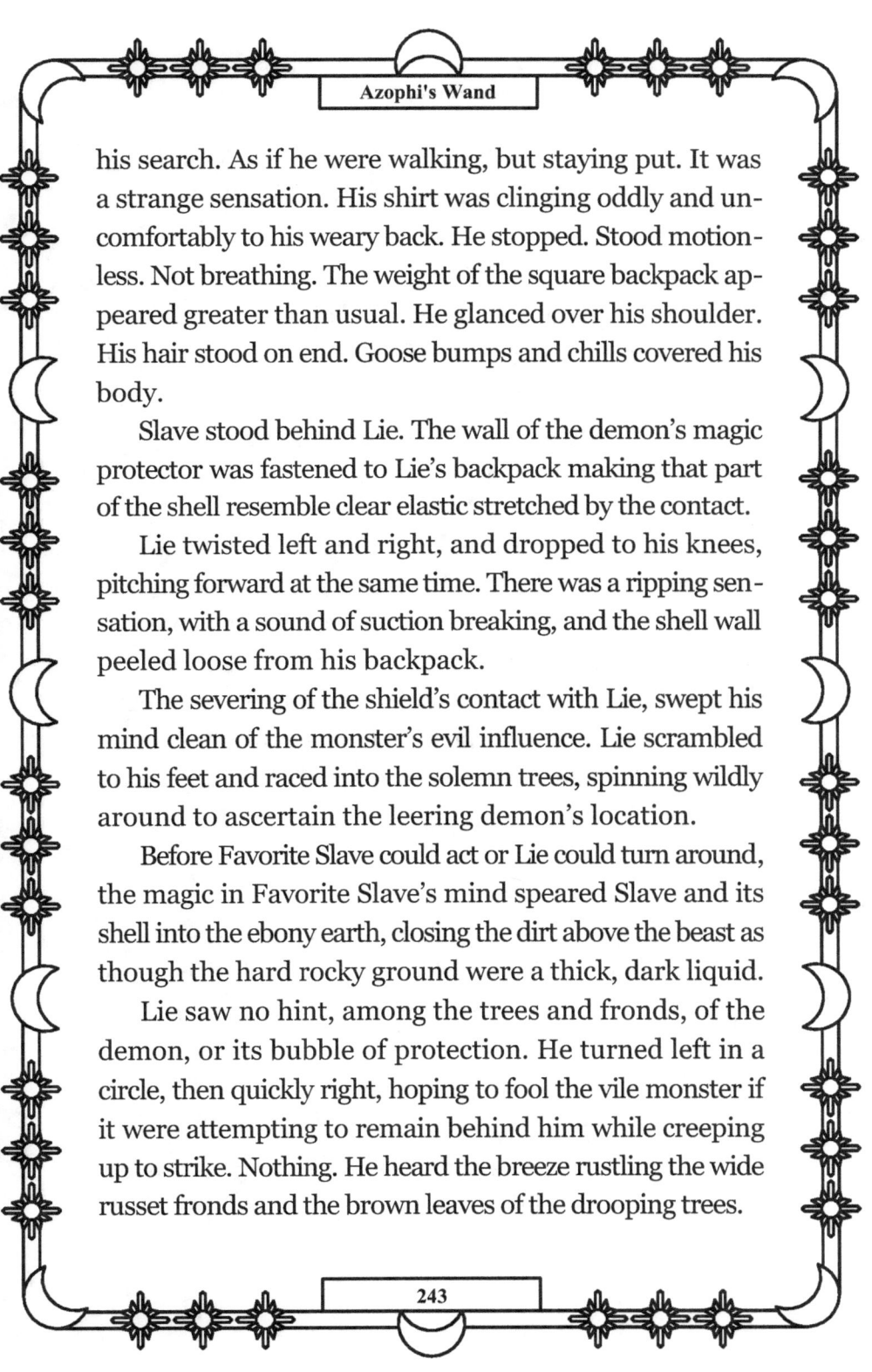

his search. As if he were walking, but staying put. It was a strange sensation. His shirt was clinging oddly and uncomfortably to his weary back. He stopped. Stood motionless. Not breathing. The weight of the square backpack appeared greater than usual. He glanced over his shoulder. His hair stood on end. Goose bumps and chills covered his body.

Slave stood behind Lie. The wall of the demon's magic protector was fastened to Lie's backpack making that part of the shell resemble clear elastic stretched by the contact.

Lie twisted left and right, and dropped to his knees, pitching forward at the same time. There was a ripping sensation, with a sound of suction breaking, and the shell wall peeled loose from his backpack.

The severing of the shield's contact with Lie, swept his mind clean of the monster's evil influence. Lie scrambled to his feet and raced into the solemn trees, spinning wildly around to ascertain the leering demon's location.

Before Favorite Slave could act or Lie could turn around, the magic in Favorite Slave's mind speared Slave and its shell into the ebony earth, closing the dirt above the beast as though the hard rocky ground were a thick, dark liquid.

Lie saw no hint, among the trees and fronds, of the demon, or its bubble of protection. He turned left in a circle, then quickly right, hoping to fool the vile monster if it were attempting to remain behind him while creeping up to strike. Nothing. He heard the breeze rustling the wide russet fronds and the brown leaves of the drooping trees.

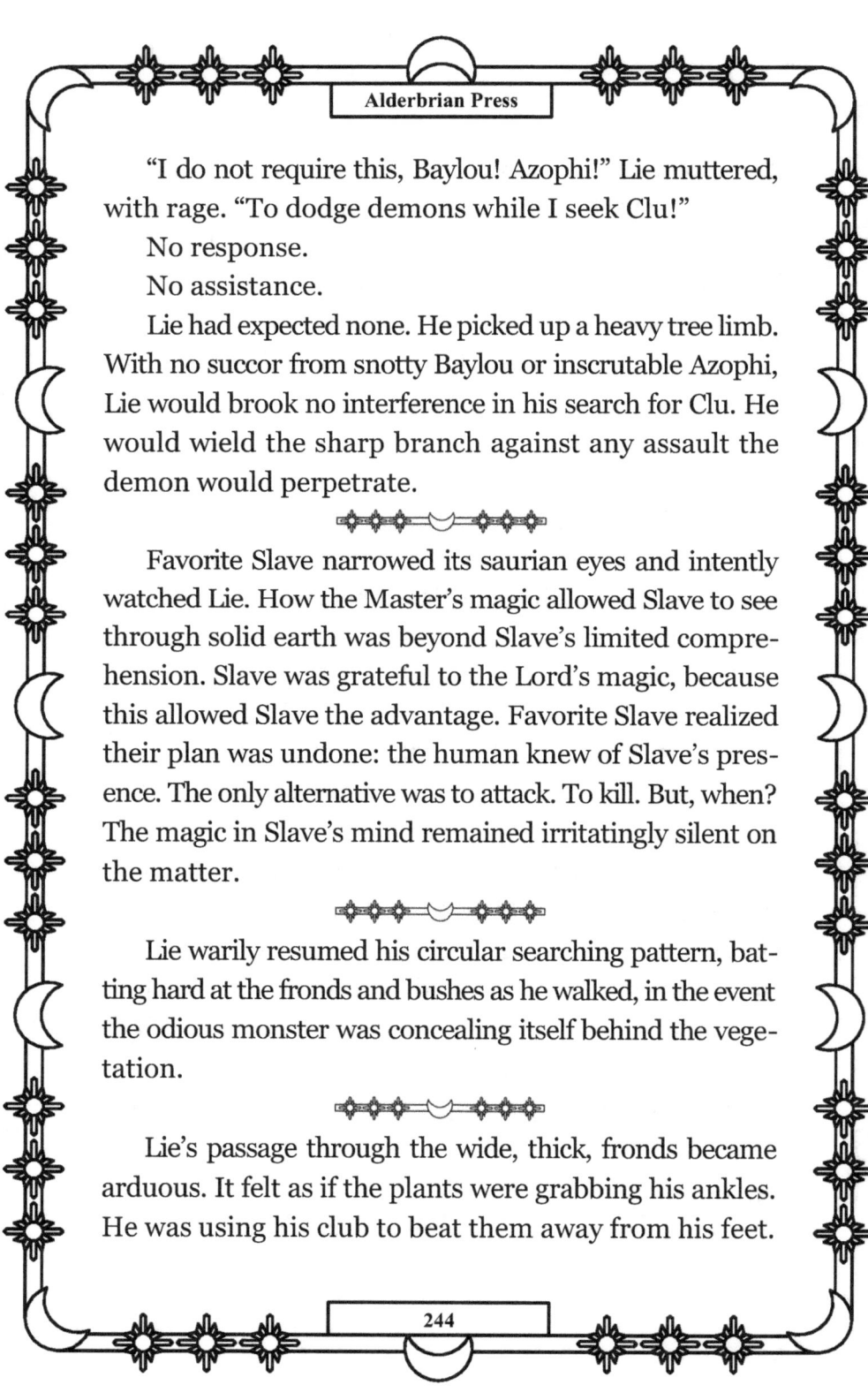

"I do not require this, Baylou! Azophi!" Lie muttered, with rage. "To dodge demons while I seek Clu!"

No response.

No assistance.

Lie had expected none. He picked up a heavy tree limb. With no succor from snotty Baylou or inscrutable Azophi, Lie would brook no interference in his search for Clu. He would wield the sharp branch against any assault the demon would perpetrate.

Favorite Slave narrowed its saurian eyes and intently watched Lie. How the Master's magic allowed Slave to see through solid earth was beyond Slave's limited comprehension. Slave was grateful to the Lord's magic, because this allowed Slave the advantage. Favorite Slave realized their plan was undone: the human knew of Slave's presence. The only alternative was to attack. To kill. But, when? The magic in Slave's mind remained irritatingly silent on the matter.

Lie warily resumed his circular searching pattern, batting hard at the fronds and bushes as he walked, in the event the odious monster was concealing itself behind the vegetation.

Lie's passage through the wide, thick, fronds became arduous. It felt as if the plants were grabbing his ankles. He was using his club to beat them away from his feet.

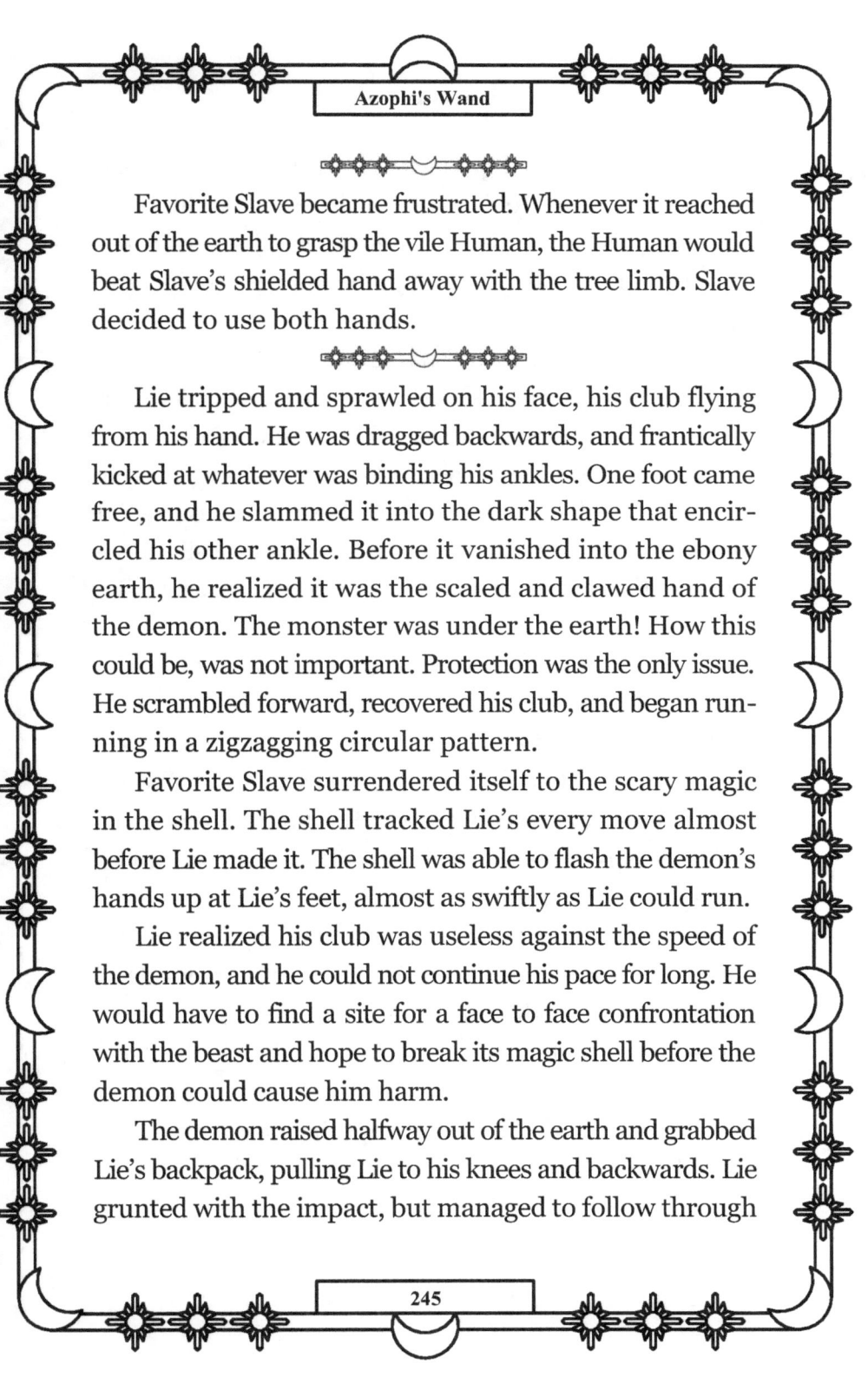

Favorite Slave became frustrated. Whenever it reached out of the earth to grasp the vile Human, the Human would beat Slave's shielded hand away with the tree limb. Slave decided to use both hands.

Lie tripped and sprawled on his face, his club flying from his hand. He was dragged backwards, and frantically kicked at whatever was binding his ankles. One foot came free, and he slammed it into the dark shape that encircled his other ankle. Before it vanished into the ebony earth, he realized it was the scaled and clawed hand of the demon. The monster was under the earth! How this could be, was not important. Protection was the only issue. He scrambled forward, recovered his club, and began running in a zigzagging circular pattern.

Favorite Slave surrendered itself to the scary magic in the shell. The shell tracked Lie's every move almost before Lie made it. The shell was able to flash the demon's hands up at Lie's feet, almost as swiftly as Lie could run.

Lie realized his club was useless against the speed of the demon, and he could not continue his pace for long. He would have to find a site for a face to face confrontation with the beast and hope to break its magic shell before the demon could cause him harm.

The demon raised halfway out of the earth and grabbed Lie's backpack, pulling Lie to his knees and backwards. Lie grunted with the impact, but managed to follow through

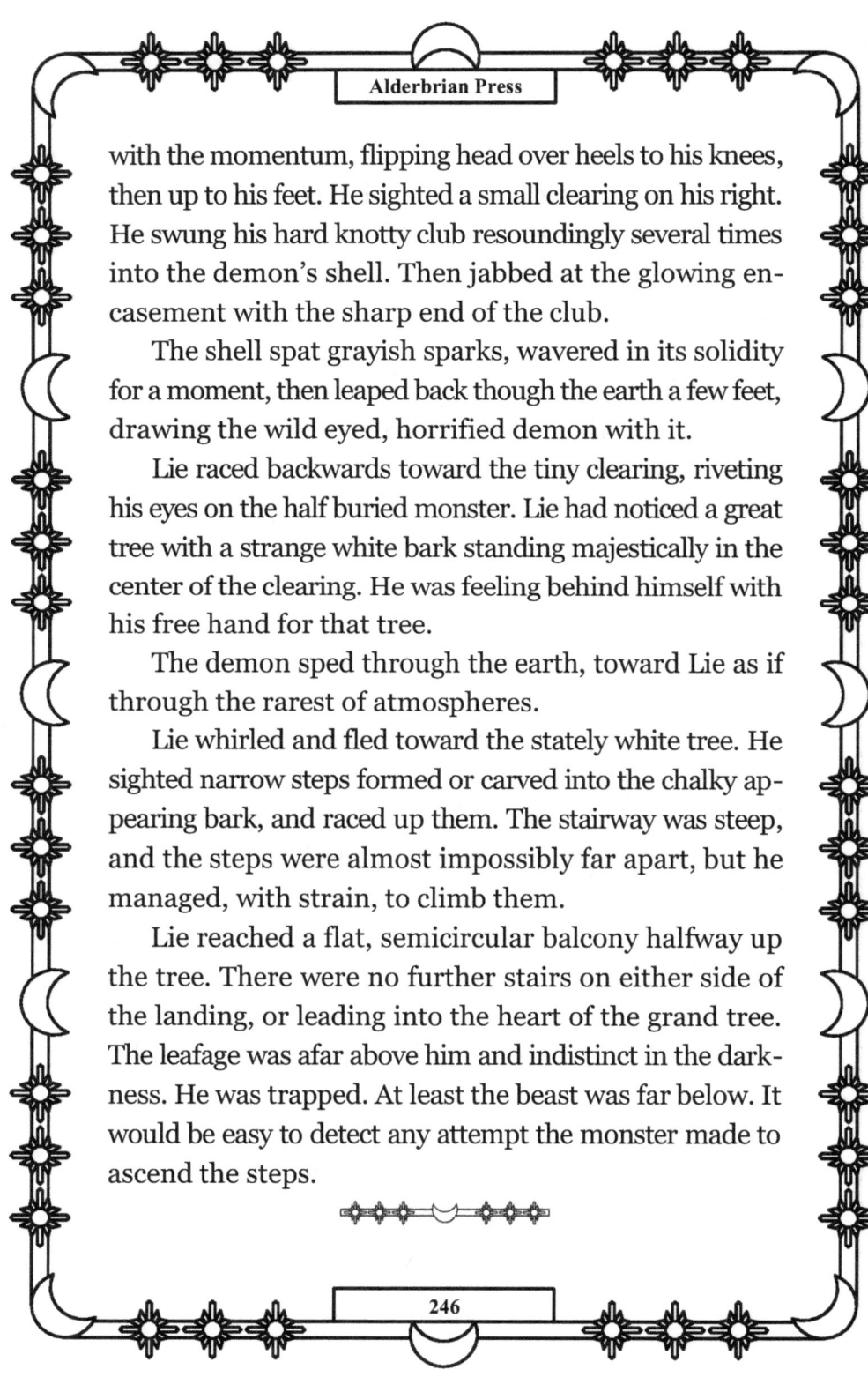

with the momentum, flipping head over heels to his knees, then up to his feet. He sighted a small clearing on his right. He swung his hard knotty club resoundingly several times into the demon's shell. Then jabbed at the glowing encasement with the sharp end of the club.

The shell spat grayish sparks, wavered in its solidity for a moment, then leaped back though the earth a few feet, drawing the wild eyed, horrified demon with it.

Lie raced backwards toward the tiny clearing, riveting his eyes on the half buried monster. Lie had noticed a great tree with a strange white bark standing majestically in the center of the clearing. He was feeling behind himself with his free hand for that tree.

The demon sped through the earth, toward Lie as if through the rarest of atmospheres.

Lie whirled and fled toward the stately white tree. He sighted narrow steps formed or carved into the chalky appearing bark, and raced up them. The stairway was steep, and the steps were almost impossibly far apart, but he managed, with strain, to climb them.

Lie reached a flat, semicircular balcony halfway up the tree. There were no further stairs on either side of the landing, or leading into the heart of the grand tree. The leafage was afar above him and indistinct in the darkness. He was trapped. At least the beast was far below. It would be easy to detect any attempt the monster made to ascend the steps.

Favorite Slave stood at the base of the odd tree. The Magic whispered to Slave and Slave laughed. It was an unnerving, growling, animal sound. Slave and its bubble sank into the rocky earth like a great drop of polluted blue water.

Lie realized his options were confined. With the gorgon absent for the moment, Lie laid his club down and ran his hands over the chalky bark at the rear of the landing. He hoped there was a hidden entrance. There was no sense carving stairs into a tree and not excavating the core of the tree for living quarters. History recorded how some of his early ancestors dwelt inside the great trees of the Southern HighLands. They fashioned ingenious entrances devilishly difficult to discover. Perhaps some of them had migrated to this misbegotten place, for some unfathomable reason.

Slave delved into the earth until the demon discerned the roots of the weird tree. To Slave's puzzlement, there were only four thick roots. They seemed to vanish forever into the deeper ebony, rocky earth. The Magic spoke in Slave's mind and Slave laughed cruelly.

The shell hurled itself at the tree, to pass into the center of the trunk, to rise up, surprise, and shred the Human. The shell resoundingly smashed into the side of the tree between two of the massive roots, rebounding as though it had struck springy, but impenetrable metal.

To the demons affright, the shell slammed itself repeatedly into the tree, frustrated at its inability to penetrate the

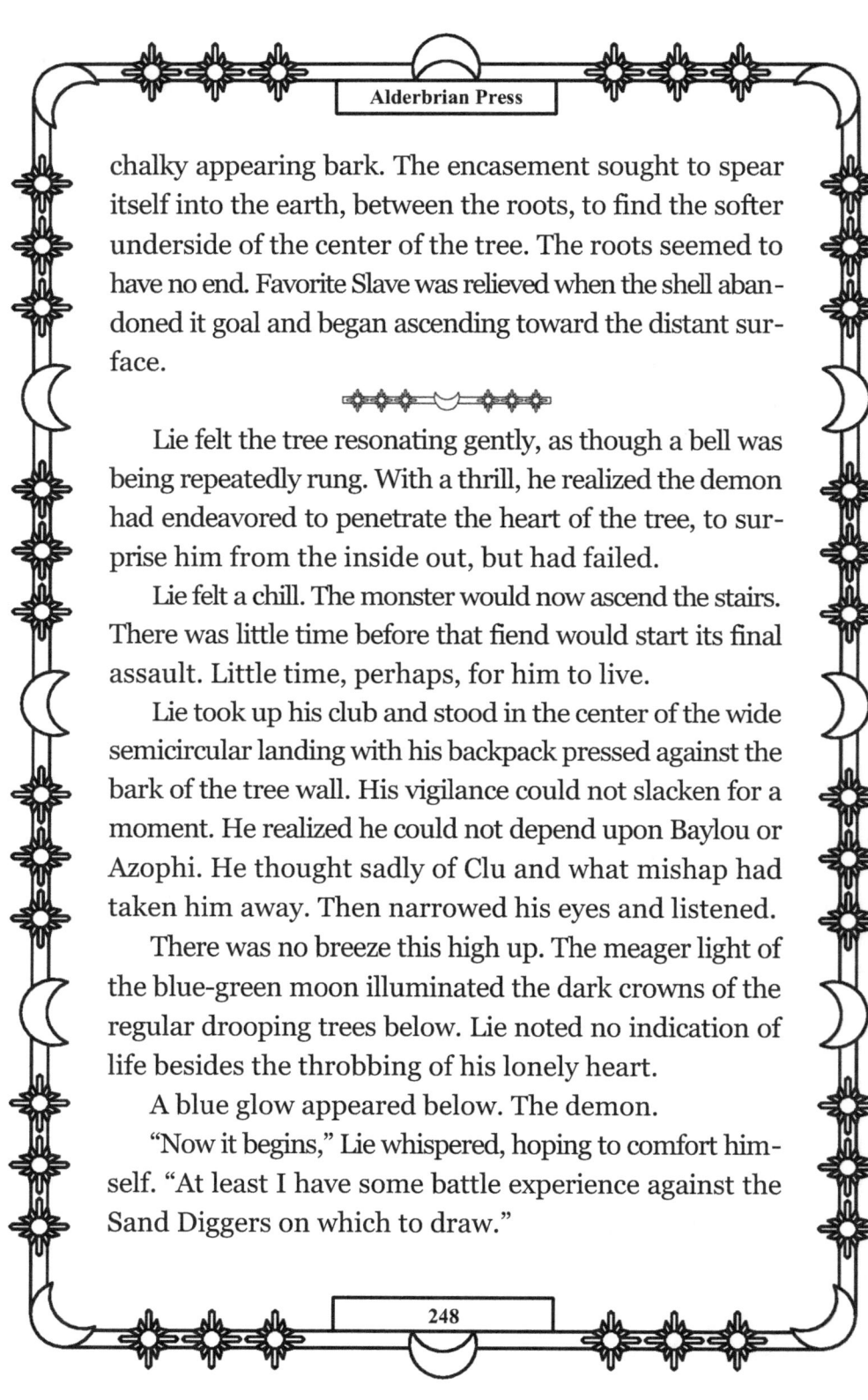

chalky appearing bark. The encasement sought to spear itself into the earth, between the roots, to find the softer underside of the center of the tree. The roots seemed to have no end. Favorite Slave was relieved when the shell abandoned it goal and began ascending toward the distant surface.

Lie felt the tree resonating gently, as though a bell was being repeatedly rung. With a thrill, he realized the demon had endeavored to penetrate the heart of the tree, to surprise him from the inside out, but had failed.

Lie felt a chill. The monster would now ascend the stairs. There was little time before that fiend would start its final assault. Little time, perhaps, for him to live.

Lie took up his club and stood in the center of the wide semicircular landing with his backpack pressed against the bark of the tree wall. His vigilance could not slacken for a moment. He realized he could not depend upon Baylou or Azophi. He thought sadly of Clu and what mishap had taken him away. Then narrowed his eyes and listened.

There was no breeze this high up. The meager light of the blue-green moon illuminated the dark crowns of the regular drooping trees below. Lie noted no indication of life besides the throbbing of his lonely heart.

A blue glow appeared below. The demon.

"Now it begins," Lie whispered, hoping to comfort himself. "At least I have some battle experience against the Sand Diggers on which to draw."

Favorite Slave waded through the earth, slowly rising until it was walking on the surface, bearing steadfastly toward the spectral tree. Slave gasped. The wild Magic of the shell whisked Slave into the air, then floated Slave toward the prey.

"This is terrible!" Lie shouted, in rage. "The damned horror can fly! If it mounted the steps, I would stand a chance! But, now!"

The demon sped toward Lie like a gleaming nightmare. Its fangs were bared and it was slavering. Its claws were wide spread and ready to wreak pitiless damage.

Desperately, Lie held his club out before him like a spear.

The shell stopped. Favorite Slave appeared surprised.

Lie sucked in a breath of hope. He did not comprehend how, but he knew the Magic in the shell was afraid of being annihilated. That he could burst it with the sharp end of his club!

Slave realized this. Its saurian insides contracted in fear. What would the part of the Master it carried within it, do now against sure failure.

Lie poked at the shell, forcing it to hover back. Had he more than one weapon, he would have chanced hurling one to pierce the foul occult bubble, without danger to himself. "Wishful thinking is a waste," he muttered, as he locked his vision on the monster.

The bubble began vibrating, bouncing the demon slightly up and down and to and fro inside it.

Lie had a hopeful realization.

Favorite Slave fearfully understood what Lie had realized. The Magic in Slave's mind was contesting with the
Magic of the shell, for control over their present situation.

"You would compel us to assault, knowing this hideous
Human will destroy the shell?" Slave said, angrily, aloud,
in a guttural language Lie could not understand.

The Master's implanted Magic spoke, using the demon's
language. It was a crackling, hissing, windy, barely audible
voice. "Yes, sniveling insect!"

"But, if the shell explodes, I die," Slave protested, "and,
if I die, you will die!"

"Not so!" the living Magic hissed. "If you perish, I shall
return in an instant, too small to measure, to my place
within the Master. Only his expendables will cease!"

Favorite Slave was awash with despair. Had the Master
lied to it about the Magic in its mind? That the Magic was
there to ensure Slave's safe return? That Slave could not
fail? Would not be slain?

The Magic whispered in Slave's conflicted brain, remind-
ing Slave of the rewards for Slave's success. Mastery of
Slave's own realm of slaves and eternal access to Pleasure Sleep. Then it reminded Slave of the punishment for
Slave's failure. A literally, eternal, slow infliction of pain.

Lie noticed the inner conflict the beast was suffering.
He crept to the brink of the landing, just within inches of
the blue shell, lifted the club above his head in both hands,
like a knife, and brought it down with all his might, plus
his weight.

The shell Magic shrieked in Slave's tormented mind.

Lie's club penetrated the orb to within an inch of horrified Slave's panicked eyes. Slave grabbed the club, sinking its claws into the knobby wood.

The shell Magic thinned itself on the rear half of its surface and directed the energy into the area around the club, preventing itself from detonating by tripling the thickness of its wall there.

Lie wrestled with the demon for ownership of the club. He had fallen off balance with the force of his desperate blow, and was sitting on the landing, with his legs dangling over it.

The Magic in Slave's mind ceded control to the demon. Slave hurled the shield forward, bearing Lie toward the white wall of the tree, to crush him.

Lie realized there was no hope of regaining his club, and he would be crushed momentarily, so he released the end of his weapon. To his horror, he did not fall free of the magic sphere! It had glued itself to his chest. He tried to roll himself left, then right, then attempted to break the suction by pushing against the shield with his hands and feet, to no avail. On the surface of the glowing globe, he saw the reflection of the wall rushing closer.

There was no escape! No hope! He had failed! Baylou was gone! Clu was gone! Lie screamed in anguish and despair.

Illustration 37

Ortourian Beast Wrought Iron Window Grillwork

Copyright © 2019 Philip Raymond Sadler

252-A

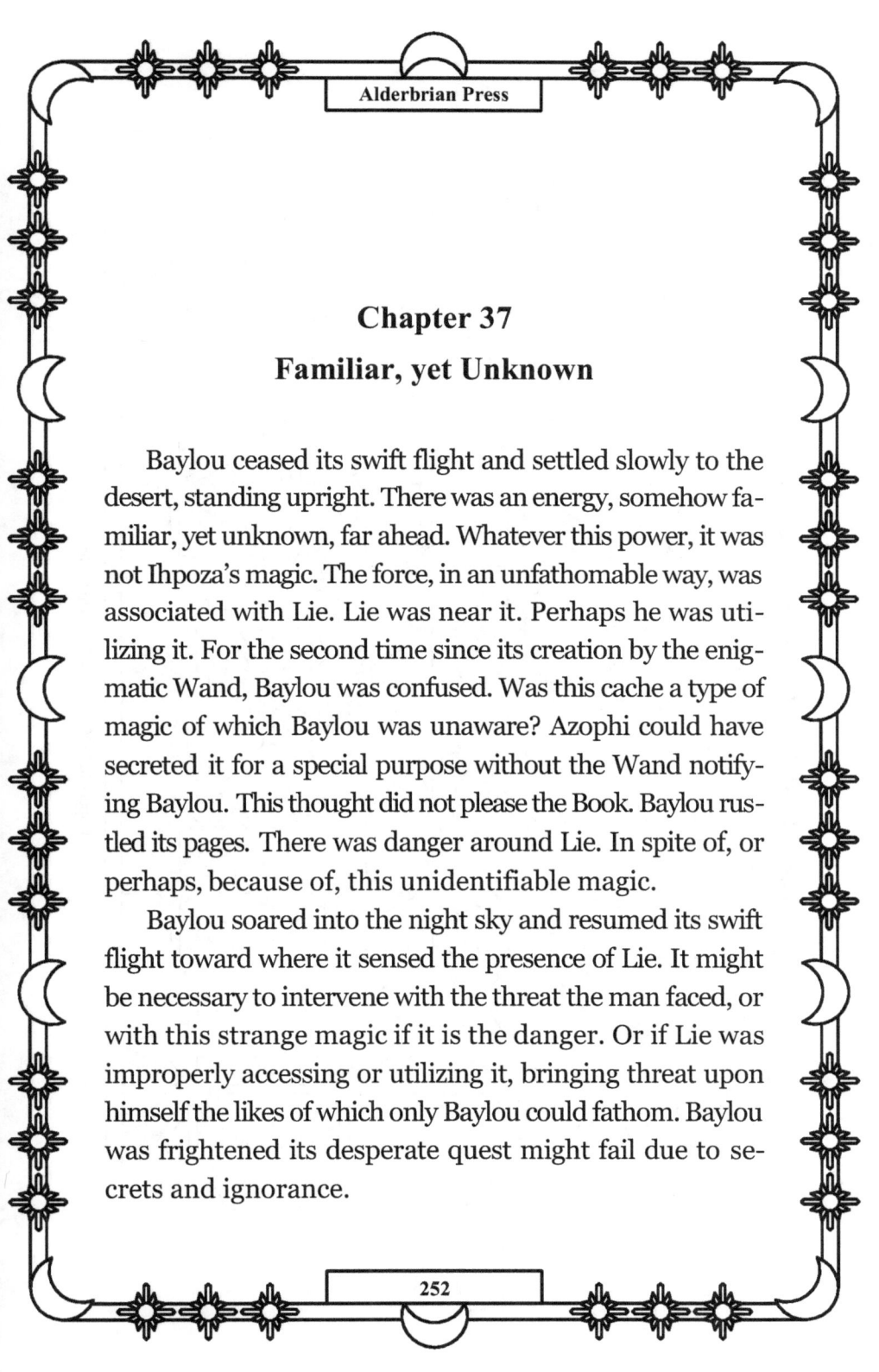

Chapter 37

Familiar, yet Unknown

Baylou ceased its swift flight and settled slowly to the desert, standing upright. There was an energy, somehow familiar, yet unknown, far ahead. Whatever this power, it was not Ihpoza's magic. The force, in an unfathomable way, was associated with Lie. Lie was near it. Perhaps he was utilizing it. For the second time since its creation by the enigmatic Wand, Baylou was confused. Was this cache a type of magic of which Baylou was unaware? Azophi could have secreted it for a special purpose without the Wand notifying Baylou. This thought did not please the Book. Baylou rustled its pages. There was danger around Lie. In spite of, or perhaps, because of, this unidentifiable magic.

Baylou soared into the night sky and resumed its swift flight toward where it sensed the presence of Lie. It might be necessary to intervene with the threat the man faced, or with this strange magic if it is the danger. Or if Lie was improperly accessing or utilizing it, bringing threat upon himself the likes of which only Baylou could fathom. Baylou was frightened its desperate quest might fail due to secrets and ignorance.

Illustration 38

Ortourian Beast Wrought Iron Window Grillwork

253-A

Chapter 38

I Regret

The bubble slammed into the white tree as if it struck burnished white iron. The impact tore Lie free of the shield, and he sailed backwards into the bright cloudy tree, flailing like he was submerged in white water.

Favorite Slave howled in frustration. It irately clawed at the bark, causing sparks to fly, but leaving no damage. The shell tried to pull Slave away from the wall, but it was as if the butt of the club had become a part of the abominable tree. Slave pushed angrily at the club. The shell sent an electric shock to the center of Slave's bones.

"Allow the insulator to wisely release the weapon," the Master's Magic sternly ordered the demon, "or you shall surely perish."

Slave stepped back against the rear of the shell and watched as the bubble pulled itself off the knobby club.

The shell contracted quickly as it came down the pointed tip of the foul weapon, producing an inner seal before it finally released the club, then redistributed its cold, evil energy to an even thickness.

Slave hovered the shell just above the landing, at the

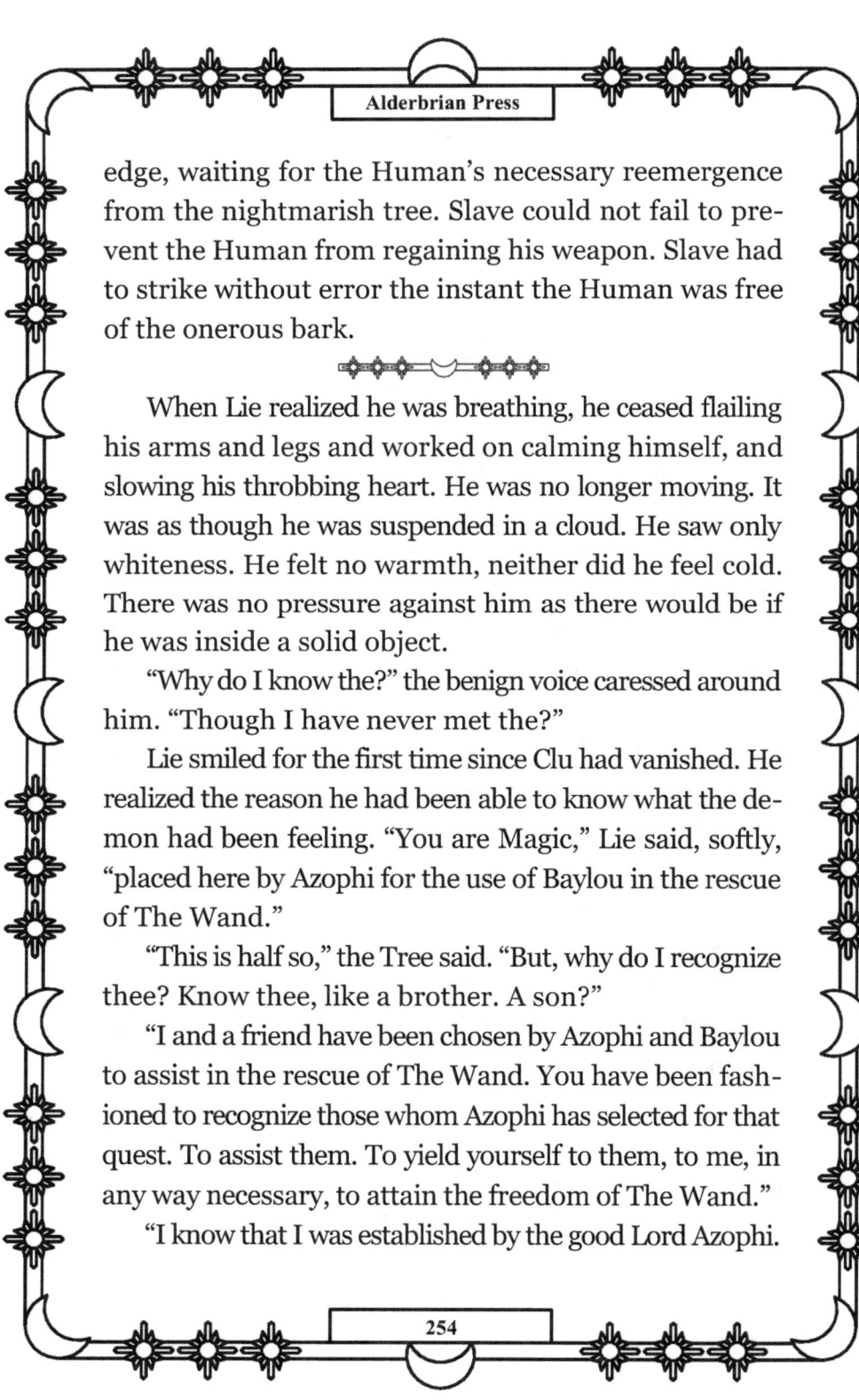

edge, waiting for the Human's necessary reemergence from the nightmarish tree. Slave could not fail to prevent the Human from regaining his weapon. Slave had to strike without error the instant the Human was free of the onerous bark.

When Lie realized he was breathing, he ceased flailing his arms and legs and worked on calming himself, and slowing his throbbing heart. He was no longer moving. It was as though he was suspended in a cloud. He saw only whiteness. He felt no warmth, neither did he feel cold. There was no pressure against him as there would be if he was inside a solid object.

"Why do I know the?" the benign voice caressed around him. "Though I have never met the?"

Lie smiled for the first time since Clu had vanished. He realized the reason he had been able to know what the demon had been feeling. "You are Magic," Lie said, softly, "placed here by Azophi for the use of Baylou in the rescue of The Wand."

"This is half so," the Tree said. "But, why do I recognize thee? Know thee, like a brother. A son?"

"I and a friend have been chosen by Azophi and Baylou to assist in the rescue of The Wand. You have been fashioned to recognize those whom Azophi has selected for that quest. To assist them. To yield yourself to them, to me, in any way necessary, to attain the freedom of The Wand."

"I know that I was established by the good Lord Azophi.

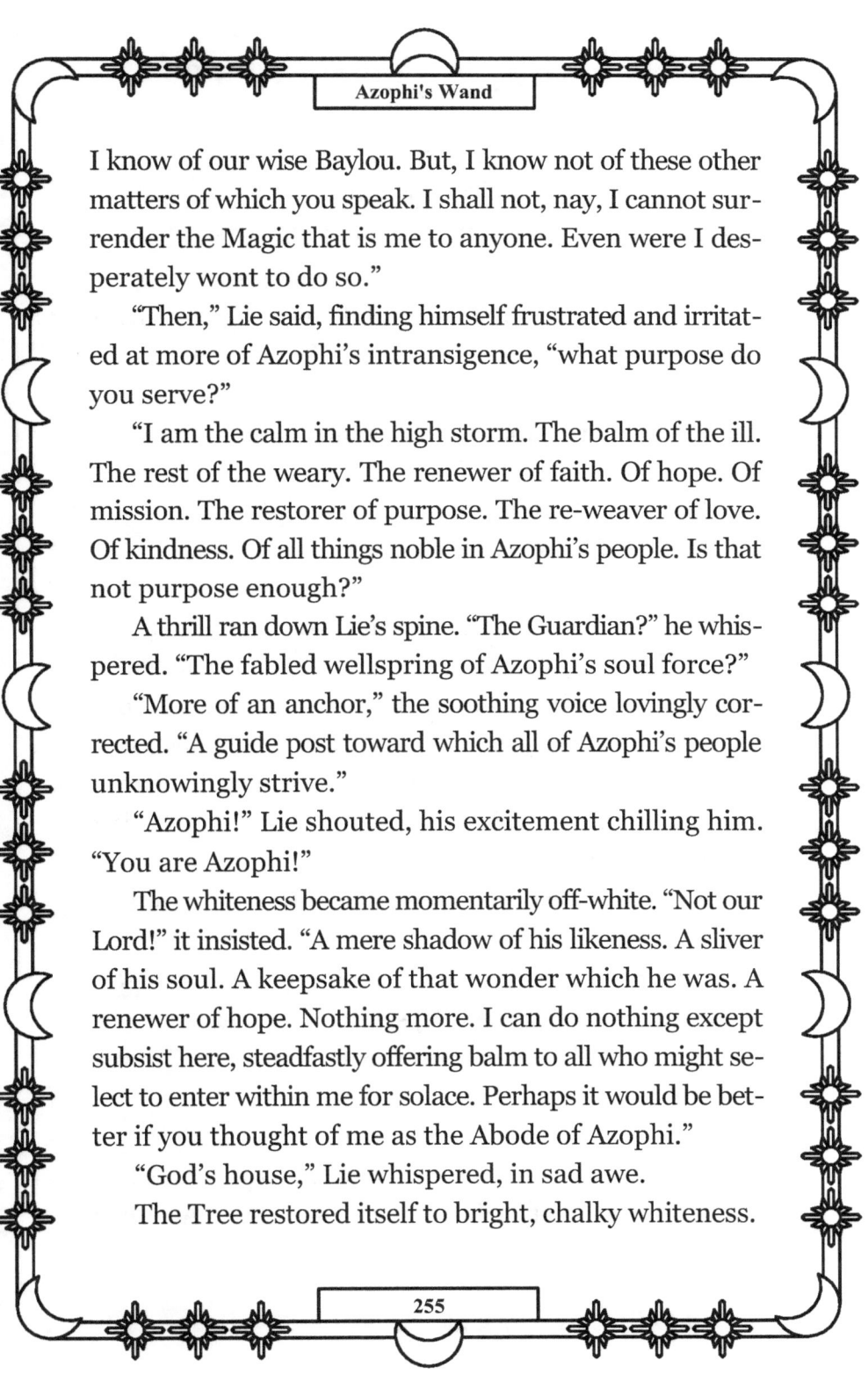

I know of our wise Baylou. But, I know not of these other matters of which you speak. I shall not, nay, I cannot surrender the Magic that is me to anyone. Even were I desperately wont to do so."

"Then," Lie said, finding himself frustrated and irritated at more of Azophi's intransigence, "what purpose do you serve?"

"I am the calm in the high storm. The balm of the ill. The rest of the weary. The renewer of faith. Of hope. Of mission. The restorer of purpose. The re-weaver of love. Of kindness. Of all things noble in Azophi's people. Is that not purpose enough?"

A thrill ran down Lie's spine. "The Guardian?" he whispered. "The fabled wellspring of Azophi's soul force?"

"More of an anchor," the soothing voice lovingly corrected. "A guide post toward which all of Azophi's people unknowingly strive."

"Azophi!" Lie shouted, his excitement chilling him. "You are Azophi!"

The whiteness became momentarily off-white. "Not our Lord!" it insisted. "A mere shadow of his likeness. A sliver of his soul. A keepsake of that wonder which he was. A renewer of hope. Nothing more. I can do nothing except subsist here, steadfastly offering balm to all who might select to enter within me for solace. Perhaps it would be better if you thought of me as the Abode of Azophi."

"God's house," Lie whispered, in sad awe.

The Tree restored itself to bright, chalky whiteness.

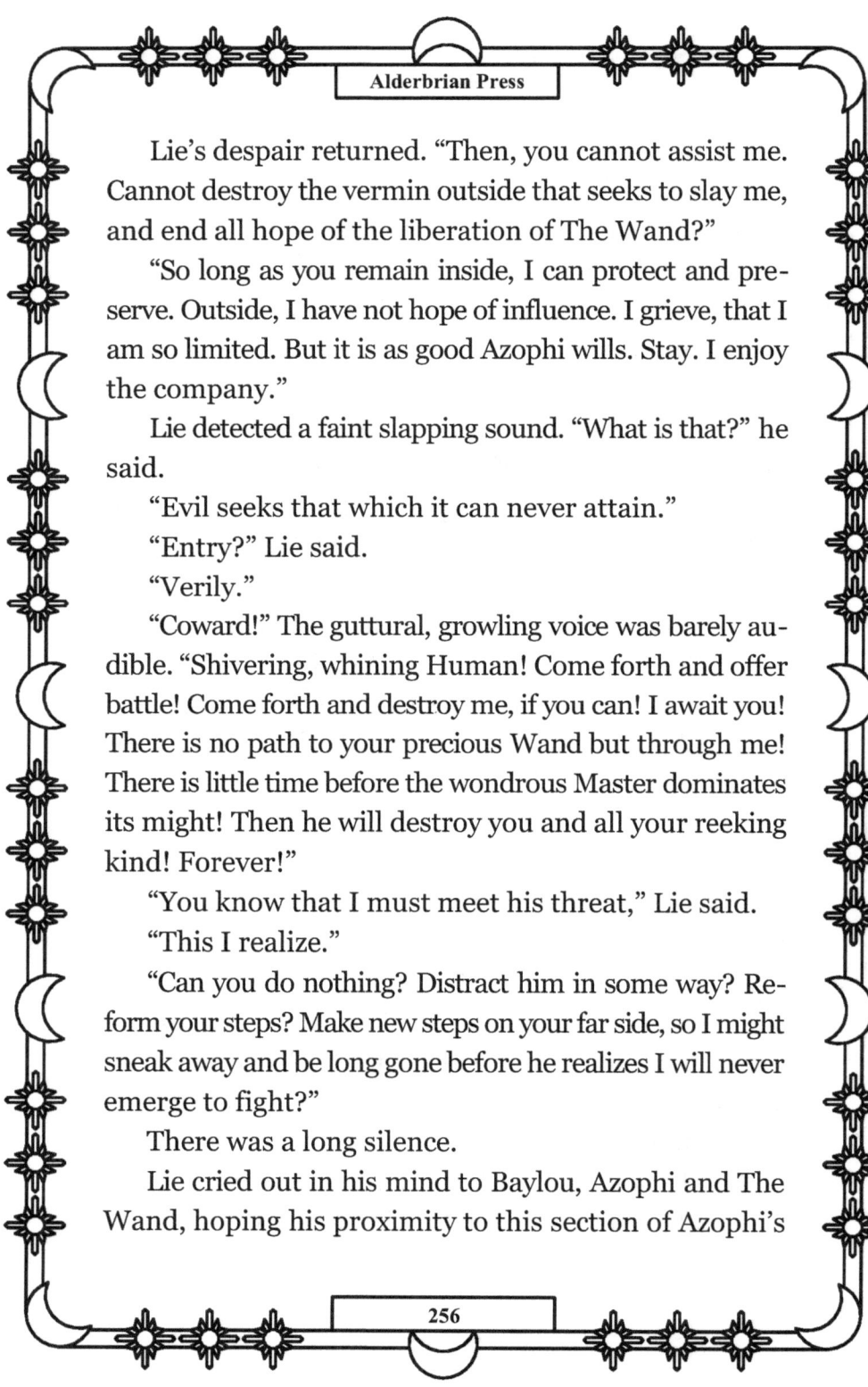

Lie's despair returned. "Then, you cannot assist me. Cannot destroy the vermin outside that seeks to slay me, and end all hope of the liberation of The Wand?"

"So long as you remain inside, I can protect and preserve. Outside, I have not hope of influence. I grieve, that I am so limited. But it is as good Azophi wills. Stay. I enjoy the company."

Lie detected a faint slapping sound. "What is that?" he said.

"Evil seeks that which it can never attain."

"Entry?" Lie said.

"Verily."

"Coward!" The guttural, growling voice was barely audible. "Shivering, whining Human! Come forth and offer battle! Come forth and destroy me, if you can! I await you! There is no path to your precious Wand but through me! There is little time before the wondrous Master dominates its might! Then he will destroy you and all your reeking kind! Forever!"

"You know that I must meet his threat," Lie said.

"This I realize."

"Can you do nothing? Distract him in some way? Reform your steps? Make new steps on your far side, so I might sneak away and be long gone before he realizes I will never emerge to fight?"

There was a long silence.

Lie cried out in his mind to Baylou, Azophi and The Wand, hoping his proximity to this section of Azophi's being might carry his thoughts to one, or all of them, and bring assistance; rescue. He sensed nothing, and slumped where he was suspended.

The Tree spoke and its simple words ached Lie's heart. "I regret."

Lie thought of Clu. That he might still be alive. That he must require Lie's help. Lie recalled Baylou's glum words: "Azon shall be a wintry planet of evil!" Lie took a deep breath of resolve. "Can I move freely within you?" he asked.

"As you desire, so shall it be." the Tree said, cheerfully.

"If I leave, can I return?"

"Always," the Tree said, lovingly. "For, never would I turn you away."

Lie thought about walking on a stone floor and his feet felt solidity. He took a step. Then another. He stopped, perplexed. "How can I find my way?" he asked.

"Verily," the Tree said.

A crystal clear corridor formed. Far ahead, stood the opaque wall sealing off the landing. Through it, Lie could see the distorted image of the insulation shell. As he approached the wall, he saw the end of his club. He took firm hold of it. "May I reclaim that which is mine?" he asked, afraid the Tree might not allow weapons within itself.

"As you desire," the Tree whispered, sadly. "But, it cannot be wielded within."

"I would not dare profane your purpose," Lie pledged.

The club wiggled, indicating it could be recovered. Lie drew the weapon through the chalky wall.

Favorite Slave howled with such a high, loud tone, even through the solidity and sanctity of the wall, the ghastly sound stung Lie's ear drums.

Lie decided a sneak attack was the wisest of his limited choices. He walked to the far right of the wall and pushed his face into the soft magical substance. When he could see clearly, he paused.

Favorite Slave was hovering at the edge of the center of the landing, just above the top step. Its slanted eyes were sweeping the wall for the slightest indication Lie was about to attack.

Lie could not determine if the demon had seen Lie's nose and eyes in the slight light of the blue-green moon. With the beast watching the wall so intently, there was little utility to a surprise move. Especially with its faster reflexes. At least, with the club, Lie's reach was greater.

Lie pulled away from the wall and walked to its center. He nodded with decision, gripped the handle of the club tightly in one hand and cradled the pointed end with his other arm. He stepped slowly into the magical white wall, keeping his breathing as shallow as possible.

Favorite Slave noted the telltale darkness growing in the chalkiness of the detested wall. It tensed every muscle, felt the high, tingling energy of Ihpoza's Magic adding to its natural prowess, and started to snarl. The moment the Human passed half-way through the wall, Slave sailed forward.

Lie waited until his courage could brook no more risk.

He flipped the club straight out before himself, grasping it with both hands, and raced forward with the sharp end aimed at the looming sphere.

Slave laughed coarsely. The bubble shot to Lie's left, then curved around behind Lie. Lie whirled, dropping to his knees and thrusting up and forward with the club.

Slave shrieked and shot the globe backward. It slammed with incredible force into the wall and rebounded at the sharp club.

Lie lunged forward.

The shiny globe shot straight up in what was a normally impossible trajectory.

Lie fell flat of his face on the white landing. He desperately rolled over and yanked the club vertical.

Slave shrieked as the bubble slammed into the club. The shield Magic created a secondary bubble around Slave, sped Slave backwards toward the edge of the landing, elongating the first bubble, which exploded with no damage to the demon. The magic had sacrificed a portion of itself to preserve the rest. Much to Slave's gratitude and relief.

Lie scrambled to his feet and hastened back into the protection of the Tree. He was gasping for breath and shaking.

"No harm can thrive here," the Tree said.

Lie's breathlessness, fatigue and fear ended as though a cool breeze had swept them away.

"If this ungainly Human is too guileful and skilled for

you," Ihpoza's Magic taunted around Slave, "I shall perform your simple task and receive all the shining glory and rewards the Master shall bestow upon a true conqueror."

Slave growled and shot rage throughout itself.

"Stop! Stop!" the Magic ordered, its hissing voice revealing pain. "I command you! I beg you! Stop!"

Slave drew itself proudly erect and grinned with fiendish delight. "You are not so impervious as you imagined, Magic!" Slave snarled. "Who will be master now?" Slave could feel the Magic, cowering in Slave's mind, now pulling itself into a small spot in the center of Slave's brain.

"I shall advise," the Magic said, with less self-assurance and no harshness.

"Then do so, for this mere Human is shaming me and you and Ihpoza. You know the good Master is monitoring us through you, and has little patience for failure."

"Remind the vermin of its lost friend."

Lie startled. The unnerving voice sounded like it was in the clear passageway. Lie knew the vermin was himself, and the friend was Clu. "I thought you could offer me no assistance," Lie said.

"I am charged with monitoring my immediate surroundings for those who are in need and would enter. I must winnow the seed from the chaff."

"We know nothing of the fate of its companion," Slave said.

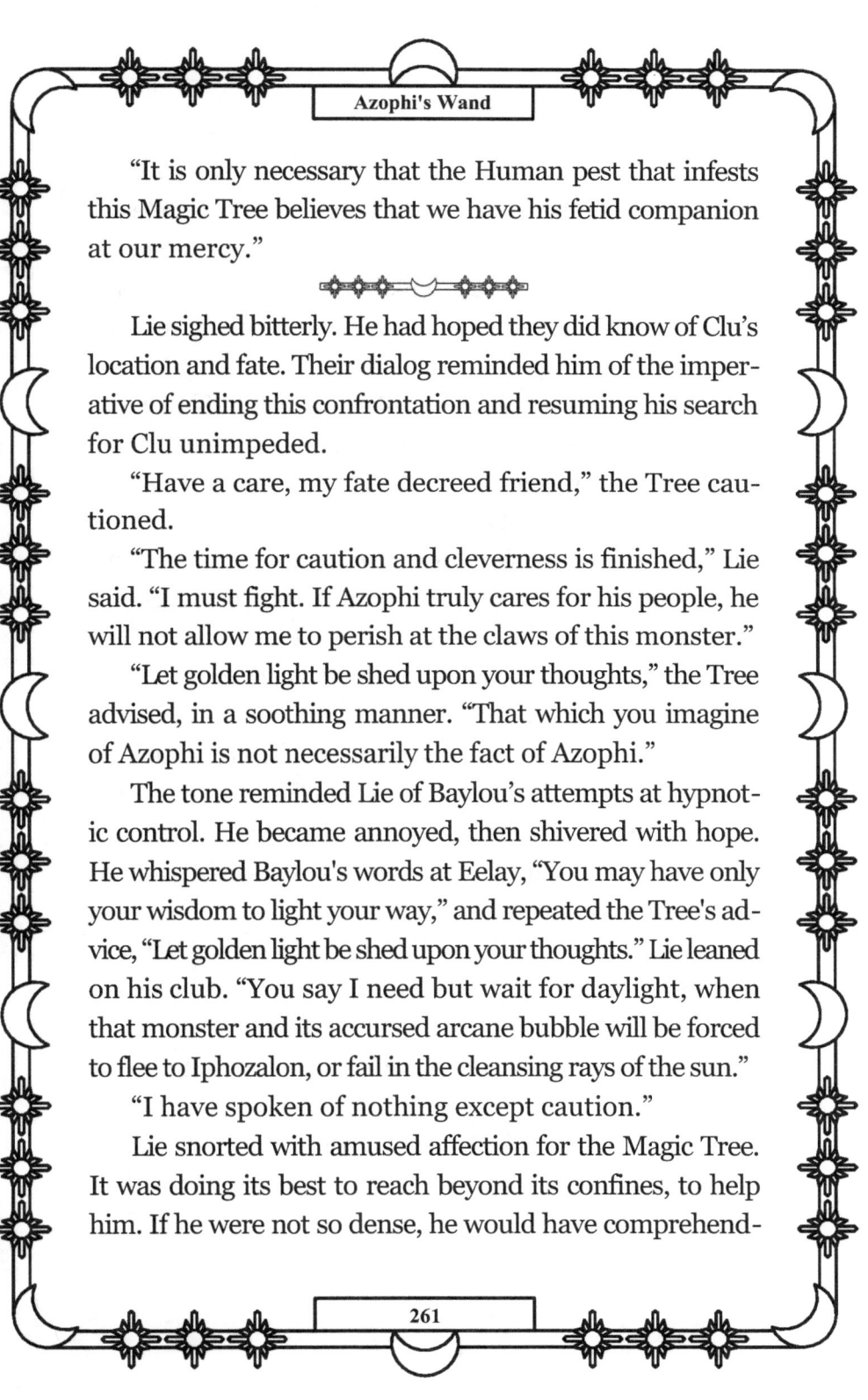

"It is only necessary that the Human pest that infests this Magic Tree believes that we have his fetid companion at our mercy."

Lie sighed bitterly. He had hoped they did know of Clu's location and fate. Their dialog reminded him of the imperative of ending this confrontation and resuming his search for Clu unimpeded.

"Have a care, my fate decreed friend," the Tree cautioned.

"The time for caution and cleverness is finished," Lie said. "I must fight. If Azophi truly cares for his people, he will not allow me to perish at the claws of this monster."

"Let golden light be shed upon your thoughts," the Tree advised, in a soothing manner. "That which you imagine of Azophi is not necessarily the fact of Azophi."

The tone reminded Lie of Baylou's attempts at hypnotic control. He became annoyed, then shivered with hope. He whispered Baylou's words at Eelay, "You may have only your wisdom to light your way," and repeated the Tree's advice, "Let golden light be shed upon your thoughts." Lie leaned on his club. "You say I need but wait for daylight, when that monster and its accursed arcane bubble will be forced to flee to Iphozalon, or fail in the cleansing rays of the sun."

"I have spoken of nothing except caution."

Lie snorted with amused affection for the Magic Tree. It was doing its best to reach beyond its confines, to help him. If he were not so dense, he would have comprehended its aid sooner. Lie strode to the wall and pushed his head through far enough to speak. "Scheme, rant and uselessly pound your fists against this barrier all you wish," he shouted, derisively, "but, take heed, harsh daylight soon approaches, bearing your well-deserved death in its rosy arms."

Ihpoza spoke to the fragment of himself in Slave's enraged mind. This spoke to the Magic of the shield. They melded, growing their might ten-fold, then spoke to Slave. Slave howled in delight and swung its right arm toward the Tree. A spear of purple energy seared into existence from before the tips of Slave's claws, flashed across the wide landing, and sank half its length into the white wall.

The great Tree shook as though the earth was suffering a seismic upheaval.

Lie struggled to remain standing in spite of the support of his club pressed against the floor of the clear passage.

"I am undone!" the Tree lamented. "I am breached! Evil has entered, and I shall be destroyed! Great Azophi! Please preserve me!"

Lie raised his club, raced forward, and slammed it into the tip of the energy spear with all the might he could muster.

The spear rang like dense metal being hit, but did not move.

Lie struck again and again and again.

The spear wiggled, slipped, then shot out of the wall and dissipated.

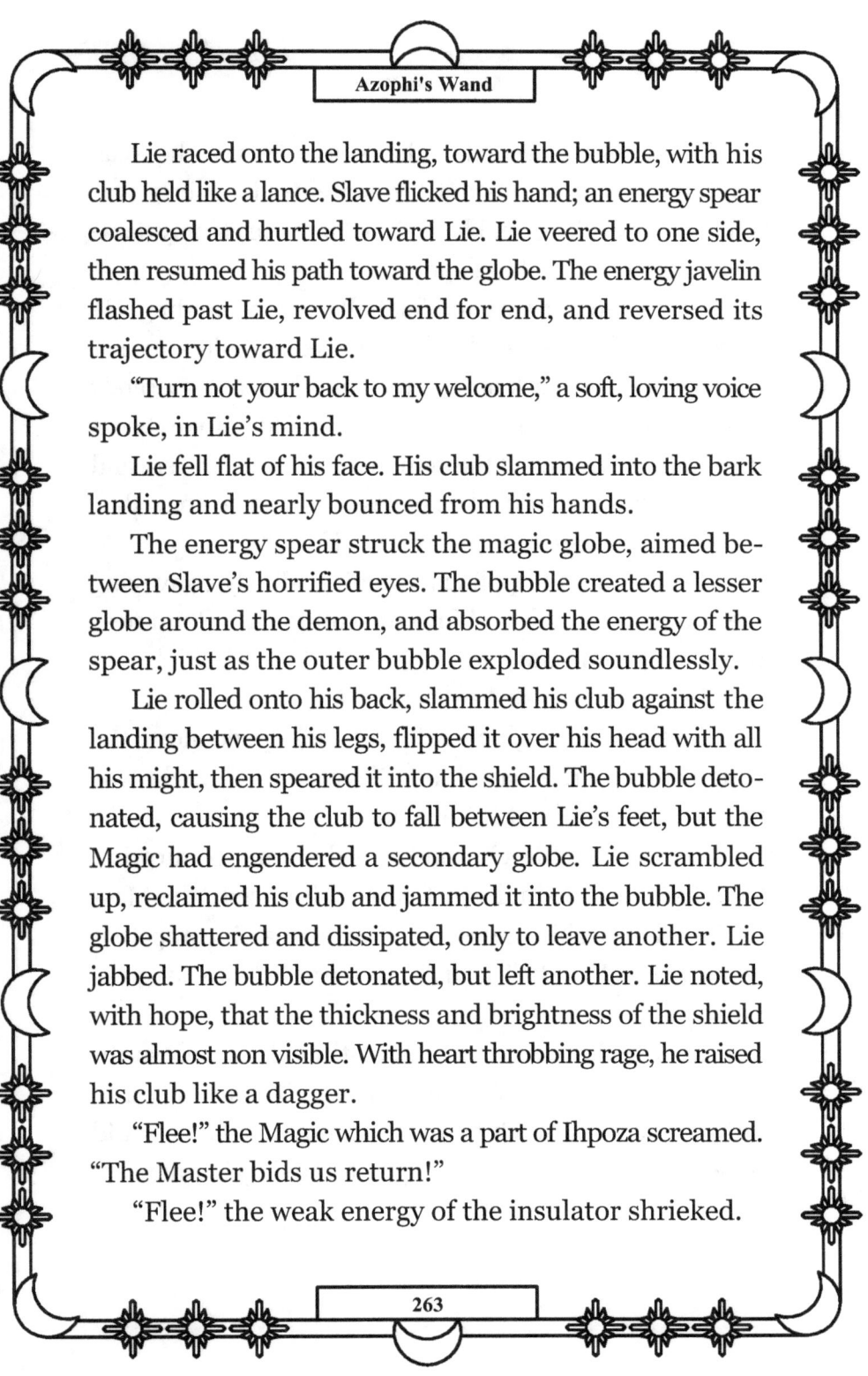

Lie raced onto the landing, toward the bubble, with his club held like a lance. Slave flicked his hand; an energy spear coalesced and hurtled toward Lie. Lie veered to one side, then resumed his path toward the globe. The energy javelin flashed past Lie, revolved end for end, and reversed its trajectory toward Lie.

"Turn not your back to my welcome," a soft, loving voice spoke, in Lie's mind.

Lie fell flat of his face. His club slammed into the bark landing and nearly bounced from his hands.

The energy spear struck the magic globe, aimed between Slave's horrified eyes. The bubble created a lesser globe around the demon, and absorbed the energy of the spear, just as the outer bubble exploded soundlessly.

Lie rolled onto his back, slammed his club against the landing between his legs, flipped it over his head with all his might, then speared it into the shield. The bubble detonated, causing the club to fall between Lie's feet, but the Magic had engendered a secondary globe. Lie scrambled up, reclaimed his club and jammed it into the bubble. The globe shattered and dissipated, only to leave another. Lie jabbed. The bubble detonated, but left another. Lie noted, with hope, that the thickness and brightness of the shield was almost non visible. With heart throbbing rage, he raised his club like a dagger.

"Flee!" the Magic which was a part of Ihpoza screamed. "The Master bids us return!"

"Flee!" the weak energy of the insulator shrieked.

Favorite Slave needed neither voice. It threw the weak orb into reverse the instant Lie perceived its energy was almost drained. The bubble vanished into the gloomy darkness, with breathtaking speed.

Lie pitched forward and fell half over the landing. He started to slide, released the club, pressed his palms against the rough chalky bark of the Tree, and shoved desperately until he slid himself back to safety. Lie rolled onto his backpack and lay panting. If the demon regained its bravery and ventured back, he would be helpless. Though he knew this, he was too exhausted for further effort.

The Tree began rippling its landing, slowly conveying Lie toward the wall, and into the comforting cloudiness of its inner sanctuary.

Slave raced the globe at break neck speed along the rough earth of the wasteland. Slave's only thought was to reach the safety of Iphozalon.

The Magic in Slave's mind issued a grunt of surprise. "You have luck beyond belief, insect," it hissed, "the Master is inconceivably pleased by your dismal, incompetent performance. You shall, actually, be rewarded for your gross bungling."

Favorite Slave said nothing, although an indescribable feeling of relief flooded through it. Slave aspired only to place as much comforting territory as it could between itself and that big, ugly, terrifying Human.

Illustration 39

Ortourian Beast Wrought Iron Window Grillwork

Copyright © 2019 Philip Raymond Sadler

265-A

Chapter 39

Death Does Own Him

"I regret that you must leave."

Lie opened his eyes. His aches and bruises were healed, and his fatigue was gone as though he had slept hours, though he had lain in the peaceful clear passageway only moments. He slowly stood up and adjusted his backpack. "I too," he said, "but Clu requires my aid. I have little, if any, time to waste."

"What of the demon? I can aid you not, on the outside."

"I must take my chances. Thank you for your hospitality. I would like to return to visit if I succeed in my mission."

"You shall be sorely missed, and heartily welcomed, each time you leave and return," the Magic Tree said, jovially. "May Azophi speed and preserve you in your travels!"

"I think I shall depend upon myself," Lie said, wryly, "for that is what has brought me this far alive." Lie walked to the barrier and cautiously pressed his face through.

"It prowls within not one circular mile of me," the Tree said. "Beyond that, Only Azophi knows."

And he is not likely to notify me, Lie thought angrily.

"Remain true to your purpose," he told the Tree.

"And you to yours," the Tree said, lovingly.

Lie stepped through the barrier and began the long trip down the steep steps. At the bottom, he found his club. It had been shattered along its length into several useless pieces.

He sighed. He had a feeling he did not have time to seek another club, however useful it might be should the demon reappear.

He had to find Clu.

He headed into the heart of the woods, sad but determined.

"We shall enact a bargain."

Lie spun around, surprised and trembling from anger.

Baylou stood six feet tall. Its bright unblinking eye was sympathetic.

Lie was startled out of his choler. "A bargain?" he said, sure of what it would be.

"Clu, for your sworn continuation of the Quest."

"You have taken him, then!" Lie accused, with relief. "I shall not barter. You will not harm him." He showed his back to the Book. "I will wait here until you return Clu. Only then, shall we press on."

"I do not possess him."

Lie faced Baylou in shock. "Who, then?" he asked.

"Death."

"You allowed him to die!"

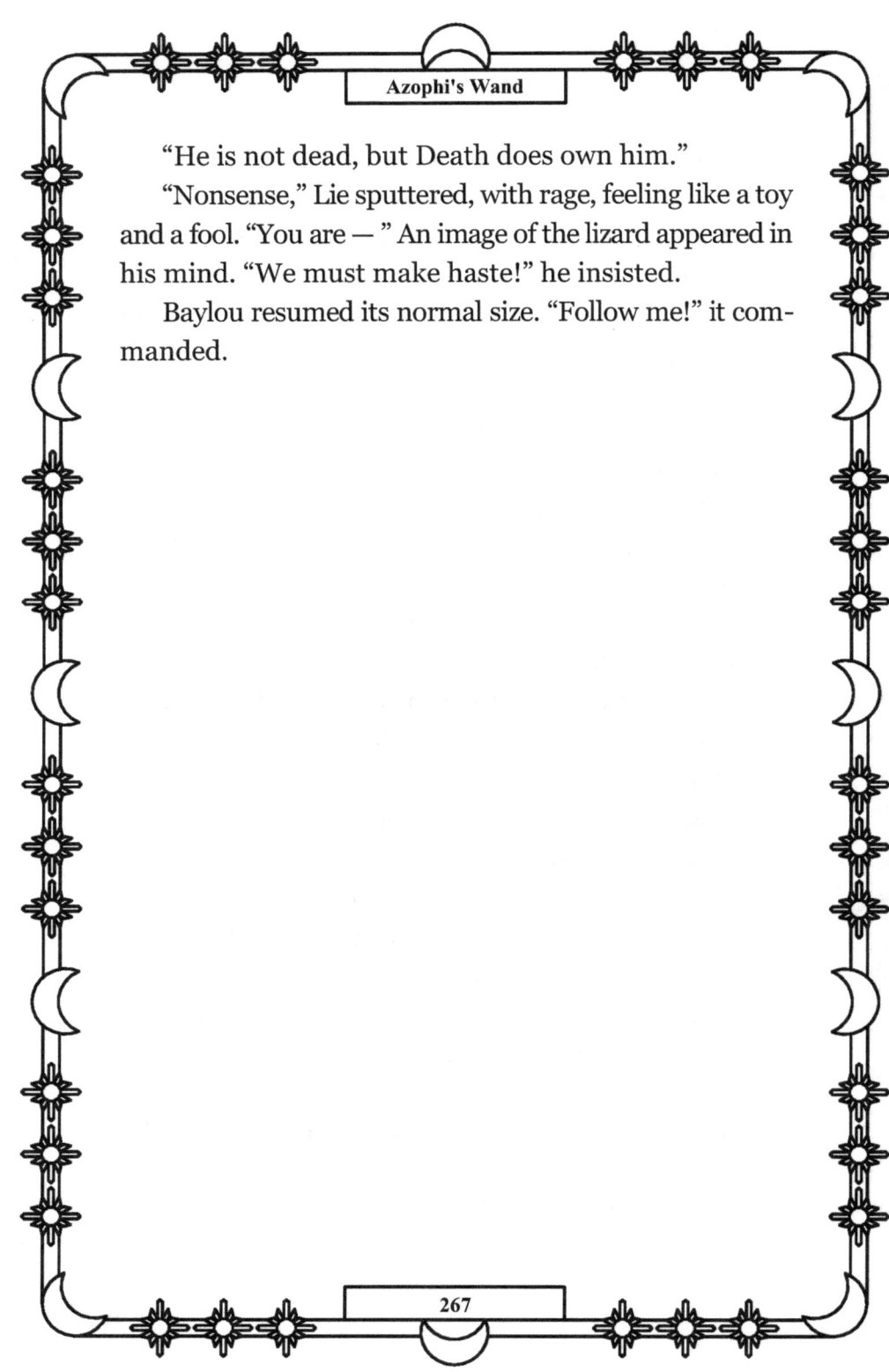

"He is not dead, but Death does own him."

"Nonsense," Lie sputtered, with rage, feeling like a toy and a fool. "You are — " An image of the lizard appeared in his mind. "We must make haste!" he insisted.

Baylou resumed its normal size. "Follow me!" it commanded.

Illustration 40

Ortourian Beast Wrought Iron Window Grillwork

Copyright © 2019 Philip Raymond Sadler

268-A

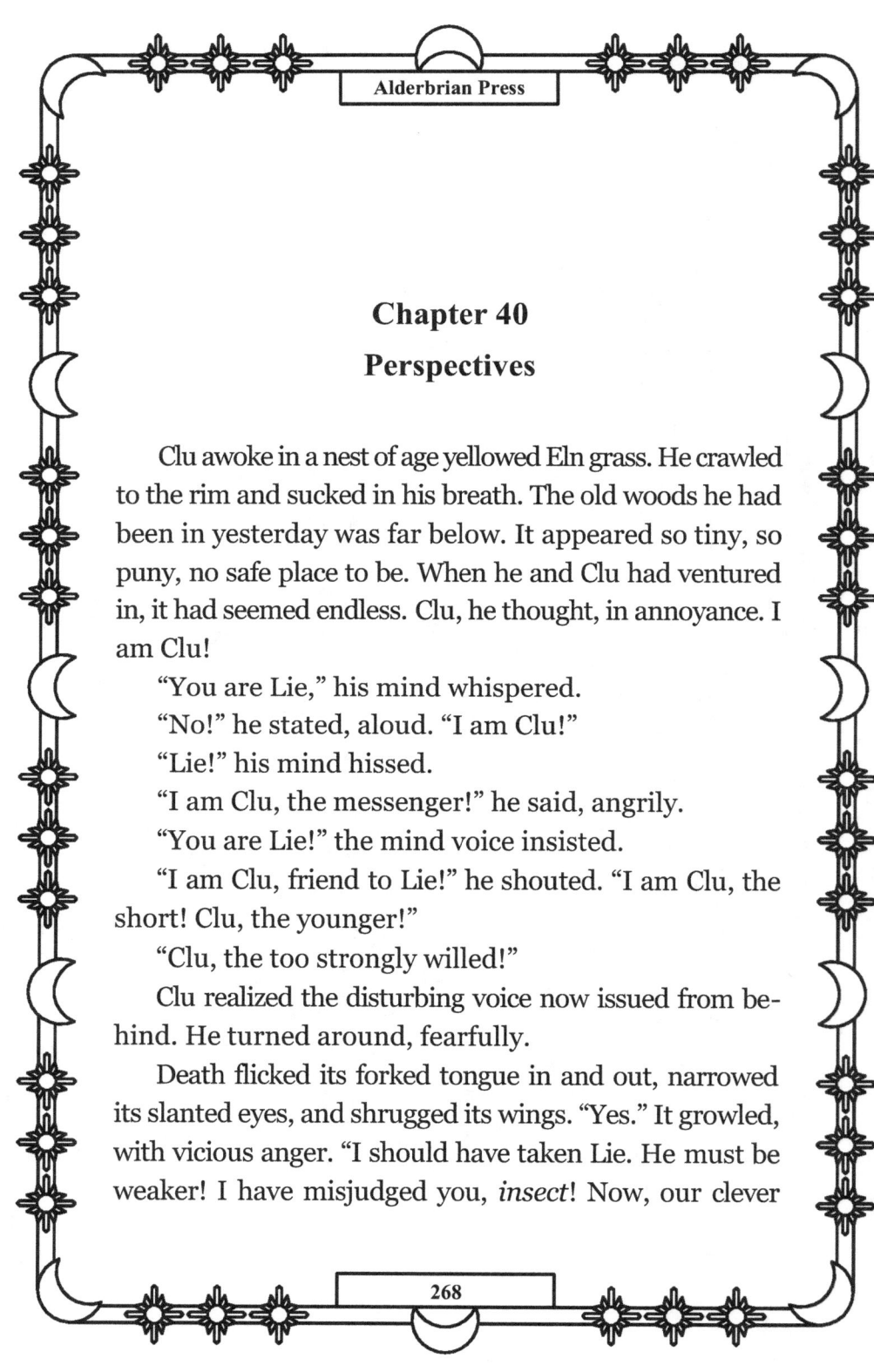

Chapter 40

Perspectives

Clu awoke in a nest of age yellowed Eln grass. He crawled to the rim and sucked in his breath. The old woods he had been in yesterday was far below. It appeared so tiny, so puny, no safe place to be. When he and Clu had ventured in, it had seemed endless. Clu, he thought, in annoyance. I am Clu!

"You are Lie," his mind whispered.

"No!" he stated, aloud. "I am Clu!"

"Lie!" his mind hissed.

"I am Clu, the messenger!" he said, angrily.

"You are Lie!" the mind voice insisted.

"I am Clu, friend to Lie!" he shouted. "I am Clu, the short! Clu, the younger!"

"Clu, the too strongly willed!"

Clu realized the disturbing voice now issued from behind. He turned around, fearfully.

Death flicked its forked tongue in and out, narrowed its slanted eyes, and shrugged its wings. "Yes." It growled, with vicious anger. "I should have taken Lie. He must be weaker! I have misjudged you, *insect*! Now, our clever plan is undone. But we shall deal with this. There is yet time!"

Clu stood motionless with terror. There was no place to run, to hide. He could only stand there waiting for Death to cut him in half with its tongue.

Illustration 41

Ortourian Beast Wrought Iron Window Grillwork

Copyright © 2019 Philip Raymond Sadler

270-A

Chapter 41

Sand and Stone

Baylou and Lie stopped near the knobby base of the lustrous column of white stone.

"Where is Clu, Book?"

Baylou tilted face down toward the sand and tripled its length and width. "Mount my back," it said. "Clu is atop the mesa."

Lie readily complied and the Book soared to the summit. Lie leaped eagerly into the old dry nest, but it was empty. He became so enraged he could neither see nor think clearly.

Baylou transformed into a small boy.

Lie was startled out of his rage.

The Child Book spoke soothingly, "Clu has not been harmed, only moved."

"To where?"

The Child Book reformed to Baylou.

The great white quartz column began to oscillate as though resonating to an indiscernible energy source. There was a wave of heat, then a burst of brilliant white light.

When his flash blindness ended, Lie found himself star-

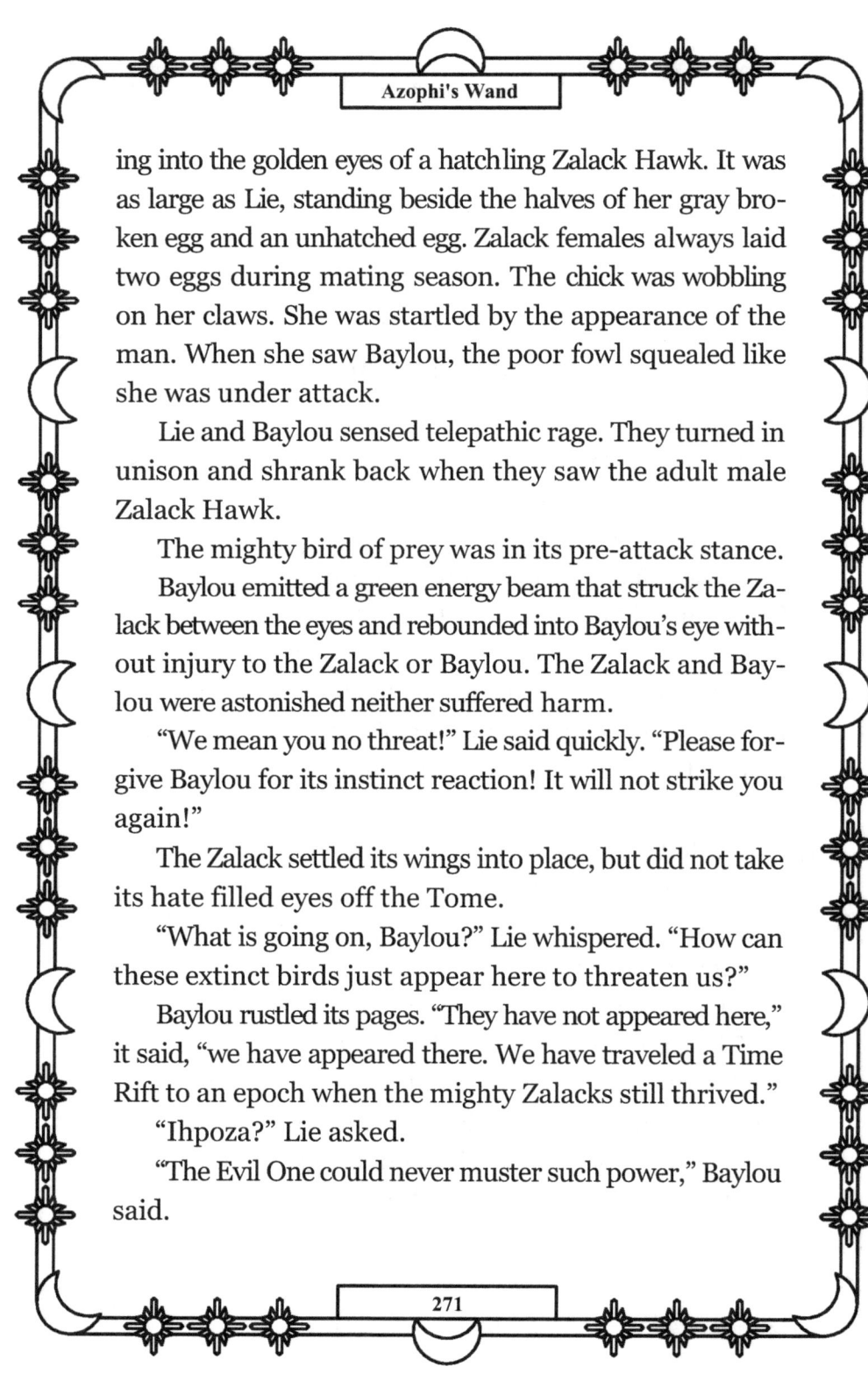

ing into the golden eyes of a hatchling Zalack Hawk. It was as large as Lie, standing beside the halves of her gray broken egg and an unhatched egg. Zalack females always laid two eggs during mating season. The chick was wobbling on her claws. She was startled by the appearance of the man. When she saw Baylou, the poor fowl squealed like she was under attack.

Lie and Baylou sensed telepathic rage. They turned in unison and shrank back when they saw the adult male Zalack Hawk.

The mighty bird of prey was in its pre-attack stance.

Baylou emitted a green energy beam that struck the Zalack between the eyes and rebounded into Baylou's eye without injury to the Zalack or Baylou. The Zalack and Baylou were astonished neither suffered harm.

"We mean you no threat!" Lie said quickly. "Please forgive Baylou for its instinct reaction! It will not strike you again!"

The Zalack settled its wings into place, but did not take its hate filled eyes off the Tome.

"What is going on, Baylou?" Lie whispered. "How can these extinct birds just appear here to threaten us?"

Baylou rustled its pages. "They have not appeared here," it said, "we have appeared there. We have traveled a Time Rift to an epoch when the mighty Zalacks still thrived."

"Ihpoza?" Lie asked.

"The Evil One could never muster such power," Baylou said.

"Then, how have we come to be here?" Lie asked. He perceived a wave of grief emanating from the adult Zalack.

"My hatchling sensed your Mind Magic energies and brought you here," the adult Zalack said, aloud, "mistaking you for young hawks."

"Why do you grieve?" Lie asked. "Your chick appears healthy."

"I mourn for my unhatched child," the adult Zalack said, staring venomously at Baylou.

Baylou turned around and psychically scanned the egg. The Tome knew it could rectify the slight problem stealing the life of the unhatched Zalack. Despite its natural, intense desire to aid the unborn hawk, the Book dared not do so.

The adult Zalack read Baylou's thoughts, sucked in his breath and thrust his beak to within a hair's breadth of the back cover of the Book.

Baylou spun around, prepared to protect Lie and itself.

"You can save my child!" the adult Zalack thundered in their minds. "You shall do this, or Lie dies!"

Baylou placed itself between Lie and the hawk, and increased in size, blocking the hawk from seeing Lie.

The Zalack laughed, with disdain.

The hatchling darted her head forward, grasped Lie by his backpack with her beak, and pulled him from behind Baylou.

Baylou emitted a finger thin beam of red energy from its back cover and struck the baby bird on her chest.

The hatchling squealed, released Lie, wobbled past

Baylou and up beside the adult hawk, pressing against him for reassurance and protection. She was not old enough to use her mental abilities to deflect Baylou's painful force beams.

"Do not press me, hawk!" Baylou rumbled inside the mind of the adult Zalack. "You shall regret it!"

The great hawk winced at the mental energy of the Book. He realized he could not force the magical Volume to save his dying chick. His grief welled.

There was a shrill cry of anger above and behind Baylou and Lie. Baylou resumed its normal size and hovered close to Lie. "I cannot defend you, and myself, against both adult birds. If I heal this chick, I will be consumed by the energy transfer. My essence says I must sacrifice myself to preserve you and Clu. You must continue the quest alone."

"That will achieve nothing except exchanging one life for another," Lie said. "The Quest would still be lost, for we are not where we are meant to be. If I cannot return to try to fight Ihpoza, your sacrifice would be useless. I am sorry, but the life of an extinct bird is not worth your life, and the lives of the people and creatures on our Azon. You must find some way to return us to our time. To do that, you must remain alive."

Baylou narrowed its eye in thought.

The adult female Zalack alighted behind Lie and Baylou. She and her mate adopted the pre-attack stance, raising their golden wings into the sun yellowed air.

Lie grasped the Book and stared into its eye. "Can you

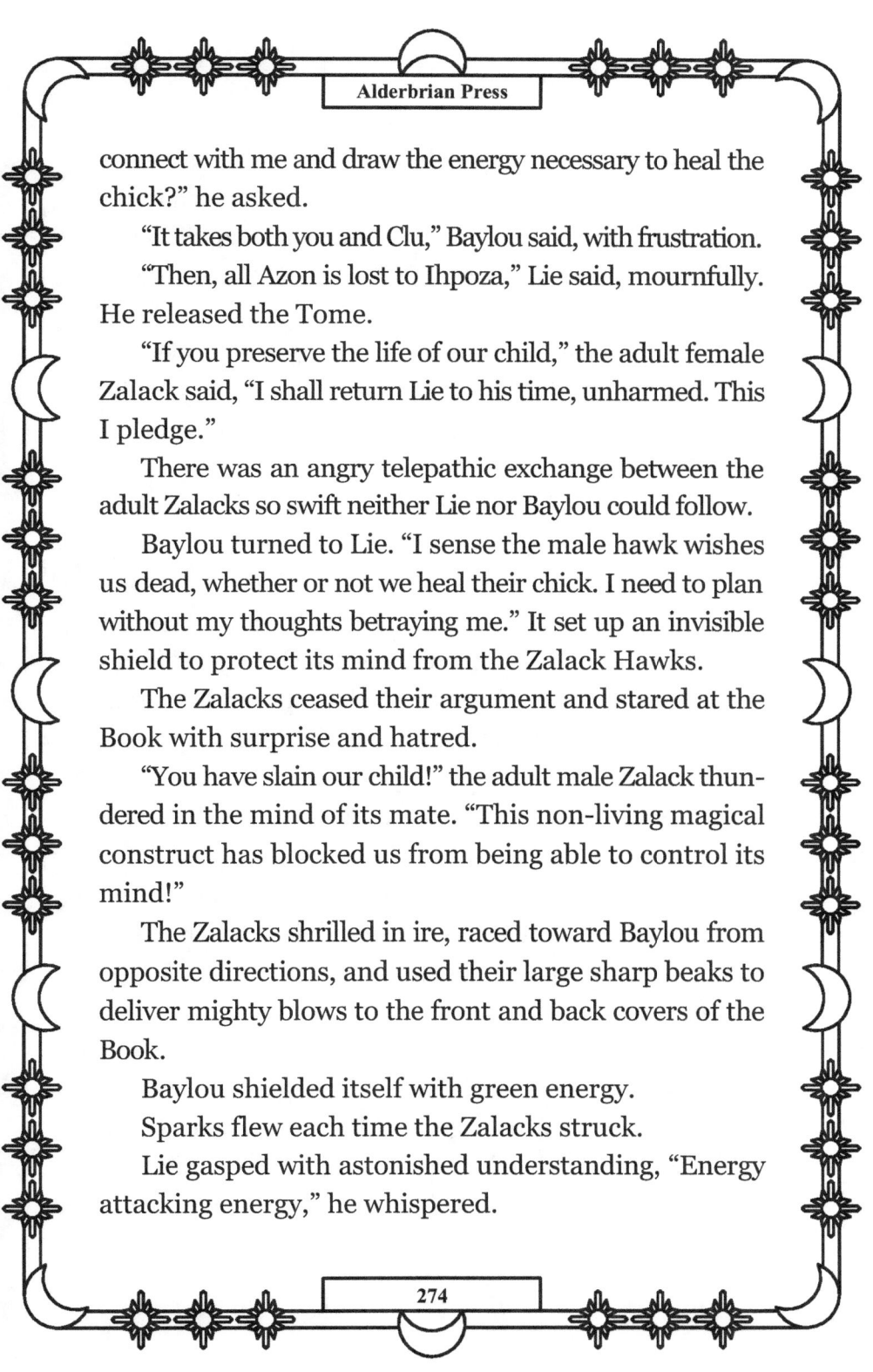

connect with me and draw the energy necessary to heal the chick?" he asked.

"It takes both you and Clu," Baylou said, with frustration.

"Then, all Azon is lost to Ihpoza," Lie said, mournfully. He released the Tome.

"If you preserve the life of our child," the adult female Zalack said, "I shall return Lie to his time, unharmed. This I pledge."

There was an angry telepathic exchange between the adult Zalacks so swift neither Lie nor Baylou could follow.

Baylou turned to Lie. "I sense the male hawk wishes us dead, whether or not we heal their chick. I need to plan without my thoughts betraying me." It set up an invisible shield to protect its mind from the Zalack Hawks.

The Zalacks ceased their argument and stared at the Book with surprise and hatred.

"You have slain our child!" the adult male Zalack thundered in the mind of its mate. "This non-living magical construct has blocked us from being able to control its mind!"

The Zalacks shrilled in ire, raced toward Baylou from opposite directions, and used their large sharp beaks to deliver mighty blows to the front and back covers of the Book.

Baylou shielded itself with green energy.

Sparks flew each time the Zalacks struck.

Lie gasped with astonished understanding, "Energy attacking energy," he whispered.

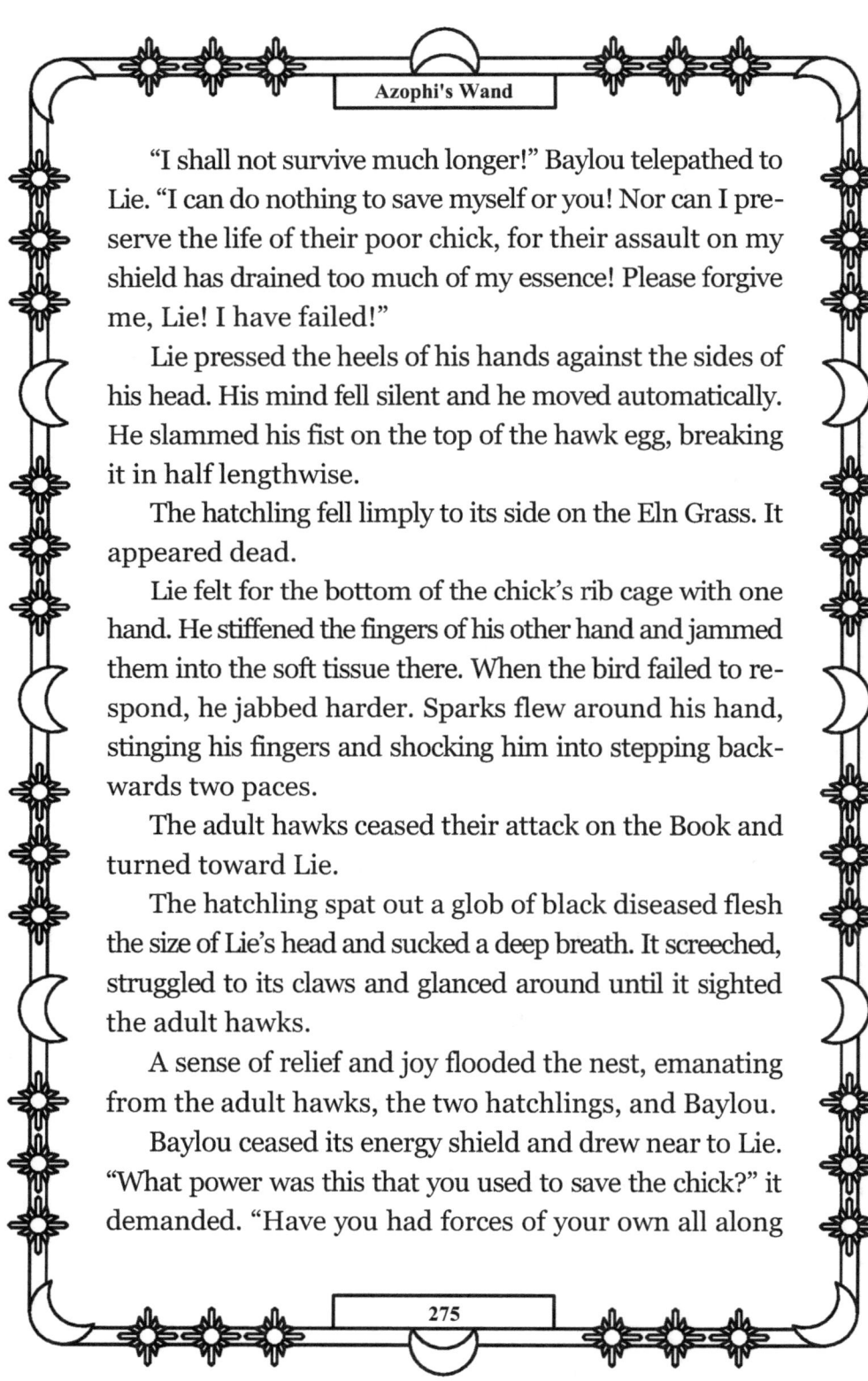

"I shall not survive much longer!" Baylou telepathed to Lie. "I can do nothing to save myself or you! Nor can I preserve the life of their poor chick, for their assault on my shield has drained too much of my essence! Please forgive me, Lie! I have failed!"

Lie pressed the heels of his hands against the sides of his head. His mind fell silent and he moved automatically. He slammed his fist on the top of the hawk egg, breaking it in half lengthwise.

The hatchling fell limply to its side on the Eln Grass. It appeared dead.

Lie felt for the bottom of the chick's rib cage with one hand. He stiffened the fingers of his other hand and jammed them into the soft tissue there. When the bird failed to respond, he jabbed harder. Sparks flew around his hand, stinging his fingers and shocking him into stepping backwards two paces.

The adult hawks ceased their attack on the Book and turned toward Lie.

The hatchling spat out a glob of black diseased flesh the size of Lie's head and sucked a deep breath. It screeched, struggled to its claws and glanced around until it sighted the adult hawks.

A sense of relief and joy flooded the nest, emanating from the adult hawks, the two hatchlings, and Baylou.

Baylou ceased its energy shield and drew near to Lie. "What power was this that you used to save the chick?" it demanded. "Have you had forces of your own all along which you have hidden from me?"

The joy turned to hatred and a feeling of the Zalacks being threatened. They snatched up their young in their beaks and sprang into the air with mighty fluttering of massive wings.

"Now, I agree!" the adult female hawk roared telepathically to her mate as they circled in the sky. "Now, they must die!"

"I have given you the life of your child!" Lie screamed angrily at the hawks. "You oathed to return us to our time! Do not violate that oath or you shall answer to Azophi!"

"He knows!" the adult male hawk shrilled telepathically.

"He knows!" the female adult hawk screamed in all their minds.

"We shall not submit! We shall not return!" the adult male hawk raged in Lie's and Baylou's minds.

With their minds, the four hawks emitted a vibrating low tone in all directions of the compass.

Other such calls answered from far away, until thousands of Zalack minds were directing their fear and loathing toward Lie and Baylou.

"What is it?" Baylou shouted. "What do you know?"

Lie stood mute. He was shuddering. His skin was pale and covered with perspiration.

Baylou spun around in a slow circle. From all directions, with incredible speed, wave upon wave of Zalacks were descending on the rock column, the nest, Lie and Baylou.

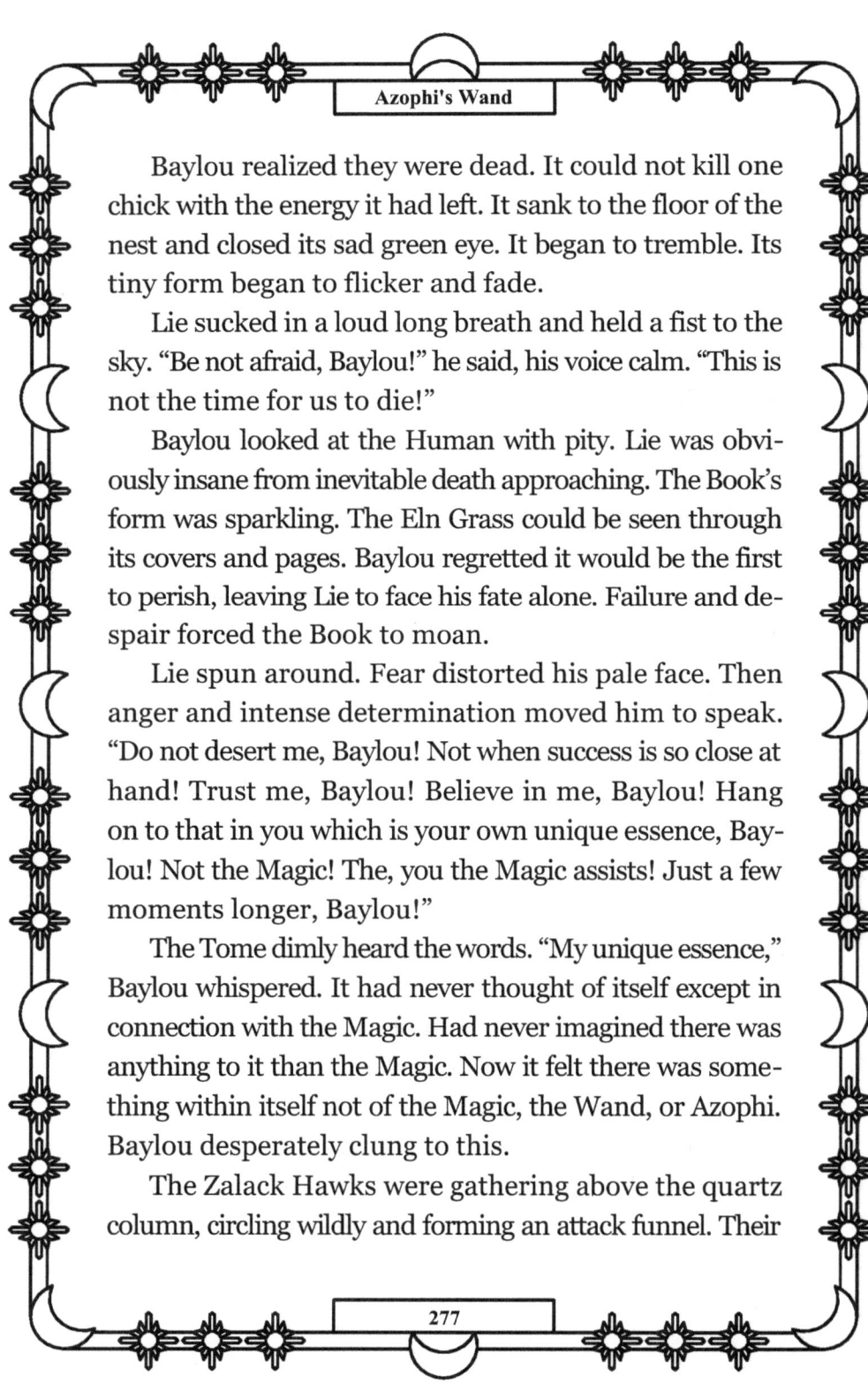

Baylou realized they were dead. It could not kill one chick with the energy it had left. It sank to the floor of the nest and closed its sad green eye. It began to tremble. Its tiny form began to flicker and fade.

Lie sucked in a loud long breath and held a fist to the sky. "Be not afraid, Baylou!" he said, his voice calm. "This is not the time for us to die!"

Baylou looked at the Human with pity. Lie was obviously insane from inevitable death approaching. The Book's form was sparkling. The Eln Grass could be seen through its covers and pages. Baylou regretted it would be the first to perish, leaving Lie to face his fate alone. Failure and despair forced the Book to moan.

Lie spun around. Fear distorted his pale face. Then anger and intense determination moved him to speak. "Do not desert me, Baylou! Not when success is so close at hand! Trust me, Baylou! Believe in me, Baylou! Hang on to that in you which is your own unique essence, Baylou! Not the Magic! The, you the Magic assists! Just a few moments longer, Baylou!"

The Tome dimly heard the words. "My unique essence," Baylou whispered. It had never thought of itself except in connection with the Magic. Had never imagined there was anything to it than the Magic. Now it felt there was something within itself not of the Magic, the Wand, or Azophi. Baylou desperately clung to this.

The Zalack Hawks were gathering above the quartz column, circling wildly and forming an attack funnel. Their

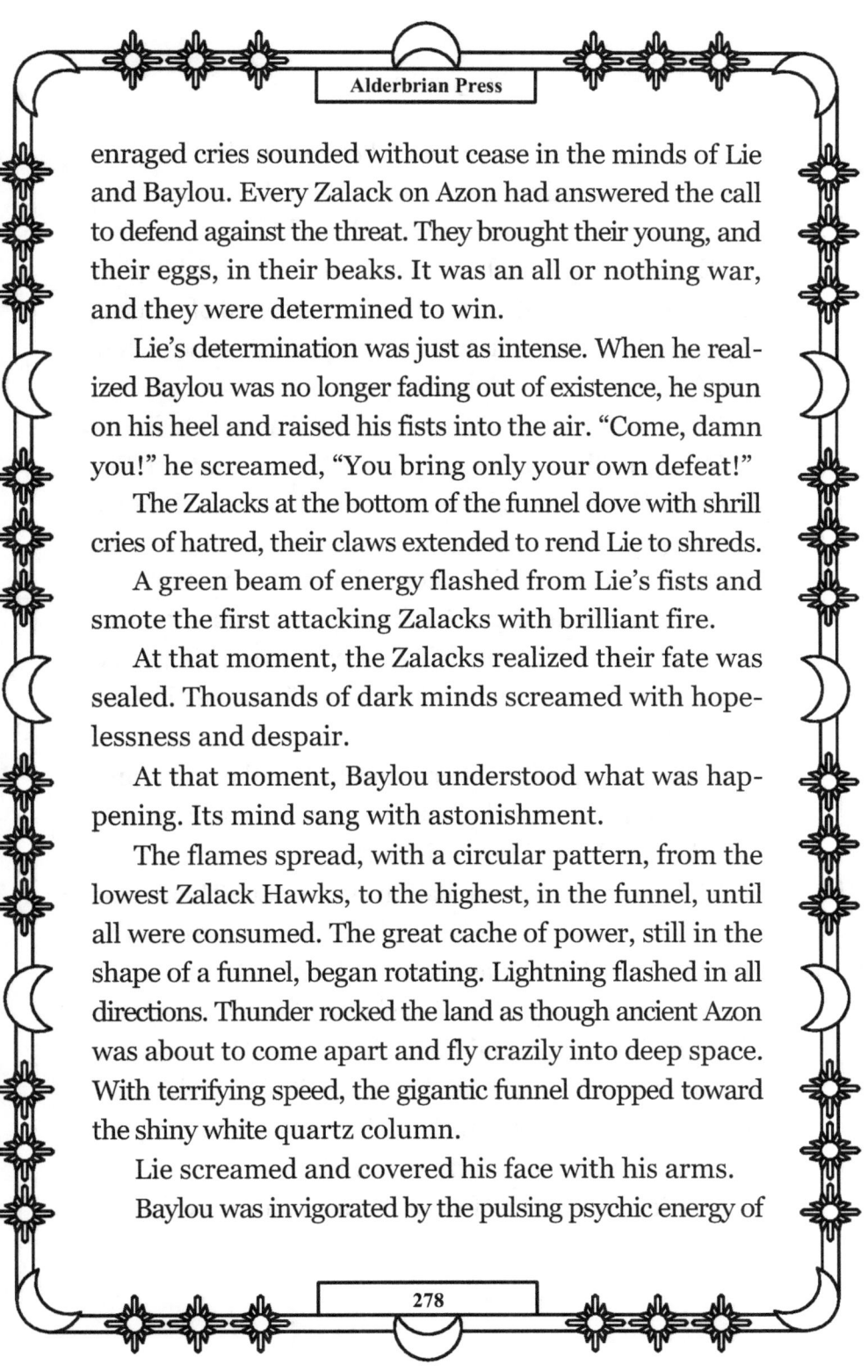

enraged cries sounded without cease in the minds of Lie and Baylou. Every Zalack on Azon had answered the call to defend against the threat. They brought their young, and their eggs, in their beaks. It was an all or nothing war, and they were determined to win.

Lie's determination was just as intense. When he realized Baylou was no longer fading out of existence, he spun on his heel and raised his fists into the air. "Come, damn you!" he screamed, "You bring only your own defeat!"

The Zalacks at the bottom of the funnel dove with shrill cries of hatred, their claws extended to rend Lie to shreds.

A green beam of energy flashed from Lie's fists and smote the first attacking Zalacks with brilliant fire.

At that moment, the Zalacks realized their fate was sealed. Thousands of dark minds screamed with hopelessness and despair.

At that moment, Baylou understood what was happening. Its mind sang with astonishment.

The flames spread, with a circular pattern, from the lowest Zalack Hawks, to the highest, in the funnel, until all were consumed. The great cache of power, still in the shape of a funnel, began rotating. Lightning flashed in all directions. Thunder rocked the land as though ancient Azon was about to come apart and fly crazily into deep space. With terrifying speed, the gigantic funnel dropped toward the shiny white quartz column.

Lie screamed and covered his face with his arms.

Baylou was invigorated by the pulsing psychic energy of

the funnel, to the level of power it held before the hatchling had drawn them through the Time Rift. The Tome threw up an emerald shield around itself and Lie.

The funnel speared harmlessly through Lie and Baylou and into the rock plateau with a horrible sound of crunching stone, leaving Lie and Baylou in stunned silence. They could see no damage to the tower.

There was a wave of heat and a brilliant white light.

When the flash blindness passed, Lie saw the thick Eln Grass had lost its green. They were in their Time Frame.

The great rock tower began to quake.

"No!" Lie and Baylou shouted, with frustration.

The great funnel of psychic force surged out of the white quartz plateau with a terrifying sound of crunching stone and a scintillating emerald light, sped into the air for a mile, and hovered soundlessly.

There was a golden glitter in the walls of the funnel and millions of Zalack Hawks, some bearing young or eggs in their beaks, flashed into existence.

The adult hawks were half the size of Lie. Their prior gigantism and intense arcane abilities were a result of the effects of the Cache Magic instilled within them.

Over the centuries, the Zalacks had feared the release of Azophi's energy would end their lives. Now, as they regained their natural state, they sang with joy, and soared away from the power funnel, to all points of the compass to seek their ancient nesting grounds.

The immense force funnel reformed into a column.

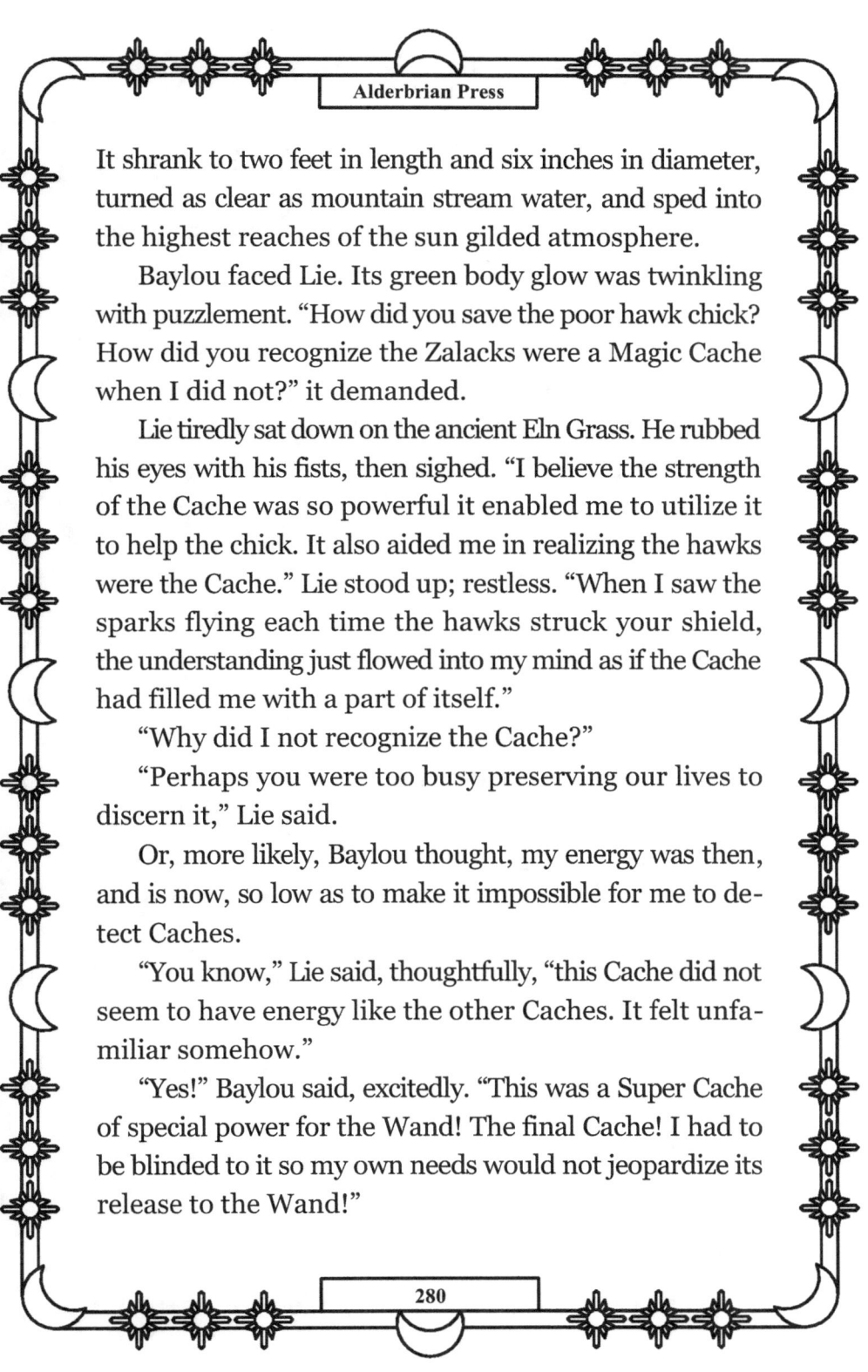

It shrank to two feet in length and six inches in diameter, turned as clear as mountain stream water, and sped into the highest reaches of the sun gilded atmosphere.

Baylou faced Lie. Its green body glow was twinkling with puzzlement. "How did you save the poor hawk chick? How did you recognize the Zalacks were a Magic Cache when I did not?" it demanded.

Lie tiredly sat down on the ancient Eln Grass. He rubbed his eyes with his fists, then sighed. "I believe the strength of the Cache was so powerful it enabled me to utilize it to help the chick. It also aided me in realizing the hawks were the Cache." Lie stood up; restless. "When I saw the sparks flying each time the hawks struck your shield, the understanding just flowed into my mind as if the Cache had filled me with a part of itself."

"Why did I not recognize the Cache?"

"Perhaps you were too busy preserving our lives to discern it," Lie said.

Or, more likely, Baylou thought, my energy was then, and is now, so low as to make it impossible for me to detect Caches.

"You know," Lie said, thoughtfully, "this Cache did not seem to have energy like the other Caches. It felt unfamiliar somehow."

"Yes!" Baylou said, excitedly. "This was a Super Cache of special power for the Wand! The final Cache! I had to be blinded to it so my own needs would not jeopardize its release to the Wand!"

"Has Azophi, then, foreseen all possibilities?" Lie asked, in awe.

"Not all," Baylou said, glumly, recalling its still nearly exhausted state due to the loss of the Cache in Slann.

Lie remembered. "Where is Clu, Baylou?" he demanded.

The Book tilted face down toward the nest and tripled its length and width. "Mount my back," it ordered.

Lie rode the Tome at its meteoric breath stealing frightful speed down to the sand and stepped off its cover.

Baylou reshaped to its normal dimensions.

"Where has the Lizard taken Clu?" Lie demanded.

"To Iphozalon," Baylou said. "To Ihpoza."

Chills traveled down Lie's spine.

Urgently, they set out for Iphozalon.

<hr />

The invisible crystal bar of energy wasted no time taking its proper place in the Universe. It speared through the vaulted ice ceiling of Ihpoza's palace and throne room and entered the spell prison, merging with the Wand.

Ihpoza sat meditating on his ornate throne, but did not note the momentous event that transpired in front of him.

Illustration 42

Ortourian Beast Wrought Iron Window Grillwork

Copyright © 2019 Philip Raymond Sadler

282-A

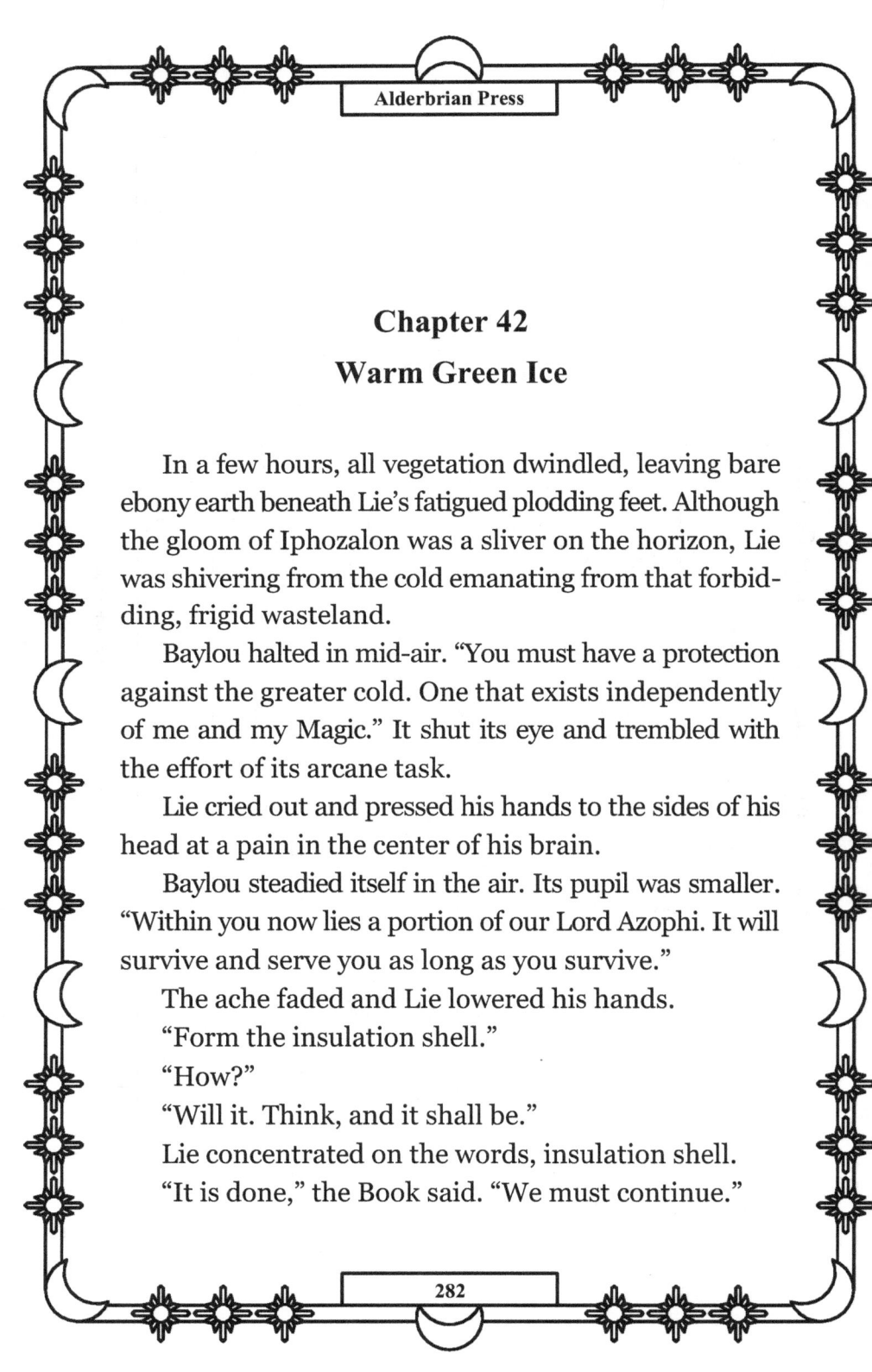

Chapter 42
Warm Green Ice

In a few hours, all vegetation dwindled, leaving bare ebony earth beneath Lie's fatigued plodding feet. Although the gloom of Iphozalon was a sliver on the horizon, Lie was shivering from the cold emanating from that forbidding, frigid wasteland.

Baylou halted in mid-air. "You must have a protection against the greater cold. One that exists independently of me and my Magic." It shut its eye and trembled with the effort of its arcane task.

Lie cried out and pressed his hands to the sides of his head at a pain in the center of his brain.

Baylou steadied itself in the air. Its pupil was smaller. "Within you now lies a portion of our Lord Azophi. It will survive and serve you as long as you survive."

The ache faded and Lie lowered his hands.

"Form the insulation shell."

"How?"

"Will it. Think, and it shall be."

Lie concentrated on the words, insulation shell.

"It is done," the Book said. "We must continue."

The cold was gone and a pale light was shining around Lie. It was as though he walked in a supple suit of head to toe warm, green ice. "Baylou, how do I breathe?"

"The shell allows air to pass in and out of itself. It also heats and cools the air as it passes through to prevent formation of the steam that would alert our enemies to our presence."

Lie nodded. Such magic could hardly be understood, only marveled at.

Illustration 43

Ortourian Beast Wrought Iron Window Grillwork

284-A

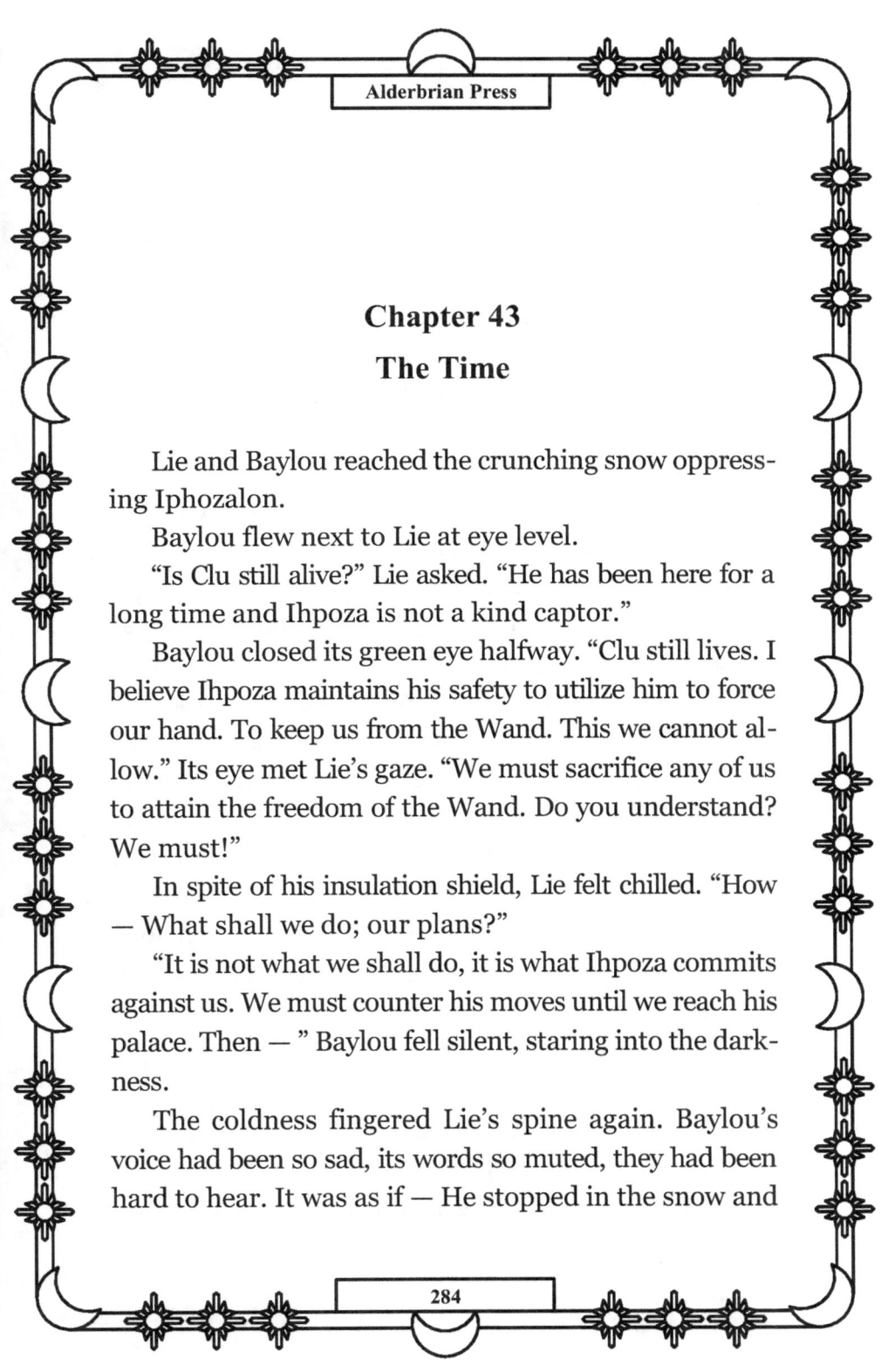

Chapter 43
The Time

Lie and Baylou reached the crunching snow oppressing Iphozalon.

Baylou flew next to Lie at eye level.

"Is Clu still alive?" Lie asked. "He has been here for a long time and Ihpoza is not a kind captor."

Baylou closed its green eye halfway. "Clu still lives. I believe Ihpoza maintains his safety to utilize him to force our hand. To keep us from the Wand. This we cannot allow." Its eye met Lie's gaze. "We must sacrifice any of us to attain the freedom of the Wand. Do you understand? We must!"

In spite of his insulation shield, Lie felt chilled. "How — What shall we do; our plans?"

"It is not what we shall do, it is what Ihpoza commits against us. We must counter his moves until we reach his palace. Then — " Baylou fell silent, staring into the darkness.

The coldness fingered Lie's spine again. Baylou's voice had been so sad, its words so muted, they had been hard to hear. It was as if — He stopped in the snow and

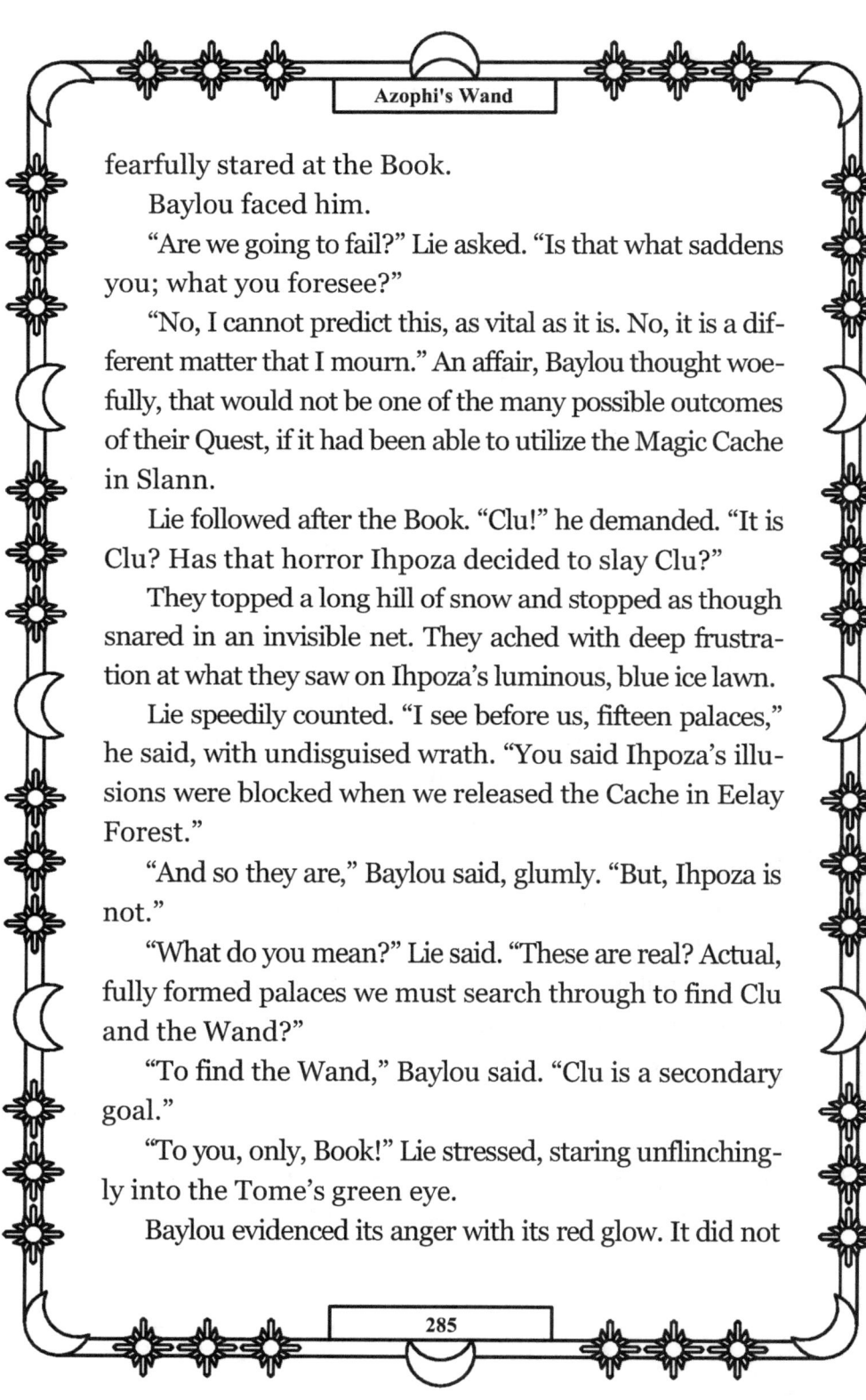

fearfully stared at the Book.

Baylou faced him.

"Are we going to fail?" Lie asked. "Is that what saddens you; what you foresee?"

"No, I cannot predict this, as vital as it is. No, it is a different matter that I mourn." An affair, Baylou thought woefully, that would not be one of the many possible outcomes of their Quest, if it had been able to utilize the Magic Cache in Slann.

Lie followed after the Book. "Clu!" he demanded. "It is Clu? Has that horror Ihpoza decided to slay Clu?"

They topped a long hill of snow and stopped as though snared in an invisible net. They ached with deep frustration at what they saw on Ihpoza's luminous, blue ice lawn.

Lie speedily counted. "I see before us, fifteen palaces," he said, with undisguised wrath. "You said Ihpoza's illusions were blocked when we released the Cache in Eelay Forest."

"And so they are," Baylou said, glumly. "But, Ihpoza is not."

"What do you mean?" Lie said. "These are real? Actual, fully formed palaces we must search through to find Clu and the Wand?"

"To find the Wand," Baylou said. "Clu is a secondary goal."

"To you, only, Book!" Lie stressed, staring unflinchingly into the Tome's green eye.

Baylou evidenced its anger with its red glow. It did not

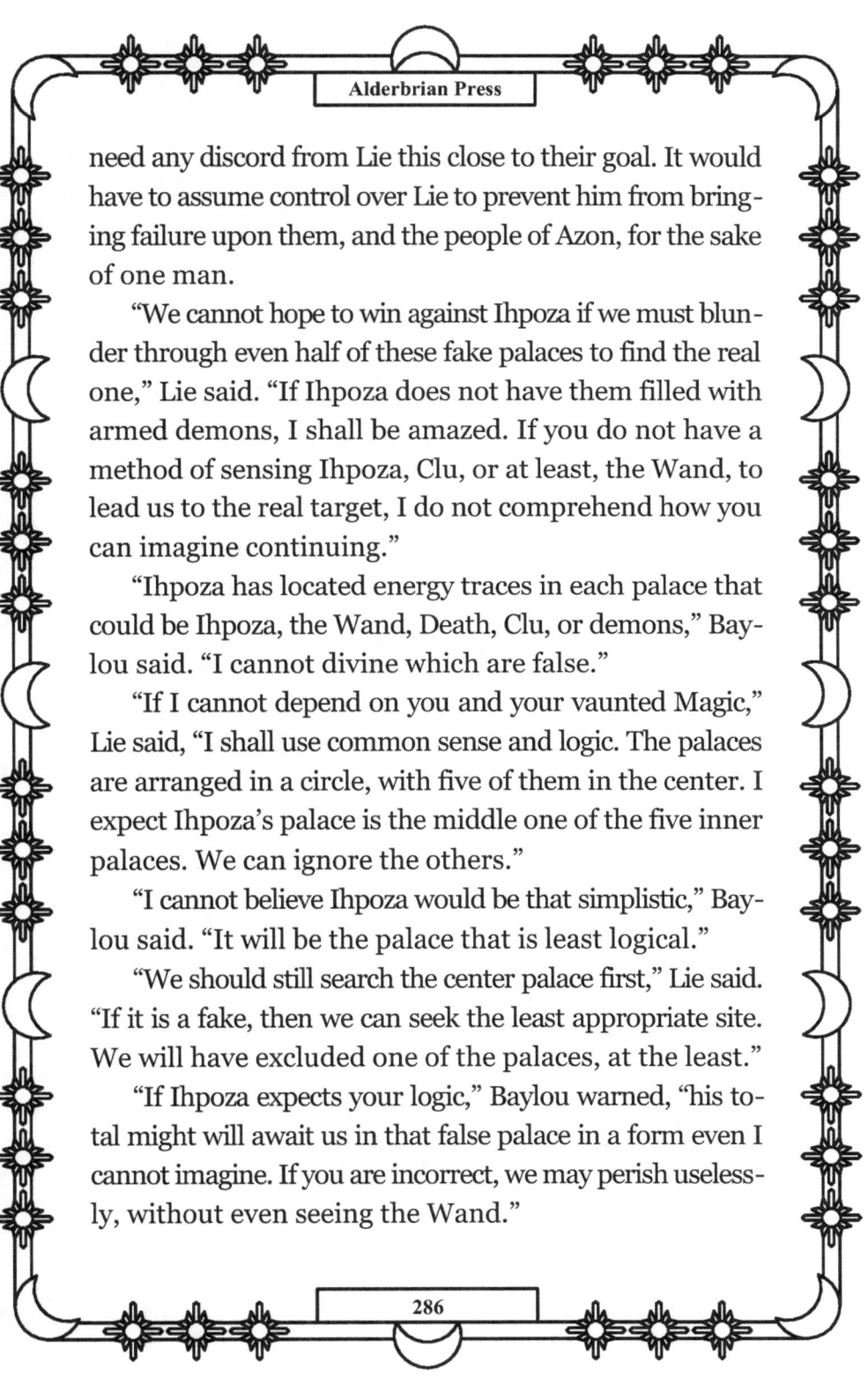

need any discord from Lie this close to their goal. It would have to assume control over Lie to prevent him from bringing failure upon them, and the people of Azon, for the sake of one man.

"We cannot hope to win against Ihpoza if we must blunder through even half of these fake palaces to find the real one," Lie said. "If Ihpoza does not have them filled with armed demons, I shall be amazed. If you do not have a method of sensing Ihpoza, Clu, or at least, the Wand, to lead us to the real target, I do not comprehend how you can imagine continuing."

"Ihpoza has located energy traces in each palace that could be Ihpoza, the Wand, Death, Clu, or demons," Baylou said. "I cannot divine which are false."

"If I cannot depend on you and your vaunted Magic," Lie said, "I shall use common sense and logic. The palaces are arranged in a circle, with five of them in the center. I expect Ihpoza's palace is the middle one of the five inner palaces. We can ignore the others."

"I cannot believe Ihpoza would be that simplistic," Baylou said. "It will be the palace that is least logical."

"We should still search the center palace first," Lie said. "If it is a fake, then we can seek the least appropriate site. We will have excluded one of the palaces, at the least."

"If Ihpoza expects your logic," Baylou warned, "his total might will await us in that false palace in a form even I cannot imagine. If you are incorrect, we may perish uselessly, without even seeing the Wand."

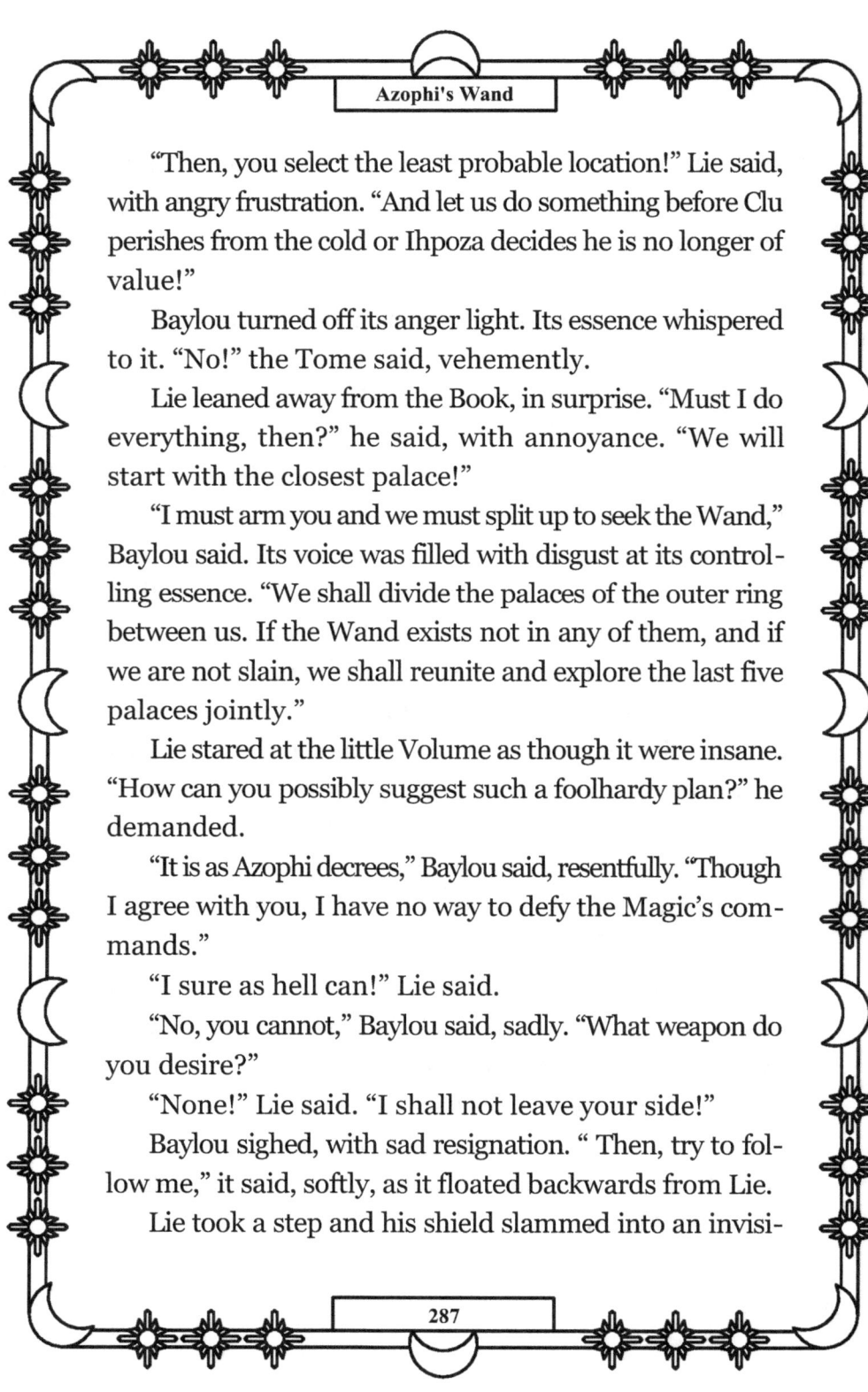

"Then, you select the least probable location!" Lie said, with angry frustration. "And let us do something before Clu perishes from the cold or Ihpoza decides he is no longer of value!"

Baylou turned off its anger light. Its essence whispered to it. "No!" the Tome said, vehemently.

Lie leaned away from the Book, in surprise. "Must I do everything, then?" he said, with annoyance. "We will start with the closest palace!"

"I must arm you and we must split up to seek the Wand," Baylou said. Its voice was filled with disgust at its controlling essence. "We shall divide the palaces of the outer ring between us. If the Wand exists not in any of them, and if we are not slain, we shall reunite and explore the last five palaces jointly."

Lie stared at the little Volume as though it were insane. "How can you possibly suggest such a foolhardy plan?" he demanded.

"It is as Azophi decrees," Baylou said, resentfully. "Though I agree with you, I have no way to defy the Magic's commands."

"I sure as hell can!" Lie said.

"No, you cannot," Baylou said, sadly. "What weapon do you desire?"

"None!" Lie said. "I shall not leave your side!"

Baylou sighed, with sad resignation. " Then, try to follow me," it said, softly, as it floated backwards from Lie.

Lie took a step and his shield slammed into an invisi-

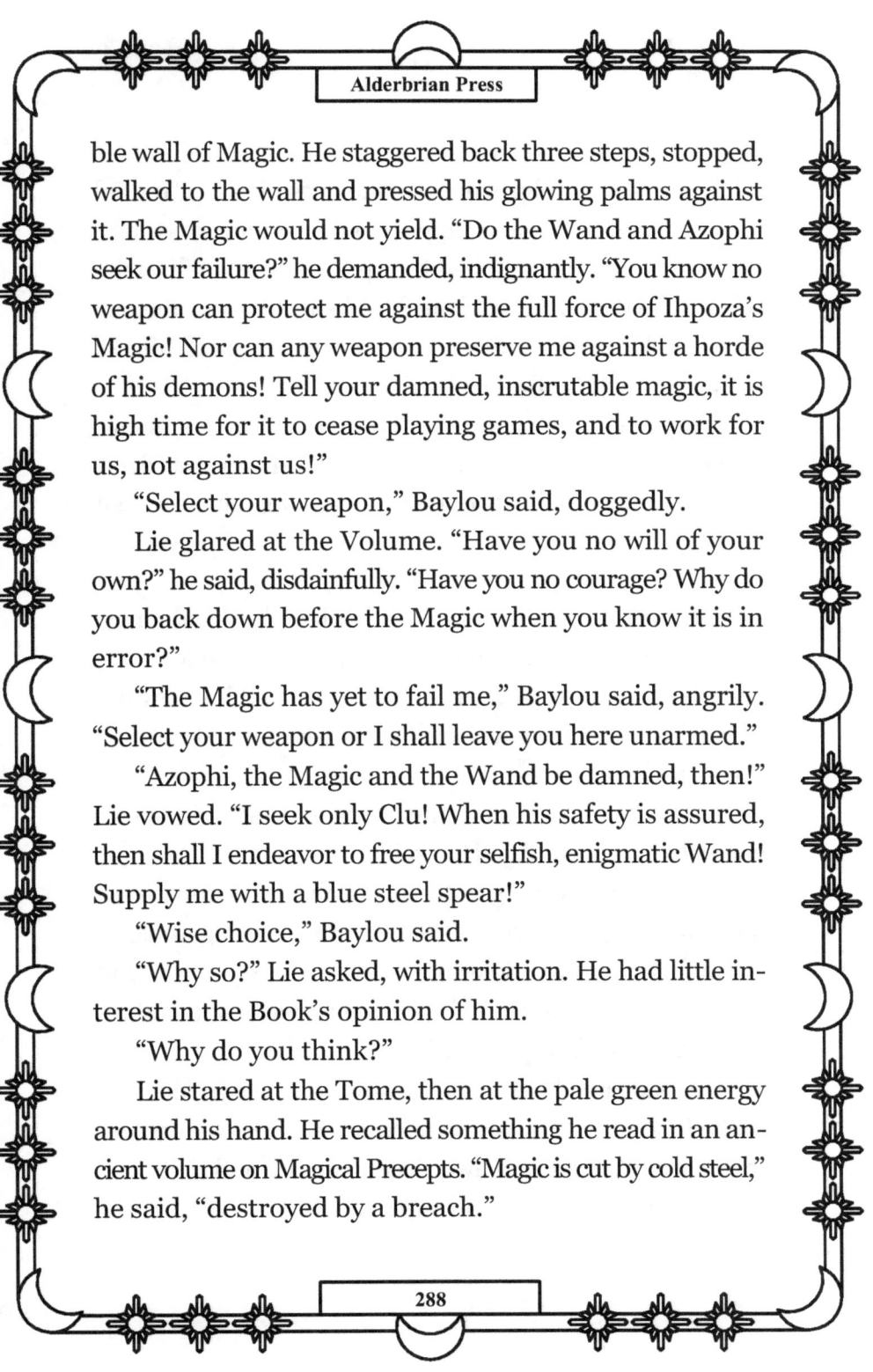

ble wall of Magic. He staggered back three steps, stopped, walked to the wall and pressed his glowing palms against it. The Magic would not yield. "Do the Wand and Azophi seek our failure?" he demanded, indignantly. "You know no weapon can protect me against the full force of Ihpoza's Magic! Nor can any weapon preserve me against a horde of his demons! Tell your damned, inscrutable magic, it is high time for it to cease playing games, and to work for us, not against us!"

"Select your weapon," Baylou said, doggedly.

Lie glared at the Volume. "Have you no will of your own?" he said, disdainfully. "Have you no courage? Why do you back down before the Magic when you know it is in error?"

"The Magic has yet to fail me," Baylou said, angrily. "Select your weapon or I shall leave you here unarmed."

"Azophi, the Magic and the Wand be damned, then!" Lie vowed. "I seek only Clu! When his safety is assured, then shall I endeavor to free your selfish, enigmatic Wand! Supply me with a blue steel spear!"

"Wise choice," Baylou said.

"Why so?" Lie asked, with irritation. He had little interest in the Book's opinion of him.

"Why do you think?"

Lie stared at the Tome, then at the pale green energy around his hand. He recalled something he read in an ancient volume on Magical Precepts. "Magic is cut by cold steel," he said, "destroyed by a breach."

Baylou said nothing.

A blue steel javelin, similar to the ones Lie and Clu used against the Sand Diggers, appeared in a standing position in front of Lie. He snatched the spear before it fell to the snow. When he shot a last hate filled look at Baylou, the tiny Tome had already vanished over one of the small hills of snow, toward the first of its five palaces.

Lie started slogging through the last of the crunchy snow. When he reached the glowing ice lawn, his energy suit slightly glued his feet to the frozen water providing him excellent traction.

Lie circled the glowing, spired palace. To his dismay, there was only one entrance and no apparent windows. He grasped his javelin with both hands, turned it sideways, parallel with the ice lawn, and cautiously stepped through the vaulted doorway.

Lie found himself standing at the entrance of the second palace he was obliged to explore.

"Is there something in the first palace you don't want me to find, Ihpoza," Lie whispered, "or something unpleasant in this palace you do want me to find? Are you trying to trick me into wasting time by second guessing you and returning to the first palace?"

Lie made a full circuit of the structure. It was identical to the first. He cautiously stepped through the vaulted entrance way. A narrow hallway lead to his left and right, and a wide vaulted corridor lead straight ahead forever. He saw

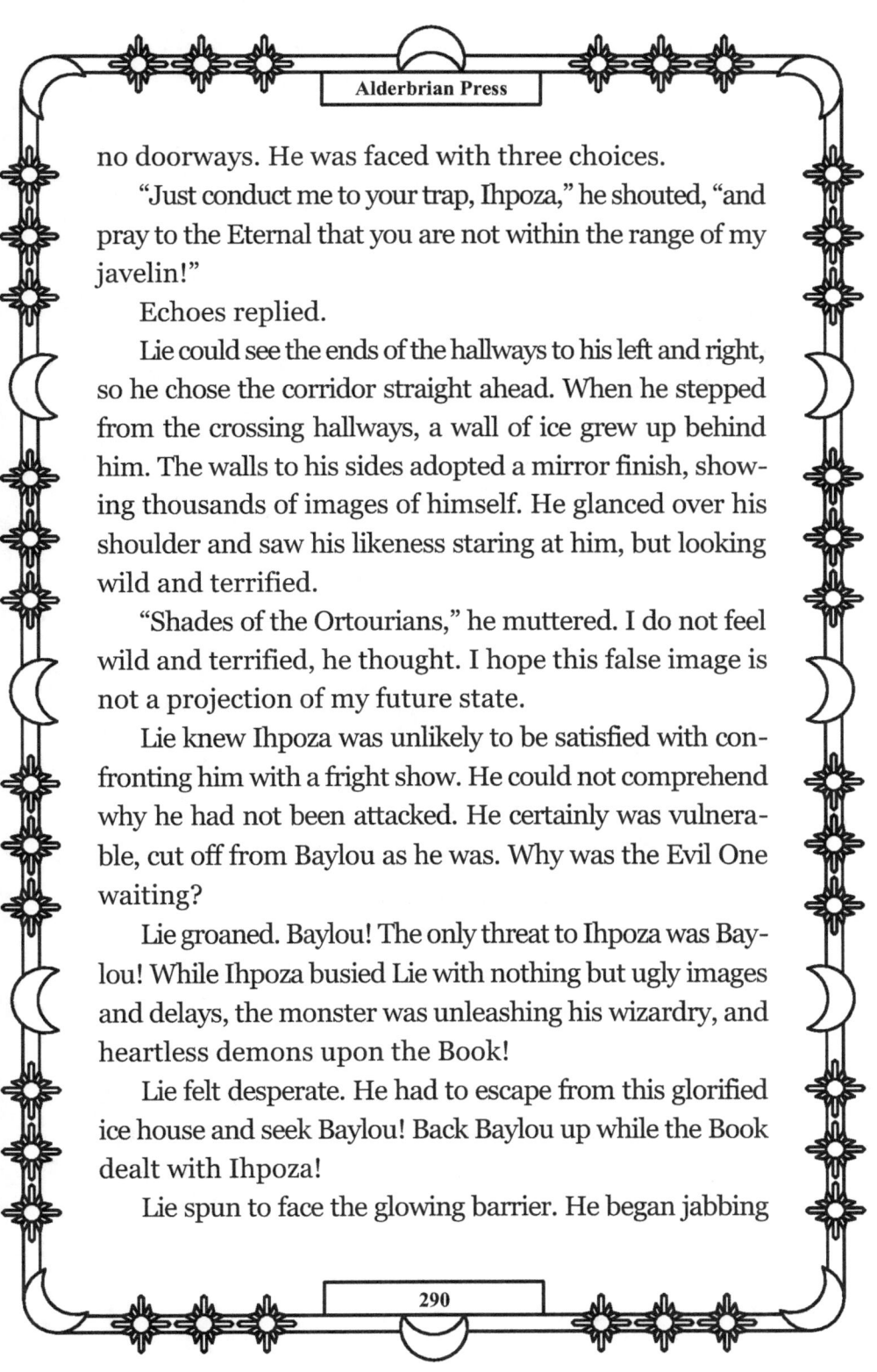

no doorways. He was faced with three choices.

"Just conduct me to your trap, Ihpoza," he shouted, "and pray to the Eternal that you are not within the range of my javelin!"

Echoes replied.

Lie could see the ends of the hallways to his left and right, so he chose the corridor straight ahead. When he stepped from the crossing hallways, a wall of ice grew up behind him. The walls to his sides adopted a mirror finish, showing thousands of images of himself. He glanced over his shoulder and saw his likeness staring at him, but looking wild and terrified.

"Shades of the Ortourians," he muttered. I do not feel wild and terrified, he thought. I hope this false image is not a projection of my future state.

Lie knew Ihpoza was unlikely to be satisfied with confronting him with a fright show. He could not comprehend why he had not been attacked. He certainly was vulnerable, cut off from Baylou as he was. Why was the Evil One waiting?

Lie groaned. Baylou! The only threat to Ihpoza was Baylou! While Ihpoza busied Lie with nothing but ugly images and delays, the monster was unleashing his wizardry, and heartless demons upon the Book!

Lie felt desperate. He had to escape from this glorified ice house and seek Baylou! Back Baylou up while the Book dealt with Ihpoza!

Lie spun to face the glowing barrier. He began jabbing

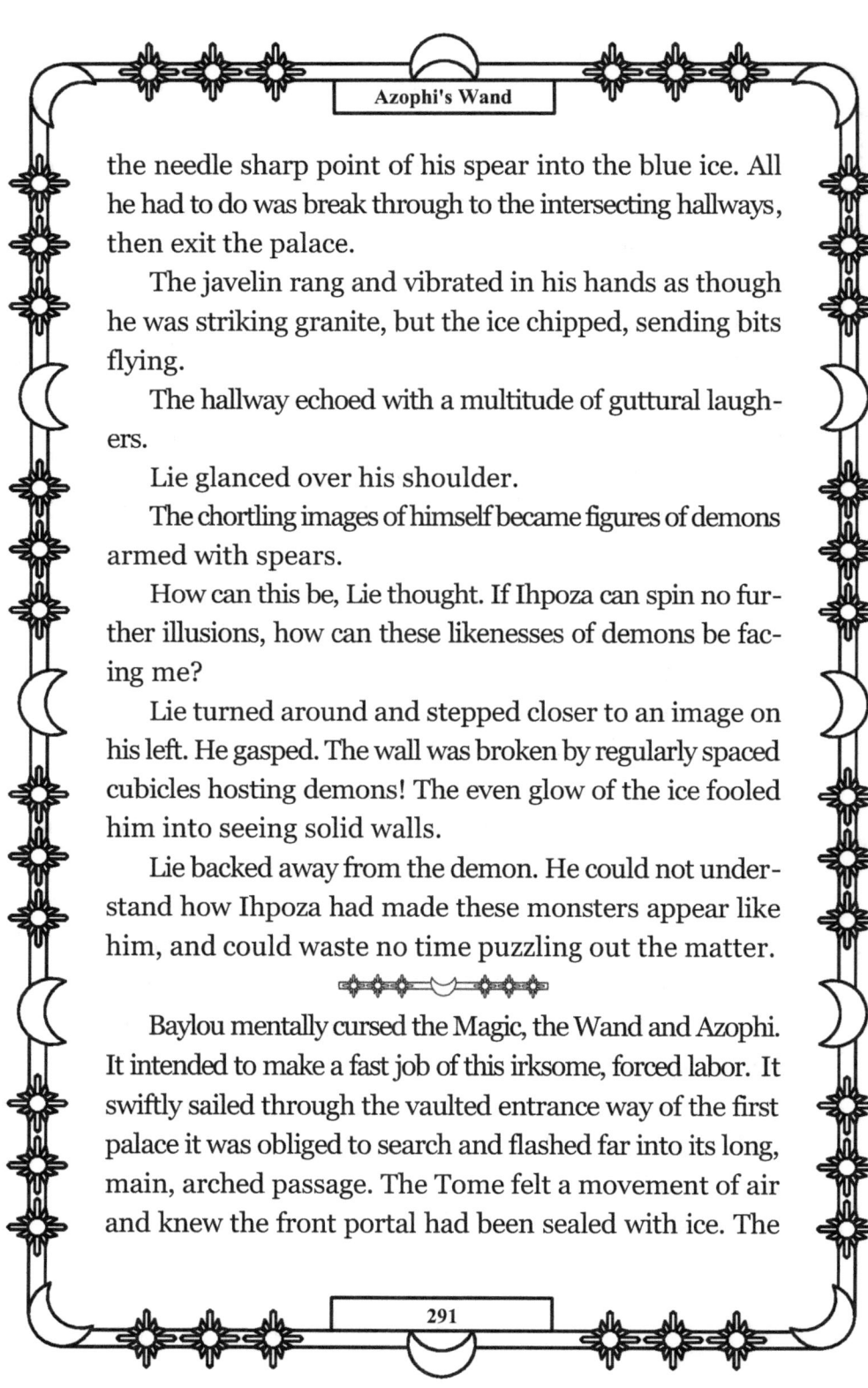

the needle sharp point of his spear into the blue ice. All he had to do was break through to the intersecting hallways, then exit the palace.

The javelin rang and vibrated in his hands as though he was striking granite, but the ice chipped, sending bits flying.

The hallway echoed with a multitude of guttural laughers.

Lie glanced over his shoulder.

The chortling images of himself became figures of demons armed with spears.

How can this be, Lie thought. If Ihpoza can spin no further illusions, how can these likenesses of demons be facing me?

Lie turned around and stepped closer to an image on his left. He gasped. The wall was broken by regularly spaced cubicles hosting demons! The even glow of the ice fooled him into seeing solid walls.

Lie backed away from the demon. He could not understand how Ihpoza had made these monsters appear like him, and could waste no time puzzling out the matter.

Baylou mentally cursed the Magic, the Wand and Azophi. It intended to make a fast job of this irksome, forced labor. It swiftly sailed through the vaulted entrance way of the first palace it was obliged to search and flashed far into its long, main, arched passage. The Tome felt a movement of air and knew the front portal had been sealed with ice. The walls of the corridor presented hundreds of images of Ihpoza.

Baylou chuckled and emitted a hot white light in all directions.

Like shiny blue wax, the palace began to melt.

The speed with which the ice thawed surprised Baylou. Surely, Ihpoza is not simply going to delay me, it thought. Only an assault upon me will be of any use to him.

Baylou shuddered. Lie and Clu! If Ihpoza captures Lie and brings him together with Clu, the Evil One will be able to link telepathically with them and tap into their Mind Magic Enhancement abilities. Ihpoza will be able to fool the Wand into believing Lie and Clu are there to rescue it! The Wand will open itself to them!

Baylou spun around, headed for the melting wall at the front of the long corridor, blasted through and slammed into a new wall. Baylou increased its heat, melted through, saw the stars in the entrance of the palace, soared into the night, and paused. Baylou scanned the area, but could not determine in which palace Lie was. It hoped Lie followed his reasoning and started his exploration with his first palace. If Ihpoza has not already taken him, Baylou thought, Lie should still be there.

Death rested its head on Ihpoza's knees and gazed into its Lord's eye sockets.

"The insects have entered the web, my Pet," Ihpoza said.

Death did not reply. It continued telepathically enhancing its adored Master's Mind Magic as Ihpoza worked his wonders.

Ihpoza returned his concentration to the tiny flickering images in the blue ice in front of his footstool. He was following several scenes. The Magic Cache in Slann had not been strong enough to blank out his Distance Sight in the heart of his realm. He would make good use of this ability now.

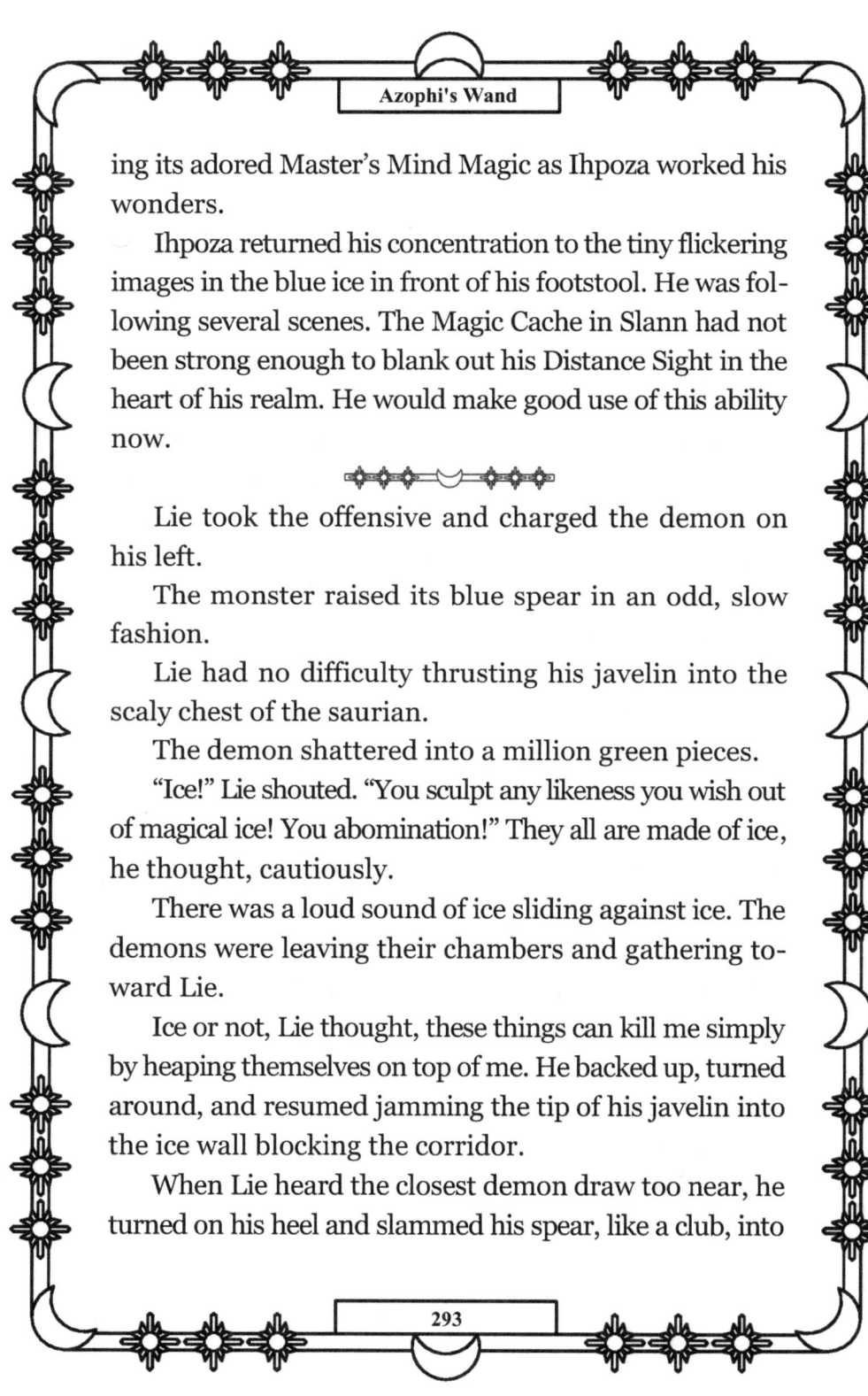

Lie took the offensive and charged the demon on his left.

The monster raised its blue spear in an odd, slow fashion.

Lie had no difficulty thrusting his javelin into the scaly chest of the saurian.

The demon shattered into a million green pieces.

"Ice!" Lie shouted. "You sculpt any likeness you wish out of magical ice! You abomination!" They all are made of ice, he thought, cautiously.

There was a loud sound of ice sliding against ice. The demons were leaving their chambers and gathering toward Lie.

Ice or not, Lie thought, these things can kill me simply by heaping themselves on top of me. He backed up, turned around, and resumed jamming the tip of his javelin into the ice wall blocking the corridor.

When Lie heard the closest demon draw too near, he turned on his heel and slammed his spear, like a club, into

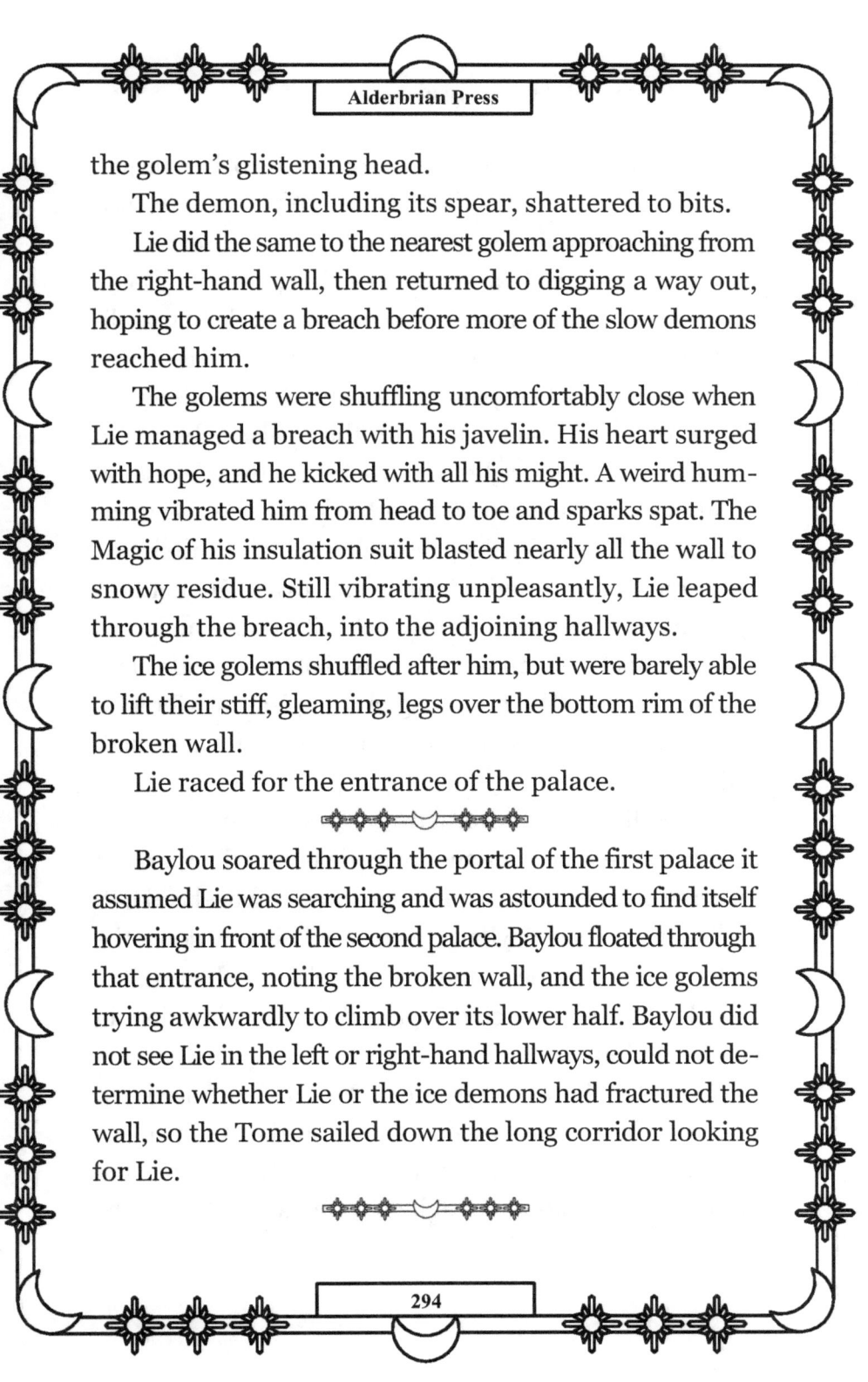

the golem's glistening head.

The demon, including its spear, shattered to bits.

Lie did the same to the nearest golem approaching from the right-hand wall, then returned to digging a way out, hoping to create a breach before more of the slow demons reached him.

The golems were shuffling uncomfortably close when Lie managed a breach with his javelin. His heart surged with hope, and he kicked with all his might. A weird humming vibrated him from head to toe and sparks spat. The Magic of his insulation suit blasted nearly all the wall to snowy residue. Still vibrating unpleasantly, Lie leaped through the breach, into the adjoining hallways.

The ice golems shuffled after him, but were barely able to lift their stiff, gleaming, legs over the bottom rim of the broken wall.

Lie raced for the entrance of the palace.

Baylou soared through the portal of the first palace it assumed Lie was searching and was astounded to find itself hovering in front of the second palace. Baylou floated through that entrance, noting the broken wall, and the ice golems trying awkwardly to climb over its lower half. Baylou did not see Lie in the left or right-hand hallways, could not determine whether Lie or the ice demons had fractured the wall, so the Tome sailed down the long corridor looking for Lie.

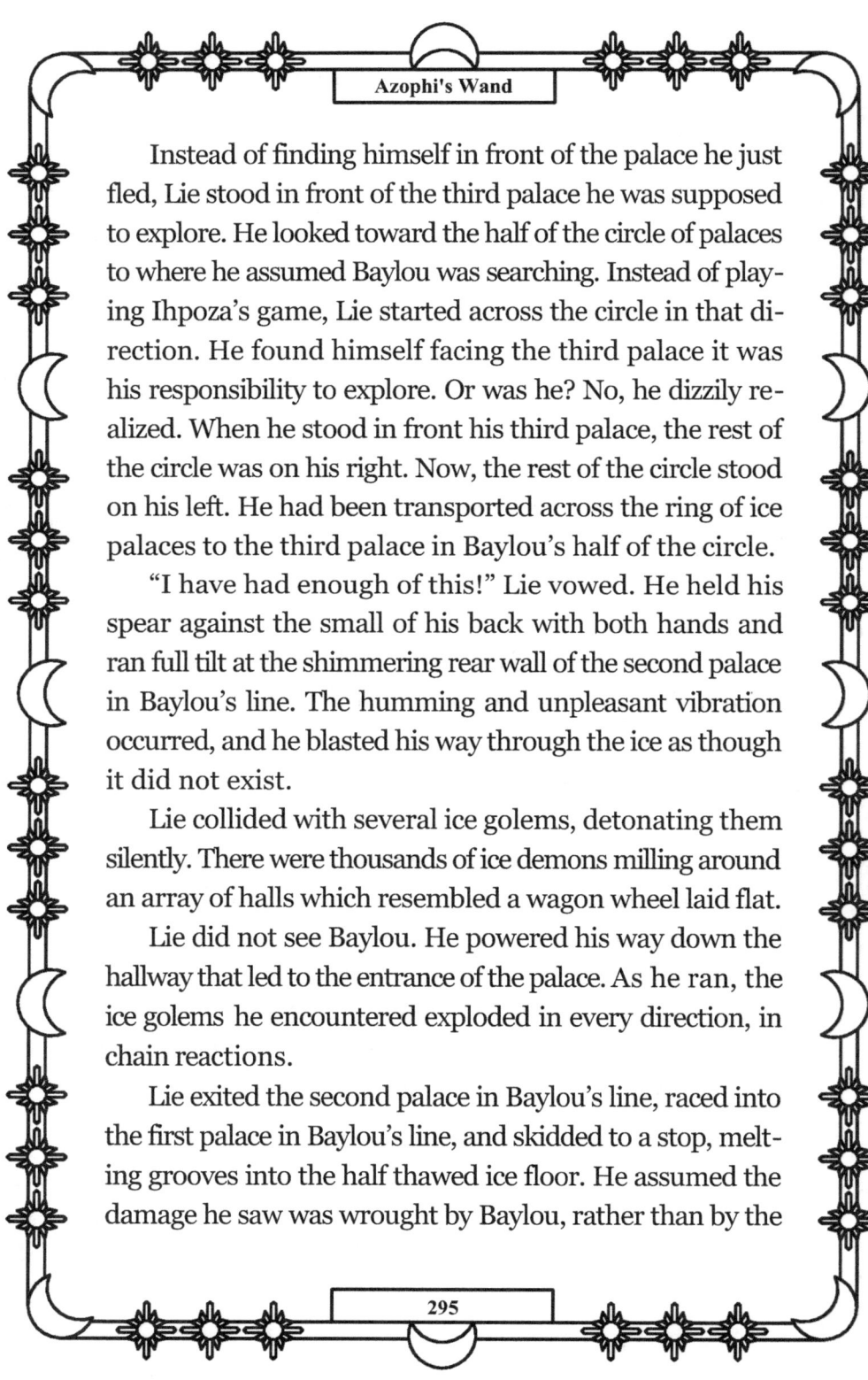

Instead of finding himself in front of the palace he just fled, Lie stood in front of the third palace he was supposed to explore. He looked toward the half of the circle of palaces to where he assumed Baylou was searching. Instead of playing Ihpoza's game, Lie started across the circle in that direction. He found himself facing the third palace it was his responsibility to explore. Or was he? No, he dizzily realized. When he stood in front his third palace, the rest of the circle was on his right. Now, the rest of the circle stood on his left. He had been transported across the ring of ice palaces to the third palace in Baylou's half of the circle.

"I have had enough of this!" Lie vowed. He held his spear against the small of his back with both hands and ran full tilt at the shimmering rear wall of the second palace in Baylou's line. The humming and unpleasant vibration occurred, and he blasted his way through the ice as though it did not exist.

Lie collided with several ice golems, detonating them silently. There were thousands of ice demons milling around an array of halls which resembled a wagon wheel laid flat.

Lie did not see Baylou. He powered his way down the hallway that led to the entrance of the palace. As he ran, the ice golems he encountered exploded in every direction, in chain reactions.

Lie exited the second palace in Baylou's line, raced into the first palace in Baylou's line, and skidded to a stop, melting grooves into the half thawed ice floor. He assumed the damage he saw was wrought by Baylou, rather than by the death of the Book. If so, at least the Tome had been inside this palace. But, where was Baylou now?

Lie retraced his steps through the palace, then the second palace, then ran into the third gleaming palace in Baylou's line.

Baylou came up short at the end of the corridor. There were no side hallways and no Lie. The way Ihpoza was magically erecting ice walls at whim, Lie could be only feet from Baylou.

The Book radiated heat and the great palace began melting. The ice golems squealed like steam from kettles and exploded at random, sending jagged bits sailing in all directions.

Baylou ceased its heat and used its power to shield itself. It soared at the vaulted ceiling and blasted into the starry sky. Below, Baylou saw the pale green shine of Lie's insulation shell moving into the third palace the Book had been assigned to explore. Baylou saw the same light entering the third palace Lie had been directed to search. Baylou realized both could not be Lie. But, which was the traitor goat? Or, were both?

The rear wall of the third palace of Baylou's line exploded without sound and Baylou saw Lie's glow.

Baylou zoomed down to hover outside the rear of the third palace on Lie's line. The wall burst to chunks and a glowing green figure ran stiffly toward the Book. Baylou emitted a red beam and the icy figurine of Lie was vaporized. The Book shot across the circle of palaces toward the fourth palace on Baylou's line, where it had seen Lie's shield shine entering that portal.

Lie caught the red glow with the corner of his eye. He skidded to a stop and stood inside the entrance of the fourth palace in Baylou's line. After easing his breathing, he crept toward the doorway and peeked around the icy door jamb.

"That which has appeared to be Baylou, in the past, has proven not to be," Lie whispered. He readied his blue steel spear. "In this hell of living ice, I must be wary to extremes."

Baylou slowed, then hovered in surprise.

Clu was running from behind the third palace of Baylou's line. Demons with spears were pursuing him.

Baylou could not determine if this was Clu, or another of Ihpoza's ice doppelgangers. They were not moving with the stiffness of the first ice demons Baylou had seen.

If this was Clu, Baylou could rescue him, then latch onto Lie, and the three of them could join telepathically to enhance Baylou's Magic and make the success of their quest for the Wand an almost foregone conclusion!

Baylou threw itself like a missile toward the tiny figure that was swiftly losing ground against the howling demons.

Lie gasped. If that was Clu, there was no way Lie could reach him in time to protect him against those monsters!

There was a sickening hissing.

Lie turned to see Death's forked tongue bearing toward his head. He attempted to dodge and strike the black tongue aside with his javelin, but the tips of the tongue snapped against his green shield at the center of his forehead, and sparks flew. Lie was horrified to find himself reeling backwards, and feeling weak. He became terrified because his power suit looked less substantial. This monster is sapping the energy out of me and my insulation shell, with its tongue, he realized. I cannot stand and fight. He spun on his heel to flee the palace, but slammed into several ice demons and recoiled into the palace. His suit was too weak to destroy the golems. He turned toward the real threat.

Death had vanished.

Lie had no time to allow relief to wash over him. He whirled around with his javelin held like a club and slammed it into the heads of the three closest ice golems shuffling toward him. The rimy demons detonated.

The ice particles cleared, and Death was revealed.

Lie threw himself onto his back and hurled his keen spear.

Death deflected the javelin with its forked tongue.

Lie scrambled to his feet and raced into the bowels of the palace.

Baylou could not risk the steel javelins of the demons, so the Tome circled around and stationed itself in front of Clu. With bitter disappointment, Baylou blasted the ice creature to snow, then vented its red acrimony against the rimy demons, vaporizing them. The Book reasserted its path toward the palace where it had last seen Lie.

In the distance, Baylou saw Death. The Book hesitated, slowing its approach. It remembered the Lizard's power draining tongue and the pain. It sighted the glow of Lie's insulation suit which appeared to be less bright than it should. Baylou knew why. The Kile Lizard had stricken Lie's protector at least once.

Baylou's hatred for evil inspired the Book. It sped toward the great Lizard like a missile, with the air whistling around it.

Before Death could follow Lie, it heard an unnatural sound and turned half around. Fear coursed through the leviathan saurian. It scrambled into the palace and fled down the corridor to the left. It made several course corrections before it found the passage it desperately sought. This hall led down at a steep angle into the ice lawn. When the Lizard passed below the surface, the ramp filled with ice, turning the hallway into a dead end.

Baylou braked inside the palace. The Lizard was nowhere to be seen. Neither was Lie. Baylou noted boot prints barely melted into the ice floor. Baylou glowed with hope. Lie could not be far away. Baylou sped down the hallway, but stopped with dismay. It was in the center of a hub of intersecting corridors. The Book could not detect further boot prints. It went back and reexamined the last pair of tracks to see if it could determine the direction Lie had gone. They appeared to lead straight. Baylou had no choice. It resumed its journey along what it hoped was the path Lie had taken.

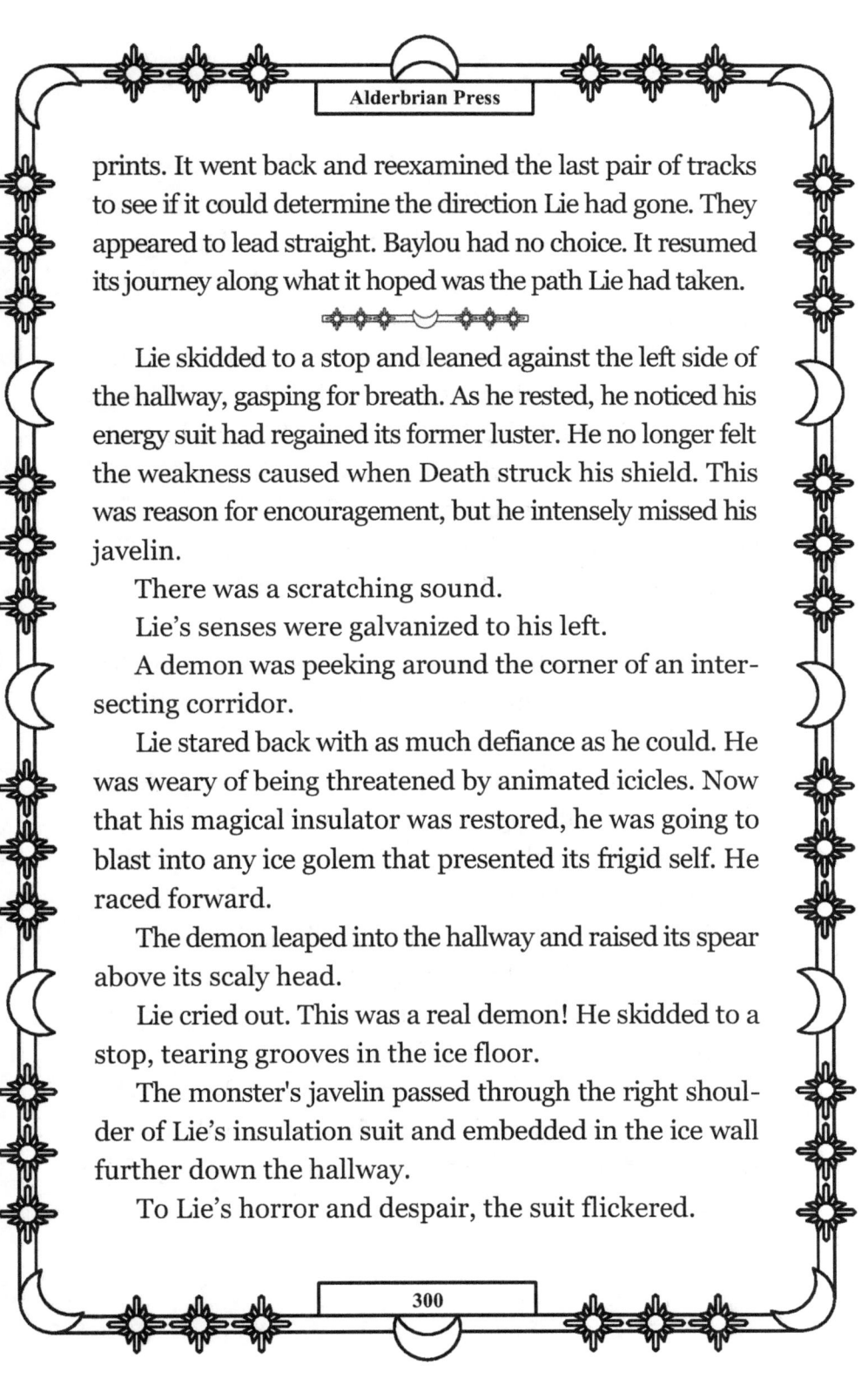

Lie skidded to a stop and leaned against the left side of the hallway, gasping for breath. As he rested, he noticed his energy suit had regained its former luster. He no longer felt the weakness caused when Death struck his shield. This was reason for encouragement, but he intensely missed his javelin.

There was a scratching sound.

Lie's senses were galvanized to his left.

A demon was peeking around the corner of an intersecting corridor.

Lie stared back with as much defiance as he could. He was weary of being threatened by animated icicles. Now that his magical insulator was restored, he was going to blast into any ice golem that presented its frigid self. He raced forward.

The demon leaped into the hallway and raised its spear above its scaly head.

Lie cried out. This was a real demon! He skidded to a stop, tearing grooves in the ice floor.

The monster's javelin passed through the right shoulder of Lie's insulation suit and embedded in the ice wall further down the hallway.

To Lie's horror and despair, the suit flickered.

To the horror of the Demon, Lie's insulator repaired and was as strong as before. The saurian turned to retreat. Several demons, armed with spears, raced around the corner of the hallway. They swept their reluctant comrade toward Lie.

Lie uttered a sound of panic, spun on his heel and slammed into the wall of the passage. It exploded out of his way, and he continued fleeing. Wall after wall detonated soundlessly and rained blue snow and hail everywhere. When Lie exploded through the shining rear wall of the fourth palace, he veered left and headed for the center palace of the five which stood in the middle of the ring of palaces.

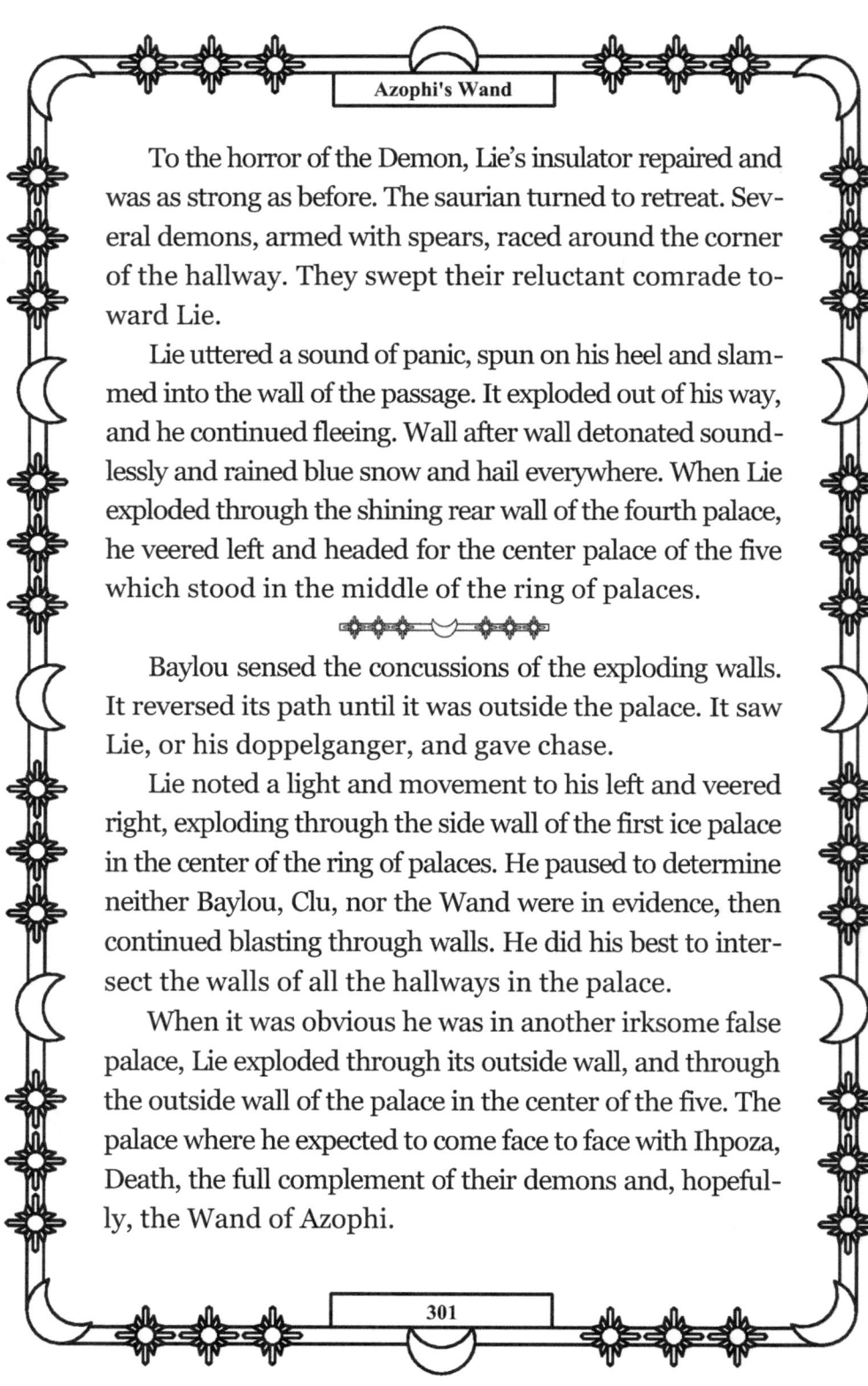

Baylou sensed the concussions of the exploding walls. It reversed its path until it was outside the palace. It saw Lie, or his doppelganger, and gave chase.

Lie noted a light and movement to his left and veered right, exploding through the side wall of the first ice palace in the center of the ring of palaces. He paused to determine neither Baylou, Clu, nor the Wand were in evidence, then continued blasting through walls. He did his best to intersect the walls of all the hallways in the palace.

When it was obvious he was in another irksome false palace, Lie exploded through its outside wall, and through the outside wall of the palace in the center of the five. The palace where he expected to come face to face with Ihpoza, Death, the full complement of their demons and, hopefully, the Wand of Azophi.

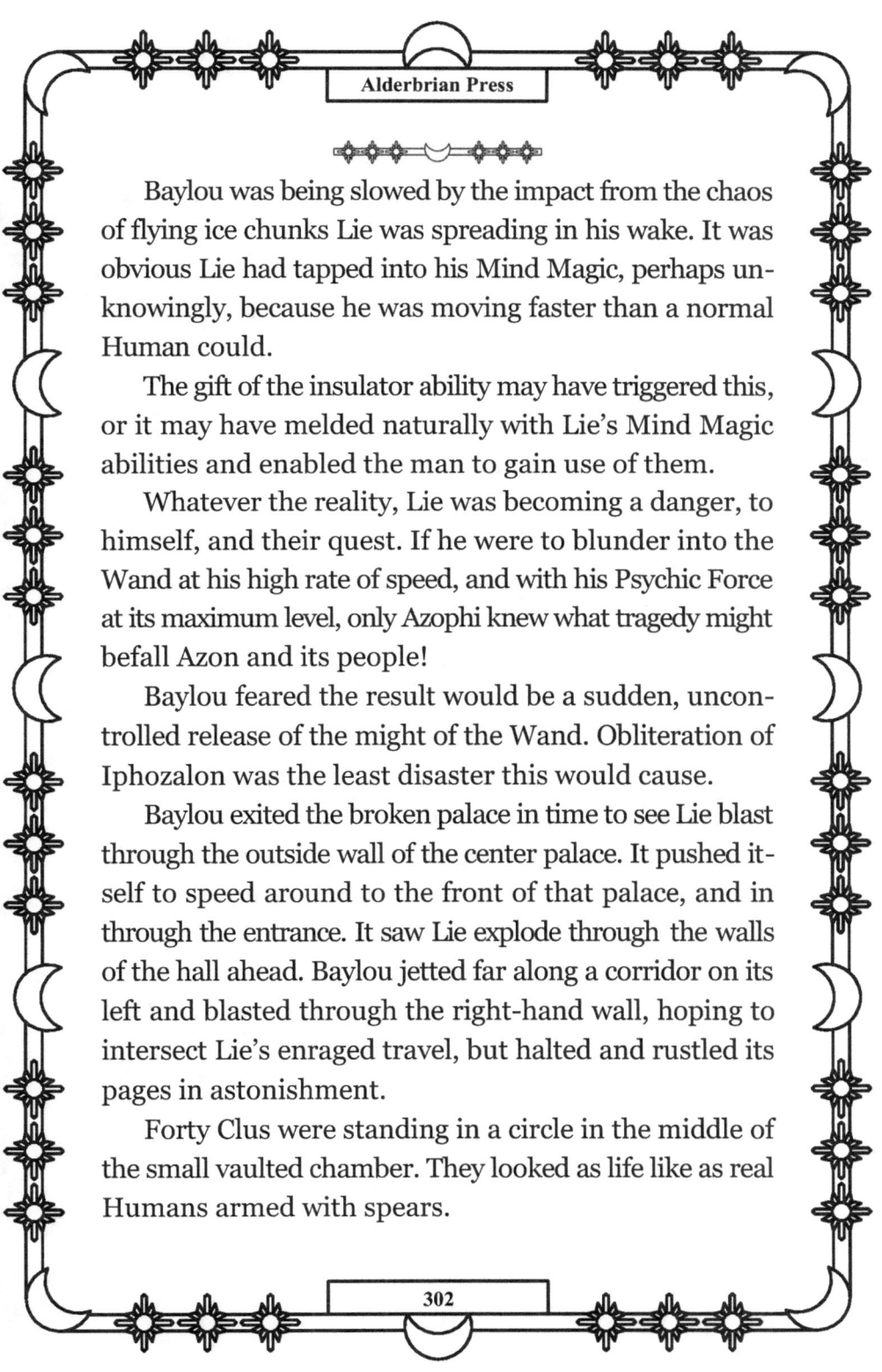

Baylou was being slowed by the impact from the chaos of flying ice chunks Lie was spreading in his wake. It was obvious Lie had tapped into his Mind Magic, perhaps unknowingly, because he was moving faster than a normal Human could.

The gift of the insulator ability may have triggered this, or it may have melded naturally with Lie's Mind Magic abilities and enabled the man to gain use of them.

Whatever the reality, Lie was becoming a danger, to himself, and their quest. If he were to blunder into the Wand at his high rate of speed, and with his Psychic Force at its maximum level, only Azophi knew what tragedy might befall Azon and its people!

Baylou feared the result would be a sudden, uncontrolled release of the might of the Wand. Obliteration of Iphozalon was the least disaster this would cause.

Baylou exited the broken palace in time to see Lie blast through the outside wall of the center palace. It pushed itself to speed around to the front of that palace, and in through the entrance. It saw Lie explode through the walls of the hall ahead. Baylou jetted far along a corridor on its left and blasted through the right-hand wall, hoping to intersect Lie's enraged travel, but halted and rustled its pages in astonishment.

Forty Clus were standing in a circle in the middle of the small vaulted chamber. They looked as life like as real Humans armed with spears.

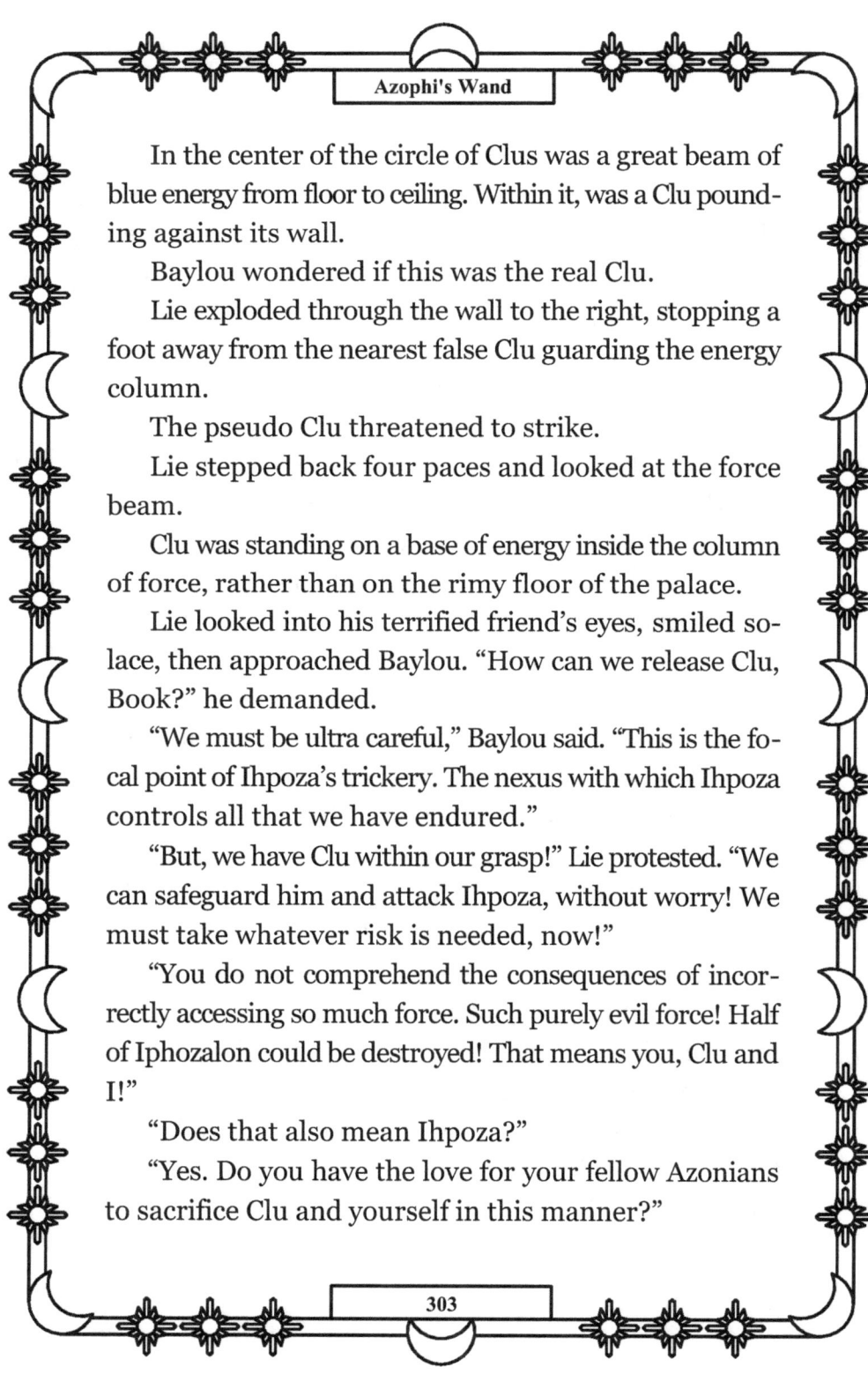

In the center of the circle of Clus was a great beam of blue energy from floor to ceiling. Within it, was a Clu pounding against its wall.

Baylou wondered if this was the real Clu.

Lie exploded through the wall to the right, stopping a foot away from the nearest false Clu guarding the energy column.

The pseudo Clu threatened to strike.

Lie stepped back four paces and looked at the force beam.

Clu was standing on a base of energy inside the column of force, rather than on the rimy floor of the palace.

Lie looked into his terrified friend's eyes, smiled solace, then approached Baylou. "How can we release Clu, Book?" he demanded.

"We must be ultra careful," Baylou said. "This is the focal point of Ihpoza's trickery. The nexus with which Ihpoza controls all that we have endured."

"But, we have Clu within our grasp!" Lie protested. "We can safeguard him and attack Ihpoza, without worry! We must take whatever risk is needed, now!"

"You do not comprehend the consequences of incorrectly accessing so much force. Such purely evil force! Half of Iphozalon could be destroyed! That means you, Clu and I!"

"Does that also mean Ihpoza?"

"Yes. Do you have the love for your fellow Azonians to sacrifice Clu and yourself in this manner?"

The false Clus raised their spears as if saluting someone.

To the left of Baylou and Lie, a tall, rectangular section of ice wall vanished, and twelve of the Vile One's demons entered, bearing spears. They formed a semicircle before Lie and Baylou.

Lie experienced a chill of realization. "We know the guard Clus are not real. However life like they appear, they must be of Ihpoza's magical ice. I am willing to gamble, these demons are also ice. You destroy the fake demons and I shall eliminate the Clus. This will give us time to deal with freeing Clu, absent any threat to us."

Baylou blocked Lie's path. "How do you know the Clu within the beam is not ersatz? One of the ring Clus might be your friend. Ihpoza may have taken control of his mind, issued him a spear and positioned him in the guard ring to slay us. This is more the way Ihpoza's evil mind functions."

"In Eelay, you said Ihpoza could control Clu and me and use us to enhance his powers," Lie said. "Do you believe Ihpoza would risk our killing Clu and preventing that possibility?"

"If Ihpoza believes that is the only way he can preserve his life and maintain ownership of the Wand, he would not hesitate to enact such a scheme. The power he could attain from you and Clu may enable him to harness the Wand, but not the only way. It is nothing compared to ownership of the Wand. Nothing compared to Ihpoza's life."

"Ihpoza risks nothing, even if he loses both Clu and

me. And he gains all of Azon if he slays you."

The demons began growling. They slowly approached with their javelins held in both hands, near one hip, prepared to jab.

Baylou shot red rays at the beasts at the ends of the semicircle. They exploded in a flurry of greenish snow.

The Clu inside the pulsating power column shouted: "Mr. Lie! I am Clu! I am not ice! Remember the Ortourian Beast! Remember the mirror stones! Remember Merra-Lynn and AarLee! Help me! Kill the false Clus! For Azophi's sake, save me!"

Baylou shot ten red rays and destroyed the remaining ice demons. When the green snow cleared from of the air, the Book turned to Lie. "I sense the imprisoned Clu is the true Clu, not a construct being fed telepathic information Ihpoza has gleaned from you or Clu. Your hunch was accurate. If you will engage the pseudo Clus, I will endeavor to safely extract Clu from the force beam, and we shall have the means to put the fear of Azophi into Ihpoza!"

Lie raced toward the nearest Clu and slammed into it. He rebounded, with stupefaction.

The false Clu laughed, sounding like Ihpoza and Death, together.

Baylou paused in the air above Lie. "Ihpoza has encased these beings in his force shields. You cannot harm them with your insulator."

Lie lunged forward, grabbed the spear away from one of the startled false Clus, leaped back three times, and flung the blue javelin with all his might.

The unarmed doppelganger tried to dodge, but the spear sank into its chest, and the creature exploded with a slight rumble. Energy sparks and white snow flew in all directions.

The other Clus rushed toward Lie.

Lie whirled on his heel and fled out the opening he had blasted through the wall.

The doppelgangers pursued the Human, roaring in rage, sounding like Ihpoza's demons.

Baylou flew toward the column of energy.

Clu ran to the part of the power beam that faced the Tome. He waved to the Book, encouraging it. "Hurry, Baylou! You know Ihpoza will send his real demons! Or he will send Death! If he comes, himself, we will be lost! We must hurry to help Lie!"

"Stand as far back as you can," Baylou ordered.

Clu complied, eagerly.

Baylou pressed itself against the side of the blue pillar of might, and began vibrating its own green energy. The power beam started resonating in a similar tone. Baylou moved into the column of power for about an inch.

"It's working!" Clu shouted, happily.

There was laughter in the room, from Ihpoza and Death.

The power pillar changed its tone to a shrill squeal. Blue lightning flashed. Baylou was hurled from the power beam and up against the ice wall behind the Book. The Tome struck with an echoing, final sounding, thud, flipped

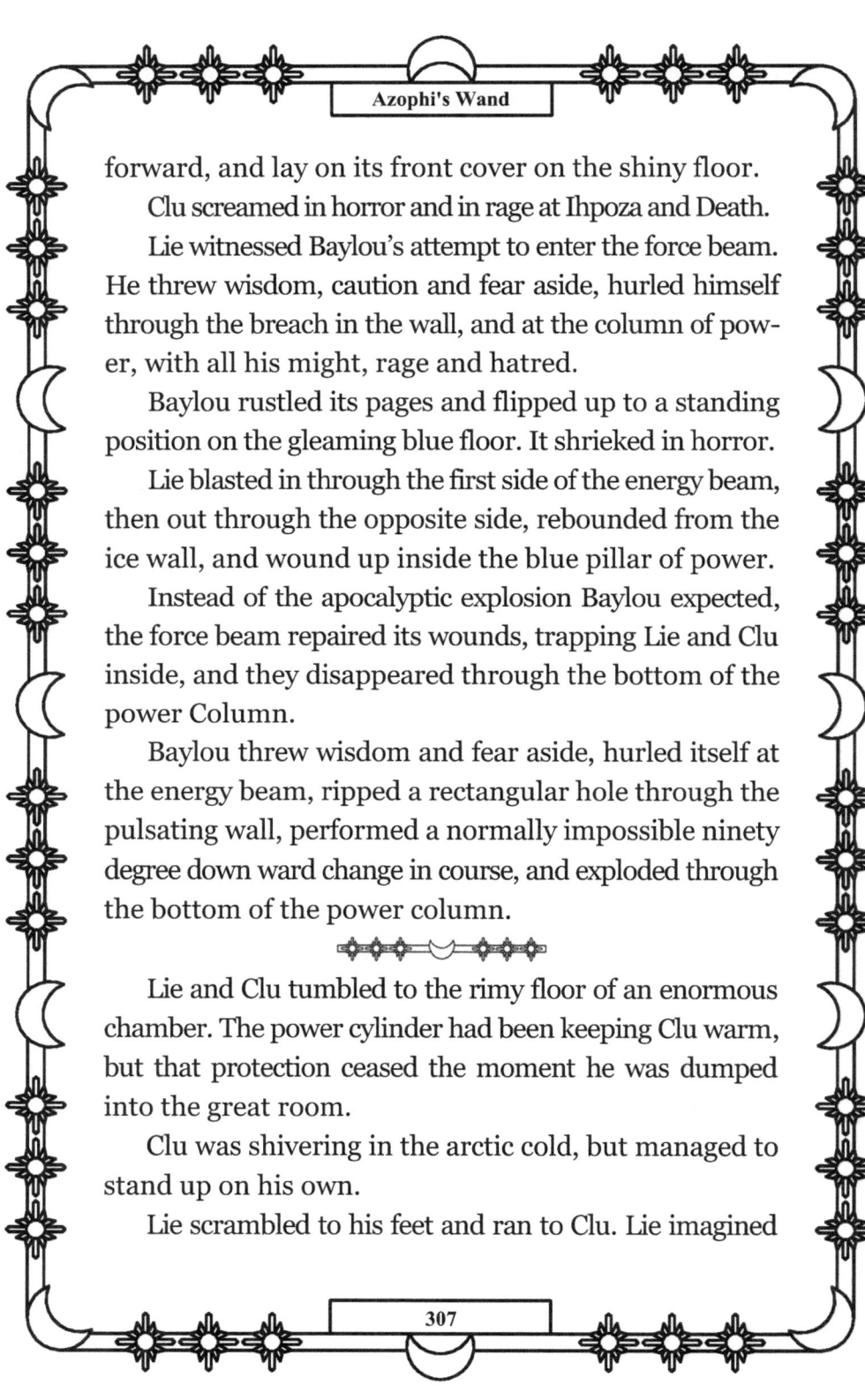

forward, and lay on its front cover on the shiny floor.

Clu screamed in horror and in rage at Ihpoza and Death.

Lie witnessed Baylou's attempt to enter the force beam. He threw wisdom, caution and fear aside, hurled himself through the breach in the wall, and at the column of power, with all his might, rage and hatred.

Baylou rustled its pages and flipped up to a standing position on the gleaming blue floor. It shrieked in horror.

Lie blasted in through the first side of the energy beam, then out through the opposite side, rebounded from the ice wall, and wound up inside the blue pillar of power.

Instead of the apocalyptic explosion Baylou expected, the force beam repaired its wounds, trapping Lie and Clu inside, and they disappeared through the bottom of the power Column.

Baylou threw wisdom and fear aside, hurled itself at the energy beam, ripped a rectangular hole through the pulsating wall, performed a normally impossible ninety degree down ward change in course, and exploded through the bottom of the power column.

Lie and Clu tumbled to the rimy floor of an enormous chamber. The power cylinder had been keeping Clu warm, but that protection ceased the moment he was dumped into the great room.

Clu was shivering in the arctic cold, but managed to stand up on his own.

Lie scrambled to his feet and ran to Clu. Lie imagined

his insulation suit expanding to include his friend. This happened in an instant.

A suctioning of air rocked the two men. The wall in front of them vanished, revealing a vast tunnel.

Death stood in the center of the icy doorway. It hissed. Instead of striking the men, the Lizard directed its deadly lingua to the section of the insulator joining them. A breach was formed.

Lie and Clu cried out in despair, but their fears were not realized. The energy suit split down the center and formed a separate version of itself around each, before the frigid temperature could harm them.

Lie and Clu backed toward the towering wall.

"It can sap your energy with its tongue!" Lie warned. He had an innate understanding: The splitting of his insulator to protect them would prevent him from blasting through the ice walls as before. He threw his arm around Clu. Perhaps, if they worked together, they could perform that feat.

There was a creaking behind them and to their left and right.

Death laughed, cruelly.

"The walls!" Clu shouted. "Ihpoza is growing the walls at us! To force us toward Death!"

"Shall I slay them, my Master," Death said, "or fetch them to you so you may drain them of their Magic and life essence?"

"Bring them!" Ihpoza's sinister voice resounded along

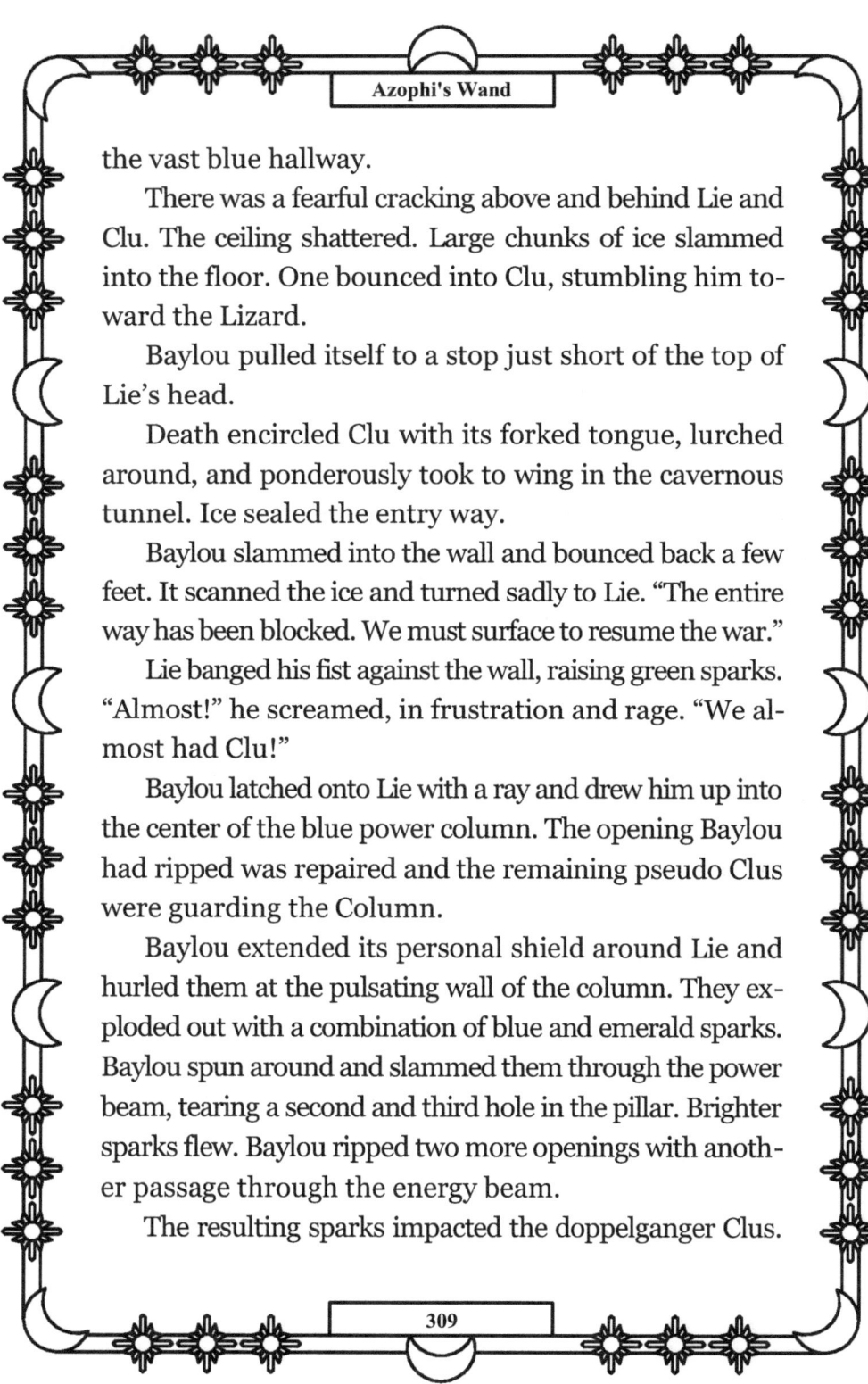

the vast blue hallway.

There was a fearful cracking above and behind Lie and Clu. The ceiling shattered. Large chunks of ice slammed into the floor. One bounced into Clu, stumbling him toward the Lizard.

Baylou pulled itself to a stop just short of the top of Lie's head.

Death encircled Clu with its forked tongue, lurched around, and ponderously took to wing in the cavernous tunnel. Ice sealed the entry way.

Baylou slammed into the wall and bounced back a few feet. It scanned the ice and turned sadly to Lie. "The entire way has been blocked. We must surface to resume the war."

Lie banged his fist against the wall, raising green sparks. "Almost!" he screamed, in frustration and rage. "We almost had Clu!"

Baylou latched onto Lie with a ray and drew him up into the center of the blue power column. The opening Baylou had ripped was repaired and the remaining pseudo Clus were guarding the Column.

Baylou extended its personal shield around Lie and hurled them at the pulsating wall of the column. They exploded out with a combination of blue and emerald sparks. Baylou spun around and slammed them through the power beam, tearing a second and third hole in the pillar. Brighter sparks flew. Baylou ripped two more openings with another passage through the energy beam.

The resulting sparks impacted the doppelganger Clus.

They exploded with a series of slight rumbles.

Baylou sailed them away from the beam of might and released Lie from its shield. Lie used his hands to shade his eyes against the brilliant sparking of the pillar.

Ihpoza's focal energy column was disrupted beyond repair and could no longer maintain the ice palaces. It exploded through the ruined tenth ice palace, into the starry sky, transformed into a mist, and flowed down through the odd towers of Ihpoza's palace, returning to its evil Master.

***

Ihpoza stroked the flat top of his beloved Lizard's head. "Despite our ingenuity, the web is broken, my pet," he said. "The war begins in earnest, now."

Death stared into its Master's empty eye sockets still enhancing the Evil One's power.

Ihpoza telepathically issued orders to Favorite Slave.

***

The false ice palaces broke apart like pale blue nightmare flowers opening their jagged petals, and flowed like water into the great flat ice lawn, leaving Lie and Baylou near a bank of snow hills. They stared at each other. Ihpoza's palace had not been among the ring of doppelganger ice palaces. They had been chasing phantoms with no hope of achieving any of their vital goals.

The demon howled only yards away. It had been lying flat on its chest, virtually invisible to detection.

Lie could barely see the beast's silhouette against the

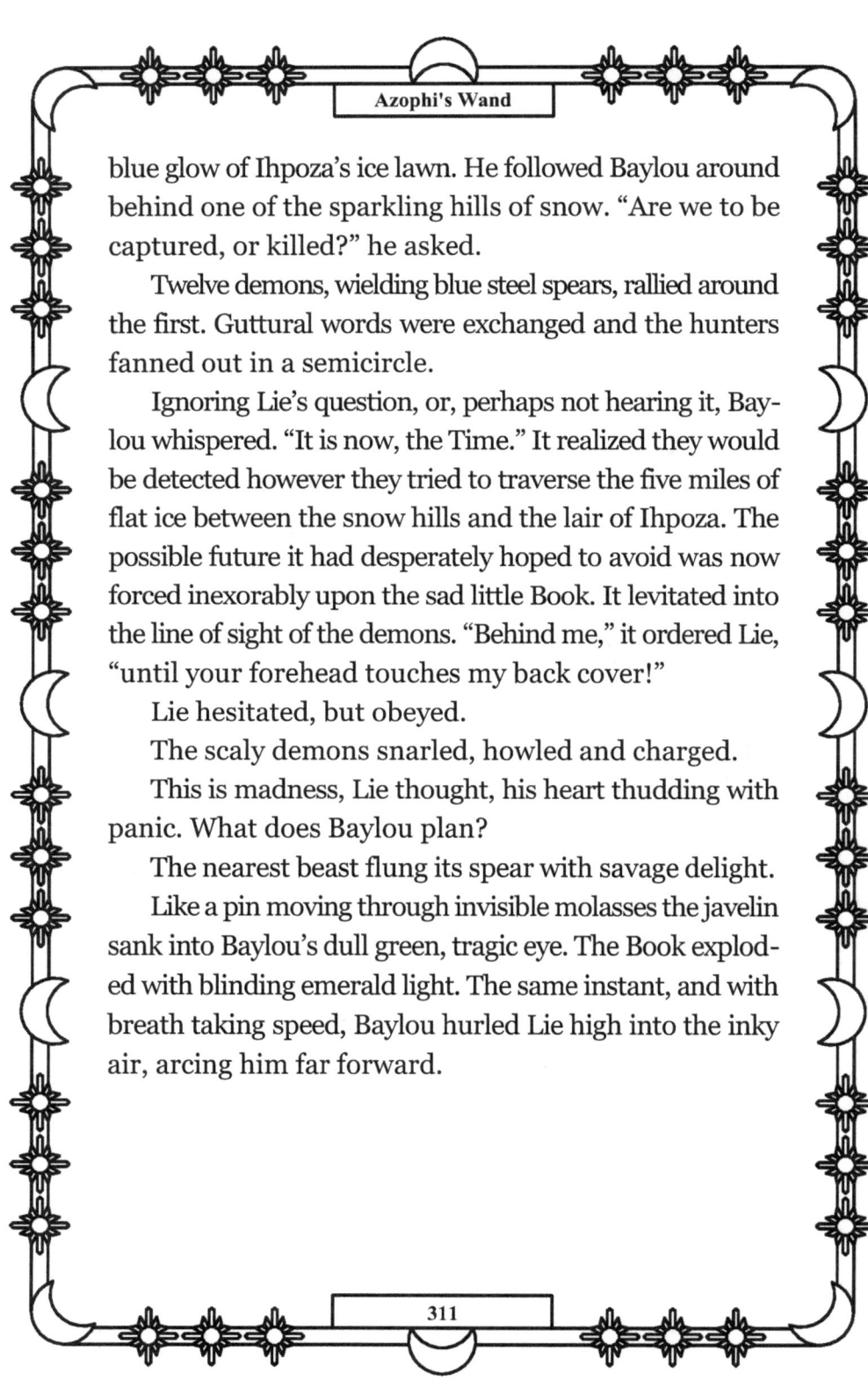

blue glow of Ihpoza's ice lawn. He followed Baylou around behind one of the sparkling hills of snow. "Are we to be captured, or killed?" he asked.

Twelve demons, wielding blue steel spears, rallied around the first. Guttural words were exchanged and the hunters fanned out in a semicircle.

Ignoring Lie's question, or, perhaps not hearing it, Baylou whispered. "It is now, the Time." It realized they would be detected however they tried to traverse the five miles of flat ice between the snow hills and the lair of Ihpoza. The possible future it had desperately hoped to avoid was now forced inexorably upon the sad little Book. It levitated into the line of sight of the demons. "Behind me," it ordered Lie, "until your forehead touches my back cover!"

Lie hesitated, but obeyed.

The scaly demons snarled, howled and charged.

This is madness, Lie thought, his heart thudding with panic. What does Baylou plan?

The nearest beast flung its spear with savage delight.

Like a pin moving through invisible molasses the javelin sank into Baylou's dull green, tragic eye. The Book exploded with blinding emerald light. The same instant, and with breath taking speed, Baylou hurled Lie high into the inky air, arcing him far forward.

Illustration 44

Ortourian Beast Wrought Iron Window Grillwork

Copyright © 2019 Philip Raymond Sadler

312-A

Chapter 44
The Wrath of the Wand

Ihpoza listened, gloating, to the final sad echo of the detonation. He stroked the lizard's head. "It is accomplished, my pet," he rejoiced. "It is finished!"

"The Book has expired," Death hissed, with delight. "Azon, and the Wand, shall soon be yours!"

Favorite Slave, and two of its comrades, survived the assault on the Magic Book. Still dazed by the concussion of the explosion, they stumbled into the throne room and stood unsteadily before their evil master.

"Because you have won us the Southern Hemisphere," Ihpoza decreed, "you shall govern as overseers of the slaves I shall create of the pitiful people of Azophi!"

Something, an energy, a presence, for mere seconds, crackled in the air. The astounded demons incinerated with intense green flames. The might which consumed them left not even ashes to remind History of their warped existence.

Ihpoza leaped to his feet in a blind panic. "The Wand!" he shrieked. "The Wand, is free!"

"It is the ghost of Baylou wreaking vengeance upon its

murderers!" Lie shouted. He strode into the blue throne room carrying one of the steel spears the slaves had discarded before they dared approach their vile master. "You may have slain the Baylou, and my friend," he threatened, "but you shall not control Azophi's sacred Wand!"

Death, affronted by the Human's audacity, tensed to spring.

Lie hurled the javelin at the glistening blue power block which had imprisoned the Wand of Azophi for centuries.

Baylou, a mere ghost of itself, appeared momentarily above the icy throne.

Ihpoza screamed with despair.

The lustrous spell prison shattered with the sound of breaking glass. The blue shards vaporized into mist and vanished. The spear passed over the top of the Wand and embedded in the ice footstool.

Imperially, the Wand rose into the air.

Ihpoza, weakened by the heat of the crystal clear radiation of the Wand, fell backwards onto his throne. "The dream!" He gasped, with horror. "The dream!"

"It cannot! It must not be!" Death sibilated. It sprang to its wings, with its powerful, sharp, forked tongue unfurling and slicing toward the center of the Wand.

There was no sound, no alteration in the intensity of the Wand's glow, nothing to indicate a discharge of power, yet Death transformed into ice, plummeted, and shattered against the frozen floor with an appalling thud of finality.

Ihpoza fell limp. His forehead became red. Almost like blood flowing from a wound, a spark of evil, the real Ihpoza, jumped from the corpse to escape the vindictive heat of the Wand's energy. It placed itself inside the block of ice that was Death's brain, absorbing the vile Kile Lizard's warped mind into his own insane, cowering consciousness.

The Wand encased the ice chunk in a shimmering square of green magic.

There was the sound of fists pounding against a solid object.

Lie's heart skipped a beat, with desperate hope. "Clu!" he shouted. "Is that you, Clu?" He raced around the shining throne.

A rectangular box of ice was attached to the back. There were air holes in the sides. Clu was kneeling within, hammering his shielded fists against the thick, bluish top. "Mr. Lie!" he shouted, hopefully. "Help me, Mr. Lie! Hurry! Get me out of here before those monsters come back!"

Lie summoned his Mind Magic, struck his fists against the box, and shattered it into harmless snow.

Clu stood up, brushing his shield free of ice flakes. He was about to hug Lie, with gratitude, when he noticed the crystal Wand hovering in midair. He smiled sheepishly. "I missed it all, didn't I?" he said.

"I don't think quite all," Lie said, thoughtfully.

"As I was instructed by Azophi," the Wand hummed. "So shall I act!" Its words were stern, and resonated the blue crystalline palace and ice lawn. "Look upon this deed,

Ihpoza," it commanded, "and discover the secret of control for which you have yearned and searched, lo, these many long centuries!" It floated to the right side of the pallid corpse and placed its top against the arm-less shoulder. The mutated body stirred in a disturbing manner.

Lie glanced at the spear in the frozen footstool, uncertain, ready to act, but Clu pulled him to a kneeling position.

The Wand shaped into an arm. Not of a scaled beast, but of a human being. The body began to change. Its head reformed, the horn became short white hair, and eyes filled the sockets. The visage of a kindly old man appeared, the body scales modified into a work jumper and boots, and the regeneration was complete.

"This was our true mission," Lie whispered. "The second birth of our Lord."

Azophi smiled at Lie and Clu. "There is no need to kneel," he said. "I have come to serve, not to be served." He smiled with affection and waved his right hand.

Baylou, awash in the bright greenish shine of its occult vitality, was brought back into the world of the quick, hovering over the blue, glowing footstool.

Ihpoza wailed once inside its frigid spell prison, then phased into extinction. The blue gleam of the Evil One's power vanished from the palace and ice lawn.

Azophi warmed Iphozalon and illuminated it with the golden light of his Magic.

FIND AN ERROR?

Please email this information to thenuttyformatter1@gmail.com:

- *the author name*
- *title of the book*
- *screenshot of the error*
- *suggested correction*